MW00325804

Noel Street

❄ RICHARD PAUL EVANS ❄

Noel Street

FROM THE NOEL COLLECTION

GALLERY BOOKS

NEW YORK   LONDON   TORONTO   SYDNEY   NEW DELHI

An Imprint of Simon & Schuster, Inc.
1230 Avenue of the Americas
New York, NY 10020

This Gallery Books hardcover edition October 2020

GALLERY BOOKS and colophon are registered trademarks of Simon & Schuster, Inc.

For information about special discounts for bulk purchases,
please contact Simon & Schuster Special Sales at
1-866-506-1949 or business@simonandschuster.com.

The Simon & Schuster Speakers Bureau can bring authors to your live event.
For more information or to book an event, contact the Simon & Schuster Speakers
Bureau at 1-866-248-3049 or visit our website at www.simonspeakers.com.

Interior design by Erika Genova

Manufactured in the United States of America

3 5 7 9 10 8 6 4

Library of Congress Cataloging-in-Publication Data
Names: Evans, Richard Paul, author.
Title: Noel Street / Richard Paul Evans.
Description: First Gallery Books hardcover edition. | New York :
Gallery Books, 2019. | Series: The Noel collection ; book 3
Identifiers: LCCN 2019032745 (print) | LCCN 2019032746 (ebook) |
ISBN 9781982129583 (hardcover) | ISBN 9781982129590 (ebook)
Subjects: LCSH: Christmas stories.
Classification: LCC PS3555.V259 N653 2019 (print) |
LCC PS3555.V259 (ebook) | DDC 813/.54—dc23
LC record available at https://lccn.loc.gov/2019032745

ISBN 978-1-9821-2958-3
ISBN 978-1-9821-2959-0 (ebook)

To Diane. Thank you for the decade.

Noel Street

PROLOGUE

It's been more than forty years. In sharing this story, I've decided to include some of my diary entries from those days—not as much for your sake as for mine. I find that in retelling our stories, the recounting eventually begins to take on more credence than the actual truth of the event.

—Elle Sheen

Every story is a road. And on all roads there are potholes and bumps, detours and unexpected encounters. This stretch of my story took place back in 1975 in a small mountain town you've never heard of—Mistletoe, Utah. It was a harsher than usual winter, and everything, it seemed, was frozen—including my life as a single mother working as a waitress at the Noel Street Diner.

Then, on one of those cold days, something came along that changed everything for me. More correctly, some*one*. It was the day I found William Smith lying under a truck on Noel Street.

Nineteen seventy-five seems both like just yesterday and a millennium ago. It was a different world. In many ways, a different country. Gas was fifty-seven cents a gallon, and Foster Grant sunglasses set you back a five spot. Jimmy Hoffa disappeared, and the videocassette recorder appeared. Stylish women wore long print dresses and knits, and men wore polyester leisure suits in colors the fashion industry is still scratching their heads over.

New York City was on the verge of bankruptcy, while *Jaws*, *The Towering Inferno*, and *Funny Lady* reigned at the box office. The year's soundtrack was provided by the likes of the Eagles, Aerosmith, Alice Cooper, Elton John, and Queen, while a nation with just three television networks watched *The Six Million Dollar Man*, *Kojak*, *All in the Family*, *M*A*S*H*, and *The Carol Burnett Show*.

Just the year before, President Nixon had resigned in disgrace over the Watergate break-ins. America was a cauldron of social unrest, and demonstrations and riots were evening news staples. Some of those demonstrations were over the Vietnam War. Some were over racial or gender inequality. All concerned me. I was a single white mother with a black child whose father had been killed in Vietnam. Dylan, my son, was now nearly seven years old. He knows his father only from my stories and the few photographs I have of him.

Mistletoe, Utah, was an unlikely place to raise a black son. It was as homogeneous and white as a carton of milk. Dylan was not only the sole black person in the small town, he was the only one some of the locals—mostly farmers and ranchers—had ever met. I know that to you who live in big cities or in the South that seems hard to believe, but that's how many of these small western towns were.

Nineteen seventy-five was the year Saigon fell and that nightmare of a war ended. At least historically. Parts of it would never die to me, not even now as I write this. But it was that footnote in history that, perhaps, played the most significant part of that winter's story.

While global chess pieces were being moved around the board by the forces that be, my little world was following its own rickety path, which took a major detour that holiday season, starting with, of all things, a burned-out clutch.

Will it ever stop snowing? I wondered as I walked to the car. The snow had piled up to almost six inches in the driveway of our duplex. I hadn't shoveled; I didn't have the time. Besides, it was going to just snow more. I pushed the snow off my car with a broom. "Come on, Dylan. We've got to go."

"Coming, Mama."

Dylan, who was tall for his age, came out of the house wearing a red-and-green stocking cap that one of the waitresses at the diner had knitted for him last year and his new winter coat that, in spite of his size, was still way too large, the sleeves coming down past his knuckles. I had bought it that big out of necessity. He had grown out of his last coat in less than a year, and I didn't have the money to keep up.

"Is the door shut?"

"Yes, ma'am."

"Then hop in, we're late."

I laid the broom against the house and got in the car. As

I backed out of our driveway, the Fairlane backfired, which made Dylan jump.

"Someone just shot at us!" Dylan shouted. He was imaginative.

"No one shot at us," I said. "It's just the car."

"It exploded."

"I'll give you that."

The Fairlane had been left to me in my grandfather's will. It had been a blessing and a curse. It was more than a decade older than Dylan and things on it were starting to go, something I was financially not prepared to handle. I had just replaced the alternator two months earlier.

What now? I thought.

CHAPTER

one

To call that winter a junction in my life would be like
calling the Grand Canyon a ditch.
                                          —Elle Sheen's Diary

I don't know much about cars, even my own—a '57
Ford Fairlane that collectors would die for today but
that I couldn't give away back then. That morning as
I started the car something felt different, which, from my
experience—in both cars and relationships—was rarely
good. And there was the smell of something burning,
which was *never* good.

"Do you smell something?" I asked Dylan. He had
sensory processing disorder—something we didn't know
about back then—and was highly sensitive to smells.

"It wasn't me," Dylan said.

I grinned. "I'm talking about the car."

"It smells like burnt toast," he said.

I sighed. "Looks like you're going to be late to school
today. We need to see Mr. Renato again."

"I don't like Mr. Renato," Dylan said.

"Why don't you like Mr. Renato?"

"He smells funny."

"That's not nice," I said, even though it was true. Mr. Renato smelled more like garlic than a roasted clove. "He just smells a little like garlic."

"What's gar-lick?"

"Garlic is something you put in Italian food like spaghetti sauce and pizza. I know you like those."

"Yeah."

"Mr. Renato is Italian, like pizza. And if you say anything about how he smells in front of him, I'm going to ground you from watching TV for a whole week."

I looked over to see if he was getting it. He was frowning. "Can I tell him he smells like a garlic?"

"No!"

Mr. Renato owned Renato's Expert Auto Repair, but since his was the only auto body shop in Mistletoe, everyone just called it Renato's—a name that outsiders often mistook for an Italian restaurant.

Renato was of direct Italian descent, immigrating to America when he was nineteen. Like everyone else in town, including me, you had to wonder how he ended up in Mistletoe. It was a woman, of course. He met her in the bustling metropolis of New York and followed her back to a town so small that the McDonald's had only one arch. Actually, that's not true. We didn't have a McDonald's.

That was a joke. I had a whole repertoire of "our town is so small" jokes, mostly shared with me by truck drivers passing through. I've heard them all. *This town is so small that all the city limits signs are on the same post. A night on the town*

3

takes six minutes. The New Year's baby was born in September. (That last one was actually true. Not a lot of births in this town, as most people leave to get married. I'm a sad example of what happens if you don't.)

The truth was, Mistletoe was so small that even people in the state of Utah didn't know it existed. Renato's love interest eventually left—both him and Mistletoe—but Renato stayed put. Unfortunately, my car kept us in frequent contact.

Renato's shop was on the way to Howard Taft Elementary, Dylan's school. The repair shop had three bays and a front office that perpetually reeked with the pungent scent of new tires.

"It smells in here," Dylan said as we walked in. I wasn't sure if it was a reference to the tires or the shop's proprietor.

I gave him a stern glance. "Remember what I told you. I mean it."

"Yes, ma'am."

"What you're smelling are the new tires. I like it."

"You're weird."

"No one's going to argue that."

Just then a short, olive-skinned man walked out of a back office holding a clipboard. He had a pen tucked behind his ear, partially concealed by his salt-and-pepper hair. He wore a long-sleeved, oil-stained cotton work shirt with an embroidered patch with his name on it. His hands were clean, though permanently dyed by motor oil. He smiled when he saw me.

"*Ciao, bella.*" He walked over and kissed me on both cheeks. "You are too beautiful."

It was nice to hear, even from Renato, who was a living, breathing Italian caricature and pretty much said it to every woman he encountered.

I was pretty in a simple way. Or, at least, I used to be. I was raised in the small town of Cedar City, the only daughter of a military officer turned rancher, and looked as wholesome as my beginnings suggested. I looked like my mother, which, I suppose, was a good thing, as she had been chosen Miss Cedar City in her youth. I had flaxen hair, a small mouth, but full lips and large brown eyes. I was trim, with curves. I wasn't tall, but, at five foot five, I was still taller than my mother. My height was something I got from my father, who was six one.

My father used to say, "I prayed to God that my daughter would be pretty, but not too pretty. Too pretty messes up one's head." Then he'd wink and say, "But God doesn't always give us what we ask for." He also used to say, "Pretty is as pretty does." I'm still not totally sure what that means.

No matter the standard, I didn't feel very pretty in those days. In the mirror of my self-image I just saw a lonely, quietly desperate woman hidden behind a mask of exhaustion.

"Hi, Renato."

He smiled even more broadly, the furrows on his face growing still deeper. "*Mamma mia, sei troppo bella,*" he said, sighing dramatically. Pretty much everything he did was dramatic. "Every time I see you it reminds me that I was born twenty-five years too early."

"Maybe I like older men."

"*Perché mi stuzzichi.* How you tease an old man." He glanced down at Dylan. "How are you, *bambino?*"

"My name's not 'bambino,'" Dylan said.

Renato smiled. "*È vero.*" He looked back up at me. "What brings you to my shop, *bella?*"

"The usual," I said. "My car's acting up again."

"Your curse, my blessing," he said. "Your naughty car brings you back to me. What is the problem this time?"

"Our car exploded this morning," Dylan said.

"*La machina cattiva.*" Renato looked out the glass door toward my car. "The car exploded?"

"It backfired," I said. "But that's not the problem. I think it's the clutch. It doesn't feel right."

"What does it feel like?"

"It feels . . . kind of loose. And it smells bad."

"You said something smells bad," Dylan said. "You said not to say that." I closed him down with a glance. I turned back to Renato.

"It smells like something is burning."

Renato frowned. "That is not good. Do you ride the clutch?"

"I don't know what that means."

"Do you keep your foot on the clutch when you drive?"

"I don't think so."

He breathed out loudly. "Your clutch may be going out on you."

"That sounds expensive," I said anxiously. "Is that expensive?"

He nodded side to side, then raised his hand to explain. He always used his hands to speak. (How do you shut up an Italian? You tie up his hands.) "The clutch plate is only twenty-five dollars."

"Thank goodness," I said. "I can almost afford that."

"It is not the part that is the problem," Renato said, his face pressed with pain. "Replacing the part is the devil. That is what costs the money."

"How much?" I asked.

"Usually costs about five hundred."

My stomach fell. It might as well have been five thousand. "Five hundred?"

"I'm sorry, but do not panic yet. I will have my man check it out first. You have your keys?"

"Right here." I fished my keys from my purse, which was a little embarrassing since my key chain weighed about a pound and had two massive plastic key chains that Dylan had made for me at school that said "World's Best Mom."

Renato smiled at the bundle. "Good thing you have a big purse," he said.

"I wish it was to hold all the money I had."

"We should all have that problem," he said. "I'll have William check your car."

"Who's William?"

"He is my new guy."

"What happened to Nolan?"

"Nolan left."

"Left? He was here forever."

"Thirty-three years. I am not happy about it. He moved back to Montana to raise cattle on his brother's ranch. Fortunately, this man, William, showed up two days before he left. He used to be a mechanic in the army." He walked to the door to the garage and opened it. Somewhere in the garage a radio was playing Simon and Garfunkel's "Sound of Silence."

"William."

A man I guessed to be about my age looked up from beneath the hood of a car. It was rare to see a new face in town outside the diner. He was tall, thin, with dark brown hair and dark features. Ruggedly handsome, I guess. At least I thought that at first. It didn't last long. "Yes, sir," he shot back, like he was still in the military.

"I love it when he says that," Renato said to me. He turned back to his man. "I need you to check the clutch on a Fairlane."

"Yes, sir. Keys in the ignition?"

"I have them." He threw him my bundle. The man caught them.

The man, William, suddenly looked at me and Dylan with a strange expression. As the mother of a nonwhite child, I was used to this. "I'll need to take it around the block."

"Of course," I said, like I had any idea what he needed to do.

He opened a bay door and walked out to my car.

"He is going to take it for a drive so he can feel the clutch," Renato explained.

"Or smell it," I said.

Dylan looked at me and I shook my head.

"Can I have a gumball?" he asked.

"Let me see if I have a penny." I reached in my purse and took out my change purse. It was mostly filled with pennies. "There you go."

"Thank you." He ran to the gumball machine.

"He is such a polite boy," Renato said. "He has a good upbringing."

"Thank you."

About five minutes later the new guy pulled my car into one of the bays and climbed out.

"What do you think?" Renato asked.

"It's definitely slipping," he said. "I can smell it."

I frowned. "That's what I said."

I looked at Renato hoping for some good news but he only frowned. "I am sorry, *bella*. It is going to need a new clutch."

My heart fell. It seems I was always paying for something. I had just finished paying off the alternator. Now this. And Christmas was coming. "Can you fix it?"

"Of course. I'll work with you on the price. I will give you the family discount. Can you make payments?"

"How much would you need?"

"I can do fifty dollars a month. I will do the tune-up for free, no charge."

"Okay." I didn't have a choice. Dylan and I were barely

RICHARD PAUL EVANS

making it as it was. I'd have to pick up an extra shift each month just for the clutch and pray something else didn't give out. Or that I didn't.

"Thank you," I said softly.

"*Prego, signorina.*"

"How long will it take to fix?"

"Maybe four to six hours. William is a fast worker. Can you leave it with me?"

"I kind of need a car. You don't have a loaner, do you?"

"Not today. I will have one tomorrow morning after Mr. Anderson picks up his car."

"Will my car last another day?"

"William, how much longer can she drive her car?"

"The clutch probably has a week or two left on it."

"Will I damage the clutch more?" I asked.

Renato shook his head. "The damage is done. But if it goes out completely you could damage your engine."

Just then William shouted, "Hey! Get off that!"

I spun around. He was shouting at Dylan, who was standing on top of an oily machine next to a stack of tires. "That's not a toy."

Dylan was paralyzed with fear. He wasn't used to being yelled at. I walked over to him. "Sorry," I said to William. "He doesn't know better."

"Then you should keep an eye on him. This isn't a playground."

"I'm sorry," I said again. I turned to Dylan, who was still cowering. "Come on, Dylan. Let's go. Don't touch anything." *So much for Mr. Rugged Good Looks,* I thought.

"He's scary," Dylan said as I took his hand.

"Yeah," I said under my breath. "Very." I walked Dylan back into the front office. Renato was already there behind his counter writing on a pad.

"So here is the work order. We are going to replace your clutch and give you a free tune-up."

"So this new guy of yours. Mr. Personality."

Renato looked at me. "Mr. Personality?"

"How's he working out?"

"William is a hard worker," Renato said. "He is doing a very good job."

"But not much of a personality," I said.

Renato's expression didn't change. "Do not be too quick to judge."

I wasn't sure how to handle Renato's uncharacteristic seriousness. And I was still reeling a little from his employee reprimanding my son and me, as well as the devastating financial news. "I'll see you tomorrow."

Renato nodded. "I am sorry for the bad news, *bella*. But I will give you the family discount."

"Thank you."

As I left the place, it was all I could do not to cry. *Why couldn't I catch a break?*

CHAPTER

two

These are days when I feel like Sisyphus of Greek legend,
forever pushing the stone up the hill. But I mustn't stop.
My son's future is at the top of that hill.

—Elle Sheen's Diary

As I pulled out of Renato's, the Fairlane seemed to drive even worse, though I'm not sure if it really was or if it was just that now I really knew something was wrong with the car and was looking for it.

Dylan was still quiet as I pulled into the school parking lot.

"You okay?" I asked.

He nodded unconvincingly.

"That was kind of scary to be yelled at," I said.

He nodded again. "I wasn't going to break anything."

"Maybe he was just afraid you were going to break yourself." I didn't believe it, but it didn't matter. I wasn't protecting the jerk, I was protecting my son. And he was probably just another bigot. I parked the car in the vacant bus lane in front of the school, then turned to Dylan and held out my hand. "Spit out your gum."

"But it still tastes."

"You know they don't allow gum in school."

He spit it out into my hand. I wrapped it in a tissue and put it in my purse. "Come on. School waits for no one."

Dylan was more than a half hour late for school so I had to sign him in. I held his hand as we walked into the front office.

"Good morning, Elle Bell," the school secretary, Cheryl, said brightly. Much too brightly for where my mind was.

"Morning, Cheryl," I said, purposely leaving off the *good*. "Late start?"

"Car problems."

She shook her head. "Again?"

"Different ailment, same car."

"I have the same problem with my husband," she said. "Dylan, please take this note to Mrs. Duncan." She handed him a pink slip of paper. Dylan turned to go.

"Wait," I said. "What about my kiss?"

Dylan looked embarrassed, furtively glancing around to see if anyone might see him.

"Come on. No one's around."

He screwed up his mouth. "All right."

He quickly pecked my cheek. I pulled him into a big hug that he tried to escape from. I released him. As he backed away from me I said, "Don't forget your lunch." I handed him a brown paper sack. "I'm working late tonight. Fran will be picking you up from school. You got that?"

"Bye, Mom." He ran out of the office.

"He's a good boy," Cheryl said.

"Probably the one thing in my life that's not going wrong," I said.

"Well, if you had to choose something to not be broken, that's the thing."

I drove from the school to the diner. I could smell my burning clutch as I got out of the car. As usual I parked behind the restaurant and walked in through the back door.

"Sorry I'm late," I said, shutting the door behind me.

Loretta, the diner's owner, looked up at me. "Everything okay?"

"No. Another car problem."

She shook her head. "Is it serious?"

"Five hundred dollars serious."

She frowned. "I'm sorry."

"Me too. Just when I get one bill paid off, another pops up."

"Pray for big tips."

"I already am," I said. "If they don't pick up I'm going to be short on next month's rent."

"I'm sorry, baby," Loretta said. "Miracles happen."

"I could use a miracle right about now." I put on my apron. "But I won't be holding my breath."

CHAPTER

three

*I always knew this day would come. So why was I
so unprepared? I suppose it's the nature of humanity to
avoid contemplating unpleasant inevitabilities. Which is
why so few buy their own grave plots.*
                                    —Elle Sheen's Diary

I t was a normal day, as far as my days went, made up of
the usual mix of regulars and strangers—elderly locals
who were lonely or bored, as well as the occasional
trucker. Like my clientele, my schedule was equally predictable. When I worked the late shift I got home from
work at ten—eleven on weekends. When I walked in that
night, Fran, my sitter, was sitting at the kitchen table
doing homework. Fran went to school at Weber State
during the day to study music, evidenced by the violin
case on the floor next to her. Fran was lovely, with an
eclectic taste in music. I never knew what she'd be playing on her 8-track player when I got home—Chopin or
Bob Dylan. Tonight there was neither as she was intent
on her studies.

"How was he?"

"Amazing as usual. He made this for you."

She held up a blue-green marbled ball of Play-Doh, with toothpicks sticking out, four on the bottom, two on top.

I took it from her. "What is it?"

"It's a reindeer," she said, grinning. "Can't you tell?"

I grinned back. "I love it."

"He loves you." She put her homework in a bag and then said, "I should probably tell you, Dylan asked me something different tonight."

I looked up from the reindeer. "What?"

"He asked if Santa was a Negro."

It was the first time he'd used that word. "What did you say?"

"I said, Santa is a spirit. He's the color of giving. I don't know what that means, but he seemed good with that. I hope that's okay."

My eyes watered. "Thank you. You said the right thing."

"He's a sweet boy."

I gave Fran a hug. She picked up her case and walked to the door. "See you tomorrow."

"Good night."

I walked to Dylan's room and opened the door. As usual, he was asleep, the covers pushed down to his waist. Fran was right; he was a sweet boy. He was also a beautiful boy. He had light, mocha-colored skin and was lanky and handsome like his father, though with the more subtle facial features from my Swedish-Welsh heritage. He was exotic looking, as he had blue eyes, something that people would sometimes stare at in disbelief. One time a woman asked me if his eyes were "real." I didn't answer her. I still have no idea what she meant by that.

I lifted the covers up to his chin and kissed his forehead. "I love you, little man." I shut his door, then went to my room and undressed.

Where had he heard the word *Negro*? I wasn't surprised that he'd asked. As the only black person in an all-white farming town, it was only a matter of time. I just hoped I'd be a little better prepared.

The next morning I got Dylan up and while he ate breakfast I made his usual sack lunch—a peanut-butter-and-jam sandwich, chips, and the donut I brought home every night from the diner. I checked my watch and then said, "C'mon, sport. Time to go."

"Can I watch *Fat Albert*?"

"You know better than that. It's time for school. After school you can watch TV."

As we climbed into the car Dylan asked, "Will our car explode again?"

"I don't know. It might." I pulled out into the snow-covered street. "That reminds me. I'm not going to be in the same car tonight."

Dylan's face grew animated. "Are we getting a new car?"

"No. We're just borrowing a car until Renato fixes ours."

He frowned. A few moments later he asked, "Mom, what's a Negro?"

I looked over at him. "Where did you hear that word?"

"Marsha at school says I'm a Negro."

Take a deep breath. At least I knew where he'd learned it. "Well, that means you're super smart and very handsome."

Dylan looked confused. "She said I'm a Negro because my skin is brown."

"Well, that's part of it," I said. "Of course, everyone has different colors on their body. Some have different color hair, different color eyes, some have different color skin."

"She said I can't go to her house because I'm a Negro."

I bit down. "Well, there you go. People at Marsha's house must not be very smart or handsome, so they're intimidated by you."

"What's inti . . . date?"

"Intimidate. It means to be scared."

"Why are they scared?"

"Because they're not as smart or handsome. Did you even want to go to Marsha's house? It doesn't sound like a very fun place to be."

"She's having a birthday party."

I tried not to show my anger. I sighed heavily. "Some people are just . . ." I stopped short of calling her dumb. ". . . don't get out much," I finally said. I pulled up to the curb of the drop-off zone. "I love you, buddy."

"Love you too, Mom."

I watched him walk up to the front of the school and fall in with the other kids, all of them white. As I pulled away I started to cry.

I drove over to Renato's and sat in the parking lot until I regained my composure. I wiped my eyes and then walked into the garage's office, a spring-loaded bell above the door announcing my entrance. To my dismay, the new guy, William, was standing at the counter. I stiffened at the sight of him. I still hadn't forgiven him for scaring Dylan. Or me. After this morning I was especially sensitive.

"Good morning, Elle," he said with surprising gentleness. Even more surprising was that he knew my name.

"Is Renato here?"

"No. He won't be in until this afternoon. But he told me you would be bringing your car in this morning. He has a loaner for you. It's that green-and-white Plymouth Valiant out there." A smile crossed his face. "I know what you're thinking. It's too sexy to drive."

I almost smiled but didn't want to encourage him. "Thank you. How long will my car take?"

"I'll have it done by three," he said. "That includes the tune-up. That won't take much time."

"What time do you close?"

"Five."

I frowned. "I don't get off work until eight. Can I pick it up tomorrow?"

"No problem."

"And the Valiant?"

"There's no hurry on that. We don't need it."

"Thank you."

He handed me the keys to the loaner, which had somehow been connected to a golf ball with a bright yellow smiley face beneath the trademarked phrase "Have a Nice Day."

I smiled at the sight of it. Someone had a key chain almost as impractical as mine. "This is . . . unusual. Not as big as mine, but unusual."

"Keeps it from getting lost."

As I turned to go, he said, "I'm sorry I got mad at your son yesterday. The machine he was playing on could have hurt him. I'm just a little jumpy. I didn't mean to upset him. Or you. Please forgive me."

I looked at him. He was definitely sincere. There was also a vulnerability to him that I hadn't seen the last time.

"Thank you for watching out for my son. As well as the apology."

"You're welcome."

"So Renato will be back this afternoon?"

"He said he would. He'll call when it's done."

"Thank you."

"One more thing. The driver-side door on the Valiant sticks a little. You just need to give it a good tug. Oh, and the brakes are a little touchy. They're fine, just a little sensitive."

Like me, I thought. "Thanks for the warning."

I walked out to the Valiant, which had a two-tone paint job, an olive-green body with a white hardtop. As warned, the door stuck. I yanked it open and climbed in. Whoever had driven the car last was at least half a foot taller than me, as my feet didn't even reach the pedals. I adjusted the seat, put on my seat belt, then started the engine. It roared like an injured lion.

Some sexy, I thought.

As I drove to work, I prayed that the Fairlane's clutch wouldn't be as bad as they thought. I knew there was no hope for it, but I prayed anyway.

"How's it going, Jamie?" I said, walking into the diner. Jamie was the waitress I worked with most. She was five years older than me and off-and-on married so often that I sometimes forgot her marital status. She was born in Mistletoe and had worked at the diner since she was sixteen. She was now thirty.

"You know, different day, same problems. You got a new car? Those Valiants are crazy sexy."

I laughed. "No, I didn't get a new car. It's a loaner Renato gave me while he fixes mine."

"Oh, right. Loretta told me your car was on the fritz. You should have had Mark look at it. Maybe he could have fixed it." Mark was her second ex-husband, though she often acted like they were still married. Actually, that was true of her relationship with all her exes.

"It's the clutch. It's no easy fix."

She shook her head. "You can't catch a break, can you?"

"Not lately."

"Well, I'll pray for large tips. For both of us." As we walked out into the dining room, Jamie's eyes widened. "Oh, no."

"What?"

"Ketchup Lady is back."

I groaned. "I'm starting my shift with Ketchup Lady. Can this day get any worse?"

"Sorry, honey. I'd take her, but you know she's headed to your station."

"It's okay. I'll eat the frog."

"What frog?"

"You know the saying. Start the day eating a frog and nothing worse will happen to you all day."

"If only," she said. "I'd eat a frog omelet every day."

I watched as the Ketchup Lady, as usual, walked past the PLEASE WAIT TO BE SEATED sign and sat herself at the table she had claimed as her own. Actually, she sat at the table next to the one she usually sat at, though not without a brief attempt to reclaim her territory. For almost a minute she just stood looking at the people sitting at "her table" when one of the men—a burly trucker—looked over and asked her what she wanted. Without answering, she turned away and sat down at the next table.

No one knew the woman's name or where she lived. She had shown up at the diner the previous spring and had stopped by every week since. We called her Ketchup Lady because she put ketchup on everything, from pancakes to fried chicken and mashed potatoes. Her plate looked like a crime scene. The first time I took her order I gagged as I brought it out from the kitchen. None of the waitresses were fans, which had less to do with her culinary affinity than her personality, which, at times, was as nasty as her palate.

This morning she was wearing a red T-shirt that read:

I Like Ketchup
On My Ketchup

I walked up to her table. "Good morning," I lied. "What can I get for you today?" *Besides ketchup*.

She looked at me as if she'd never seen me before. "What *may* you get for me? Learn proper grammar, you'll go further in life. I'd like the ham-and-cheese omelet smothered in ketchup. Also a side of sausage—patties, not links—with ketchup. And your buttermilk biscuits with ketchup."

The biscuits were a new addition to her culinary repertoire. The idea of putting ketchup on a biscuit made me sick.

"We have a policy that we don't put things on our biscuits," I said. It was a policy I had made up on the spot. "But you're welcome to put anything in it you like."

She looked annoyed. "Then I'll need an extra bottle of ketchup. This one is nearly gone."

The plastic ketchup bottle on the table was more than half-full. *Was she planning on drinking it?* I wouldn't have been surprised.

"Sure thing," I said. "Would you like anything to drink? Tomato juice, perhaps?"

She just looked at me, either missing or ignoring my snark. "No."

"Very well. I'll be right back with your meal."

I took her order to the kitchen. Our chef, Bart, looked it over. "So she's back," he said. "The first lady of ketchup."

"Back like a bad cough," I said.

"Some people shouldn't leave their homes," Bart said.

I liked Bart—we all did. He had been with the diner since it opened, when he was young and still had a life, or, at least, dreams. Now he was obese, old, and tired, and lived alone in a Winnebago equally dated and disheveled, on the outskirts of Mistletoe near the town's landfill. The waitresses were the only family—male or female—he had.

As I left the kitchen, a group of men walked in. They were all wearing the same kind of trucking company shirt. I walked over and greeted them, led them to a corner of my section, then got their menus and water. As I passed by Ketchup Lady she said, "How long will it be?"

"Not long," I said.

"Check on my meal before you take that large table's order. I have a busy morning."

I bit my tongue. Literally. I wanted to empty the bottle of ketchup on her head. I went back to the kitchen. To my surprise, Ketchup Lady's order was done.

"Why so fast?" I asked Bart.

"The sooner the ketchup princess eats, the sooner she's gone."

"You're a prince," I said.

"And you're my queen," he replied.

I carried the woman's meal out along with an unopened bottle of ketchup, setting them down on the table in front of her. Ketchup Lady looked up at me with annoyance.

"I said *smothered*."

The omelet was almost drowning in a pool of tomato. "You can add more ketchup yourself if you'd like."

"I didn't come here to make my own food," she said. "That's what I pay you for."

Again I bit down. "Here," I said. I took the opened bottle of ketchup and poured out the rest of its contents onto the plate, pretty much covering everything in a sea of red. I noticed the men at the table next to us were laughing.

"How's that?" I asked.

She looked at it for a moment and then said, "That will do."

I walked back to the kitchen, shaking my head. Fortunately she didn't stay long. As I cleared her table I noticed her plate was clean. Like it had been licked clean. And she left a tip with a note.

Here's your tip. I shouldn't have to ask for more ketchup.

Around a quarter to five, a little before the dinner rush, Loretta came out of her office. "Elle, you've got a phone call. It's Renato," she said with unveiled enmity. Loretta knew Renato. Biblically, I mean. She'd once had a fling with him. I think just about every unmarried woman in Mistletoe had. I was an exception.

I wiped my hands on a dishcloth. "My car must be done." I walked back to her office. The receiver was sitting to the side of the telephone.

"Hello."

"Elle," he said, forgoing his usual terms of endearment. "I have bad news."

My heart panicked. "It cost more than five hundred dollars?"

"No, it is something else. The reason your Fairlane backfired was not because it needed to be tuned up. Your timing belt is going out."

"The timing belt? What does that cost? I mean, it's just a piece of rubber, isn't it? It can't be too much."

"It is like the clutch; it is not the part, it is the labor. The belt is only fifty dollars, but there are a lot of engine parts that need to be removed to replace it."

"Can I drive without it?"

He gasped. "No, *bella mia*. The car will not run without a timing belt. It is more serious than even the clutch."

I groaned, rubbing my eyes with my hand. "How much?"

From the length of his hesitation I knew his answer would be bad. I just didn't anticipate how bad. "Six hundred." He quickly added, "But I will work with you on it. Family discount."

"Six hundred more. With the clutch, that's more than a thousand dollars." I breathed out heavily. "I don't even know if the car's worth that."

"Old cars do not become new," he lamented. "I checked the blue book on your car. It is worth almost two thousand. Maybe you should get a new car."

"But then I'd have a monthly payment . . ."

"Yes, but you have one now anyway. If you sold the car, you could pay off the repairs and use the money toward a monthly payment. It would at least buy you a few months."

I pushed away my panic. "I'll think about it."

"So do you want me to fix it?"

I thought over my predicament. "I can't sell a car that doesn't run," I finally said. "I'll figure something out."

"I'm sorry, *bella*. I wish I could just do the work for you. But it is hard enough keeping the shop open as it is. I got the taxes and payroll. It is killing me."

"I understand. I'd never ask that. When will it be ready?"

"We have to order the belt from Ogden, but William is fast. It should be done by tomorrow night. You'll have it for the weekend."

"Thank you." I hung up and tried not to cry. Maybe I should have. I'm told that crying waitresses make more tips.

C H A P T E R

four

There was a bit of excitement in town today. A man climbed under his truck. For this town, that's front-page news. I'm not making fun of this. In larger towns, good news days tend to be bad days for humans.

—Elle Sheen's Diary

"I told the kids at school we got a new car, so they think we're rich," Dylan said the next morning on the way to school.

"We're not rich," I said. "Why did you tell them that?"

"Albert's family got a new car. His dad's a plumber. He's rich."

I looked over. "Is being rich important to you?"

"We only have old things."

"You're not old. I'm not old."

"You're kind of old."

"Didn't need to hear that today," I said.

"But you're still pretty."

I smiled. "Okay, you've redeemed yourself."

"What does that mean?"

"It means Mama Gator ain't going to eat her young."

I dropped Dylan off, then hurried to the diner. Loretta

was sitting at her desk counting receipts. "Good morning, honey."

"Not so good," I said, stopping at the door to her office. "I need to work more shifts."

Loretta looked up. "You got it, honey. You can start tonight if you like. Cassie just called in sick again. She's got that influenza that's going around. I swear, that girl catches everything. She's a walking petri dish. Trying to earn a little extra for Christmas?"

"Christmas is the least of my worries." I frowned. "I'm pretty sure the universe has conspired to bankrupt me before the year's out."

"Don't flatter yourself, honey. The universe doesn't care that you exist."

"That's . . . so depressing."

Loretta looked at me sympathetically. "I'm sorry, honey. Sometimes it feels like we're running just to stand still."

"I'm running and still going backward."

"Now *that's* depressing," Loretta said. "So I'm going to start putting out the Christmas decorations today."

"Don't do it all yourself," I said. "I want some fun."

"I'll have Bart bring down the boxes when he's got a minute."

I loved it when we decorated. The diner, like the street it was named after, was made for the holiday and wore it well.

"Hey, Elle," Jamie said, invading the back room. "Dennis is here. He's waiting for you."

"Thanks, doll."

I walked through the kitchen toward the front. Bart smiled when he saw me. "Elle."

"Morning, chef-man. Dennis is here. The usual."

"The Dennis usual," he echoed. "Eggs fried hard, side of ham, drizzle of mustard on the side."

"You got it."

Dennis was one of my regulars, as predictable as a snowdrift in December. He was an older gentleman, eighties I guessed, a widower, tall with oversized ears and a massive red nose and silver eyebrows as thick as rope. He wore a gray wool Irish flat cap that I'd never seen off his head, his silver hair peeking out from under it like weeds growing out from under a fence. I had considered that his hair was woven into his hat so he couldn't remove it.

Dennis was sitting in his usual corner booth. He smiled when he saw me. "Hey, Elle."

"Good morning, Dennis."

His brows rose. "But is it?"

"Not really," I said. "But it's a pleasant fiction."

"Indeed," he said. "Got your Christmas shopping done?"

"Haven't even started. How about you?"

He swatted at the air in front of him. "Humbug. I'm too old for that craziness . . ." He shut his menu. I don't even know why he looked at it as he always ordered the same thing. "I'll have the usual with a drizzle of mustard on the side."

"I know. I already put your order in."

"You did, did you?"

"The second Jamie told me you were here. I thought I'd save you some time. Busy man like you."

"Busy man like me," he said, making a low growl. "I'm about as busy as a sloth on sleeping pills. Who knows, I might mix things up on you sometime and order a short stack and hash browns just to keep you on your toes."

"You've come at the same hour, sat in the same booth, and worn the same hat for the last five years. I don't think you'll be mixing things up on me."

"Seven," he said. "You weren't around before that."

"I'll make you a deal. Change the hat and I'll wait for your order."

He grinned. "Fair enough."

Outside the diner came a loud, prolonged honk followed by a staccato chorus of others. The front of the diner was all windows and along with everyone else, I looked out to see what was happening. From what I could see, there was an older model olive-green Ford pickup parked in the street in front of the diner. The driver's-side door was open and, peculiarly, there was no one inside.

"What in tarnation?" Dennis said. "Looks like some fool just ditched his truck in the middle of the road."

Just then Lyle Ferguson, a chunky red-faced man who owned the local hardware store, stormed through the front door of the diner. "Someone call the police."

"What's going on?" Loretta asked, walking out from the kitchen.

"There's a man under that truck," Lyle said.

"He was run over?" Loretta asked.

"No, he just got out and crawled under it."

I walked to the front door and looked out. I could see a man lying on his stomach underneath a truck. "What's he doing?" I asked.

"He's crazy," Lyle said. "He's shouting things in Chinese or something crazy."

"The police are here," I said.

A blue-and-white police car with no siren but lights flashing maneuvered around the stopped cars and pulled up to the curb next to the diner. Two officers got out. I knew both men, as they were diner regulars.

The driver of the police car, a lanky, red-haired officer named Andy, knelt down beside the truck. Then the other officer, Peter, a stocky, thick man with a crew cut, did as well.

Pedestrians stopped on the sidewalk to watch as the drama unfolded. A few drivers, at least those stuck behind the stationary truck, got out of their cars.

"He's under his truck," Dennis said. "That crazy got under his truck."

"That's what I just said," the red-faced man affirmed. "He's lost his mind."

"Probably on drugs," Dennis said. "It's that LSD."

"He should be locked up in an asylum," Lyle said. "Man's mad as a hatter."

I had no idea what was going on, but my heart felt for him. "Maybe he needs some coffee." I poured some coffee into a paper cup and walked out into the cold.

Andy and Peter were still crouched down next to the

truck, which was still idling, the fumes of its exhaust clouding the air around the scene. Like Lyle had said, the man underneath the truck was shouting in a foreign tongue. I didn't understand what he was saying, but I understood the tone—he sounded angry. Or scared.

"Is everything okay?" I asked.

Officer Andy glanced up, surprised to see me. "Stay back, Elle."

The man kept shouting, his voice growing in ferocity.

In spite of the warning, I moved a little closer and crouched down to see who it was. To my surprise, I recognized him. It was William, the new guy at Renato's.

"I know him," I said.

Both officers looked at me.

"You know him?" Andy asked.

I nodded, still looking at the man. Then I said, "William, can you hear me? It's me, Elle. From the shop. Can you hear me? You're going to be okay."

His gaze met mine. He suddenly stopped shouting. The intensity left his face, replaced by a look of confusion.

"I brought you some coffee."

William looked to me like someone who had just woken from a dream. He wiped his eyes. Then he lay on his side and groaned a little, as if recovering from the outburst.

"Are you okay?" I asked.

"Yeah," he said, shielding his eyes.

"Sir," Andy said. "We need you to come out from under the truck."

William looked back over. He still looked a little disoriented. Or maybe embarrassed. "Yes, sir," he said. He slid out from under the truck, sitting on the wet asphalt. The front of his sweatshirt was soaked and dirty. He put his head in his hands.

Andy turned to Peter. "I think we're okay. Go direct traffic."

Peter stood and walked around behind the truck.

Andy turned back to William. "Are you all right?"

"I'm sorry," he said. "I'm not sure what happened."

I moved in closer to William. "I brought you some coffee," I said again. I offered him the cup. "It's black."

William hesitated for a moment, then took the coffee. He drank the entire thing in two gulps, then lowered the cup to his side. "Thank you."

"You're welcome. Would you like me to take the cup?"

He handed it to me.

"We need to get your truck out of here," Andy said to William. "Do you mind if I have Peter drive it?"

"I can move it," he said.

"I'd like my deputy to move it," Andy said.

William rubbed his face. "The keys are inside."

"Thank you," Andy said, though he already knew. The truck was still idling. He turned toward his officer and shouted, "Pete. Move the truck."

"On it," Peter shouted back. As Peter came back around, I said, "Can we get his coat?"

"Grab his coat," Andy said.

Peter grabbed William's thick army-green jacket and handed it to me, then climbed inside the truck.

"Where are you going to take it?" William asked.

"Not far," Andy replied. "Just down to the station. I'll drive you there. We just need to ask you a few questions. Make sure you're all right."

William nodded. Andy stood and offered William his hand. He helped him up. "My car's right here," Andy said.

"Here's your coat," I said.

He took it from me and put it on. "Thank you."

"You're welcome."

William followed Andy to the police car. I just stood there watching as Andy opened the back door and William climbed in. Andy glanced back at me, then got in the driver's seat. The police car drove off followed by William's truck. I walked back inside the diner.

"What was that about?" Loretta asked.

"I honestly don't know," I said.

"It's that LSD," Dennis said. "Kids and drugs these days. I tell you, the world's coming apart at the seams."

CHAPTER

five

Music can open doors our hearts have locked and dead bolted.

—Elle Sheen's Diary

L ater that afternoon I called Renato's. Renato answered the phone.
"Hi, it's Elle."

"*Ciao, bella.*"

"Did you hear what happened with your new guy?" I asked.

"*Si.* William told me. He did not look well so I sent him home. That means your car is not going to be done by tonight."

"I understand."

"Not to worry, *bella.* You can keep the Valiant for the weekend. It is a sexy car."

"Thank you," I said. "Is William okay?"

"I do not know," he said. "But he is a good man. We can hope."

I woke the next morning to eighteen inches of new snow. Dylan wanted me to take him tubing and was upset when I told him that I had to work.

"But you don't work Saturday mornings," he said.

"I know. We just need a little more money right now."

"I hate money," he said.

I hugged him. "So do I. But I wish I had more of it."

Fran watched Dylan while I worked a double. Andy and Peter, the police officers, came in during the dinner shift.

"Hey, Elle," Andy said.

"Hey," I said. "Sit wherever."

"Thanks." Andy always walked stiffly. He once told me that, as a teenager, he had broken his back riding a motor- cycle and had never fully recovered.

I grabbed some water glasses and brought them over to the table. "Need a menu?"

"No," Andy said. "We know it by heart."

Peter, who was the more quiet of the two, just shook his head. "I'm good too."

"Wouldn't go that far," Andy said.

"What can I get you boys?" I asked.

Andy said, "I'll have the open-face turkey sandwich smothered in gravy with mashed potatoes, cranberry sauce, and mixed vegetables."

"One Thanksgiving come early," I said. "And what would you like to drink?"

"Ginger beer. And save me a piece of that pecan pie if you still got some."

"We didn't get any today."

"What you got?"

"Apple."

"Apple is good."

"Apple it is."

"I'll have the meatloaf special," Peter said, rubbing a thick hand through his spiky brown hair. "Gravy on top *and* on the smashed potatoes."

"Smash the potatoes," I said. "Did you want some pie?"

"I'll have the apple."

"À la mode?"

"I'll have cheese with it."

"Apple with a chunk of cheddar. Hold the à la mode."

I went back to the kitchen and put in the order. Then, while the chef was cooking, I took a short break to eat my own dinner. I was halfway through my meal when the kitchen bell rang.

"Order up, Elle."

"Thanks, Bart."

"Did you finish your dinner?"

"Do I ever?"

"That's why you're so thin. I'll cook slower next time, let you put some meat on those pretty little bones."

"I've got enough meat on my bones." I grabbed the plates. "And you cook slow enough."

"Oh, you're cold, girl," he said. "Cold as a Mistletoe winter."

"I may be cold, but you're slow." I grinned. "Slow but good."

"That's what all the ladies say," he said.

"You're incorrigible."

I carried the plates out to the police officers. "Here you go, gentlemen."

They both thanked me. Then Andy said, "Hey, I wanted to say, that was really nice of you to take that coffee out to that guy. He really appreciated it. He mentioned it several times."

"So, are you guys friends?" Peter asked.

"No. I just met him a few days ago. He's a mechanic over at Renato's. He's working on my car."

"From under your car to his," Peter said, amusing himself.

"Why did he crawl under his truck?" I asked.

"That's the crazy part," Peter said. He turned to Andy. "You tell it."

Andy cleared his throat. "You know, we see some weird junk on our beat, but I've never seen anything like that. I don't know the term for it, but that guy is a Vietnam vet . . ."

"Shell shock," Peter said. "It happened to a cousin of mine. His brain never really came back from the war. He ended up hanging himself."

Andy nodded. "Apparently he saw a lot of bad stuff over there."

"He told us he lost half his patrol in an ambush," Peter said.

Andy continued, "So yesterday, he was in front of your diner waiting for the light to change when a song came on the radio that, like, triggered him. He suddenly thought he was under attack from the Viet Cong."

Peter shook his head. "Man, you should have seen his face when we got there. It was like staring down the devil. That's something I don't think I'll ever forget. Down at the station he told us he thought we were Viet Cong soldiers. He was shouting at us in Vietnamese."

"I didn't know soldiers had to learn Vietnamese," I said.

"They don't if they don't have to," Andrew said.

"He was a POW for almost four years. He was in that famous Hanoi Hilton," Peter added.

"Oh dear," I said.

"I can't imagine what that would do to your brain," Andy said, shaking his head. "He was with one of the last groups to come home."

My heart was pounding. "You didn't give him a ticket, did you?"

"No. I mean, if I were going by the book, I should have cited him, but sometimes you got to go by the spirit of the law. He fought for our country."

I thought about how harshly I had judged him. "Where's he from?"

"He moved here three weeks ago from Colorado, but originally he's from Indiana."

"What a way to start a new life in a small town," I said.

"It's like they say," Peter said between bites, "wherever you go, there you are."

"Is he okay?" I asked.

"I think so," Andy said. "We took him over to the hospital in Ogden and let someone there check him out. They've got a psychiatric ward there."

"Hopefully they can help," I said.

"That was a tough thing, that war," Peter said, slowly shaking his head. "A lot of those boys never really came back."

Suddenly I teared up. Andy looked over at him. "You idiot."

Peter looked at me. "I'm sorry, Elle. I forgot."

"You *forgot* to plug in your brain this morning," Andy said. "So sorry, Elle. We shouldn't have brought it up."

"It's okay," I said, wiping my eyes. "I asked." I took a deep breath. "I'll stop bothering you boys and let you eat."

"You're never a bother, Elle," Andrew said. "That's why we always come back."

I forced a smile. "You always come back because Loretta's got the best pie in town."

"That too," Andy said, turning back to his plate. "Bless you, Elle."

I started to go, then turned back. "What was the song?"

Andy looked up from his turkey. "The song?"

"The song that set him off."

"Creedence Clearwater Revival," he said. "'Run Through the Jungle.'"

CHAPTER

six

*The sermon today was on gratitude. I've always believed
that there are none so impoverished as those who deny the
blessings of their lives.*

—Elle Sheen's Diary

S unday was the only day I had off all week. It was also
my only day to spend with Dylan. The day began
as it always did, with me making Dylan waffles with
whipped cream and then taking him to church. We were
nearing Thanksgiving so the sermon was on gratitude and
the power of thankfulness. I was grateful to hear it. I needed
to hear it. When you're struggling with lack, it's easy to become obsessed with all you don't have and forget what you
do. It was nice to be reminded of all I had to be grateful for.

After church we came home and I made chili and
homemade bread, using half the dough for fried scones.
(In Utah, the term *scones* is used for what the rest of the
world calls fry bread or elephant ears.) My homemaking
habits were more than economical. They were reminiscent
of my own upbringing. Growing up in Cedar City, my
mother made homemade bread every week. At least she
would when she wasn't on a bender.

After lunch, Dylan asked if we could go outside and make a snowman. There was enough snow in our little backyard that we could have made an army of them—which Dylan advocated for, but I persuaded him to stop at two: an effigy of each of us.

Afterward we came back inside and, after peeling off layers of snow-covered clothing, we made Christmas cookies. I had a collection of five Christmas cookie cutters: a star, a stocking, an angel, a Christmas tree, and a reindeer, the latter being Dylan's favorite. (Fortunately I had some of those little cinnamon candies to put on the reindeers' noses.)

While waiting for the cookies to cool, I let Dylan eat an unfrosted one and watch TV while I took a forty-five-minute nap—by far my greatest luxury of the week. Then we frosted the cookies and finished our night with our Sunday-evening tradition of lying on my bed and watching *The Wonderful World of Disney* (which, no doubt, would have been much better in color. The last of the networks had switched over to color just a few years earlier).

I looked forward to this, as it was the one time that Dylan would still cuddle with me and let me hold him. I knew it wouldn't always be that way—a fact I mourned. He was my little guy. He was my life. Even with the hardships of those days, I still often thought that I would have loved to freeze that time of Dylan's life. But even then I knew it would be a mistake. To hold the note is to spoil the song.

"Mom, do you think we'll ever get a color TV?" Dylan asked as I put him down for bed.

"That would be nice," I said, which was my standard answer for things I couldn't afford.

"Everyone has a color TV."

"Not everyone. Some people don't even have TVs."

He looked absolutely amazed. "What do they watch?"

I kissed the top of his head. "Life."

Monday morning it was back to the usual grind. The diner's traffic was typical: the local regulars, a half dozen truckers hopping off I-15, the odd salesman stopping by for breakfast.

Dennis came in at his usual time. He was wearing the same hat, of course. In spite of my earlier threat, I didn't put his order in.

"Morning, Elle."

"Good morning, Dennis. How's your day?"

"I'll let you know when it happens," he said. "I'll have the usual. If you didn't already have your guy back there make it."

"No, I waited. A drizzle of mustard."

"A drizzle of mustard."

A few minutes later I brought out his food.

"That was some excitement last week," he said. "Did you ever hear what happened to that guy who was run over by the truck? I looked in the obituaries this morning but there wasn't anyone who had died in a truck-related accident. Had two cancers and maybe a suicide. I had to deduce that, of course. They never state the cause of death if it's a suicide unless you're Hemingway or Marilyn Monroe. And the latter was suspect. You know she was involved with the Kennedys."

Dennis's memory wasn't great. Somewhere over the weekend he must have told himself a different story about the event. Before I could correct him he continued.

"Anyway, the suicide was old Creighton up in Farr West. Certainly not famous or involved with the Kennedys—just not doing well since Lois died. Saw him four weeks ago at the Masonic lodge. He told me that waking was the worst part of his day, next to every other moment."

"I'm sorry to hear that," I said.

Dennis once told me he read the obituaries every day to see if he was in them. If he wasn't, he got dressed.

"He wasn't run over by the truck," I said. "He climbed under it."

Dennis's brow furrowed. "Why would he do that?"

"I guess he wasn't feeling well," I said.

"That makes no sense. Most of the time I don't feel well, but I've never once crawled under my car." He shook his head. "He must still be alive. He wasn't in the obituary."

CHAPTER

seven

Too many people turn to the end of another's story even before the final chapter has been written.
                                    —Elle Sheen's Diary

I was working a double shift and the only time the diner could afford for me to be gone was between two and four, our slow time. I was eager to get my car back, but by the time the dinner rush ended, Renato's would be closed.

A little before noon I found Loretta in her office. "Loretta, I need to take a break after the lunch rush."

She looked up from her paperwork. "Did the school call?"

"No. I need to pick up my car before the shop closes."

"Fine with me, sugar plum. You hear that, Jamie?" she shouted. "You're pulling double duty this afternoon while Elle gets her car."

"Got it," Jamie said. She was putting on mascara in the bathroom outside Loretta's office. I don't know how Loretta even knew she was there. She had a sixth sense that way.

Before becoming a waitress, Jamie had worked a previous life as a hair stylist, and she saw her body, all six feet of it, as a blank canvas to be painted on—with makeup and hair dye being her preferred media. She wore thick eye shadow the colors of the rainbow with drawn-on eyebrows, overcompensating for what God had neglected.

Truthfully, I wasn't positive what color her hair was, though I guessed it was light brown on its way to gray. Since the day I met her, her hair had been platinum, dishwater blond, strawberry blond, lavender, umber, black, light brunette, chestnut, and flaxen—pretty much the gamut of follicular possibility. Her color du jour was ginger, something that agreed with her.

"Thanks, honey," I said.

"Don't mention it. I'm praying for a miracle healing for your clutch."

I wasn't looking forward to getting my car back. I hated my car. And I was terrified to see the repair bill.

I drove over to Renato's a little before three.

"She's right there," Renato said, pointing toward my car. He handed me the keys with a sheet of yellow paper. "And here is the bill."

I took the paper from him. It hurt to see it. It was for seventy-seven dollars, twenty more than I hoped it would be.

"Seventy-seven?"

"Yes, *signorina*."

I breathed out slowly, then looked into his eyes. "I know you're giving me a good deal, but right now, that's a little steep for my monthly budget. Is it possible we could stretch it out a little more and make the monthly payment in the fifty-dollar range?"

"That is not a payment," Renato said.

I looked at him quizzically. "I don't understand."

"That is the whole bill. *Tutto il conto.*"

It took a moment for me to understand. "But you said it would be more than five hundred just for the clutch. And more for the broken belt."

"That bill is just for parts. There is no charge for labor."

"But . . ." I looked at him with gratitude. "You can't do that."

"Well, I didn't," he said. "William did. He repaired your car on his own time. It took him until four in the morning. You can thank me for the heating bill and him for the labor. *Un bacio* will be fine," he said, turning his cheek to me.

I kissed it, then said, "He fixed my car for free?"

"Except for the cost of parts," Renato said.

I couldn't believe it. "Is he still here?"

"No. He was sick over the weekend so he's taking the day off."

"He was sick while he was working on my car?"

"Very sick. He was coughing like an old tractor. I think he has the influenza," Renato said. "I could barely understand him this morning." He leaned forward even though there was no one else there. "He sounded a little *pazzo.*"

"*Pazzo?*"

"A little delirious. Very sick."

I was speechless. Then I pulled my checkbook from my purse. "I'll pay this now." I wrote a check for seventy-seven dollars and handed it to Renato. "Why did he do that?"

"He said you were kind to him," Renato said.

"All I did was take him a cup of coffee."

"I told you, remember? Do not judge him too harshly."

"I'm sorry," I said. "That was foolish of me." I took a deep breath. "I would like to thank him. Do you know where he lives?"

He scrawled a number on the back of my receipt. "He lives in that apartment building on the end of Noel Street. The one with the *schifoso* yard, just three blocks down from the diner."

"I know the one," I said. "Thank you."

"*Prego, bella.*"

I got in my car and started it. It sounded beautiful. I suddenly began crying. *Why would he do such a thing for me? How could I have misjudged the man so badly?*

CHAPTER

eight

For the last seven years my life has felt like a financial Whack-a-Mole game.

—Elle Sheen's Diary

As I walked back into the diner, Jamie looked me over. "Oh, honey." My eyes must have been red because she hugged me. "I'm so sorry. You'll get through this. I've got a little stashed away, I can help."

Her response only made me cry more. "That's not why I'm crying. He fixed it for free."

"Renato fixed your car for free?" Loretta said, walking into the conversation. "That's a first. That man would charge a baby for diapers."

"It wasn't Renato," I said. "It was the new guy who works for him. William."

"The guy who stopped traffic the other day?" Jamie said. "The one you said was a beast?"

"I'm so sorry I said that. He worked on my car until four in the morning."

"Why would he do that?" Jamie asked.

"I don't know. All I did was take him a cup of coffee."

Loretta shook her head. "That must have been some coffee. Is he single?"

"Is he cute?" Jamie added.

"You two have a one-track mind."

"At least someone's on that track, baby girl," Loretta said. "You're derailed."

"I don't know if he's single."

"Well, you better find out. What did you say to him?"

"I didn't say anything. He wasn't there. Renato said he was sick. He was sick when he worked on my car."

"That's really sweet," Jamie said. "Maybe you should take him some chicken soup."

"That's a good idea," I said.

"I'll donate a crock of chicken noodle to the cause," Loretta said. "And whatever else you want to take him. We got the pecan pie in today. A man fixes your car for free, you better take care of him."

"I'll take him some dinner," I said. "But I don't get off until ten."

"I don't have anything tonight," Loretta said. "You can take off at seven thirty, after the rush."

"Thank you."

"You never answered me," Jamie said. "Is he cute?"

I thought a moment, then said, "Yes. He is."

Loretta nodded. "That always helps."

I was surprised to find myself growing excited about the prospect of seeing William, though, frankly, I had no idea how the encounter would go. I'd seen the man three times. The first time he yelled at my son and then scolded me, the second time he apologized, and the third time he was under a truck hiding from an imaginary enemy. Realistically, I should probably run. But he had blessed my life more than anyone in the last five years and he didn't even know me. Who was this man?

CHAPTER

nine

I went to his apartment anticipating staying for a few minutes, not the night.

—Elle Sheen's Diary

I don't know if it's true of all small towns, but people generally eat early in Mistletoe, and by seven o'clock there were only eight customers in the diner.

Loretta came up behind me as I was filling a drink order. "You can go now, darlin'," she said. "Go see the man." She was carrying a paper bag and a large plastic container with its lid taped down. "I got him a few days' worth of soup." She had gotten more than just soup. She had filled the bag with the morning's pastries, a loaf of hard bread, and some pecan pie. "I threw a few bags of chamomile tea and some packets of sugar in the bottom of the sack. Nothing better for the system when you're sick."

As generous as Loretta was to those in need, I was a little surprised at how fully she'd embraced reaching out to this guy. "That's really kind of you."

"Whatever I can do. Thing is, he helped you, so that

6 6

helped me. Otherwise I'd likely have been obliged to give you a raise."

"You were thinking of giving me a raise?"

"Yes, but I came to my senses and talked myself out of it. Now you have a good night and don't go catching anything. I already lost Cassie. I can't afford to have you sick too."

Loretta was peculiar about money. She was simultaneously generous and tightfisted—the kind of person who would give you the shirt off her back and then charge you to wash it.

I carried the food out to my car. It wasn't lost on me that I was driving my car because of him. Instant karma.

I knew the apartment building. Everyone in Mistletoe did, as it was the only one in town. No one I knew had ever lived there, and, from all appearances, its only inhabitants were drifters, strangers, and men in trouble with their wives. The locals just called it "that apartment," but it had a name: the Harrison. It had once been a hotel, named after President William Henry Harrison, whose presidential run lasted a lackluster thirty-one days, as he died of pneumonia after giving his inaugural address in freezing temperatures without a coat. I have no idea why anyone would name a hotel after the man; you would think they would have chosen a president who had accomplished something while in office—or at least had the sense to wear a coat.

The hotel was built more than a hundred years back when Mistletoe was a prosperous mining town. As usually happened, when the veins of ore ran dry, so did the town, leaving a few farmers, homesteaders, and those too old to pick up and start their lives over again. The hotel passed into bankruptcy and eventually it was left to the owner to either tear down or find a way to repurpose it. He chose the latter.

It was dark out, had been for several hours, and the Harrison apartments were near the south end of Noel Street in a bit of a run-down area. In a bigger town this might have been considered dangerous or scary, but this was Mistletoe and its days of newsworthy crime were pretty much past.

There were no lights on this end of the street and a sickle moon lit the area, sparkling off the recently fallen, crystalline-crusted snow.

No one had shoveled the sidewalk in front of the apartments and there was a single set of footprints that led into the building. William's olive-green pickup truck was parked around the side, visible from the street.

I parked my car at the curb out front of the building, got the food out of the back seat, and carried it up the snow-encrusted walkway to the front doors and into the apartment building's dimly lit lobby.

The inside of the building looked as derelict as its exterior. There was a bag of garbage, a bicycle with a flat tire leaning against one of the walls, and a pile of mail on the floor beneath an inset brass mailbox as if the building's residents, past and present, hadn't picked up their mail for a few months.

The place looked like I imagined it might, as if the

owner was absentee and the place's inhabitants were more squatters than renters.

A spiderweb-covered bronze chandelier flickered a little but gave enough illumination to reveal a dirty black-and-white-checkered tile floor. The lobby still looked like it belonged to a hotel. There was a curved stairway with a carved wooden banister leading to a second-story landing with a spindled balustrade.

The base of the stair flared out and, on each side of the stairs, a columnar newel post supported an intricately carved wooden pineapple that had likely once been beautiful but now was chipped and dusty and covered in spiderwebs.

I was startled by a brindled brown-and-black cat that darted across the lobby and disappeared down the darkened hallway.

I took the receipt from my pocket where Renato had written the number of William's apartment. Number 205. I climbed one flight of stairs and walked down the hall to the third door on the right.

Curiously, the door to the apartment was already open a few inches. I set the bag of food down on the floor, then rapped on the door with the back of my hand. There was no answer—at least not from *his* apartment. The door across the hall opened and quickly shut again before I could see who was there.

I rapped again. There was still nothing, though my knocking had opened the door a little more, wide enough to reveal the room's interior, lit by a single yellowish light from a brass floor lamp. I could hear the metallic ticking of a radiator.

"Hello?" I said, then louder, "Is anyone home?"

There was no response.

"William?"

There was a spasm of coughing followed a few moments later by heavy, slow footsteps. A hoarse voice asked, "Who is it?"

I swallowed. "It's Elle. From the diner." Then added, "You fixed my car."

William staggered over to the door. I almost didn't recognize him. He wasn't wearing a shirt; just gray cotton sweatpants that hung loosely from his thin waist. He was lanky and lean in form, but muscular. His right shoulder was covered in a tattoo. He looked sick; his face pale and his hair matted to one side as if he'd been sleeping. His chin was covered in thick stubble. He leaned against the door for support.

"What can I do for you?" he asked, even though he clearly wasn't in a condition to do anything for anyone, including himself.

"I came to thank you," I said, feeling like getting him out of bed was doing more harm than good. "I heard you were sick, so I brought you something to eat." I squatted down and lifted the food. "I brought you some soup. It's still warm."

He coughed, covering his mouth with his forearm. He looked unsteady and in no condition to carry what I'd brought him. "If you don't mind, I'll just put this on your counter."

He nodded slightly. "Thank you." He stepped back from the entrance, though still leaned against the door. I walked past him into the room.

The room smelled dank and musty, old like it was. The apartment still looked like a hotel room, boxy and curtly divided with a small coat closet near the front door. The front room included a small kitchen with a chin-high refrigerator and a small hot plate. The floral wallpaper was faded and torn in places.

What furniture there was looked to be remnants from the hotel days. There was a small table, two chairs, and a low couch upholstered in a threadbare green velvet from the fifties.

On the other side of the apartment, the bedroom door was open and I could see the unmade bed he had just crawled out of. I set the food on the counter.

"Would you like me to pour the soup into a bowl?" I asked.

"No," he said softly. "Thank you."

I sensed that he really just wanted to be left alone. "I'll just leave everything here." I looked back at him. "I'm sorry you're so sick."

"Thank you," he said, the words sounding like they'd taken great effort. He was still leaning against the door like it was holding him up. As I walked back toward him, he put his head down as if he were dizzy. Then he collapsed to the floor with a dull thud.

"William!"

He was unconscious. I put my hand on his forehead. He was burning with fever. I knelt at his side, my hand on his arm. "William," I said softly. "William."

Suddenly his eyelids fluttered open. He gazed at me with a confused expression. "Who are you?"

"I'm Elle. Remember? You fixed my car."

He closed his eyes for a moment, then said, "What are you doing here?"

"I brought you some food. I came to thank you."

He didn't respond.

"We should get you to the hospital," I said. "You're very sick."

"No," he said, squinting with pain. "No hospital. No doctor."

I wasn't sure what to do. Frankly, I wasn't even sure what I was doing. I barely knew this man. Of course, he barely knew me, yet he helped me. I couldn't help but feel somewhat responsible for his sickness, since he'd no doubt gotten sicker working through the night on my car.

"What can I do for you?" I asked.

He closed his eyes and breathed heavily but said nothing. He looked vulnerable and weak, nothing like the powerful, scary man I first encountered at the auto shop.

"Is there someone I can call?"

After a moment he said softly, "There's no one."

The words made my heart hurt. "Don't you have anyone to take care of you?"

"I don't need . . ." He didn't finish the sentence.

I sat there for a moment looking at him. His lips were dry and cracked. I guessed he was dehydrated. "I can help," I said. When he didn't object to my offer I asked, "When was the last time you had something to drink?"

His response came haltingly. "I don't know."

"I'm going to get you some water."

I got up and began looking through his cupboards for a cup. There were only three, two coffee cups and a cheap plastic one. Then I looked inside his refrigerator to see if he had cold water. It was surprisingly bare. There was only a carton of milk, a half-empty jar of Miracle Whip, a small jar of mustard, and an opened package of hot dogs.

I filled the cup with water from the tap and brought it to him. I knelt down next to him and said, "Let me help you drink." I put my hand behind his head. His hair was matted and wet with sweat. "I'm going to help you lift your head."

He groaned a little as I lifted. Then I raised the cup to his lips, supporting the back of his head with my hand. He drank thirstily, though some of the water dribbled down the corner of his mouth, down his stubbled chin. When he had finished the water, he laid his head back. I dabbed the water from his face with my coat sleeve. He shivered.

"You have the chills," I said. "And your fever . . ." I touched his head again. I'd never felt a fever that hot. I wished I had a thermometer but, considering the austerity of his apartment, I doubted he had one. The situation reminded me of a few months back when Dylan was running a fever and I had sat up with him through the night. "Do you have a thermometer?"

"No."

"I'm going to get a cold cloth for your forehead." I looked around his counter and through his drawers until I found a dishtowel. I opened his freezer looking for ice. There was only a frosted package of peas. I wrapped them in the dishcloth and brought them back over to him.

"Tell me if it's too cold."

He coughed again, then closed his eyes. I held the bag of peas to his forehead. I glanced down at my watch. It was past eight. Fran would have already put Dylan to bed. Fran rarely minded staying late, or even spending the night, but I needed to tell her. William shivered again.

"I need to go home and check on my son," I said. "But I'm going to come back. Okay?"

"You don't need to," he said.

"I think I do. Let me help you to your bed. Or do you want to lie here until I get back?"

"My bed."

"I'll help you up." I set my makeshift ice pack to the side and leaned over him. "Put your arms around my neck."

He lifted his arms around my neck locking his fingers together. His breath was warm on my neck. It was strange to think it, but it was the first time in a long time that a man had put his arms around me.

"Let's sit you up first and let you get settled for a moment. I don't want all the blood rushing away from your head." I sat up, and he pulled himself to a sitting position.

A moment later I said, "Tell me when you're ready."

"Ready."

"All right. Up we go."

As I stood, he pushed himself up, using me more for balance than lift. I put my arm around his waist and we walked to the bedroom. He sat down on the side of his bed, then lay back, groaning with the motion. I lifted his legs onto the bed and pulled them a quarter clockwise.

"You just rest. I'll be back in about a half hour."

"Thank you." He rolled his head to the side. For a moment I just looked at him. My heart hurt for his pain but equally for his loneliness. Lately I had obsessed over how hard my life seemed, but I didn't suffer from loneliness. I had friends. I had Dylan. For all I could see, he had no one.

I walked out of his bedroom, shutting the door behind me. I checked his apartment door to make sure it wouldn't lock behind me, shut it, and went down to my car. It had started snowing again, and the windshield was covered with a thin batting of white.

I turned on the windshield wipers and drove down the deserted Noel Street past the diner. The diner was quiet as well and I could see Jamie and Nora inside filling the salt and pepper bottles—one of the things we did before going home each evening.

My duplex was only eight minutes from the diner. I walked in to find Fran sitting on the couch reading a book. She jumped when I walked in.

"I scared you," I said.

"It's the book. It's a suspense novel."

"What is it?"

She held up the book so I could see its cover: *Where Are the Children?*

"That sounds scary. Who wrote it?"

"It's a new writer." She glanced at the cover. "Mary Higgins Clark. She's good."

"And how was Dylan?"

"He went right down," she said. "How was your night?"

"Different than I expected. Would you be okay staying a little longer? I'm taking care of someone."

"Who?"

"Just a friend," I said. "He's new in town. He's sick and doesn't have anyone else."

"No problem," she said. "I can finish the book. Should I spend the night?"

"If you don't mind."

"I don't mind. Is it still snowing out?"

"A little."

"The weatherman said it was going to snow all night. All the more reason to stay put."

"Thank you. I just need to gather a few things."

I looked in on Dylan. He was sleeping soundly, though he'd pulled off most of his covers. I pulled them back up to his chin, kissed his forehead, then went to my room and got a heating pad, a bottle of aspirin, a thermometer, and a couple of washcloths. I grabbed an ice pack and filled it with ice from the freezer, then put it all in a large canvas bag.

"I don't know when I'll be back," I said to Fran on my way out.

"Don't worry about a thing," she said.

"I never do when you're here."

The snow was already coming down heavier. I carried everything out to my car, then drove back to the Harrison. It was nearly ten o'clock when I opened the door to William's apartment. As I walked in I heard a strange guttural noise that sounded more like a growl than a groan. Then I heard William shout out. "No!"

I walked to the door of his bedroom, slowly opening it. "William?"

His eyes were open and he was looking at me, but *not* at me—like he was looking through me. He looked scared.

"Charlies are everywhere, Lieutenant! Let's Zippo it and get out of here."

I didn't know what to do. Was it dangerous for me to be here? He was powerfully built. What if he mistook me for something else?

Sympathy won out. "William, it's just me. Elle. You're in your bedroom. I'm the only one here. Everything's okay."

He stopped, breathed out slowly, then lay back down.

My heart was still racing as I walked to the side of his bed and sat down.

"Hey." I put my hand on his forehead. He was still burning up. I took the thermometer from my bag. "William," I said softly. "I'm going to check your temperature."

He didn't open his eyes but turned back toward me.

"I'm going to put this thermometer under your tongue. Don't bite it." I held his bristled chin as I slid the thermometer between his lips and under his tongue. I held it there for a full minute and then pulled it out. A hundred four degrees. I had spent enough late nights in the ER with Dylan to know this wasn't good.

"You're a hundred and four," I said, setting the thermometer on the windowsill.

"I'm not that old," he said.

In spite of the circumstances, I grinned. "I really should take you to the hospital in Ogden. Would you let me?"

He didn't say anything.

"I can't carry you. Do you think you could walk out to my car?"

"No hospital. No doctors."

I sat there a moment as I thought what to do next. "Well, we need to do something. I brought you some aspirin. Let's at least get that in you."

I went back out to the kitchen and refilled his cup with water, then poured the aspirin into my hand.

"I've got some water and three aspirin. It will help with the fever. Open please."

He opened his mouth and I individually set the pills in.

Then I pressed the cup to his lips. He swallowed the pills with half the cup of water, then lay back.

"I brought you an ice pack," I said.

I set the cup down and pulled the ice pack from my bag. I propped his pillow up so it would hold the pack up to his forehead. It only took a minute for him to fall back asleep, his breathing taking on a calm, slow cadence. "I'm sorry you're so sick," I said. "I won't leave you."

I thought he was asleep—maybe he was—but a single tear rolled down his cheek.

The lights were off, but it wasn't that dark. The moon reflecting off the snow lit the room in a brilliant blue. For nearly an hour I sat on the side of his bed watching him, his face half illuminated like a waning moon. He was so broken. Broken yet beautiful.

At one point he rolled over onto his stomach and the blanket came down from his shoulders. What I saw made my heart jump a little. There were rows of thick scars running vertically down his back. I pulled the blanket down to the small of his back. There were ten-inch scars, more than a dozen of them, raised and angry. I lightly touched one. "What did they do to you?" I asked softly.

Maybe half an hour later I sat down on the floor next to his bed with my back against the wall and closed my eyes but couldn't sleep, which was rare for me.

William got up only once in the night, to use the bathroom. He was disoriented, and I helped him to the toilet. When he came back to bed he said, "Thank you, Nurse," which I think he believed.

I again put the ice pack on his head, then lay down on the floor. I think I fell asleep around one. William woke again around three thirty. He was tossing from side to side. He kept saying, "Don't. Don't. I don't know. I told you." I knelt at his side and gently touched his arm. "You're dreaming. You're okay. You're okay."

His eyes opened and he breathed out heavily, almost panting. Then he caught his breath and looked over at me. Even in the darkness I could see the clearness and intensity of his gaze. This time he was looking directly at me, not at some figment of a nightmare, but into my eyes. Then he said, "I see why he loved you."

I looked at him. "Who?"

He closed his eyes and went back to sleep. I watched him for a moment, then went back to the floor and fell asleep.

I woke a little before seven, the brazen winter sun shining through the blinds, illuminating the room in golden stripes. I didn't know where I was at first, just that my back ached from sleeping on the hard floor. I sat up and yawned. William was still sleeping, lightly snoring.

I leaned over him just to make sure he was asleep, then I put my hand on his forehead. He was still feverish but not as hot as the night before. I pulled the covers up over him and was about to go when he slowly rolled over. His eyes were open. For a moment we just looked at each other.

"You're still here," he said in a raspy voice.

"I said I would be. I need to get my son off to school, then I'll come back." He just stared at me. I leaned over him and touched his forehead and said, "I'll be back."

CHAPTER

ten

*Guilt and expediency should not be allowed to coexist in
the same mind.*

—Elle Sheen's Diary

The night's storm had blanketed my car in nearly a
half foot of snow. I got a snow brush from my back
seat and scraped off the windows, then drove home.
Fran was wearing one of my sweatshirts. She was in the
kitchen making oatmeal.

"Morning, Florence Nightingale," she said.

"Good morning. Is he still asleep?"

"He's taking a shower."

"How'd he sleep?"

"He doesn't even know you were gone. How are you?"

"Exhausted. I slept on the floor."

"That sounds painful." She brought me over a cup of
coffee. I took a sip. "Thank you."

"Don't mention it. So who's your sick friend?"

"His name is William. Actually, he's not really a friend. I
don't know him very well."

"But you spent the night . . ."

"It's not what you think," I said, drinking my coffee. "I went over to thank him for fixing my car and he was so sick that he passed out. He was all alone. What was I supposed to do?"

"Is he cute?"

"That's not the issue."

"That's always an issue," she said. "So he's not."

"I didn't say that."

Just then Dylan walked into the kitchen. He looked at me curiously—probably because I looked like I had slept in my clothes and my hair was a tangled mane. "Morning, honey."

He didn't say anything about Fran being there. "Hi."

"I've got some oatmeal for you, little man," Fran said.

Dylan walked to the refrigerator and took out a jar of strawberry jam and carried it over to the table.

"Thanks for staying," I said.

"You're welcome. If you're okay, I'll head on home."

"We're okay," I said. "Is it all right if I pay you next Wednesday?"

"You know I'm good," she said. "I left the book on the nightstand if you want to read it."

"You're not going to tell me who dun it?"

She smiled. "Not this time." She walked over and kissed Dylan on the forehead. "Have a good day, handsome little man. I'll see you after school." She looked at me. "Would you like me to pick him up?"

"If you don't mind."

"No problem," she said. "Think you'll be late again?"

"I don't know."

"I'll bring my makeup just in case." She blew me a kiss, then walked out.

I got myself a bowl of oatmeal, put in a spoonful of brown sugar and raisins, then sat down across from Dylan. "How did you sleep?"

Dylan looked up from his bowl. "Good."

"What did you do last night?"

"We did Spirograph. Then we read a book."

"What book?"

"*Andy Buckram's Tin Men*. It's about robots."

"Classic."

His brow fell. "Do you have to work tonight?"

"Yes."

He frowned. "You *always* have to work."

"Someone has to buy the oatmeal," I said. "I don't *always* work."

"It seems like it sometimes."

"I know. It does to me too. But I don't work this Saturday, and on Sunday I don't work until three, so we can go somewhere."

"Where?"

"I don't know. Maybe tubing? If it's not snowing."

"Yeah!" Dylan pumped his fist. "And hot chocolate?"

"It's not really tubing if you don't have hot chocolate after, right?"

He nodded. "Right."

"Now go brush your teeth and pack up your school bag. We need to get going."

Dylan ran off to the bathroom while I put our bowls in the sink to soak. He was right. It felt like I was always working, which wasn't my choice. So why did I have to feel guilty about it too?

CHAPTER

eleven

*I saw him again today. Twice. Then I ruined everything
by opening my mouth. Or maybe it was my heart.*
—Elle Sheen's Diary

I dropped Dylan off at school, then ran by the diner and
grabbed some orange juice and a couple of oatmeal
muffins.

"You're here early," Loretta said as I walked in.

"I'm just picking up some things for William. I'll put it
on my tab."

"William?"

"The soldier."

"Ah. How did that go last night?"

"I ended up spending the night at his place."

Loretta clapped her hands. "There is hope yet!"

"It's not that," I said. "He was so sick that he passed out.
I ended up taking care of him all night."

"Well, that's not bad either."

"I'm taking him something for breakfast. I'll be right back."

"Take your time, darlin'. You can't rush love."

"I'm not. I'm rushing breakfast."

I drove back down Noel Street to William's apartment. I

rapped twice on his door and then let myself in. The apartment was still dark and quiet. "I'm back," I said, soft enough not to wake him if he was still sleeping but loud enough not to startle him if he wasn't. Still carrying the juice and muffins, I walked to the door of his bedroom, lightly rapped on it, and then pushed it open. He was in bed but awake.

"Hi," I said.

"You came back."

"I said I would."

"Were you here all night?" he asked.

"Yes."

He looked at me with a curious expression. "Why did you stay?"

"Because you needed me."

He smiled. It was only a slight smile, but it was the first smile I'd seen on him. It was like the sun rising after a cloudy day.

"You have a nice smile," I said.

His smile grew a little more. "Thank you."

"Why did you fix my car?"

"Because you needed me," he said, using my words back at me.

"You have no idea how much you helped." Suddenly the emotion of it caught up with me and my eyes welled up.

"I could say the same. You helped me when I was out in the street."

"All I did was bring you coffee."

"You brought me more than coffee." He slowly shook his head. "You brought me back to reality."

I didn't know what to say to that. After a moment I said,
"You must be hungry." I lifted the bag. "I brought you some
orange juice and a muffin from the diner." I reached in and
took out the muffin. "Here you go."

He peeled the paper off the muffin and hungrily de-
voured it.

"Would you like the orange juice?"

He nodded and I handed him the cup. He drank it
down nearly as fast as he ate the muffin.

"You look a lot better than you did last night," I said.

He set the empty cup down on the stand next to the
bed. "What did I look like?"

"Death."

"I felt like death."

"I brought another muffin." I handed it to him.

"Thank you."

He ate while I watched. After he finished the second
muffin, he looked up at me. "You're probably wondering
why I climbed under the truck."

"I know why," I said. "The police officers who helped you
are regulars at the diner. They told me what happened."

"You must think I'm a complete nutcase."

"I think you've been through some very hard things."
Then I said softly, "When I was taking care of you, I saw
the scars on your back."

I could see that mentioning this brought him pain.
"They're kind of hard to miss."

"I'm sorry."

"You're not the one who should be sorry."

I sighed lightly. "I need to go to work." I stood. "I didn't get a chance to get groceries, but I can take a break from work a little later."

"You don't need to do that. You've done enough."

"It's my pleasure. I brought you some soup and bread last night. It's in the refrigerator. You can have that for lunch. Loretta sent you enough food to last a few meals."

"Loretta?"

"She's my boss. She owns the diner."

He nodded. "Please thank her for me."

"I will. There's also pecan pie. I don't know if you like that."

"I love pecan pie," he said. "Back in Indiana I used to buy those little Bama pies, you know the ones?"

"My husband used to like those," I said, softer. "I also brought some chamomile tea. It will help you feel a little better."

"You're making me feel better." For a moment he just looked at me, then he said, "May I ask you something?"

"Of course."

"Why are you being so good to me?"

"Why wouldn't I?"

"I could think of a hundred reasons," he said.

I smiled. "And I can't think of one."

Loretta was still in her office when I got back to the diner. "How's your soldier?"

"He's doing a lot better. He asked me to thank you."

"If you see him again, tell him he's welcome."

"I'll be seeing him again."

"I was hoping as much."

That evening, I left work early again for William; this time so I could stop at the grocery store. I didn't know what he ate, so I bought some basics: oatmeal, bread, butter, milk, eggs, cheese, sliced sandwich meat, and three cans of Campbell's soup. The bill came to almost twenty dollars, but when I thought about the hundreds of dollars he'd saved me it seemed like a small price to pay.

I drove back to his apartment, knocked on the door, and let myself inside, carrying a grocery sack under each arm. His bedroom door was shut. "It's just me," I said.

As I set down the groceries I noticed a saucepan in the sink with residue from the soup I'd left for him. At least he'd been up and eaten something. I quietly opened his bedroom door and looked inside. He was sleeping, so I walked back to the kitchen and put everything away.

"Elle." His voice surprised me, not just because he was awake, but because he had spoken my name. I liked the way he said it.

I walked back to his room and opened the door. "Hi."

"Hey," he said, smiling.

"How are you feeling?"

"Tired, mostly."

"I see you ate something."

"I had some of the soup you brought. It was good."

"Can I make you some chamomile tea?"

He nodded. "I'd like that."

"Do you have a kettle?"

"No. Just the pan I warmed the soup in."

"I can work with that."

William coughed. "I can help."

"No, you stay there. You need rest."

"As you wish," he said.

I smiled. "I wish." I walked back out to the kitchen. I turned on the water in the sink and washed the pan, then filled it halfway with water.

Then I turned on the hot plate and set the pan on its glowing coils; the water hissed as the coils grew bright orange. Once the water was boiling, I opened the cupboard and grabbed one of the coffee cups. One said Winchell's Donuts. The other was a glossy black mug with a white skull and the letters USMC. I chose the donut cup as it seemed more life-affirming and, considering his condition, he needed it. I filled it with hot water and put in one of the teabags.

"Do you like your tea with honey or sugar?"

"Sugar," he said.

I tore open a sugar packet and stirred it in. I let the tea steep for a minute, then took out the teabag and brought the cup to him.

"There you go."

"Thank you." He blew on the drink, then took a sip.

When he set the cup down I reached over and put my hand on his forehead. "You're not as hot as you were. You were a hundred and four last night."

"You took my temperature?"

I nodded. "You don't remember?"

"No." He looked at me for a moment, then said, "From my mouth . . ."

I laughed. "Yes. From your mouth."

"That's good to know. I was kind of vulnerable."

"Yes, you were."

We looked at each other, smiling; was it chemistry?

"I can't stay late tonight," I said. "I've got to get back to my son. But I brought you some groceries."

"Thank you," he said. "How much do I owe you?"

"Nothing," I said.

"Come on. Let me pay you."

"After what you did, it would be embarrassing for me to take your money."

"It would be embarrassing for me to take a handout from a single mother."

I nodded. "Then you're going to have to be embarrassed."

He looked at me gratefully. "Thank you."

"You're welcome."

"You don't have to stay here. You've wasted enough time on me."

I looked at him for a moment then, to my own surprise, said, "I've enjoyed being with you."

"It's mutual," he said. He sipped his tea and then asked, "Do you know what day it is?"

"It's November eighteenth."

"What day of the week?"

"Tuesday."

He looked confused. "I think I missed a few days."

"No doubt." I smiled. "Well, I better go." I started to leave, then stopped and turned back.

"Last night you said something peculiar."

"Yes?"

"You said, 'I see why he loved you.'"

He was quiet a moment, then shook his head. "I must have been delirious."

"You were very sick." I breathed out. "Well, I better run." I looked at him again and then said, "Would you like to do something sometime, maybe get something to eat?"

"Thank you. That's a really kind offer, but . . ." He looked me in the eyes. "Could I say no?"

I flushed with embarrassment. "Of course. I didn't mean anything, I just . . ." I wasn't sure how to finish the sentence.

"I really appreciate all you've done for me."

"It's nothing compared to what you've done for me," I returned. "Besides, I'm partially to blame for you being sick. If my car wasn't broken down, you wouldn't have been working all night in the cold. You could have died from exposure." I forced a grin. "Like the guy they named this apartment building after."

"Harrison," he said. "But I'm not dead yet."

The moment fell into awkward silence. Finally I said, "Well, I better go. If I can do anything for you . . ."

"I hope I didn't offend you."

"No," I said. "You didn't." Then I added, "Maybe bruised my ego a little."

He grinned. "Then I'm sorry for the bruises."

"Forgiven," I said. "I'll see you around." I walked out of his apartment. As I descended the stairs, my eyes welled up in embarrassment. It seemed that I was undesirable to everyone but old men and lonely truck drivers. My heart ached as I drove home to take care of my son.

CHAPTER

twelve

I guess he changed his mind about me. I wonder what happened.

—Elle Sheen's Diary

The next morning at work Jamie asked, "How's your patient?"

"He's fine," I said.

"That wasn't very convincing."

"He's not my patient anymore. He's better."

"But you'll still be seeing him?"

"Apparently not."

"What do you mean?"

"I asked him if he'd like to go out sometime. He turned me down."

"Loser," she said, shaking her head.

"He's not a loser," I said.

She looked at me with surprise. "Oh my. You're defending him. Feelings, perhaps?"

"No," I said. "There are no feelings."

"Really?" she said. "So he's just another fish in the sea?"

"I don't have a sea," I said. "I don't have any bait and I'm too tired to fish. I just want to get back to work."

"Oh, you got bait, girl," she said after me. "You just forgot how to use it."

It was a long day. I operated on little enough sleep as it was, but that late night caring for William had finally caught up to me. It was after the dinner rush when Jamie came to the breakroom to find me. "Elle, you've got to come out and see who just walked in."

"Who now?" I asked.

I followed her out. She pointed toward the door. "That's him, right?"

William was standing inside the door next to the PLEASE WAIT TO BE SEATED sign. He still looked a little pale. I admit it was a little painful to see him. "Yes, that's him."

"He's gorgeous."

"Then you should ask him out," I said. "Maybe he won't turn you down."

"No, he's yours," Jamie said. "Go get him."

I took a deep breath, then walked over to him. He smiled when he saw me.

"Dinner for one?" I asked, trying not to sound hurt or distant and probably failing at both.

"It's just me," he said. "As usual."

"You can sit wherever."

He looked around, then said, "Where are you serving?"

"That section," I said, gesturing to my zone with a

menu, which I handed to him. "You can seat yourself. I'll get you some water."

"Thank you."

A moment later I brought him a glass. "Do you know what you want?"

"A chili cheeseburger and fries."

"And to drink?"

"A Dr Pepper."

"Anything else?"

"I would like to apologize."

I looked up from my pad. "For what?"

"You asked if I wanted to do something sometime, and I said no."

It hurt just hearing it again. "Don't worry about it."

"I haven't stopped worrying about it since you left. I came to see if I could take you out to dinner."

"Why do I feel like you're doing this out of pity?"

"Because I am," he said.

"Oh, really?" I said.

"Not for you," he said quickly. "For myself. Any man who would turn down an offer like that from a beautiful woman like you is pretty pitiable. Or maybe he was just a recluse who was out of his head recovering from an illness."

"You were pretty sick," I said.

"Delirious," he said. "Totally out of my head."

"I might be able to cut you a little slack—being sick and all."

He grinned. "You are as merciful as you are beautiful."

I smiled.

"Are you busy tomorrow night?"

"I'm off," I said. "But I'll need to find a sitter for Dylan. Can I call you?"

"I don't have a phone at my apartment, but you can call me at Renato's."

"You're already back at work?"

"I start back tomorrow. Renato needs the help. He came over this morning to see if I had a pulse."

"Apology aside, do you still want the food?"

"A man's got to eat."

"Yes, he does."

Back in the kitchen Jamie said, "How did it go?"

"He came to apologize and ask me out."

"Did you accept?"

"Of course."

Jamie smiled. "Smart girl."

William didn't stay long. He wolfed down his burger and was gone. He left me a ten-dollar bill for a four-dollar meal.

CHAPTER

thirteen

I'm so scared. It's been more than nine years since I went out on a date. Back then I was childless. The playing board has changed substantially, but the pawn is still vulnerable.

—Elle Sheen's Diary

A few minutes after he left, I called Fran to see if she could watch Dylan. As usual, she was happy to help.

The next morning I called William at Renato's. It took him a while to come to the phone.

"Sorry. I was under a car."

"Again?" I said.

He laughed. "It's getting to be a habit."

"So, I got a sitter."

"That's good news," he said happily. "Can I pick you up at six?"

"Six is good."

"Is there anyplace in particular you'd like to eat?"

"Anyplace but the diner."

He laughed again. "Fair enough. Do you like Italian food?"

"I love Italian food."

"Renato recommended a place in Ogden. DiSera's Italian. Have you been there?"

"No, but I've heard it's good."

"I'll make reservations," he said. "I'll see you at six."

"See you then."

I hung up. It had been years since I'd been out on a date. Let's be honest—it had been years since I'd been out anywhere. I couldn't wait.

CHAPTER

fourteen

William took me to a fancy Italian restaurant. He
listened too well and I talked too much. In other words, I
still have no idea who he is.

—Elle Sheen's Diary

I finished work that day at two. On my way out, Loretta
stopped me at the back door.

"I hear you have a date," she said. "With the soldier."

"Word spreads fast."

"It's a small town. Where are you going on this date?"

"DiSera's. In Ogden."

"Oh, he's a big spender," she said. "That's pricey."

"You've been there?"

"Many times. Renato loves that place. Their lasagna is
delicious, as is their gnocchi and sage-butter spaghetti."

"You're making my mouth water."

"Which is what I hope your date does for you."

"You're incorrigible."

"Yes, I am. I was hoping it might rub off on you."

I drove home, showered again so I didn't smell like coffee and cigarettes, then went through my closet looking for

something to wear. I didn't have many things to dress up in. The life I was living didn't require anything. I ended up in a high-necked blouse with ruffles on the cuffs that Loretta had given me the previous Christmas and a long denim skirt.

Fran arrived at a quarter to six. "You look nice," she said. "Love the blouse. Where are you going?"

"I'm going out on a date," I said proudly.

She looked at me like I was speaking a foreign language. "A date?"

"Try not to look too surprised."

"Who's the lucky man?"

"William," I said. "He's the one I was taking care of earlier this week."

"Ah," she said.

"What does that 'Ah' mean?"

"It means that I wondered if there was a little flame there. I mean, you did spend the night."

"I didn't 'spend the night.' He was sick," I said. "It's just a first date."

Just then Dylan came out of his room. "Where are you going, Mama?"

"I'm going out to dinner with a friend."

"Can I go?"

"No, not this time, buddy."

He looked puzzled. "How come?"

I realized that this had to be strange for him. Outside of work, I rarely, if ever, went anywhere without him. "Sometimes moms need time for themselves."

"How come?"

"They just do," I said.

Thankfully, Fran interjected. "Dylan, I thought you were going to watch TV with me."

"I want to go with my mom."

"We can watch *The Waltons*."

"I don't want to watch *The Waltons*."

"How about *The Six Million Dollar Man*?"

"All right," he said.

A few minutes later the doorbell rang.

"That's him," I said. "I don't know when I'll be home. We're going to dinner in Ogden."

"The big city," she said. "What time do you want Dylan in bed?"

"He can stay up late. Maybe nine."

"Do you want me to stay the night? Just in case?"

"In case of what?" I said. I opened the door. William stood in the doorway. He was dressed in bell-bottomed jeans and a knit sweater. His hair was nicely combed and he was clean-shaven.

"You look nice," he said.

"Thank you, I was thinking the same about you. I just need to get my coat. Come in."

As I walked over to the closet, Fran approached William.

"I'm Fran," she said, looking a little too interested.

"I'm William. It's nice to meet you. Thanks for babysitting."

"It's cool," she said.

"All right," I said, walking between them. "I'm ready." I looked around. "Dylan? Where are you?"

Dylan was hiding behind the kitchen table. I forgot that Dylan and William had unresolved history.

"Dylan, come here."

"No."

"Dylan," I said more forcefully.

William raised his hand. "It's okay." He walked into the kitchen, crouching down a couple of yards from Dylan. "Dylan, my name is William. We got off to a rocky start, so I brought you something. It's a peace offering."

"What's that?"

"A peace offering is something you bring someone to say you're sorry. In this case, it's a candy bar." He brought a Hershey's Chocolate bar from his jacket. "Do you like chocolate?"

Dylan nodded.

William turned to me. "Is this okay?"

"It's too late now," I said. "He's seen the goods."

He smiled, then turned back. He handed Dylan the candy bar. "I'm sorry I yelled at you. I promise I won't do that again."

Dylan took the chocolate. "It's okay."

William put out his hand. "Then we're cool?"

"We're cool," Dylan said, taking his hand.

"All right," William said, standing. "Big relief."

"Since you boys have it together," I said, "can we go?"

"Have a good time," Fran said to William.

Then she leaned in and whispered, "He's cute."

"Maybe you should sleep over," I said. I put on my coat and walked out with William into the cold.

"I'm in the Cadillac," he said, motioning to his green pickup.

"I remember."

He opened the door for me and helped me in, then he walked around and climbed in the other side. There was a Little Trees air freshener hanging from the mirror.

"I'm sorry, it smells like motor oil in here. I bring my work home with me."

"You work on cars at home?"

"I meant the oil," he said. He started the truck and pulled out into the road.

"By the way, good job with Dylan," I said. "You won him over."

"The magic of chocolate. Does wonders with kids."

"I've got news for you. It's not just kids. It's pretty much catnip for women."

He looked over and smiled. "That's good to know."

DiSera's was one of the nicest restaurants in Ogden, evidenced by the full parking lot. I followed William into the crowded lobby, passing several people grumbling about the long wait.

William walked up to the hostess, who, understandably, looked a little frantic.

"May I help you?" she asked.

"We have reservations for seven," William said. "It's under Smith."

She looked at her guest book, then looked back up. "William Smith for two?"

"Yes, ma'am."

"It will just be a few moments while they clear the table, Mr. Smith for two."

"Thank you."

I looked around the dimly lit restaurant. Outside of the diner, I hadn't been in any restaurant for several years. I watched the waiters and waitresses scurrying about with a kind of shared empathy, wondering what it would be like to work in an environment where people dressed up to eat.

"Follow me, please," the hostess said.

William motioned for me to go first and I followed the hostess to a candlelit table in the corner of the main dining room. William pulled out the chair for me and I sat down. The hostess unrolled our napkins and handed us menus in faux leather frames.

"Charlotte will be right with you," she said.

William looked at me and smiled. "Does it feel different being on the other side of the menu?"

"It feels different sitting down to cloth napkins." I looked over the menu. The prices of the meals were triple those at the diner. I instinctively began looking for the cheapest item.

"I hear the lasagna is good," he said.

"I've heard that too," I said. "It's expensive. Everything on the menu is expensive."

"You're worth it," he answered.

I smiled at him. "I may be, but you don't know that."

"Maybe I do," he said. "You're easily the best nurse I've ever had."

"Maybe I missed my calling in life."

"Would you like some wine?" he asked.

"Yes." I loved wine but, with the exception of Loretta's Christmas party, I hadn't had any in two years. "I love red wine."

"They have some excellent Chiantis," he said.

"You've been here before?" I asked.

William shook his head. "No. Renato told me. He speaks reverently of this place. I think food is akin to religion in Italy."

Our waitress came with a basket of breadsticks. "May I take your order?"

"Please," William said, deferring to me.

I ordered the lasagna. William ordered the spaghetti with clams and requested a wine list. A few minutes later the restaurant's sommelier came out with their list and his recommendations. He returned with a bottle of a Ruffino Chianti Classico and poured our glasses.

I sipped the wine. "This is really nice. I don't want to know how much it cost."

"You don't need to worry about that. We're celebrating."

"What are we celebrating?"

"Whatever we want," he said.

"Maybe I should get a job here," I said. "Getting tips on this menu would change my world."

"How much of your income is in tips?"

"Most of it. It's not a lot, obviously."

We both took a drink of wine. "That is good," he said.

"Heavenly," I said.

He set down his glass. "Were you born in Mistletoe?"

"No. I'm from Cedar City."

"Where's that?"

"It's a town in southern Utah. It's not as small as Mistletoe. I didn't even know Mistletoe existed until the day I arrived there. It's one of those towns you drive past on the way to somewhere else."

"How did you end up there?"

"Now that's a story."

"I'm up for a story," he said.

"It may cost you another drink," I said.

William smiled as he refilled my glass.

I took another sip of wine. "So, how I ended up in Mistletoe. Basically, I ran away from home. At least what was left of it. My parents disowned me or maybe I disowned them. It went both ways."

"What happened?"

"I married someone they didn't want me to marry."

"They didn't like him?"

"They never met him," I said. "He was black."

He nodded knowingly. "Where did you meet?"

"In school. We fell in love. But I knew my parents would never approve of me marrying a black man, so after a year of dating, we were secretly married and living a double life.

"I wish we had been more open, but neither of us had any money. Finally, he dropped out of school to work." I paused. "That's when he was drafted into the war." I took a drink, then a second.

"He didn't believe in the war. He said he had some friends moving to Canada to avoid the draft, but I wasn't going to do that. I was still a small-town girl. I didn't think there was life outside Cedar City, let alone America. I couldn't leave my friends and family." I sighed heavily. "If only I'd known how things would turn out. I lost my family *and* him." I took another drink. William just looked at me sympathetically. I was drinking too much. It certainly loosened my tongue.

"The thing is, my family bleeds red, white, and blue. My great-grandfather served in World War I as a general, my grandfather was a colonel in World War II, and my father served in the Korean War. I told my husband that if we ever hoped to have my father accept us, he'd have to serve. So he did, for me." My eyes suddenly moistened. "I asked too much. He never came back."

"I'm sorry."

"Me too," I said. I took another drink of wine. "But he left me something. We didn't know it at the time he was deployed, but I was pregnant. My parents, of course, were apoplectic. They thought I was an unmarried pregnant woman."

"You didn't correct them?"

"Not at first. I knew that the truth, to them, would be worse. When they finally learned that I was married and that my baby would be black . . ." I shook my head. "Let's just say they weren't real pleased.

"I thought they'd change their mind after Dylan was

born. I thought, who could reject a baby? But they did. About six months later we got in a big fight. My mother said he wasn't their grandson and never would be. I remember looking at my father, waiting for him to come to my defense, but he said nothing. I think that silence was worse than my mother's rejection." I breathed out. "That pretty much destroyed any chance of reconciliation. I told them that if they disowned their own grandson, then I was disowning them. That's when I left. I had a hundred and fifty dollars and the Fairlane my grandfather had given me.

"Unfortunately, I pretty much left without a plan. I drove north, looking for a job. I couldn't find anything. I wasn't exactly a stellar candidate—a single college dropout with a six-month-old baby. Dylan and I slept in the back seat of the car. After a week I was desperate. I was exhausted and almost out of money.

"That's when I found Mistletoe. I was driving at night. It was snowing so hard, I was afraid I'd drive off the interstate. Then I saw this light ahead. It was the diner. I was down to my last few dollars and gas. I was just praying that something would work out.

"I carried Dylan inside the diner. When I walked in, the place was almost deserted. There were Loretta, Jamie, and a couple of truckers. One of the truckers spun around in his chair, looked me over, and said, 'Well look what the storm blew in.'

"Loretta was on him like sesame seeds on a bun. She got in his face and said, 'You say one more word like that and that's the last meal you'll eat at my place. You got me?'

"The man backed down like a scolded schoolboy. He said, 'Yes, ma'am.'

"Then Loretta came up to me and said, 'What's his name, darlin'?' I told her. She took Dylan from me and then said, 'Sit down, sweetie, before you fall down. What do you want to eat?' I said, 'Just some coffee and toast. I don't have much money.' She said, 'You're in luck, girl. We've got a special on dinner tonight. It's free ninety-nine.' She kept bringing me food; then, after I was done eating, she asked where I was spending the night. I said, 'We've been sleeping in the car.' She said, 'That's no place for a baby. Where are you headed?' I said, 'Wherever the road takes us.' She said, 'Well, honey, it's taken you here. And I have a room in back you can stay in. Lord knows we've got plenty to eat.'"

"What a good woman," William said.

"Yes, she is." I smiled sadly. "She saved my life. I found out later that her only son had committed suicide just two months earlier and she was still raw."

William seemed to process this. Then he asked, "She offered you a job?"

"No, she never really hired me. It more or less just happened. At first I started helping out just to thank her. I did dishes, helped in the kitchen, then I started pouring water and bussing tables for the waitresses. They started sharing their tips.

"The other waitresses were sweet as can be. It was like Dylan had a plethora of mothers. They helped watch Dylan and I helped them all I could. I don't know where I'd be without them."

"What about your parents?"

"I haven't talked to them since I left home. They're pretty much dead to me."

"What was your relationship like before you left?"

His question surprised me. "It was good, once. My father and I used to be really close. When I was sixteen, I didn't get asked to my first prom. That night I was in bed, crying. He knocked on my door and then came in. He said, 'Why aren't you dressed? We have reservations.' He had bought me a corsage. He took me out to dinner and dancing." I looked down, the memory freshly burning. "We used to be close."

"What about your mother?"

"We never really got along. My mother drank a lot. She really struggled, but the demon owned her. I used to ask my father why he stayed with her, but he just said, 'A soldier never leaves his post.'"

I swished what was left of the wine in my glass. "You have to give him credit. He was loyal. At least to her. Not so much to me. Maybe that's what makes it hurt so much."

"I'm really sorry," he said.

"So here I am. I always thought, once my husband gets back, everything will change. I might even finish school."

"What did you want to do?"

"I wanted to be a writer."

"Like . . . books?"

I nodded.

"Maybe someday I'll write my story."

"I'd read it," he said.

"Thanks. I'll autograph it for you." I breathed out. "Enough about me. What about you? What brings you to Mistletoe?"

"My truck," he said.

"Something brought you here," I said. "No one arrives in Mistletoe by accident."

"I'm sure that's true," he said. He took a drink of wine, looked at me, then said, "I figured it was a nice place to die."

I wasn't sure if he was joking or how to respond, but the moment was interrupted by our waitress. "Sorry for the wait, here is your Spaghetti alle Vongole," she said, setting the plate in front of William. "And your lasagna, ma'am. Would you like some Parmesan cheese?"

"Yes, please."

The waitress grated cheese over my pasta. "And you, sir?"

He raised a hand. "No, thank you. I have it on good authority that Italians never put cheese on seafood."

"Very well," she said. *"Buon appetito."* She walked away.

I picked up the conversation. "So, you won't tell me what brought you here, maybe you'll tell me where you came from."

"Denver. Most recently."

"What did you do there?"

"I worked at a car dealership for a while, maintaining cars."

"Did you always want to be an auto mechanic?"

"It was more something I did than aspire to. I was raised in Fort Wayne, Indiana. I guess being that close to the

Indianapolis Speedway, cars got into my blood. I always wanted to race cars."

"But you moved to Denver?"

"After the war . . ." He hesitated. "Things changed."

We ate a moment in silence. Loretta was right; the lasagna was delicious.

William took another drink of wine, then said, "The thing about war is, everything you think you know about humanity, or about yourself, is challenged. Especially in a conflict like Vietnam." He looked at me over his glass. "Did you know that Vietnam wasn't even a war? It was never approved by Congress, so technically it's considered a conflict." He shook his head. "Semantics and politics. When bullets are flying at you, it doesn't matter what you call it."

"Were you drafted?"

"Sort of," he said.

"What does that mean?"

"If I tell you, you're going to totally wonder what you're doing with me."

I smiled. "I already am."

"Then I have nothing to lose," he said, grinning lightly. "So I'm what they call a two-or-ten."

"Two or ten?"

"The judge pounded his gavel and gave me a choice: two years in 'Nam or ten years in prison. I chose the former."

"What did you do?"

"Got in with the wrong crowd, mostly. I ended up

spending time in prison anyway—the Hanoi Hilton. I would have done better at home." His voice fell an octave. "At least they're not allowed to torture you in US prisons."

I let his words settle. "You served your country. That was an honorable thing."

"I wish it were that simple," he said. "I risked my life and had no idea what I was fighting for—a corrupt dictatorship that represented almost everything we're fighting against?" He took another drink of wine. "Needless to say, I'm pretty much a hot mess."

I had never before heard the term but liked it. "A hot mess. That sums us both up."

"The difference between you and me is that you can't afford chaos," he said.

"Why do you say that?"

"Because you care about your son more than yourself," he said. "You're a good person."

"So are you," I said.

He looked at me skeptically. "Now that's the wine talking."

I reached over and touched his hand. "No, it's my gratitude talking. What you did for me . . . Aside from Loretta, no one has ever helped me like that. Dylan and I are barely getting by. It would have taken me years to pay off that debt. You didn't even know me and yet you helped us. Hot mess or not, you have a good heart."

He took another drink and said nothing. He went to pour more wine into my glass but I put my hand over it. "That's enough. Are you trying to get me tipsy?"

"I'm just trying to make you feel good."

I looked at him for a moment, then said, "It's been a long time since anyone has tried to do that."

"Am I succeeding?"

I smiled. "Spectacularly."

We split a piece of tiramisu and, I confess, I had another glass of wine. It was the most relaxed I had felt in years.

Around nine o'clock he asked, "What time do you need to be back?"

"It doesn't matter. My sitter is spending the night."

"Can I show you something?"

"Sure."

"Come with me."

It was late and the restaurant was only half-full as we left the parking lot. William drove us about six miles up alongside a small canyon I'd never been to before. The canyon road was narrow and snow-packed. About four miles up the canyon he stopped his truck next to a large snowbank. It was dark, and the granite walls were mostly concealed by snow-frosted pines whose tops disappeared into the darkness of night.

"Is this it?" I asked.

"No. It's down that road a quarter mile. But there's more snow than I thought there'd be. I don't want to get the truck stuck. And you're not dressed for walking in snow."

"What is it that you wanted to show me?"

"It's just a place," he said.

"What kind of place?"

He turned to me. "A peaceful place."

I looked at him for a moment and then said, "I want to see it."

"You'll get cold. Especially your feet."

"It's a small price to pay for peace."

"Are you sure?"

I nodded. "I'm sure."

He got out of the truck and walked around to my door and opened it and helped me down. He took my hand. "If it gets too cold, just tell me and we'll come back."

"It's a deal."

Hiking through the snow was harder than I expected. The snow was up to our knees in places as we trudged along a narrow, uncleared path surrounded on both sides by columnar trees, white and frozen, lining the path like marble pillars. The cold air froze our breath in front of us.

Suddenly we came to a clearing that overlooked the valley below. William stopped. "This is it."

"Oh my," I said. In front of us was a waterfall, the exterior draped in an intricate lacework of ice. The sound of laughing, rushing water escaped the ice veil and fell below into a river whose banks were piled with snow. Everything around us was white, crystal, and blue, lit by a full moon that hung naked in the winter air.

"They call this Lace Veil Falls," he said.

"It's beautiful," I said, my voice muffled in the blanket of winter that surrounded us. I looked at him. "How did you find this place?"

"I found it the day after I moved to Mistletoe," he said. "I sat up here one night and just looked out over the valley."

"In the cold?" I asked.

"In the cold . . ."

His words trailed off in silence.

After a while I said to him, "Thank you for sharing this with me."

"You're welcome," he said softly. He turned and looked at me. I had my arms crossed at my chest and I was shivering.

"You're freezing."

"I'm a little cold."

"Let's get you back." We walked about twenty yards when he looked at me and said, "Your feet must be frozen."

"It's not much farther," I said.

"I can carry you."

"Really, you don't have to . . ."

He reached down and lifted me, his muscular arms embracing me. "This is better."

I was thinking the same thing. It felt good to be in his arms as he effortlessly carried me through the thick powder. He carried me all the way to his truck, set me down, and opened the door, then lifted me in. It was the most romantic thing I'd experienced in years. When he got back in the truck he was quiet. Then I noticed that his eyes were wet.

"What is it?" I asked.

He didn't look at me. He just started his truck and then reached over and turned on the heater, turning the vent toward me.

"What is it?" I asked again.

"It's nothing."

I reached over and touched his arm. "Something just happened, didn't it?"

He took a deep breath, then said, "Thank you for sharing that with me. I wanted to share that with someone."

We drove in silence back to my duplex. It was almost midnight when we arrived. We parked at the curb, and William walked me to the door.

"Thank you for tonight," I said. "It was really nice talking to you."

"Would you like to go out again?"

"I would love to."

He thought a moment, then said, "Is tomorrow too soon?"

I was happy that he was so eager. "I'd love to but I work tomorrow night."

"How about Saturday?"

"I work at night, but during the day I could do something." I caught myself. "I'm sorry . . . I promised Dylan I'd take him tubing."

"We can do that," he said.

"You want to go tubing with us?"

"It sounds fun. As long as you wear the shoes for it."

I smiled. "I wasn't going to wear boots to a nice restaurant."

"And the evening was the better for it," he said. "So, as far as the tubing goes, I have inner tubes and an air compressor at the shop. The tubes will fit better in the back of my truck than in your Fairlane."

"You talked me into it," I said.

"What time would you like to go?"

"Is nine good?"

"It's good for me."

Our words gone, we stood there quietly looking at each other. I wondered if he was going to kiss me. I was hoping he would. Instead he put out his hand. "Thank you."

I took his hand. "You're welcome. Good night."

I opened the door and stepped inside. I couldn't wait to see him again.

CHAPTER

fifteen

Why is it that the people with the smallest minds have the biggest mouths?

—Elle Sheen's Diary

"How did the date go?" Jamie asked the next morning, pouring cream into a coffee cup.

I must have smiled. It was kind of automatic.

"That good, huh?"

"He was really sweet. And the restaurant was amazing."

"So, is there a sequel to this romance?"

"I wouldn't call it a romance."

"What would you call it?"

I smiled wider. "Fun."

"That's even better," she said. "So when are you seeing him again?"

"We're going tubing with Dylan tomorrow."

"Getting in with the son. That's fast."

"It's not that. He asked me out and I'd already made plans with Dylan, so he offered to come along."

"Sounds like romance to me," Loretta said, walking past us to the kitchen.

"That woman should work for the CIA," Jamie said.

"Thought about it," she shouted back.

About an hour into my shift I got a call from Fran. She sounded awful. "Elle, I'm so sorry. I've come down with something. I'm so sick I had to miss school."

"What do you have?"

"Everything. I've got a sore throat, chills, fever. I could feel it coming on last night. I don't think I should watch Dylan."

I wondered if I passed it on to her from William. "I'm sorry. I'll pick up Dylan and bring him here."

"Are you sure?"

"Of course. You get some rest. Get better."

"How was your date last night?"

"It was nice," I said. "You take care of yourself. I need you."

"I need you too. Bye."

It wasn't the first time I had to bring Dylan with me to the diner. Fortunately, Loretta was always good about it. In fact, I think she enjoyed it.

A little after two o'clock I picked Dylan up from school, stopped by home to get him something to do, then came back to work. Loretta was in her office when we walked through the back door.

"I'm sorry, Loretta. Fran's sick, so I had to get Dylan."

She smiled at Dylan. "Lucky us," she said. "How's my handsome man?"

"Good, Ms. Loretta. Can I have a hot chocolate?"

"Of course you can. With whipped cream?"

"Yes, ma'am."

"You have such nice manners that I'm going to get you a donut to go with that."

"Just sugar him up," I said.

"Someone's got to," Loretta said.

I said to Dylan, "Hang up your coat, then take your bag out to the corner table. You can do your Spirograph. Just don't bother anybody."

"I won't." He hung up his coat and walked out to the table in the farthest corner of the dining room. There's a reason I had told him not to bother anyone. Dylan was always well behaved, but he was naturally curious as well as a consummate socialite and liked talking to strangers. And, frankly, now and then there were people in the diner I didn't really want him talking to.

I took him his hot chocolate and donut, then went back to work.

Around six o'clock I was taking an order when I noticed William walk through the front door. He was wearing a green army jacket with his hands deep in his pockets. I waved to him and he smiled and tipped his head. I finished taking the table's order and then walked over to him.

"Hi. What brings you here?"

"I just thought I'd come get something to eat."

"Oh," I said. "Then your being here has nothing to do with me?"

He grinned "Maybe a little."

I felt like a smile was commandeering my face. "I had such a good time last night."

"Me too," he said. "You're pretty good company. Sorry about the snow hike."

"Frostbite aside, it was my favorite part of the night," I said. "I'm serving this side, so just grab a table. Dylan's back there. Why don't you go on back and say hello?"

"Dylan's here?"

I nodded. "My sitter called in sick."

"I won't be eating alone after all," he said. He headed back toward Dylan. Dylan looked up with a big smile which, of course, translated to an even larger smile on my face.

A few minutes later I took William's order. It was interesting watching Dylan respond to being with him. He ordered the same thing William did—a toasted tuna salad sandwich with coleslaw and fries. And a large dill pickle. I don't think I'd ever seen Dylan eat a pickle before.

A few minutes later Andy walked in. He was in uniform but alone this time. I sat him just a few tables from William before wondering if, considering their last encounter, that was such a great idea. As I walked back to the kitchen I noticed that William got up and walked over to Andy's table and shook his hand.

It was about twenty minutes later when I was just coming back to the kitchen after serving Dylan and William that Jamie said, "Sorry, baby, she's baaaaack." I looked over. Ketchup Lady was there.

"Oh no."

"My section's light, I can take her."

"No, I'm good, if you don't mind seating her."

"That woman seats herself, but I'll take her a menu."
Jamie walked out to the woman, while I walked back and
grabbed a pitcher of water. I passed Jamie on the way to
the dining room. "She sat herself at sixteen. Her usual."

She was seated just a few tables from Dylan and William. Honestly, I was kind of glad William was there. It
would give us something to laugh about later.

"Thanks, doll. Did you check the status of the ketchup
at her table?"

"Yes, the bottle is half-full."

"No, it's half-*empty*," I said. I grabbed a full bottle of
ketchup and, still carrying the pitcher, walked over to her.
When I got to her table, Ketchup Lady looked more agi-
tated than usual.

I set the water and ketchup down, then said, "What can
I get for you?"

"I can't sit here."

You seated yourself, I thought. "Is there a problem?"

"I would say so. Why is that nigger boy in here?"

My chest froze. I glanced over at Dylan, who was
showing William how to use the Spirograph. "That boy is
my son," I said, my face hot. "Don't you ever call him that
again!"

The woman didn't flinch. "Well, I don't like him here."

I was so angry I was shaking. "You get out of here right
now before I shove this bottle of ketchup down your
throat."

She looked at me in complete shock. "How dare you!"

"How dare *you*!" I shouted back.

She began looking around the diner for support. I hadn't noticed but Loretta was standing near the cash register within earshot of the altercation. "Did you hear that?" Ketchup Lady shouted to her. "Did you hear what this insolent *waitress* just said to me?"

Loretta walked over, glaring at the woman. "I heard what you said. You get out of my diner right now. And if I ever see you here again, I'll throw you out."

The woman's face was almost as red as the ketchup. "I . . . I . . ." She glanced over at Andy. "This woman just threatened me. Do your duty. This is our country!"

Suddenly I realized that William was standing next to me. He looked fierce. "This boy's father died protecting *your* country," he said slowly but forcefully. "Do you know how many black brothers of mine died so you could fatten your face? Now get out of here before I drag you outside and throw you into the gutter where you belong."

Ketchup Lady looked utterly terrified. She turned to Andy, who was watching the exchange. "He threatened my life, Officer. Arrest him."

Andy stood and walked over. "No, all I heard was you threatening him. Get out now or I'll arrest you for causing a public disturbance."

The woman was trembling now. She looked back at Dylan. I sensed she was about to say something to him when William said, "You say one word to that child and you'll regret it for the rest of your life."

"How dare you threaten me! I have connections. You're going to see the inside of a jail, mister."

William almost looked amused. "You think that scares me? You have no idea what I've seen and what I'm capable of."

The woman looked faint. Loretta stepped forward and grabbed her by the arm. "Get out of here."

Ketchup Lady stood. She looked a little wobbly, then she stumbled toward the door. Jamie walked over to the table, grabbed the bottle of ketchup, and went to the door and threw it in the direction the woman had walked off in. I heard the bottle shatter.

"Take that, you gross slob," she shouted.

I broke down crying.

CHAPTER

sixteen

There's a reason movies use ketchup to simulate blood.
                              —Elle Sheen's Diary

L oretta put her arm around me. "Come to the back, honey. Come back and sit."

"I can't," I said. "I've got to talk to Dylan." I looked over at him. He was visibly upset.

"Did he hear what she said?" I asked William.

He shook his head. "I don't think so."

Dylan ran over to me. "Why are you crying, Mama?"

I knelt down and hugged him. William squatted down next to us. "Everything's okay," he said. "There was a mean lady, but we made her leave." William turned to me. "Elle, go back with Loretta, I'll take care of Dylan." Then he said to Dylan, "Would you like to share a milkshake?"

"No, I want my own."

"Even better," he said. "What flavor should we get?"

"Let's get strawberry."

"Perfect. I love strawberry."

Loretta smiled at him. "I'll get two strawberries. And thank you, sir, for your service."

"You're welcome."

She turned to me. "Your friend has things under control. Now come on back, darlin'."

As we walked back she said to Andy, "Your dinner's on me, Officer. Dessert too."

"Always my pleasure," he said. "We don't need that kind of crazy in Mistletoe."

CHAPTER

seventeen

William said something tonight I won't forget: "Never live someone else's crazy."

          —Elle Sheen's Diary

Loretta let me go home early. Actually, she made me. William stayed with Dylan the whole time I was in the back with Loretta. They were arm wrestling when I came out, William pretending to lose.

I was wearing my coat and carrying Dylan's over my arm. "It's time to go, Dylan."

"Okay." He started stuffing all his toys back in his bag.

William sidled up to me. He asked softly, "Are you okay?"

I just nodded. I was afraid that if I opened my mouth I'd start crying.

"May I give you a hug?"

"Yes. Please."

He put his arms around me. For a moment he just quietly held me. I almost forgot we were in public. He felt so good—his warmth, his strength.

"Can I drive you home?" he asked.

"I have my car."

"We can pick it up tomorrow after we go tubing. If you're still up for it."

"I don't know."

"We should go," he said. "We can't let crazy people dictate our lives."

He squeezed me one last time, then released me and turned back to Dylan. "Hey, tough guy. Want to go home in my truck?"

"Yay!" he said.

I took Dylan's hand and we walked out the diner's front door. I noticed something different in William's moves. He seemed aware of the movement around him; every car and every human. He was still a soldier. When he pulled up to my house he was just as vigilant, walking me to the door. I felt sorry for anyone who might think to cross him.

I opened the door. "Go inside, Dylan," I said.

He looked at William. "Can we play Rock 'Em Sock 'Em Robots?"

"It's too late tonight. But Mr. William is coming over tomorrow."

"I'll be over tomorrow morning," William said. "To take you tubing. I'll bring more chocolate."

"Yes!"

"But only if you go right to bed."

"Okay."

"And brush your teeth."

"All right."

He ran inside. I looked up at William. Before I could thank him he said, "Are you okay?"

"I'm still a little shaken up."

"There will always be people like that. Don't give them your time or your sanity."

I looked into his eyes. "Thank you for being there."

"You're safe now," he said. "You can trust me."

I looked at him for a moment, then said, "I do. I don't know why, I barely know you, but I do." I leaned my head forward against his chest.

He put his arms around me and kissed my forehead, then leaned back. "You are an amazing, beautiful woman. No wonder . . ." He stopped.

I looked up at him. "No wonder what?"

He paused. "No wonder everyone loves you."

I looked at him, not believing that that was what he had been going to say. I took a deep breath and stepped back. "I'll see you tomorrow."

"Tomorrow," he said. "Lock your door."

"I will." Up until that day I never had.

CHAPTER

eighteen

*In the middle of a snowstorm we tubed down a steep hill,
blind and out of control. That pretty much describes my
life these days.*

—Elle Sheen's Diary

I woke the next morning feeling refreshed and excited for the day. William arrived at my place at five minutes to nine. He wore army boots, wool gloves, and his green army jacket. I figured it was the only coat he had.

Dylan answered the door. "Hi, Mr. William. Did you bring the chocolate?"

"Dylan," I said, walking up behind him. "You don't just ask people for chocolate."

"No, he's just keeping me honest," William said. "I promised him." He brought a chocolate bar out of his jacket. "Did you go to bed?"

"Yes, sir."

"Did you brush your teeth?"

"Yes, sir."

He held out the chocolate bar. "Then you've earned this amazing bar of chocolate."

"Smart man," I replied. "Earning points with the kid."

Dylan took the candy and turned to me. "Can I?"

"Chocolate for breakfast?" I said. "Sure, why not?"

He quickly tore open the wrapper.

"Dylan, where are your gloves and hat?"

"I don't know."

"They're in your closet."

"If you knew, why did you ask?" Dylan said.

I breathed out. "Just get them."

William laughed. "He got you."

As Dylan went to his room I said to William, "Thank you again for last night."

"I would say it was a pleasure, but it wasn't."

"You're a strong man."

"When I'm not under trucks," he said.

When Dylan returned, the bar of chocolate was gone and the corners of his mouth were stained with chocolate. We walked out to William's truck and climbed into it. The bed was filled with two large inner tubes, both dusted with snow.

"Where are we going?" he asked.

"There's a little park just before the canyon," I said. "It's not far from here. The hills are just the right size for Dylan."

"Just point the way."

Twenty minutes later we arrived at the park. There were maybe a dozen others, riding tubes and sleighs.

It was snowing fairly hard and even though I had told Dylan that we wouldn't go in the snow, it was only because I was afraid to drive in it. William had no such problem.

We picked a medium-sized hill and William carried the two inner tubes up the incline while I walked up behind him holding Dylan's hand.

At the hill's summit we linked ourselves together with our legs and slid down together, screaming and laughing. At least I screamed. Dylan just laughed. I hadn't seen him that happy for some time. The falling snow limited our visibility, which added both to my fear and our general excitement. We tubed for about two hours, until we looked like animated snowmen; our clothes soaked through and almost frozen, we drove back to my house.

"That was so cool!" Dylan exclaimed, still excited from the day.

"That was a good place to tube," William said.

"It's not too steep or too crowded," I said. "Especially in the snow." I looked at him. "The county lets you cut Christmas trees there," I said. "Jamie and I cut one once. It was only a little one but we still had trouble carrying it out."

"I could help with that," he said. "If you decide to do it again."

"I might take you up on that." I leaned over and whispered, "A tree is not in the budget this year."

William whispered back, "Does Dylan know?"

I glanced over at him and then shook my head. "Not yet. I'm still hoping something might work out."

He nodded. A moment later he said, "Do we have time to stop for a hamburger?"

"I just need to be at work by three."

"Plenty of time."

William drove us to the Arctic Circle, a small local hamburger joint just a mile from Mistletoe up I-15. As we walked into the restaurant Dylan froze. There was a young black man standing behind the counter. Seeing black men in Mistletoe was rare enough, but a black teenager was a first for him.

For a moment the two of them stared at each other. William approached the counter. "How's it going?"

The young man looked away from Dylan. "Not bad. What can I get for you?"

"I'd like two Ranch burgers and an order of fries with your famous fry sauce." He turned to me. "What would you like?"

"I'll have half of what you're getting. Dylan will have the corn dog."

Dylan still just stood there staring at the young man. William turned to him. "Do you want fries with that?"

Dylan nodded.

"Got to have the fries," William said. "We'll also have two Cokes and a lime rickey. That will do it." He took his wallet from his back pocket. "Thank you."

"No problem," the young man said.

As we sat at the table Dylan suddenly said, "He's a Negro."

William nodded. "There are black people everywhere. In the army my best friends were black. This is just kind of a different town. There aren't many black people."

"How come?"

"Good question." William turned to me. "How come?"

"More are in the big cities than in small towns like ours," I said.

"Why?" Dylan asked.

"I'll have to think about that."

"Let us know when you figure that out," William said, grinning.

"So how's the corn dog?" William asked.

"Good," Dylan said.

"You know, where I used to live, sometimes they fed us fish heads."

I was surprised that he was talking about it.

Dylan stared at him, not sure if he was kidding or not. "Honest?"

"I'm telling God's truth. I wish I wasn't."

"Did you eat them?"

"You'll eat anything if you're hungry enough." He leaned forward. "Even rats."

"Ooh," Dylan said.

William nodded. "Tastes like chicken."

On the way back to town William said, "We still need to pick up your car."

I had forgotten that we had left it at the diner. "I'm glad one of us remembered."

A few moments later William stopped his truck behind

the diner next to the Fairlane, which was covered with snow. "What time do you need to be back here?"

"Not until three," I said. "I have ninety minutes. Would you like to come over for some hot cocoa?"

"I would love to."

"Can Mr. William play Rock 'Em Sock 'Em Robots?" Dylan asked.

"I'm sure Mr. William has better things to do."

"Better than playing Rock 'Em Sock 'Em Robots?" he replied. "I think not." He turned to Dylan. "Are you good?"

"Yeah."

"We'll see," he said.

He turned to me, "Give me your car keys."

"How come?"

"So I can warm up your car while I clear off the snow."

I took my keys out. "You don't need to . . ."

He put his finger on my lips, stopping me. "Let me be good to you."

It was the sweetest thing I had heard in months.

He got out, pried my car door open—which had frozen shut—started my car, then, with a broom he took from the bed of his truck, cleared the snow off my windshield. Five minutes later he opened my door and offered me his hand. "It's ready. Your car's warm."

"Thank you," I said, taking it. I stepped in. "Meet you at my duplex?"

"I'll see you there."

"Can I ride with Mr. William?" Dylan asked.

"It's fine with me," William said.

"Sure."

Back at my duplex we kicked off our boots and then went inside. Dylan took William's hand and led him into his room while I went to the kitchen and heated up some milk in a saucepan, then poured in the cocoa powder. When it was hot, I poured three coffee cups full and dropped in marshmallows. I carried all three cups into Dylan's bedroom, something waitresses are good at. I gave them their drinks, then sat down on the floor next to William to watch them box.

"You're really good at this," William said to Dylan.

"You're not so good," Dylan said.

"Dylan," I said.

"He's right," William said. "I stink at this. He keeps knocking my block off."

They played a little longer until I made Dylan get in the bathtub. While he was bathing, William and I sat at the kitchen table with our cocoa. "I like your place," he said.

"Thank you. You have a nice place too."

He looked at me quizzically. "I thought you had been there."

I laughed. "I have."

"So you're either being cloyingly polite or have trouble seeing in the dark."

I smiled. "It was a little dark. And I'm a little cloying."

William laughed.

"Who lives in the other side of the duplex?"

"Mr. Foster."

"What's he like?"

"Old, mostly. He rarely comes out."

"But he's quiet?"

"Not really. I mean, he is; it's not like he's having wild parties, but his hearing's going, so he turns the TV all the way up. Fortunately, he goes to bed before Dylan does."

"Is he nice?"

"Yes, and he pays Dylan a dollar to take his garbage to the curb. That's like a nickel a foot."

"What does Dylan do with all that money?"

"I make him put it in his college fund."

We drank our cocoa.

"Today was a nice day," I said.

"Yeah, it was. Dylan's a great kid."

"He's my reason, you know? He's proof of God's love."

"He's proof of your love," William said.

"I worry about him. Like, maybe I'm going to ruin his life by living here."

"Why do you think that?"

"He's the only black child in his school. He's the only black child in this whole town. You saw how he reacted to that young man at the hamburger place. Then add to that the fact that he doesn't have a father."

"He has you. And father or not, you've done a great job with him."

"I just wish I could give him a better life."

"You give him love. That's better than anything material you could give him."

"I know. I just wish I could give him more time. I work so much." I shook my head. "I keep waiting for things to get easier, but they don't."

"Who watches Dylan when you're working?"

"Fran."

"She's the one I met the other night?"

"Yes. She's like a second mother to him."

"How did you find her?"

"She worked at the diner for a while, but she didn't last long. She's in college now."

"Speaking of the diner . . ." He glanced down at his watch. "It's almost time for you to go to work. I better go."

Just then Dylan came out of the bathroom wearing only Flash Gordon underwear. "Want to play Rock 'Em Sock 'Em again?"

"Hmm," William said. "Let's see, do I want to be beaten and humiliated again? I don't think so."

"Please?"

"As fun as it sounds, I think I'd better go home. Your mom needs to go to work, and your sitter will be here soon."

Dylan turned to me. "Can Mr. William watch me?"

"No, honey. Fran is coming."

Dylan looked disappointed.

"I'll be back," William said. He looked at me. "If it's okay with your mother."

Dylan looked up at me. "Is it, Mama?"

"Absolutely," I said. "Now say goodbye to Mr. William, then I'm going to step outside to talk to him."

"Goodbye, Mr. William."

"Goodbye, Dylan."

I led William outside, shutting the door behind me. "That's quite an honor. He wants you to watch him instead of Fran."

"Probably because he can beat me at the boxing robots."

"Probably," I said with a half smile. "Thank you for taking us tubing. And to lunch. Dylan had a really good time."

"Do you think Dylan's mother had a good time too?"

I smiled. "She had a good time too."

"Good," he said. "I was kind of going for that."

"So, before you go, I wanted to ask you something." As he looked at me I suddenly felt a little nervous.

"Yes?"

"I wanted to ask what are you doing for Thanksgiving?"

"Thanksgiving. What Thanksgiving?"

"So you don't have plans."

"No, I have plans. I've got a date with myself and a turkey-and-mashed-potatoes TV dinner. Hold the TV."

"I'd hate to interrupt that feast, but would you like to have dinner with Dylan and me? I can pretty much guarantee that the food will be better."

"Not to mention the company," he said. "I absolutely bore myself. Sometimes I get in arguments with myself just to stir things up."

I smiled.

"What can I bring?"

"Just your boring, argumentative self," I said. "I get almost everything from the diner."

"Then how about I bring some wine?" he said.

"I won't turn you down on that."

"I didn't think so. So do I have to wait until Thanksgiving to see you again?"

I smiled. "I'm off Tuesday at three."

"Can you find a sitter?"

"I'll get a sitter."

"I promise I'll make it worth your while."

CHAPTER

nineteen

We do not always believe things because they're true. More often than not, we believe things because they're expedient.

—Elle Sheen's Diary

MONDAY, NOVEMBER 24

M onday night after work, Fran met me outside the duplex, which is something she never did unless she was in a hurry to get somewhere. She stood in front of the door as if she were guarding it. "You'll never believe what happened," she said.

"I'm sure I won't," I replied. "Is it a good or bad thing?"

"Two things. First, Dylan is still up."

Bad thing, I thought. "It's a school night."

"I know, but I made a judgment call. I think you would have done the same. Something special happened." She opened the door and I walked in. In the middle of our living room was a six-foot Christmas tree. It was mostly decorated and Dylan was standing next to it laying strands of tinsel across its boughs. His smile was epic. "Look, Mama! We got a tree!"

I turned to Fran. "Where did it come from?"

"Well, we all went on an unexpected little field trip."

"A field trip?"

"Literally. William came by in his truck and we went to a field and cut it down. He set it up, and Dylan and I did the decorations."

I glanced around. "Where's William?"

"He left a couple hours ago. He said 'Merry Christmas' and he'll see you tomorrow." She shook her head. "It's kind of a Christmas miracle."

"He's kind of a Christmas miracle," I replied.

I found I was thinking about him all the time. I couldn't wait until Tuesday. How different my life felt having something to look forward to.

William wouldn't tell me what we were doing as he wanted it to be a surprise. His only instruction to me was to dress for winter and wear warm boots. So I threw on a turtleneck sweater and jeans and wondered if we were going hiking again. We didn't. He picked me up a little after four o'clock and we drove north up I-15.

We were going for a sleigh ride. It was dusk when we arrived at Hardware Ranch about an hour north of Mistletoe near Hyrum. The ranch was state-owned and encompassed nearly twenty thousand acres.

Dylan would have loved it, but I'm glad we went alone. William and I snuggled up together under a blanket for the hour-long ride, which took us through miles of pristine wilderness and past the largest herd of elk I'd ever seen. Our driver told us that the herd had started with a couple dozen and then grew over the past decade to nearly a thousand animals.

After the ride we drove to the nearby town of Brigham City (named after the Mormon prophet Brigham Young) and had dinner at a little restaurant called the Maddox Ranch House. The restaurant was one of the oldest in Utah and had garnered a reputation of having some of the state's best fried chicken, bison steaks, and hot buttered rolls.

We both ordered comfort food. William ordered the breaded trout while I had the chicken-fried steak with mashed potatoes.

"Thank you for the tree," I said again. "You should have seen how excited Dylan was."

"I did," he said.

"Of course. Was it hard getting the tree out?"

"A little. I could have used a horse to help pull it out," he said, buttering a roll. "Speaking of which, you seemed comfortable around the horses tonight."

"I grew up with horses," I said. "My father raises them. At least he did. I have no idea if he still does."

"So your dad was a horse breeder."

"My dad was into a lot of things. He was in the military until he was thirty-five, then he retired and bought the ranch in Cedar City. He's an entrepreneur and an investor. We never wanted for anything.

"Growing up, we lived frugally—my father wore old clothes, mowed his own lawn, drove an old car—but I realize now we were well off. My dad wasn't showy, and he's not obsessed with money; it just kind of flows with him." I looked at William. "Does that make sense?"

He nodded. "I knew people like that in the military."

"I certainly didn't inherit it from him. I've been poor since the minute I left home."

He grinned. "You mean you're not getting rich at the diner?"

"No. Are you getting rich at Renato's?"

"What do you think?"

"I hear Renato is as tight as a tourniquet."

"That's a little harsh. Renato has been good to me," William said. "I'm not getting rich, but I don't really need much either. When I got back from the war, I had a lot of back pay from the military, so I've got savings. I'm doing okay."

"This is an odd question, but do you get paid as a POW?"

"It's considered time served. POWs also get a little extra—sixty-five dollars a month, for imminent danger pay. Sounds absurd hearing it that way: I made an extra two dollars a day for putting my life in greater danger."

He took a bite of his fish, then said, "You also progress through the ranks, so your salary goes up." He smiled darkly. "I didn't get to do a whole lot of shopping in Hanoi, so the money just stacked up."

"You said you were sent to Vietnam by a judge."

He nodded. "I was facing hard jail time."

"That's hard for me to believe."

"Why is that?"

"Because you're one of the sweetest men I've ever met."

He smiled at the comment. "I put on a good show."

"I don't think so. I'm a pretty good judge of character," I said. "What's your family like?"

"Dead."

His reply stunned me. He noticed.

"Sorry," he said quickly. "That was . . . crass."

"That's okay," I said.

"The truth is, I had a great family and an idyllic childhood. I had both parents at home, two little sisters, Little League baseball on Saturday, church on Sundays. We were pretty much the Cleaver family—until they were killed in a car crash."

"Your whole family?"

He nodded. "Everyone but me. I was supposed to be with them, but I got in a fight with my mother before leaving and said I wouldn't go. I was stubborn. I locked myself in my room. My dad wouldn't have put up with that nonsense. He would have knocked my door down and dragged me out, but he wasn't there. He was in Ohio on business. He was an auto parts salesman. My mother and sisters met up with him and were headed to Cincinnati for the week."

"What was the fight about?"

William shook his head. "I don't remember. I should have been with them."

"You would have died if you were."

"I'm not sure that would have been such a bad thing."

The comment hurt my heart. "Maybe you weren't supposed to be with them. Maybe God was looking out for you."

"I'm not that fatalistic," he said. "It would make me wonder why He wasn't looking after them." After a while he breathed out. "After they died, I had no one. We had one of those isolated families where neither of my parents had any familial connections. My father didn't get along with his family, and my mother didn't have one. I think she was an accident. She was an only child and born late in her parents' lives. Her father was sixty-five when she was born. Her mother was fifty-two. Her father died when she was nine, her mother passed away the same year I was born.

"So with no family and since I wasn't yet eighteen, I became a ward of the state and was put in the foster care system. It didn't go well. At that age, I was too old to assimilate into another family. Not to mention, I was pretty messed up. My family had just died and the last thing I had said to my mother was that I hated her. The guilt and shame were eating me alive. I think some part of me blamed myself for their deaths."

"You know that's not true."

"I know—I knew it then—but I didn't *believe* it. Belief and knowledge aren't the same thing. Belief is much more powerful.

"During that time I actually tried to join the army, but I was too young. So I ended up as a foster child with a caseworker. I honor anyone who takes in a foster child, but the family I was put with was a mistake. They owned a dry-cleaning business and were basically looking for free labor. I was working sixty hours a week cleaning and pressing clothes. I told my caseworker that I was a slave, but she just thought I was exaggerating. Finally, after a year and a half of that, I ran away.

"I couch-hopped for a while, then I got a job with one of my dad's old clients at a car dealership detailing cars. It was a pretty good gig. Then one day, at the dealership, I ran into a group of guys a few years older than me. I thought they were cool. They talked tough, and they had hot cars and foxy girlfriends. They all shared an old home together, kind of like a commune. None of them worked; they just, like, hung out all day. One of them invited me to move into their place. They gave me cigarettes and beer. I thought I was pretty cool because they liked me.

"It never occurred to me how they were supporting their lifestyle. I didn't realize they made their money stealing or that they brought me in because they were grooming me for something. One night after a few months, they came to me and said, 'You've been living off us far too long. It's time you earned your keep.' I had no idea what they were talking about, but they told me that if I didn't help them break into the car dealership I worked at, they were going to beat me up for freeloading and then make me pay them back for all the food and beer and back rent.

"I offered them all the money I had, but they came up with some ridiculous amount of money I owed them, like five thousand dollars, nothing I could have afforded.

"So I helped them break in. They stole two cars. Then one of the security men walked in on us. One of the guys had a gun and shot him. It didn't kill him, thankfully, but it was considered attempted murder.

"The security guard recognized me and we were caught. I had just turned eighteen a week before, so I was tried as an adult. Those guys I thought were so cool showed their real colors; they told the court it was all my idea. Since I worked at the dealership, the judge believed them. It was their word against mine.

"That's when he gave me the option to go to Vietnam or prison. I had already tried to join the army, so it was pretty much a no-brainer for me."

"And I thought I had it tough," I said.

"What I went through doesn't make your life any easier," he said. Then he forced a smile, saying, "That conversation turned heavy fast. Let's talk about something lighter."

I smiled back. "Like what?"

"Like, did you know your name is a palindrome?"

"What's a palindrome?"

"It's something that reads the same forward and backward. Like the words *radar* or *racecar*."

I worked it out in my head. "*Racecar*. That's kind of cool."

"They can be more than one word," he said. "My favorite palindromes are *Do geese see God?* and the world's first greeting, 'Madam, I'm Adam.'"

"You know, the man they named Noel Street for was a palindrome. His name was Leon Noel."

"I assumed they named it Noel Street because the town's name is kind of . . . Christmassy." He looked at me. "Is that a word?"

"Christmassy. Works for me," I said. "Mistletoe is definitely Christmassy. You arrived just in time for the Noel Street Christmas Market."

"I saw them putting up booths in the park," he said. Suddenly his expression softened. "Fort Wayne used to have something like that. They called it 'Christmas in the Park.' It was only one day, but there'd be horse-drawn wagon rides and groups singing carols. They had booths with crafts and things. There were food vendors, hot wassail, eggnog, and fresh donuts." His eyes had the soft glaze of nostalgia. "We used to go there every year as a family . . ."

"Dylan and I look forward to the market every year. This year will be the best ever."

"Why is that?"

I looked at him and smiled. "Because you're here."

William dropped me off at home a little before midnight. He walked me to the door. "So I'll see you on Thursday?"

"What's Thursday?" he asked.

I glared at him.

He grinned. "Oh, right. Thanksgiving."

"Oh, Thanksgiving," I mocked.

"I'll come hungry," he said.

"I promise you won't leave that way."

"I believe you." He looked into my eyes. The mood grew more serious. "I had a really good time tonight."

"Me too."

Then he leaned forward and we kissed for the first time. It was delicious.

After we separated I said, "Thank you again for tonight."

"I'll see you Thursday."

He turned and walked back to his truck. I waved as he drove off, then went inside. Fran was at the kitchen table doing homework. She looked up at me wearily. "How was the date?"

I smiled. "Perfect."

"Perfect," she repeated. "I think that's good."

My brow fell. "Why do you say that?"

"I don't know. It's just, where do you go from perfect?"

CHAPTER

twenty

For better or worse, this is a Thanksgiving I will never forget.
—Elle Sheen's Diary

Thanksgiving was special. For starters, I got the day off with pay. The diner was closed. It's not that there wasn't enough business. The opposite was true. Thanksgiving always provided a stream of travelers, truck drivers, and Eleanor Rigbys but, as a courtesy to her staff, Loretta shut the place down.

What made the day even better was a self-imposed tradition started by our chef Bart. The day before Thanksgiving Bart made a meal for all of our families, which included his delectable cornbread stuffing, pecan-crusted sweet-potato soufflé, Parker House rolls (just the dough so we could serve them hot), and mashed potatoes with turkey gravy. For dessert I purchased one of Loretta's famous Granny Smith apple pies, the kind with a cinnamon-and-sugar latticework crust. Instant Thanksgiving, just add turkey.

Or, in our case, roast chicken. Dylan liked chicken more than turkey, and since it was the right size for the two of us, that's what we usually had. But this year with William coming, I opted for the larger species of bird.

What I will always remember about that Thanksgiving is that the day started out good, ended good, and the dash between the two ends was a nightmare.

It was snowing again when William arrived at noon. I had just brought out the turkey and the rolls were almost brown, so I asked him to carve the turkey, something he was keen to do, while I brought out the piping-hot rolls and saw to the rest of the meal. We set all the food out on the kitchen counter, then sat together around our tiny kitchen table.

"I'll pray," I said. "Let's hold hands." I cleared my throat. "God, we thank Thee for the remarkable abundance of our lives. We are grateful that William has chosen to spend this day with us. Please bless us to serve all Thy children, especially those that are without. Amen."

"Amen," my men echoed.

I wondered if William had had a decent Thanksgiving since his childhood. He ate three plates of food, and two helpings of pie.

"Remarkable," William said, "I don't think I've ever been this full. I might pop."

Dylan looked concerned. "Really?"

"No. But you should probably wear a raincoat just in case."

Dylan looked at me. "He's kidding," I said.

"Only about the popping part," he said. His face suddenly took on a softer expression. "How life can change.

173

There was a time I was so hungry that I chewed on my shoe just to taste something."

"Yuck," Dylan said.

I looked at William sympathetically and took his hand.

"Why didn't you just go to the refrigerator?" Dylan asked.

He looked at Dylan, then suddenly smiled. "I should have thought of that."

After dinner Dylan went to his room to play while I made William and myself some coffee.

"Cream and sugar?" I asked.

"Both, please."

I brought the cups over.

"This is good," he said. "What is it?"

"It's a special Kona coffee bean that Loretta buys. We don't serve it; it's too expensive for our customers' tastes. But she gives it to us at cost."

"Membership at the diner has its privileges. Including this amazing dinner."

I looked at him happily. "What you said earlier, about chewing your shoe. Was that true?"

"Yes."

"How did you keep going?"

"Some say it's the survival instinct. But I don't think so."

"Why is that?"

"Nearly a million people take their lives each year. It's not about survival; it's about finding meaning in living. Even in our suffering."

"And you found meaning?"

"In a twisted way, I didn't want to let them win." He shook his head. "Whatever it takes, I guess."

"It got you here," I said.

Just then there was a loud crash in the front room. William and I entered the living room. There was a grapefruit-sized stone in the middle of the floor. Dylan came out of his room to see what the noise was. William said to Dylan, "Stay here." William ran to the window and looked out, but whoever had thrown it was gone.

We both walked over to the stone. Written on it in Magic Marker was one word: NIGGER.

William pushed the stone under the couch with his foot. "We're getting out of here," he said.

I think I was in shock. "Where?"

"My place." He said in a voice surprisingly calm, "Dylan, how would you like to play at my house?"

"Can I?" he asked.

"We'll all go," I said.

Where I was paralyzed with fear, William seemed to be activated by it. "Do you want to pack some things?"

I went into Dylan's room and came out with his back-pack. We drove in William's truck to the side of his building, walking through thick snow to the lobby. The brindled cat I'd seen the first day was sitting on the balustrade looking down on us.

"You have a cat?" Dylan asked.

"He's not mine," William said. "He doesn't belong to anyone. He just lives here. He might be the landlord."

"What's his name?"

"I've named him Ho Chi Minh. Because he likes to sneak up on you when you're not looking."

We walked up the stairs to William's apartment and went inside. I took Dylan's coat off and then my own. I noticed William left his on.

"Can I have the keys to your house?" he asked.

"Yes." I took them out of my purse and handed them to him. "How come?"

"I'm going to get some cardboard and patch up your window so the snow doesn't come in. I'll be back in an hour. Don't let anyone in."

"Do you think we're in danger?"

"No. But I don't take chances."

He walked out. "Where is Mr. William going?" Dylan asked.

"He just went to fix something," I said.

"How come someone threw a rock through our window?"

I didn't know that he had comprehended what had happened.

"I don't know. Sometimes people do strange things because they're afraid."

Dylan looked more puzzled. "What are they afraid of?"

"Things they don't understand," I said. "What scares you?"

"Bears," he said.

I nodded. "Me too."

"Did a bear throw that rock?"

"Maybe," I said. "Maybe."

While William was gone I cleaned his apartment: washed the dishes, dusted, even mopped the floor with a cloth. The air was a little stale, so I turned up the heat and cracked a window to let some fresh air in. An hour and a half later William returned. He looked around his apartment.

"You cleaned."

"I had to keep busy," I said. "How did it go?"

"I boarded up the window. I cleaned up the glass and then took the stone over to the police station. That one officer was there."

"Andy?"

"No, the short one with a crew cut."

"Peter," I said. "What did he say?"

"He asked if we saw anything. I told him we didn't, so he's going to check with your neighbors to see if they saw anything." He looked at me intensely. "He asked if you had any enemies they should know about."

The question angered me. I didn't have time to make enemies. I just lived my life the best I could.

"Not that I know of," I said.

"I told him about the Ketchup Lady."

"What did he say?"

"The other officer had already told him about what happened at the diner. He's driving over to her house later today to interrogate her."

"He knows who she is?"

"Loretta did. She looked her up once—just in case she ended up causing any problems."

My heart hurt. I looked over at Dylan, who was still in the bedroom. "So what do we do now?"

"I say we go for a ride and not let this nastiness ruin our holiday."

"Where?"

"How about Salt Lake?" he said. "I heard that they turn the lights on at Temple Square Thanksgiving night."

"Whatever you think," I said. The truth was, I was tired of always being in charge and having to figure out what to do. For once I just wanted to be looked out for. "When?"

"Now."

I walked back to the bedroom. "Come on, Dylan. We're going for a ride."

CHAPTER

twenty-one

My heart feels like a kite in a hurricane.
                                        —Elle Sheen's Diary

The drive to Salt Lake was slow. I-15 was slick and we found ourselves following a caravan of snow-plows. I didn't care. We weren't in any hurry.

When we arrived at the downtown area we were sur-prised at how empty the square was. William stopped at the curb near the center and got out. He asked someone wearing a name tag what time they turned the lights on. He walked back to me. "Well, I messed that up. They turn them on the day after Thanksgiving."

"It's okay," I said. "It's still pretty. Let's walk around the grounds."

The truth was, I wasn't disappointed. In my state of mind I wasn't really in the mood to fight crowds. It just felt good to be somewhere else. Mostly, it felt good to be with William.

We walked around the Temple grounds and then through one of the nearby indoor malls called the ZCMI Center. Our Thanksgiving gluttony had started to wear off, which we satiated with Chinese noodles, caramel apples, and saltwater taffy.

The evening was calm and pleasant and, by dusk, I'd almost forgotten why we'd left Mistletoe to begin with. On the way back home Dylan fell asleep on my lap.

"Looks like we wore him out," William said, glancing over.

"It's usually the other way around," I said.

"Sorry I mixed up the night."

"I wouldn't change a thing," I said.

"You can lean against me, if you want."

I lay my head against his shoulder. We didn't speak much, in part because Dylan was sleeping, but mostly because the silence was enough. We drove back to his apartment.

"I think you should stay at my place tonight," he said softly. "You and Dylan can sleep in the bed. I'll sleep on the couch."

I just nodded. William carried Dylan inside and I tucked him into the bed that I had slept next to when I was taking care of William that first night.

"I don't have anything to wear," I said. In my hurry to leave I'd only packed for Dylan.

"I might have something," William said. He opened a drawer and pulled out a T-shirt with the Harley-Davidson logo on it. "Try this. It might be long enough."

He stepped out of the room. I took off everything except my underwear and donned the long T-shirt. It fell to my knees. I opened the door. "It fits."

He looked at me. "You look cute."

"If the shirt fits . . ."

For a moment he just looked at me. Maybe longingly. Or maybe I just hoped.

"Is there anything else I can get for you?" he asked.

I walked over and hugged him. "Thank you for being so sweet. Today should have been awful. But I feel happy."

"So do I," he said. "Thank you for inviting me to dinner."

"Thank you for coming."

As I looked into his eyes I felt drawn to him. Into him. We began kissing. It was several minutes before I pulled away. "I better go to bed," I said reluctantly.

He just looked into my eyes. "Are you sure?"

I nodded. "Yeah. Good night."

"Good night," he said. He kissed me once more, then sat down on the couch. "Sleep well."

"You too," I said.

I went back inside the bedroom and shut the door behind me.

I couldn't sleep. I could still taste his lips on mine. For more than an hour I just lay in the dark thinking about him. Wanting him. I looked over at Dylan to make sure he was asleep, then I pulled the covers up to his chin and got out of bed. I walked to the door, opened it, stepped out, and quietly pulled it shut behind me. William was asleep on the couch. He was mumbling a little.

I knelt down on the floor next to him, then put my hand on his side. He stopped talking. Then he slowly turned around, his eyes open. "I want to lay with you," I whispered.

He just looked at me, his eyes gently studying my face, then moved as far back against the couch as he could and rolled onto his side, giving me a small perch to rest my body next to his. I climbed onto the couch, our faces just inches apart from each other. The darkness caressed his shadowed face. For a long time we just gazed into each other's eyes. Then I said, "I'm falling for you."

He just looked back at me with soft eyes. "Don't. I'm broken."

"I know."

His eyes suddenly welled with tears, which pooled above his nose and fell down his face. I gently touched the tears with my fingers and wiped them off. Then I pressed my lips to his and we kissed, softly, sweetly at first, then passionately. Everything around us dissolved into nothing. Only once before in my life had I felt that kind of love.

CHAPTER

twenty-two

Sometimes we need the darkness to reveal our light.
                              —Elle Sheen's Diary

FRIDAY, NOVEMBER 28

I woke the next morning in William's bed next to Dylan. Somewhere in the night William must have carried me back to his room. I was disappointed to not feel his body next to mine, but I was glad. It would have been confusing for Dylan had he come out of the room and found us together.

With Dylan still asleep, I got dressed and went into the living room. William was gone. I didn't know what that meant.

Ten minutes later I heard the front door open. William walked in. His shoulders had snow on them and he was carrying a bag from the grocery store.

"I got us something for breakfast," he said.

I took the sack from him and set it on the counter. Then I helped him off with his jacket, which he flung to the floor, and I put my arms around him, my head against his chest. He wrapped his arms around me. I wanted to be held by him more than I could say. I didn't know how he felt about what had passed between us during the night but I knew what I felt. I said softly, "I meant what I said last night."

He kissed the top of my head. "I know."

I knew he was having trouble saying how he felt about me. Of course, I wanted to hear it, but I didn't care right then. He had already said it, just without words. He had shown me he cared in a hundred ways. He had shown me with his strength and anger and gentleness and vulnerability. I would rather have someone show me love and not tell me than tell me and not show me. I think we're all that way.

"Is Dylan still asleep?"

I smiled. "You'd know it if he wasn't," I said. "Do you have any eggs?"

"Maybe half a dozen."

"I can make French toast. Would you like that?"

"Yes."

"Sit down at the table. Let me serve you."

"I'd rather be next to you."

I smiled. "Me too."

He stood behind me with his arms around my waist. It was romantic but not very practical to cook like that. I finally turned around and we kissed. After several minutes I breathlessly said, "Maybe you should sit on the couch or we'll never eat."

He smiled, kissed me again, then walked over and sat down. As I worked I occasionally glanced over at him. His eyes were always on me, as if he were transfixed by me.

I made coffee and cocoa and French toast, then took the remaining French toast batter and cooked it up into a light scramble.

"I don't have syrup," he said.

"You have sugar," I said. "I can make that work." I dissolved brown sugar and water together, then buttered a couple of pieces of toast for Dylan and put the rest on a single plate and poured syrup over the top. Then I scooped up the egg and put it next to the toast. I brought the plate to the table. "Breakfast is served."

"Where's your plate?"

"I'll share yours."

He took a bite, then forked a bite for me. I opened my mouth and he fed me. I stared at him as I ate as if I couldn't take my eyes off him. We ate the whole meal this way.

"Do you have to work today?" he asked.

"Tonight." I looked at him. "How about you?"

"Usual day."

"Could you drop by the diner after work? I'll feed you."

"I'll stay until closing if you want."

I smiled. "That would be nice."

He sat back. "Until we find out what happened, it would probably be best if Dylan didn't go back to your place." He added, "He could stay here."

"I think it would be better if he stayed with Fran. It would be more natural."

"Whatever you think is best."

I fed him the last bite of French toast. "Could you drive me to my car?"

"Your car's already downstairs."

"How did you get it here?"

"I got Sam at the grocery store to drive it over."

"Thank you."

"You're welcome." He lifted our plate and stood. "I better get to work." He took our plate to the sink and set it in water. "Would you like me to find someone to repair your window?"

"No, I'll call the landlady. She's good about things like that."

"All right. I guess I'll go." He just looked at me as he breathed out slowly. "You make it hard to go."

I walked over to him and we kissed. "Thank you for making me feel safe."

"Thank you for letting me."

CHAPTER

twenty-three

*I'm afraid I'm falling for him. That's a lie. I've hit the
ground without a chute.*

—Elle Sheen's Diary

Dylan and I returned to our duplex a little after
noon. Not only had William picked up the broken glass from the window and put cardboard
over it but he'd cleaned up after the Thanksgiving meal as
well, wrapping the leftovers in plastic wrap or putting them
in Tupperware. He had even vacuumed, which to me is one
of the most romantic things a man can do.

Gretchen, my landlady, was her typical efficient self and
had someone there to repair the window even before it
was time for me to leave for work. Dylan sat in the living
room watching the man replace the window and chatting
the poor man's ears off.

Fran arrived around two as the window repairman was
finishing up. Outside our door was the previous window's
frame with its remaining shards and Fran had walked in
past it, leaving her visibly upset.

"Did they catch who did it?" she asked.

"Not yet," I said.

"People are sick."

I looked at her softly. "Some are."

I got Dylan off with Fran and then drove to work.

Word about the stone being thrown through our window had already spread around the diner and Loretta was eager to talk to me about it.

"I'm sure it's that vile Katherine woman," she said. "It can't be a coincidence."

"Who's Katherine?" I asked.

"Aka Ketchup Lady. You know I gave Andy her address. He and Peter went out to interrogate her."

"I don't know if it was her or not," I said. "I just don't ever want to see her again."

"You know you won't see her here. She steps one foot in here and she gets the boot. She can slurp her ketchup somewhere else."

"Thanks for the support."

"That's what I'm here for, baby girl."

William came in around seven. He sat himself in my section and got up and kissed me when I came out to him.

"Did you get your window fixed?" he asked.

"Yes. And the strangest thing, my house was clean. Sparkling, even."

"Christmas elves," he said.

"Apparently," I said. "I wonder why they came only after you moved into town."

"Coincidence, maybe."

"I think not." I grinned. "What are you doing tomorrow?"

"Working. Renato got backed up. I told him I'd work him out of his mess."

"All day?"

"All day, all night. Sorry, you know I'd rather be with you. I'm open Sunday, though. Do you have anything Sunday?"

"Church. But that's just until one." A thought crossed my mind. "Why don't you come to church with us?"

"I don't do church," he said.

"You might like it." I grabbed his hand. "I'll be there. Then I'll cook you a nice meal after."

"We could have Thanksgiving leftovers," he said.

"That sounds like a yes."

"Yes. What time?"

"Church starts at eleven, so if you're picking us up, ten thirty would be good."

"I'll be there."

"I have two more events to put on your calendar."

"I don't have a calendar," he said.

"That makes it easy, then. The first is Saturday night, December sixth. It's the Noel Street Christmas Festival. The second is Friday, December twelfth, Dylan's Christmas concert at school."

"You're planning things two weeks out?"

"Of course. You have to plan these things out," I said. "Don't you?"

"No, I just go with the wind," he said. "I'm a drifter."

"Well, would this drifter like to join us at the annual Christmas concert?"

"Absolutely. Sounds exciting."

"Don't get too excited," I said. "It's just the usual elementary-school production. One of the teachers plays the piano while the kids sing the classics, 'Frosty the Snowman,' 'Rudolph,' 'Jingle Bells.' But Dylan's pretty excited about it. This year he got chosen to be one of the bell ringers for 'Jingle Bells.'" I grinned. "It's a big honor."

"Sounds like it," he said.

"It's during the day. Can you miss an hour of work?"

"Renato doesn't care when I work, just that I get things done. I can go in a little early."

I smiled. "I'll let Dylan know. He'll be excited."

"That makes two of us," he said. "And I thought this was going to be a boring Christmas."

CHAPTER

twenty-four

*William taught me more about my own religious beliefs
today than a flock of pastors and a stack of Bibles ever
could.*

—Elle Sheen's Diary

As I wrote before, my Sunday routine rarely varied,
which, outside of my time with Dylan, is probably
the biggest reason why I loved the day. It was truly
a day of rest. First, unless I was filling in for someone, I
never worked on Sunday. Second, I slept in almost an hour
later than usual—a cherished extravagance—then, while
Dylan slept, I enjoyed some quiet time with some coffee
and a book. Around nine, I made Dylan his traditional Sunday waffles for breakfast.

After doing the dishes, I laid out Dylan's Sunday
clothes—usually jeans, a button-down shirt, and a clip-on
bow tie—then got myself ready for church. The only difference this Sunday was that William was coming, so I spent
more time on my makeup and hair and worried about what
to wear. I wore a long V-necked sage-green dress with an ac-
centing fabric rose made of the same material. I had bought
the dress three years earlier for one of Jamie's weddings.

I hoped William would think I looked pretty. Dylan did. "Wow, Mama. You look beautiful."

I smiled. "Thank you."

"You don't even look like yourself."

I shook my head. "Thank you."

William showed up at my apartment at ten thirty sharp. Maybe it was still the soldier in him or maybe he was just that way, but he was always punctual. He was wearing jeans and a button-down shirt beneath a navy-blue cardigan.

"Is this okay?" he asked, looking down at himself. "I wasn't sure how I was supposed to dress. I'm not really a churchgoing guy."

"You look nice."

"Thank you. Not as nice as you."

Dylan just stood there looking at William. "I don't want to wear a tie," he said.

"Nothing in the Bible about wearing ties," I said. "But you do look nice in it."

"Your mother's right," William said. "You look pretty debonair with the tie."

"What's that mean?" he asked.

"It's an old word for *handsome*," William said.

Dylan thought for a moment, then said, "I'll wear it."

The church Dylan and I had been attending was a non-denominational Christian church that met in what had been an old funeral parlor out in the countryside almost halfway between Mistletoe and the equally small town of Wilden, falling on the latter's side of the city line.

My first Sunday in Mistletoe, Loretta told me about the

church and took me but she stopped going shortly after. I continued going without her. Fran attended the church as well.

We walked into the chapel just a few minutes before the service began. The three of us sat together in the middle of a pew next to Fran, who had come early to save us seats.

The church was small and poor. Our pastor, Pastor Henderson, did yard care and blade sharpening on the side to make ends meet.

We had a pianist, Mrs. Glad, who played an old upright piano that, I was told, had come from a bar. The church had a small choral group made up mostly of elderly parishioners who used to be able to sing, but still joyfully (and by joyfully I mostly mean loudly) offered what they had left. As it was the Christmas season, they sang Christmas songs, two of which the congregation joined in on: "O Come, All Ye Faithful" and "Angels We Have Heard on High."

After Pastor Henderson made a few announcements, there was another song followed by prayer, and then a Communion of grape juice and a Ritz cracker—always Dylan's favorite part of the service. This was followed by a sermon.

I loved my church and I had come to love celebrating the holiday season there. The message of hope filled my heart with peace and gratitude, both powerful forces to get me through the daily challenges of my little life. The sermon that day was on forgiveness, and Pastor Henderson was in good form.

About ten minutes into the sermon William handed me the keys to his truck and whispered in my ear, "I'll meet you at your apartment." He stood up and made his way down the pew past the other worshippers on his way out.

I turned to Fran. "Would you take Dylan home?"

"Got it," she said, watching William leave.

I stood up and walked out after him. When I got outside the church, William was already a surprisingly long way from the chapel, walking briskly through the snowclad barren landscape toward the main road. I couldn't believe he was walking home. It was at least seven miles to Mistletoe, and he wasn't even wearing a coat.

"William!" I shouted.

He kept walking, bent against the cold.

I shouted again as I ran toward him. "William!"

He stopped and turned around. When I caught up to him I paused to catch my breath, then said, "Where are you going?"

"I just had to get out of there," he said.

"How come?"

"I don't belong."

"Everyone belongs," I said.

"I don't," he said. "All that talk about grace and forgiveness." He looked at me. "I just couldn't handle it."

"Why?"

He hesitated. "Because God will never forgive me for what I've done."

His words moved me. "That's why God came. That's what Christmas is about. Forgiveness and hope."

201

"There is no hope for me. Not after what I've done."

I pondered his words, then said, "Have you ever really shared what happened with anyone?"

"No."

"Maybe it's time." I took his hand. "I want you to tell me about it."

He looked at me like I'd just asked him to jump off a cliff. Maybe I had. "I can't."

"What are you afraid of?"

He raked his hand back through his hair and looked at me. "That you won't like me anymore."

I looked him in the eyes. "My husband wrote me about the war. I know he hid a lot from me, but I could still feel both the horror and shame he felt. You were put in a situation that wasn't your fault. Would you have done those things if you hadn't been taken from your home and ordered to kill?"

He shook his head. "No, of course not."

"The fact that you're suffering shows who you really are. You need to let it go. You don't need to worry about me not loving you. You can trust me."

"Not with this." He looked up. "I don't want to take that chance."

"You have to," I said softly.

"Why?"

"Because if you believe that I couldn't love you if I knew the real you, then you will never believe in my love."

He just looked at me for a moment, then slowly nodded. "Let's go someplace."

"Let's go to your place," I said.

"My apartment?"

"No, the frozen waterfall."

"That would be appropriate," he said.

We held hands as we walked back to the church and got in his truck. We drove up along the canyon to the waterfall. No one was there, but the wind was blowing hard, so we didn't get out of the truck. We just sat inside, the heater on high.

I knew this would be difficult for him so I started. "Where do you want to begin?"

He took a deep breath. "Christmas Day." He went quiet. I reached over and took his hand.

"Tell me."

He took a deep breath. "The day started with a Christmas service put on by our chaplain. It was nostalgic, you know. Everyone was melancholy or homesick. A few guys cried. Everyone but me. I had no one back home.

"Then they opened their care packages while we listened to a broadcast Christmas message from President Johnson. After the service, the chaplain gave everyone a Bible. It was the only present I got."

He looked over at me. "Two days later we were called up to search a small village in Quang Tri.

"It was half an hour before dawn. We were moving in through a rice paddy when a dog started barking. An old man walked out of his hut. He looked around for a moment, then he saw one of our men. I was just ten yards away and I could see it all. The old man and the soldier just stood there staring at each other. Then the old man started shouting.

"That's when all hell broke loose. A dozen machine guns shredded everything in sight. Flame throwers belched out hell. People were screaming and crying." He looked at me. "People were dying.

"Afterward I was counting casualties when I came across a Vietnamese woman huddled near the edge of the jungle. She was holding her son." William's voice suddenly choked with emotion. "He was no older than Dylan. He had been shot and his life was bleeding out on his mother. For a moment we just looked at each other. There was such fear in her eyes. Then she lifted her hand. I thought she had a grenade, so I shot her." His eyes welled up. "When I went to check her for weapons, I found that she was only trying to show me a prayer book."

"I'm sorry," I said.

He slowly shook his head. "Everything about that war was a mess. The brass couldn't figure out how to decide who was winning, so someone decided to measure success by body count. We were being pushed by a general they called the 'Butcher of the Delta.' His ambition was indiscriminate. He ordered the killing of innocent men, women, and children and counted skulls as trophies. He had a saying: 'If it's dead and Vietnamese, it's VC.'

"Four days after leveling that village, on New Year's Eve, we walked into an ambush. Half our platoon was killed. Friends of mine were killed." He looked into my eyes.

"That's when I was taken captive." He looked at me, his eyes revealing his pain.

"You've told me nothing that makes me respect you less," I said. I leaned over and kissed him on the cheek. "Tell me what it was like being a prisoner of war."

"Horror."

"Tell me."

He rubbed his face. "It was day-to-day survival. There was constant physical and mental torture. Worst of all was the unknowing. They wanted us to believe that we might never go home—that no one knew where we were or that they thought we were dead.

"The first year I was tied up in a bamboo cage in the jungle with eleven other men. Six of them died of disease or starvation. After a year or so, those of us who had survived were moved to Hanoi.

"I spent the next few years lying on a bamboo mat on a concrete floor with my legs bound. There were meat hooks hanging from the ceiling above us." His voice softened with the recollection. "That's where I got those scars on my back."

I rubbed his hand.

"We suffered from constant hunger on the edge of starvation. When they did feed us, it was usually old bread and watery soup filled with rat droppings.

"I woke every day in horror. They forced us to speak betrayal, while we struggled to defend something no one fully understood. They told us about the atrocities and corruption going on in South Vietnam. They didn't have to make up lies; they just read to us from the US newspapers.

"The South Vietnamese leaders were gorging themselves off their own people and country. They turned their own people against them. And we were there fighting to hold up one corrupt regime after another in the name of freedom.

"When our government officials lodged complaints over their treatment of their own people, they were told it wasn't any of their business. They'd take our blood and weapons, but not our counsel. We were so afraid of the world turning communist . . . The choice was between one devil or the other."

"You were a pawn in an evil game," I said. "Just like my husband. You paid for their sins. The sin will be on their heads." I looked into his eyes. "Come here."

He leaned forward. I cupped the back of his head and pulled it against my breast and held him while he cried. "I love you," I said.

He pressed himself into me. "I love you too," he said softly.

William and I arrived back at my duplex after dark. There were more snowmen in the yard. Nearly a dozen. Maybe more.

When we went inside Fran was sitting at the table studying. Dylan was already asleep in bed.

"Did you have a good night?" I asked.

Fran nodded. "We watched Disney."

"And made snowmen," I added.

"Yes, we did," Fran said. "Hundreds."

I laughed. "Looks like it."

"Do you need anything else?"

I shook my head. "No. Thank you."

"You're welcome." She looked at William and smiled. "Have a good night."

"You too," William said. "Thanks for watching Dylan."

"Always my pleasure."

After she left I invited William to stay. I felt the need to stay close to him. He was vulnerable and I didn't want him going home alone. I had him lie down on the couch. I put a warm washcloth on his face, then gently massaged his feet.

He fell asleep in our front room around midnight. I didn't try to wake him.

The first week of December passed slowly. Scientists say that time is relative. I believe this. In fact, I created my own formula: $V = D^2 + W$. Time's Velocity = Current Drudgery^2 + the next Worthwhile Event in our life.

Restaurants always pick up around the holidays, so we

all worked as much as we could. William was busy as well but we saw each other when we could. He'd either come by for dinner or, if he worked too late, coffee.

I was excited to spend some real time alone with him again. The next thing on our calendar was the Noel Street Christmas Festival.

CHAPTER

twenty-five

Something happened tonight at the Christmas Festival that I can't explain.

                    —Elle Sheen's Diary

SATURDAY, DECEMBER 6

For some streets, decorating for Christmas is like putting lipstick on a pig. But Noel Street didn't just share a holiday name, it was made for it. Dickens-era streetlamps with deep green patinas lined the cobblestone street, hung with great pine wreaths. Silver tinsel wires were strung across the width of the road and wrapped with red-and-green ribbon and blinking white and gold lights. In the center of each strand were three-foot-tall silver bells.

The old brick buildings that lined Noel Street still had their original wood-framed glass picture windows, which the local proprietors dressed inside and out, reminiscent of the days when a child could stand on the sidewalk gazing at a magical, sparkling display filled with Christmas dreams.

The street's decorations were the largest line item on the town budget, which was something the locals were proud of. The cynical of heart might write it all off to commercialization, but it was far more than that. It was magic and enchantment. Noel was a street made to be dressed.

The north end of Noel Street—the opposite end of town from the Harrison—circled Garfield Park, a grassy public square with an old wood pavilion and its centerpiece, a massive hundred-and-fifty-year-old Norway spruce. The park was where the festival was held, with the Noel Street traffic flowing into it like a river into a lake.

The Noel Street Christmas Festival was the kind of event that didn't know its potential when it started. In fact, its evolution was so natural that there was an ongoing argument among the locals about who had started it and when it actually began.

There were watermarks along its path. You could say it began sometime in the early fifties when the Downtown Merchants' Association—consisting of less than a dozen business owners—decided to petition the Mistletoe city council to decorate the large spruce. Just a year earlier someone had suggested that the tree should be donated to Rockefeller Center in New York City and almost found themselves run out of town.

With promised donations and the loan of a cherry picker, the council approved the request and the tree was decorated. Just a week later the local elementary school music teacher, Mrs. Carter (who has since passed away), decided to form the Noel Street Chorale, a hodgepodge of singers who met by the tree each weekend night during the holiday season to sing Christmas carols.

At first it was just the singers; then their families came, followed by strangers looking for entertainment in a small town with few amusements. One night, someone had the idea to bring a container of hot cocoa for the singers, a simple act of goodness that led to an unexpected proliferation. By the next year both the size of the chorale group and its audience had doubled and the local women's auxiliary set up a small but permanent stand serving hot cocoa and coffee—not just for the singers but for their audience as well—as a means to raise funds for their local service projects.

Nothing spurs success like profit, and the next year there was another stand selling homemade bread with honey butter. This was followed two weeks later by a donut stand and Mrs. Bench selling hand-knit Christmas stockings and Christmas tree ornaments her husband carved by hand from olive tree wood.

As the park's crowds grew, the members of the original Downtown Merchants' Association realized they had created something perennial, so they again petitioned the city council and reserved the square for an annual Christmas event. A committee was formed and one of the wealthier Mistletoe benefactors visited the famous Christkindlmarkt in Germany and brought back an entire notebook of ideas to bring to the small Mistletoe festival—some practical, some not.

As the Christmas festival grew, it began attracting the citizens of neighboring places, first from the small border towns of Wilden and Tremonton, then eventually drawing those from the larger cities of Ogden, Layton, and Logan.

Soon the festival filled the park and spilled out onto the neighboring streets. It was the only time of year in Mistletoe that open parking spaces weren't a given.

By 1975 the Noel Street Christmas Festival was a complicated affair with bureaucratic regulations and oversight, rented booths, merchant stalls, choir stands, a public address system, and a printed program with two weeks of scheduled performances. Vendors, now coming from outside Mistletoe, sold everything from mulled wine and baked apples to funnel cake and roasted nuts.

There was both a gingerbread house contest, sponsored by the local credit union, and a crèche display, a life-sized nativity with a real donkey and oxen, a stall of reindeer, and, of course, a huge golden throne that Santa himself (accompanied by an enterprising local photographer) inhabited weekend evenings before Christmas.

Dylan had waited all week for the evening, each day building in anticipation like Christmas. Like Christmas, he had trouble sleeping the night before.

William picked us up a little after sundown and we drove downtown, parking in one of the reserved parking places behind the diner. Then the three of us wandered up and down the crowded sidewalks, stopping to watch street performers and carolers and peruse the vendors' booths and sample their wares. Christmas music blared from every corner.

"I can't believe there are this many people," I said, pressing our way through the crowds. "The festival just keeps growing."

"People are looking for something," William said.

We stopped at a booth selling German delicacies and ate bratwurst and sauerkraut sandwiches (something I could never have gotten Dylan to eat on my own) and Spätzle (ditto) with large cups of cider served in plastic steins.

After we'd eaten, we made our way to the crowded square, holding hands with Dylan in the middle. We stopped to take pictures by the Christmas tree and then walked to the main pavilion to listen to a barbershop quartet sing "God Rest Ye Merry, Gentlemen" followed by "It's Beginning to Look a Lot Like Christmas."

"This is impressive," William said. "There are a lot of people here. I wonder where they're coming from."

"It used to just be the locals and couples on dates," I said. "Now look at all the families. They're coming from all over."

We were standing near a large box or crate wrapped in Mylar and tied with a bow to look like a Christmas present. We could see our reflection in the box. Just then Dylan looked up at me with a large smile. "Look, Mama. We're a family."

I smiled back at him, then looked over at William. To my surprise he wasn't smiling. There was a peculiar look in his eyes. He suddenly released Dylan's hand. "Hey, buddy. Want some caramel corn?"

"Yeah."

Dylan hadn't noticed William's nuanced response, but I had. William left us for a moment, then came back with a large bag of caramel corn. From that moment on, William was different. Quieter and disconnected. He was also holding something so he couldn't hold hands. I puzzled to understand what had happened.

It was still early, just a little before nine when William said, "We probably shouldn't keep Dylan up too late."

"You want to go already?" I asked.

"It would probably be best."

I hid my disappointment. "All right," I said. We walked against the flow of a still-growing crowd back to his truck. It was a little after nine o'clock when we arrived back at my duplex. I sent Dylan inside to get ready for bed, remaining outside with William.

"Would you like to come in?" I asked.

"Thanks," he said. "But I'm a little tired."

I took his hand. "Are you okay?"

"I'm fine."

I looked into his eyes. "Are *we* okay?"

The pause after my question was answer enough. "We're fine," he said.

I just looked at him, still unable to read what had happened. Whatever it was, he clearly didn't want to talk about it.

I took a deep breath, then exhaled. "All right. Good night." I stood on my toes to kiss him. He gave me just a light peck on the lips. "Good night."

He turned to go.

"Call me tomorrow?" I asked.

"Sure."

The next day William didn't call or stop by the diner. I knew something had bothered him the previous night. As much as I wanted to see him, I didn't reach out to him. Whatever he was dealing with he needed to work out. But it wasn't easy. My heart ached. It didn't help that in the days leading up to the school Christmas concert, Dylan asked me at least a dozen times if William was going to be there. I wished I knew.

CHAPTER

twenty-six

To have children is, by necessity, to be vulnerable.
—Elle Sheen's Diary

FRIDAY, DECEMBER 12

The morning of the big program my heart wrestled with the competing emotions of excitement and dread. *I still haven't heard from William since the festival. Where is he?*

Dylan was over-the-top excited about the concert and his debut performance as a first-grade bell ringer. It was a really big deal for him, which only made me more anxious about not hearing from William. Notwithstanding, I didn't want anything to take away from Dylan's day.

I put chocolate chips in his Cream of Wheat, something reserved for very special occasions, then dressed him in red corduroy pants with a long-sleeved white cotton shirt and green suspenders.

"You, little man, look like Christmas personified," I said. "Santa would be proud."

"Is Santa going to be there?" he asked.

"I don't think so."

"Is Mr. William going to be there?"

I deflected the question. "We'll see. Are you ready to ring that bell?"

He nodded. "I practiced."

Only seven kids in the entire school got to play an instrument; a fifth-grade boy who played the drum during "The Little Drummer Boy," three third-grade girls who played plastic recorders during "Silent Night," then the three children in Dylan's class who got to ring bells for "Jingle Bells." The rest of the children were assigned to general chorus duty.

As I put on his coat, Dylan asked, "Is Mr. William picking us up?"

"No. He's coming from work. We're going to meet him there."

His little forehead furrowed. "Is he coming for sure?"

My heart ached at the question. "I don't know for sure. He said he was coming. Unless there's an emergency at work, he'll be there."

"I hope there's not an emergency," Dylan replied. "This is a pretty big deal."

I still love that he said that.

Dylan and I got in the car. I started it up and turned on the heater. There was a huge burst of air, then nothing.

"No, no, no," I said.

"What's wrong, Mama?" Dylan asked.

I groaned. "This car hates me."

To my huge relief (and surprise), William was waiting for us at the school when we got there. Dylan picked out his truck in the school parking lot the moment we drove in. I didn't know where he'd been but at that moment, I really didn't care. I was just glad he was there. I just didn't want to see Dylan disappointed on such an important day.

William must have gotten there pretty early because he'd secured front-row seats for us. As usual, most of those in attendance were mothers and grandparents with a sprinkling of fathers who could get off work. William looked a little out of place. He was taller and younger than most and decidedly male. He was also dressed nicely, nothing he'd be wearing to work at Renato's.

I sent Dylan to his classroom and then walked up to the front of the little auditorium. It had been decorated for the concert with a few hundred snowflakes the children had cut out.

William stood when he saw me. "Hi," he said. Noticeably, he didn't try to kiss me.

"Thanks so much for coming," I said. "Dylan asked me at least a half dozen times if you were going to be here."

"I wouldn't miss it for the world," he said.

We sat down together. "How have you been?" I asked.

He avoided my gaze. "Just busy, you know?"

"I know," I said. I looked at him. "I've missed you."

"I've missed you too," he said softly.

"Did I do something wrong?"

He looked down, threading his fingers together. "No." Then he reached over and took my hand. For the moment I let it go at that. I wanted his touch. I didn't want to spoil anything.

Fran arrived a few minutes before the concert. William hadn't known she was coming, and all the seats around us were taken, so she said hello, then went and sat near the back of the room.

The concert started promptly at nine thirty. Howard Taft Elementary School was small, with less than two hundred students in seven grades. The kindergarteners went first, which was more an exercise in herding cats than a musical performance. They were singing "Rudolph, the Red-Nosed Reindeer" and someone had the bright idea of putting red noses—foam rubber clown noses, really—on each of the kids. Needless to say, the whole song (to the delight of photograph-snapping adults) was just an exercise in children chasing little red balls across the floor.

After the teachers had collected the noses, the next performance was Dylan's class with "Jingle Bells." The kids sang loudly and happily, and Dylan, who was taking the bell thing way too seriously, rang his bell with stoic concentration, his eyes not once leaving his teacher, Mrs. Duncan, who was directing the song.

We endured another four songs, and then William and I joined the rest of the parents in the cafeteria for milk and frosted Christmas-tree-shaped sugar cookies.

I was looking around for Dylan when I noticed him on the other side of the cafeteria with a group of children. He was pointing toward us.

"I'll be right back," I said to William. I crossed the room, smiling like only a proud mother could. "You were so great," I said when I got to him. "You really rang that bell."

Dylan just looked at me with a peculiar expression, the kind he wore when I caught him doing something he wasn't supposed to be doing.

Just then, Mrs. Duncan walked up to me. "Hi, Elle."

"Congratulations," I said. "That was awesome."

"Congratulations to you," she returned.

I smiled. "For what?"

"Dylan tells us he's getting a father." She looked across the room at William. "Is that the lucky man?"

Dylan looked at me sheepishly.

"Mr. Smith is only a friend," I said. I looked at Dylan, unsure how to respond. I was torn between making him apologize and just holding him.

Just then one of the boys said, "I told you he was lying."

Dylan ran out of the room.

"Sorry," I said to his teacher. I chased after him. I found him hiding behind a row of coats in his classroom. I squatted down next to him. "Are you okay?"

He just looked at me with tears in his eyes.

"I'm not going to get mad at you." I breathed out heavily, then sat down on the floor. "You know, it's hard not having a father, isn't it?"

He slowly nodded.

"You may not know it, but we're in the same boat, you and I. I don't have a father either. Sometimes I even cry about it. It doesn't seem fair, does it?"

He shook his head.

"You need to know something. You have a father. And he was a really great man. A special man. Your father is a hero. But you never got to see him, and that's not very fair to you. But he loved you very much, and he was so excited about coming home from the war and seeing you. He was excited about playing baseball and going tubing and taking you camping." My eyes welled up.

"But that didn't get to happen. I'm so sorry. And I know that he's sorry. But *you* have nothing to be sorry about. Because you're just a wonderful little boy in a big world, and none of this is your fault. Not one little bit. Do you understand that? You have nothing to be sorry or embarrassed about."

Dylan's eyes welled up too.

"Mr. William likes you very, very much. He's not your father, but he still cares about you and me, and that's a good thing. The other day he told me what a great kid you are. Do you know what I told him?"

Dylan shook his head again.

"I told him that he was right, that you're the best kid I know. But whether or not you ever have a father doesn't change that one little bit.

"And you know what? Someday you might have the chance to *be* a father. And that little boy or girl will be the luckiest person in the whole world except for me, because I'll always be luckier. Because you're my son, and I'm awfully glad I got to be your mother."

For a moment Dylan just looked at me. Then he came out from behind the coats into my arms. I just held him. "I love you, my little man. I love you with all my heart."

CHAPTER

twenty-seven

This afternoon, William . . .
*[I never finished writing this entry. Next to those words
there was just the stain of two teardrops. I suppose that
says more than I could have written.]*
—Elle Sheen's Diary

After a few more minutes I said, "Do you feel better?"
He nodded.

"Would you like to get a cookie?"

He nodded again.

I leaned back and kissed his forehead. "Okay. Let's go."

I held his hand as we walked back down the hall to
the cafeteria. The crowd had cleared a little but there
were still dozens of children swarming around the cookie
table.

"Do you want me to go with you?" I asked.

"No, thank you."

"Okay. I'll be over here with Mr. William." I let go of
his hand and he ran over to the cookies where the other
children were.

I looked around for William, hoping that he hadn't left.

I found him standing alone on the south side of the cafeteria, leaning against the wall. I walked over to him.

"Where have you been?" he asked. Frankly, I wanted to ask him the same question.

"I had to talk to Dylan. He was telling some of the other children that you're his father."

William looked at me with a peculiar expression. "What?"

"Don't worry, I told him to stop."

William's expression turned still harder. He looked upset. "Why would he do that?"

The intensity of his response surprised me. "Why are you so upset by this? You should be flattered. Dylan looks up to you. He just wanted to be like the other kids whose dads are here."

William didn't say anything.

"Are you telling me that it's never even crossed your mind?"

"Has what crossed my mind?" he said angrily.

My eyes welled up. I covered them with my hand. "Oh my gosh." My pain turned to anger. I looked up at him. "What's going on? Why haven't you called?"

"I told you."

"You told me nothing!" I shouted. I noticed all the other parents looking at us. "Come outside."

William followed me outside the school. I turned on him. "What is this?"

"What is what?"

"This . . . us."

"What did you think this was?"

"Clearly not what you did," I said.

"Did I ever tell you that I was looking for a relationship?"

"Not in words."

"I didn't come to this place to fall in love."

I looked at him for a moment, then said, "But you did, didn't you?"

He didn't answer.

"That's what it is, isn't it?" When he didn't answer I said, "You came here for whatever reason and fell in love and you got scared."

"What do you know about being scared?" he said.

I caught my breath. My head was spinning. "Maybe nothing compared to you. But what I know is that you went through a hell that few people could understand and you had every reason to die yet you fought to live. And now that you're back, you're afraid of living."

"What do I have to live for?"

The question stung. "I thought I was something to live for. I thought Dylan was something to live for."

He didn't speak. The rejection that burned in me turned to anger. "You're a coward. You're not afraid of death, you're afraid that life might be worth living. You're afraid you might have to forgive yourself."

"There is no such thing as forgiveness."

"That's not true."

"Really? Have you forgiven your father?"

Again, his words stung. I couldn't answer.

"Have you forgiven yourself for sending Isaac to fight in

a war he didn't believe in and never came back from? Have you forgiven yourself for sending him to his death?"

His words sent a shock through me. My knees weakened. I began to tremble. "I didn't send him to his death."

"Are you sure?"

The words were like a spear through my heart. At first I couldn't breathe. William stood there helplessly. Suddenly Fran walked out of the school. She looked at me, breathless and heaving in pain, and walked over. "Oh, honey. What happened?" She spun toward William. "What did you do to her?"

William just stood there.

"What did you do to her?!" she screamed.

He just stood there awkwardly and speechless. When I caught my breath, I looked up at him and said softly, "If I tell you you're right, will you leave me?"

"I'm so sorry," he said.

I couldn't stop shaking. "Please."

"You need to leave," Fran said. "You need to leave now."

He just looked at me, his eyes welling. "I'm really sorry." He turned and walked away.

After several minutes Fran said, "It's cold, Elle. Let's get you inside."

"I don't want to go inside. I don't want Dylan to see me like this."

Fran took my hand. "I understand. Let me walk you to the car, then I'll get Dylan. I'll take him to my place."

"All right," I said softly.

We walked together across the wet pavement to my car. Fran opened my door, hugged me, and then helped me in.

"Are you sure you can drive?"

I nodded.

"Okay. Just call when you want me to bring him back. He can spend the night if you want."

"Thank you."

She stood there looking at me with sympathetic eyes. Then she said, "What do you want me to tell Dylan if he asks about William?"

"Tell him he's gone."

CHAPTER

twenty-eight

How is it that we don't see the train until we're beneath it?
                                                —Elle Sheen's Diary

Dylan slept that night at Fran's. I couldn't sleep. I tried. I even took sleeping pills, anything to escape the pain, but nothing helped.

As I tossed in bed, somewhere in the middle of the night, something hit me. Something William had said at the school that stole any hope I had of sleep. *Did he really say what I thought he said?*

I waited until the sun came up, then, in just my sweats and a T-shirt, I put on my coat and drove to Renato's.

William's truck wasn't in the parking lot. I stormed into the repair shop's lobby. Renato was there talking to some man. They both turned and looked at me. Without speaking, I opened the door to the garage. No one was there.

I turned back to Renato. "Where is he?" I asked. "Where's William?"

Renato looked at me sadly. "William quit. He said he had to move on."

The words felt like a brick on my chest. "When?"

"He came by my house last night."

"Did he already leave?"

"I don't know," he said. "He was very upset."

I ran back out to my car. I had to see him. I had to know the truth. I drove to the Harrison with tears running down my cheeks. To my relief, William's truck was still there.

I ran upstairs and pounded on his door. It was nearly a full minute before William opened it. He said nothing, his gaze locked on mine.

"I never told you my husband's name," I said. "I never told you his name was Isaac. You knew him, didn't you? You knew my husband."

William just looked at me.

"Tell me!" I shouted. "You knew my husband!"

William's face showed neither anger nor indifference. After a moment he said, "Come in."

His apartment looked even barer than before, if that was possible. There were two large green canvas duffel bags on the floor next to the couch. There was a gun on top of one of the bags.

William sat at one end of the couch. "Have a seat," he said softly.

I sat at the other end of the couch. I just sat there, trembling.

William rubbed his chin and said, "I knew Isaac. He was my best friend. I was with him when he died."

My eyes welled up.

"It was that New Year's Eve I told you about, right after the attack on Quang Tri. Our platoon walked into an ambush. Isaac got hit right off. I carried him to some rocks next to a waterfall, but he was bleeding badly. I needed to get him out of there, but we were pinned down. We were outnumbered. The bullets were thicker than mosquitoes." The pain and fear in his eyes was fresh, as if he were reliving the moment.

"I kept telling him to hang in there, that we were going to make it. But we both knew otherwise." William swallowed. "His last thoughts were of you. He was afraid you would blame yourself for his death. He was afraid of his son growing up without a father. He asked me to find you and tell you that he loved you."

William's eyes welled up. "I was carrying him when I was captured." He looked into my eyes. "You wanted to know what kept me alive through that hell? It was that promise." He closed his eyes tight, forcing a tear down his cheek. "Actually there were two promises. He made me promise to give you something." He breathed out slowly. "I was going to mail it to you after I left."

He reached into one of the duffel bags and brought out a black velvet pouch. "You have no idea what it took to get this to you." He handed it to me.

I opened the pouch and poured its contents into my palm. It was Isaac's wedding band. I looked up at William.

"I swallowed it at least a hundred times to keep them from finding it. If they had seen me swallow it, they would have cut me open."

I looked at the ring, caressing it between my fingers. It was just a simple gold band, all we could afford at the time. I remembered slipping it on Isaac's finger. William had risked his life to bring it to me.

"When I came back to America, I realized that the promise I made to Isaac was the only thing that kept me alive."

"Then he gave you a gift," I said.

He shook his head. "It was a curse." He looked at me. "You asked me why I came to Mistletoe. I came to fulfill a promise to my friend and then do what I should have done back in Vietnam."

"What's that?"

"Die."

The word echoed in my heart. "That place you took me," I said. "The falls . . ."

"That was where I was going to take my life."

"That's why you were crying?"

"I was crying because I was carrying Isaac like that when he died."

I let the words sink in. "Why did it take you so long to find me?"

"I was a mess. I was trying to make something stick. I couldn't."

"Maybe it was the wrong thing you were trying to make stick. Maybe God had something better for you."

"There is no God."

"Then why are you so angry at Him?"

He didn't answer. For a long time there was only silence. "I don't know why I didn't see it before, but I understand now," I said. "You were afraid because you finally found a family. You found what was taken from you all those years ago."

He put his head down. I moved closer to him. I reached out and touched his cheek. He raised his head to look at me.

"Can't you see it? This is too big a coincidence. Have you considered that maybe Isaac didn't ask you to make that promise for him? That promise was for *you*. It kept you alive through that hell. It brought you to us. He gave you a gift. He gave you back a family. He gave you us."

"That's what I'm afraid of."

"It's not what you're afraid of," I said. "It's what you're afraid of losing. Why else would you have come here and taken an apartment and a job. You could have just found me at the diner and left the same day.

"William, God is giving you this. He's giving you a second chance. But you have to have the courage to take it. It's your choice now. You can have what you've always wanted. I know you're afraid of losing us. After all you've been through, who wouldn't be? But this time, this moment, is up to you but if you don't take the chance, you've already lost us."

William was quiet for the longest time, thinking, searching. The whole time I silently prayed, hoping he would have faith just one more time—hoping that he would believe. Then he looked up at me. I knew his answer before he spoke. All he said was "I'm sorry."

His words ended the conversation. My heart knew it

was over. We were over. "Me too," I said. After a minute I took a deep breath. I felt nothing but darkness. "Are you going to take your life?"

"I don't know."

"Please don't. Not that what I think matters." I looked him in the eyes. "I love you, William. More than I could ever say." I swallowed. "And I know you love me."

He looked at me for a moment, then said, "More than I've ever loved anyone or anything." Then he said something I'll never forget. "It's the only thing more terrifying than death."

"That's the price of love," I said. "The risk of losing it. But it's worth the risk."

"Is it?"

I took another deep breath. "I guess that's for you to decide."

I just sat there for a moment. Then I wiped my eyes and lifted the golden ring. "Thank you for this." I stood. "I guess I better let you get on with your life."

As he stood, I walked over and put my arms around him, my head against his chest. With his arms around me, he pulled me in close. For just a moment I pretended that this was something else, but my heart wouldn't allow it. I stepped back, kissed him, then turned and walked out of his life.

CHAPTER

twenty-nine

Broken hearts tend to take the rest of the body with them.
                                    —Elle Sheen's Diary

It was only a week until Christmas. I was alone. Dylan had been with Fran for two days.

I couldn't stand the sound of my thoughts, so I turned on the radio to one of those all-Christmas-all-the-time stations. "I Heard the Bells on Christmas Day" by Harry Belafonte played.

There is no peace on earth, I said to myself. *Never has been. Never will be.* The phrase from the song clung to my heart like a burr.

My heart was broken.

Most of all I was tired. Tired of loneliness and responsibility. And, in spite of my exhaustion, I could see no respite, no reprieve, no way out, and Christmas was looming ahead of me like an iceberg in the path of a titanic meltdown.

Dylan would be back soon. I wished I had someone to send him off with for a while. Fran would have kept him for as long as I needed, but she was leaving town for the holidays. I couldn't hide my brokenness.

My thoughts were interrupted by the doorbell. It was Gretchen, my landlady. The sight of her just made my stomach hurt more. She stood on the porch holding a plate of cookies. She looked at me, clearly shocked by my appearance. My hair was a rat's nest, and I had no makeup on. I hadn't worn makeup for days.

"Elle, are you . . . okay?"

"I've been better," I said. "Come in."

She stepped inside. "Are you sick?"

"No."

"Is it the window?" she asked. "You know they caught that evil woman."

"This has just been a hard month. It's been a hard year."

"I'm really sorry." She forced a smile. "But cheer up. I brought you my famous pepperkaker cookies. The ones that sell like hotcakes at the festival. They're always good for a smile."

"Thank you," I said. I took the plate from her and set it down on the table. I turned back. "Look, I know I'm late on rent, but . . . is there any way we could split this month across the next three months."

Gretchen looked confused. "You want to split up your rent?"

"Just for the next three months," I said. "I think I can get back on track."

"I'm sure I don't know what you're talking about."

"My rent," I said, angry that she was making my request more difficult than it already was. "You came here to collect the rent, right?"

She looked even more confused. "No, I came to bring you cookies. Your rent's paid."

"I don't understand."

"Honey, there's nothing to understand. Your rent is paid up to the end of next year, which I am very grateful for."

"You must be mistaken. I didn't pay it."

"Not you, dear. It was the man you sent."

"What man?"

"The one you sent with your rent. I've never met him before. He told me he was paying the bill for you. He paid in cash."

I let the news sink in. "Was his name William?"

She bit her lip. "I'm sorry, he didn't give me his name. He was a nice-looking gent, older, maybe in his late fifties."

"Fifties? Are you sure?"

"Oh yes. He had fabulous gray hair."

I honestly had no idea who it could be.

"I assumed you knew." She smiled. "Maybe it was someone you met at the diner." She raised her eyebrows. "Maybe you have a secret admirer."

"I don't know anyone who could have done that."

She shrugged. "Well, someone paid it. Maybe it was an angel. Maybe it's a Christmas miracle. I'm happy for you, Elle. You deserve a break. Maybe this news will brighten your day a little. Or a lot. Merry Christmas, my dear."

"Merry Christmas to you too," I said.

I shut the door after her. *Who had paid my rent?*

CHAPTER

thirty

I had an unexpected visitor today.
                              —Elle Sheen's Diary

Fran came by with Dylan a little after seven o'clock. She honked "shave and a haircut" as she pulled into my driveway—something Dylan always made her do. She was on her way to Texas to visit her family, and the back seat of her car was full of wrapped gifts and suitcases.

The passenger-side door opened and Dylan practically sprang from it, running to me and shouting, "Mama! Mama! I missed you!" I hugged him tight and kissed the top of his head. "I missed you too, buddy."

He stood back. "Look!" He held out a wrapped box. "Fran gave me a present. But she says I can't open it until Christmas."

"Go put it under the tree," I said. "I'll be right there."

He ran into the house. Fran walked up to me, leaving her car idling.

"He's had a bath and I fed him dinner." She looked at me. "Elle, I'm so sorry I can't keep him longer. You know I would."

"You've done more than enough. I'm worried about you driving at night. Are you sure you won't wait until morning?"

"I'll be okay. I'm just going to Green River tonight, maybe Laramie if the roads aren't too bad. That's not too far."

"I'm sorry I delayed your trip. But I don't know what I would have done without you."

"I think that about you all the time," she said. "And my buddy Dylan. You're my family too. I'll be back January third, okay? I'll plan on getting right back into it." She leaned forward and we hugged. "Merry Christmas, Elle. Nineteen seventy-six will be a better year. I promise. You know I'm right about these things. It's the psychic in me."

"I'm going to hold you to that," I said, forcing a smile for her. "Merry Christmas."

"I love you," she said.

"And I love you."

She walked back to her car. I shut the door behind her. I walked over to the tree. Dylan was sitting next to it. "How was your visit with Fran?" I asked.

"I can't wait to see what she got me. Is Mr. William coming for Christmas?"

"No. Mr. William had to go away."

"For . . . ever?"

"Yes."

Dylan looked sad. "But I like him."

A tear fell down my cheek. I made no attempt to hide it. "Me too, buddy. Me too."

An hour later there was a knock at my door. I had already sent Dylan to bed, and I guessed it might be Fran coming back. Maybe she had decided to wait to leave until tomorrow after all. I opened the door, ready to give her a big hug.

My father stood in the doorway.

CHAPTER

thirty-one

One cannot understand the power of grace until one has needed it. Or given it.

—Elle Sheen's Diary

I didn't recognize him at first. He was older, of course, but he looked older than I would have thought after six years. He was completely gray, the hair at the top of his head thinning. Maybe it was because I no longer feared him, but he seemed smaller and softer somehow, even though he still held himself like a military man.

"Hi, Miche," he said. He pronounced it "Meesh." Michelle was my real name, but everyone except my father called me by the abbreviated *Elle*.

For a long time I was speechless. Finally I asked, "How did you find me?"

"A mutual friend."

"We don't have mutual friends."

He cleared his throat. "Seeing me is probably a pretty big shock."

"That's an understatement," I said.

Just then Dylan walked up behind me. "Mama." I didn't want him to see my father, but it was too late. He stood behind me staring. Then he said, "I'm Dylan. Who are you?"

"Don't tell him," I said.

My father glanced at me, then back at Dylan. "You can call me Larry."

"Hi, Mr. Larry," Dylan said.

"Dylan, I need you to go back to your room."

Dylan frowned, then stomped back to his room.

"I'm sorry it's so late," my father said. "I tried to catch you earlier, but you weren't at the diner."

"How do you know where I work?"

"Same friend," he said. "May I please come in? I promise I won't stay long."

I didn't move. I think I felt that letting him in was, in some way, symbolic of letting him back into my life, something that wasn't going to happen.

"Just five minutes and I'll be gone," he said.

I thought over his request. "All right. But just five minutes."

"Five minutes," he echoed. "Thank you."

I stepped back from the door and let him in. I walked to my kitchen and brought out an egg timer. I set it for five minutes, then put it on the table. My father watched my demonstration but said nothing about it.

"You have a nice place. May I sit down?"

I nodded. I noticed he was holding a brown manila envelope under his arm. For a moment we just looked at each other without speaking.

"You don't have much time."

"I know . . . It's just been so long." He glanced at the

egg timer, breathed in deeply, then sighed. "I came to tell you that I'm sorry. What I did to you, especially at such a difficult time, was unconscionable. I am ashamed of what I did. I don't expect you to forgive me, but I wanted you to know that I'm sorry. I was wrong."

It was the first time I had heard those words come out of his mouth. It should have felt good, but it didn't. I read somewhere that we always react angrily at people for finally doing what they should have done before. I wanted to punish him.

"Wrong about what?" I said.

"Pretty much everything," he said. He looked down.

"What were you hoping would come from this?" I said. "That after all this time I was just going to let you back into our lives? Is that what you expected?"

He continued looking down, the balding crown of his head showing. "Expected? No." He slowly looked up. "But I was hoping."

I didn't respond.

"I believe that when you repent, you need to make restitution, when possible. I wanted to see if you'd let me make up for what I should have done a long time ago."

"Is that what this is? Repentance?"

"In part."

I suddenly understood. "You paid my rent."

He nodded. The bell rang on the egg timer. I glanced down at it and then back at him. "What made you think I wanted your help?"

"I didn't think you wanted my help. I just thought you probably needed it."

I wasn't sure how to respond to that. He glanced down at his watch. "Well, I've taken my five minutes. Thank you for hearing me out. I'm sorry to bother you. I just wanted to tell you in person how sorry I am." He slowly stood, his gaze catching mine. "And how much I've missed my girl." His eyes were moist. "I've made some big mistakes in my life, Miche, but none bigger than my mistake with you. Turning away my only daughter is unforgivable. I hope you can forgive me someday. Not for my sake—I don't deserve it—but yours. For your own peace."

William's words about forgiving my father echoed back to me.

My father turned toward the door and began walking toward it. "What I want doesn't matter, anyway. At least not for much longer."

"What do you mean by that?" I said.

He didn't answer, but continued toward the door.

"What did you mean by 'much longer'?"

He turned back and looked at me as if he were trying to decide whether or not to answer. "I have cancer, Miche. The doctors say I won't be around much longer."

The words affected me more than I wanted them to. "That's why you came back now? Guilt? Dying regrets?"

He looked at me sadly. "No, the guilt and regret were there long before the cancer. Up until now I didn't know where you were." He gazed into my eyes. "I've looked for you for years. I even hired a private eye, but he failed. I had no idea where you went. I didn't even know what your new last name was. For all I knew you had left the country." He sighed. "I'd given up hope of ever seeing you again until your friend showed up."

"Who is this friend?" I asked.

"Second Lieutenant Smith."

It took me a moment to understand. "You saw . . . William?"

He nodded.

The revelation angered me. My life was none of William's business. "What did he tell you?"

"Much," he said softly. He breathed out. "He told me about Isaac—the kind of man he was, the kind of soldier he was. He told me how he was killed in action." My father's voice choked. "I'm so sorry you had to go through that alone. I'm sorry I wasn't there for you."

I could see the pain in his eyes.

"He told me he was ashamed of me."

"What did you say to that?"

"He didn't tell me anything I didn't already believe. I told him that I was ashamed of myself.

"Then he told me about you and Dylan. I asked him whether he thought you'd talk to me if I went to see you. He said he didn't know, but if I had any courage left in me, I should try." He cleared his throat, blinking away the forming tears. "I can't change what I've done, Miche. I can only try to change the future. I came to do the right thing if that's possible." He looked into my eyes. "If you'll let me. I know I'm asking a lot, but it would be a true mercy."

As I looked into his vulnerable, pleading eyes, the man standing before me somehow changed to me. I no longer saw the rigid military man who had rejected my baby and me that painful night. I saw someone different. I saw a humble, broken man mourning the mistakes of his past. I saw a grieving, aging man trying to make something right, not just for him, but for the sake of right itself. I saw through the veil of mistake and circumstance a man I'd once known, a man who had provided and cared for me. A man who had held my hand and carried me on his shoulders when I was tired. A man who, in his own, sometimes flawed ways, always did his best to protect me. In short, I saw my father again.

I couldn't speak for a long time. Then I nodded. "All right."

Those two simple words had a profound impact on him—more, perhaps, than I could understand. He wiped his eyes with his forearm, then took the brown envelope from under his arm and handed it to me. "This is mostly just a lot of legal mumbo jumbo. I set up a college fund for Dylan. There's enough there for his education at a good school, also books and housing. He has several years before then, so the fund should grow a bit. It might even help him get into a house someday."

"You paid for Dylan's college?"

"There's something else. I set up another fund. It's in that same envelope. It's called the Isaac Sheen Scholarship Fund. It's for one Negro student each year at Arizona State."

"Thank you."

"It's long past due," he said.

As I looked into his eyes, I suddenly started crying. He

just stood there, almost at attention, his face full of emotion. "We once had a wonderful relationship, Miche. You were my life. My light. We had such fun." He grinned. "Well, maybe I was never much fun, but I tried."

I laughed through my tears. "You were fun. Sometimes."

He laughed as well. Then his gaze grew more serious. "My sins have brought their own punishment, Miche."

Hearing this made my heart hurt, not just for my loss but my father's as well. I thought of my love for Dylan and understood that my father loved me the same. For the first time I realized just how much he had suffered too.

I wondered if he'd gone through this alone or if my mother had changed as well. "Where's Mom?" I asked.

My father looked down. "She's gone. She tried, but . . ." He cleared his throat. "Two years ago her liver failed. We tried for a transplant, but it was too late."

I suddenly felt my own pain of loss. "I'm sorry I wasn't there for you."

"It was my own fault." His eyes welled up. "I can't tell you how many times I've looked through our photographs of us. The Christmases we spent. I've missed my daughter."

"I've missed you, Dad."

He swallowed. "May I hug you?"

"I would like that." I fell into him and we embraced. It felt so good to be held by him again.

"Thank you, Miche."

"Thank you, Daddy."

After we parted, his eyes were red. "Do you think I

could see Dylan? I won't tell him who I am. I just want to see my grandson."

"Yes." I walked to Dylan's room and opened the door. As I expected, he wasn't asleep. He was always curious when someone new was in the house.

"Dylan. I want you to meet someone."

"Is it Mr. Larry?"

"Yes."

Dylan hopped out of bed. He walked directly up to my father. "Mr. Larry, why are you at my house?"

My father crouched down on his haunches. "I came to see how you and your mother were doing. You are a handsome young man."

"I know," Dylan said. "Who are you again?"

My father just looked at him and then wiped his eyes.

"Why are you crying?" Dylan asked.

"Because I'm sorry you had to ask that."

I stepped forward. "Dylan, this is your grandpa. My father."

Dylan looked puzzled. "You said you didn't have a father."

"I was wrong," I said.

"I have a grandpa?"

"You do," my father said. "I'm right here."

Dylan still looked confused. Then he asked, "Where have you been?"

"I've been lost," he said. "Very, very lost."

"And someone found you?"

He smiled. "Yes. Someone found me. A soldier." He glanced at me, then back to Dylan. "If it's okay with you and your mother, I'd like to invite you to our house for Christmas. I'll even take you on a sleigh ride through the mountain with real horses."

"You have real horses?"

"Yes. And real cows, goats, and chickens."

"Are you a farmer?"

"Yes, I am. And I have a big farmhouse, but no one to spend Christmas with."

Dylan looked at me. "Can we go to his big farmhouse for Christmas, Mama?"

I nodded. "Yes."

I looked over at my father. He didn't even try to stop his tears.

CHAPTER

thirty-two

*Throughout history, the homecoming has been celebrated
in story and in song. I have never understood why as
well as I do today as I celebrate it in my heart.*
                              —Elle Sheen's Diary

Two days later, Dylan and I made the three-hundred-
mile drive south to Cedar City. I hadn't been there
since I'd left six years earlier. It took us five hours. It's
hard to believe that just five hours had separated so much.

I was wearing Isaac's ring on a gold chain around my
neck. It was the gold chain my father had given me at
my high school graduation. I hadn't worn it since I left,
but even in the hard times I hadn't been able to pawn
it either. Maybe, like William, I was still holding on to
something I couldn't bring myself to admit I wanted. Or
needed.

"The old Fairlane," he said, walking out to greet us. "I'm
a little surprised it's still running."

"Barely," I said. "I just replaced the alternator, clutch,
and timing belt."

His brow furrowed. "What did that set you back?"

"Not as much as it should have," I said. "William fixed

it for free. But it hasn't stopped the rest of it from falling apart." I grinned. "I think it has leprosy."

My father chuckled. "Old cars don't get new."

I smiled. "I've heard that."

Christmas Eve was a giant party. My father had cut his own tree from the forest behind his property. Unlike the small tree at home, his was massive and rose nearly fourteen feet high in his spacious living room, filling the entire room with its beautiful fragrance. It was elaborately decorated with beautiful lights, ribbons, and ornaments.

"Who decorated your tree?" I asked.

He looked at me with surprise. "I did, of course. You know I'm a Christmasphile."

I smiled with remembrance. It was true. My father loved Christmas.

My father had a lot of friends whom he'd invited over to see his returned daughter and grandson. Probably close to a hundred people came by the house. I shouldn't have been surprised, but there were a lot of single, older ladies who spent a lot of time with us. Frankly, I didn't know there were that many single women in Cedar City, but I suppose, for my dad, they were probably coming from other cites as well. There were even a few handsome ranchers that my father, not so discreetly, informed I was single.

At the height of the party my father walked to the center of the room with a glass of wine. He clinked on the glass with a spoon until the room was quiet. "I'd like to make a toast," he said. He turned to me. "As most of you know, Christmas is a special time of year for me. At least it was. There hasn't been a tree in this house since my daughter left. I swore that there would be no tree until she came back. I had begun to lose hope that there would ever be a tree in this house again."

His eyes welled. "But Christmas is about hope. The Wise Men traveled far to find a mother with her child in a simple manger. The same is true for me. I may not be wise, but I was searching. And God, in His infinite good-ness, sent me a star to find her. So I raise a toast to that star, a soldier who set me on the right path, I raise a toast to the season itself and its promise of hope. Most of all, I raise a toast to that mother and her beautiful, beautiful child. May Christmas forever live in our hearts." He raised his glass. "To Christmas."

I raised mine and said softly, "And to the Father."

All in all, it was a glorious celebration with food and music, laughter and joy, and I think Dylan had more fun than the rest of us.

After everyone had left, including a few of the women I practically had to shoo away, my father and I stayed up late and told stories of the old days, some true, some not so much. Mostly my father just wanted to know all about my life since I'd left.

In the end he asked about William and what had hap-pened between us. I was surprised at how much I was willing to share. Even though he'd broken my heart, he'd given me a precious gift. He'd given me my father back. And he'd given Dylan a grandfather. Most of all, he'd given my heart something I didn't want to believe was lacking—forgiveness.

"He loves you," he said.

I nodded. "I know. But maybe not enough."

My father nodded, then said, "Don't underestimate the power of love over fear."

My father had prepared my old room upstairs for my return and one across the hall for Dylan. Being in a strange house, I asked Dylan if he wanted to sleep with me—something he often asked to do even in our house—but, for the first time ever, he turned me down. He was pretty excited to have his own room in the farmhouse.

The next morning Dylan and I woke to the smell of coffee and Burl Ives's Christmas music playing from my father's television stereo. It was a powerful flashback for me, reminding me of many happy Christmases we had shared together.

Dylan and I walked downstairs to find the tree literally buried in a mountain of presents. There were more than twenty gifts for each of us. I don't know how my father knew what we wanted, but he did pretty well, though he later confessed that several lady friends had lent a hand in the purchasing and wrapping department.

Throughout the morning's unveilings, my father just sat in his old La-Z-Boy chair, the same one I remembered from my childhood, and watched the proceedings with a joyful smile that practically split his face from one side to the other.

The gifts he gave us were more than extravagant, and Dylan looked like he was living a dream he was afraid to wake up from. He got a cassette tape recorder, a phonograph player system with a built-in 8-track player, Jackson 5 and 5th Dimension albums, a pet rock, and a plethora of other amusements. There was even a new Atari Pong game, the expensive one Dylan sometimes talked about but knew I would never be able to afford. One of his favorite gifts was his own pair of leather cowboy boots.

"Look, Mama, boots!" he said, holding them up. "I'm a cowboy."

"Put them on," I said.

"Can I?" he asked.

"Of course. That's what they're for."

Dylan pulled the boots on over his bare feet.

"Now you look like a real cowboy," I said.

"Except for a hat," my dad said. "Every cowboy needs a hat. Wait a second, I think I got one of those too." From behind the chair he brought out a small felt cowboy hat. He threw the hat to Dylan like it was a Frisbee.

"Wow!" Dylan said. He put it on. Backward.

"Other way, partner," my father said.

Dylan turned it around.

"It's a Stetson. That's the real McCoy."

"That's really too much, Dad."

"No," he said, winking at me. "It's not."

After we'd opened the last present, my father said, "I got one more thing for you, Miche."

"You got me enough already," I replied.

"Now don't be difficult," he said, standing. "It's just one more thing. But try as I might, I couldn't get it through the door, so I left it outside. Come on, Dylan. I have something outside for you too."

"Is mine too big to come in the house too?"

"Well, yours can't come inside for other reasons," he said.

We followed my father out the side door. Sitting beneath the covered driveway was a brand-new cherry-red Valiant.

"It's the Valiant Regal sedan, six-cylinder, four-speed," he said, sounding almost like a TV commercial. "American made, of course. One of Chrysler's best new cars of the year."

"It's beautiful." I hugged my father. "Thank you so much, Dad . . ."

"Is that our new car?" Dylan asked.

"It sure is," I said.

"Can I tell Albert?"

"You can tell anyone you want," I said.

"Open the door, girl," my father said. "Nothing like the smell of a new car."

I opened the door and looked inside. It was gorgeous.

"Can I get in?" Dylan asked.

"Of course."

He jumped inside the front seat, falling back in the bucket seat. He turned to me. "It kind of stinks."

I smiled. "It's the new car smell. You'll learn to like it."

"Have you ever seen a Valiant?" my father asked.

"Funny you should ask. I drove an older model a few weeks ago. While they were fixing the Fairlane." I smiled. "Everyone kept telling me it was sexy."

"Well, I don't know about that, but it's a solid car and brand-spanking new, right off the dealership floor."

"You bought it off the dealership floor? Whatever happened to don't buy retail?"

"You remembered," he said, smiling. "Well, I still hold to the maxim. I didn't buy it at retail. I bought it from my own dealership."

"You own a car dealership?"

"Two of them: one in Cedar, the other in St. George. Both Plymouth-Chryslers. They're doing well, too. Some of those Japanese cars coming into the market have pilfered a few sales, but I don't think they'll last. They don't make them like we do here in America."

"Now what do I do with the Fairlane?"

"I'll take it off your hands. Maybe we'll keep it in the barn. Who knows, might be a collector's piece someday." He turned to Dylan. "Speaking of the barn, I got one more present to give."

The three of us walked out to the stable. My father walked up to one of the stalls. A quarter horse mare put her head over the gate and nuzzled him.

"Oh, I love you too, Summer," he said, kissing her on the head and rubbing her neck. He turned around. "Dylan, come here for a second."

Dylan walked up behind my father. He'd never been near a real horse and was a little scared.

"No need to worry," my father said to Dylan. "This here is Summer. She's a mama horse, and just six months ago she gave birth to a baby colt. Can you see him back there?"

There was a beautiful bay roan colt with a black mane and a star on its nose. "What do you think of him?"

"He's cool," Dylan said.

"Well, I'm glad you think that, because he's yours."

"That's my horse?"

"He sure is."

Dylan turned to me. "Can I have him?"

"That's between you and Grandpa," I said. "He gave him to you."

"Yes!" Dylan said. He turned back to my father. "What's his name?"

"Well. He doesn't have one. He was waiting for you to name him."

"Can I call him Mr. William?" Dylan asked.

I swallowed. "You can call him anything you like."

My father winked at me. "You might want to think about it for a while," he said to Dylan. "A name is something you want to give a lot of thought to. Let's just call him 'Horse' for now."

"Okay," Dylan said.

Thank you, I mouthed to my father.

"Well, let's get back inside before someone catches pneumonia. I've got breakfast to make." He said to Dylan, "Would you mind going with your mom to the hen house and grabbing us a few eggs? A half dozen ought to do. There's a basket for the eggs right next to the door you walk in."

Dylan nodded. "Will you help me, Mama?"

"Of course."

It was my father's Christmas Day tradition to make us whatever we wanted for breakfast. He looked like he had bought out the local grocery store just to make sure he had everything we might ask for. He made waffles for Dylan, of course, with strawberries and whipped cream, two kinds of sausages, bacon, biscuits, ham-and-pepper omelets, and gravy. It was kind of obscene how much food he made. It was obscene how much I ate.

After breakfast my father started doing the dishes.

I walked up to his side. "I can do that, Dad. You've worked all morning."

"No. You play with your son."

"Trust me, he's played enough with me. I think he needs some Grandpa time."

As I was doing the dishes the doorbell rang. "Miche, would you mind getting that?" my father shouted from the living room. "Dylan has me all tied up here. Literally."

"Sure, Dad," I said, wiping my hands with a dishcloth. "I can't believe how many friends you have."

"You know how it is. They're like crows. I try to scare them away, but they keep coming back."

"It's probably another one of your lady friends."

I walked to the front door and opened it.

William stood in the doorway. I looked at him for a moment, then said, "What took you so long?"

CHAPTER

thirty-three

Fate's pen has rewritten more than one ending.
—Elle Sheen's Diary

After kissing me soundly, William stood back and laughed.

"You were really expecting me to come back?"

"No, I didn't expect," I said, borrowing my father's words. "I hoped."

He looked in my eyes. "What gave you hope?"

"Two reasons. First, you talked with my father. My father's a smart man. He would have figured out pretty quickly that there was something between us." I smiled. "And if there's one thing about my father, the man's a fixer. He can fix anything. Tractors, dishwashers, windmills. Even relationships."

"I'll give him that," he said. "What's the second?"

"You love me."

New Year's Eve was the sixth anniversary of Isaac's death. The day was even more powerful to William. It was the day he had watched his friend die. It was the same day he'd been taken captive. Today it represented the opposite. It represented a new life and freedom.

It was shortly after midnight. My father had put Dylan to bed and then said good night and went to bed himself, leaving William and me alone on the couch. The room was lit by a single light in the kitchen.

I snuggled into his arms. "Do you believe in the spiritual law of restitution?" I asked.

He kissed me on the temple, then asked, "What's that?"

"It's the belief that everything we lose in this life will be returned to us in the next."

He pondered my question and then said, "I don't know." He pulled me in tighter. "But I know one thing about loss."

"What's that?"

"Whether we lose something or not, it's better to have had it."

EPILOGUE

Some own up to their past. Some are owned by their past.
The wise take what they can from the past and then leave
it behind.

On William's and my first date I told him that I'd like to write a book someday. Here it is. At least here's part one. My life isn't over.

In spite of my rent being paid for the year, less than a month later Dylan and I moved back home to Cedar City. Saying goodbye to Loretta, Fran, Jamie, and the rest of the regulars at the diner was excruciating, with an ocean of tears, even though I reminded them that I was just moving down the road. It was a long road, but the same one passed through both towns.

Loretta shut down the diner and threw a big going-away shindig for us. My dad and William were there. Against William's advice, I tried to hook Loretta up with my father. I figured it would be like having two people I love in the same house. It didn't take. William was right. She would have driven my father crazy. And vice versa.

William and I were married in April, the same month

Isaac and I had been. He took a job in the service department of my father's Cedar City car dealership. In less than a year he was managing the place. I believe that was my father's plan all along. I asked him if it was what he was expecting. He smiled and said, "Expecting, no. I just hoped."

As my father's health deteriorated, he turned more of the responsibility of running the dealerships over to William and me, opting to spend as much time with his grandson as he could.

My father taught Dylan to ride horses and motorcycles and tractors and pretty much anything else on his farm that moved. They went on many long rides on their horses, sometimes even overnighters with tents and packs. My father became as good a grandfather as a boy could hope for. Many times, at least when he was feeling sentimental, he told me how he regretted the years that he'd missed in our lives. But if you ask me, he made up for it and then some.

My father bravely fought his cancer like the soldier he was. The six months the doctors gave him ended up being almost six years. The doctors called it miraculous. I just think he finally had something to live for. That's something we can all understand.

My father passed away five years and thirty-five days after he found us that winter in Mistletoe. His death was Dylan's first real lesson in grief and it was painful to watch. I suffered with him. But I was grateful for every one of those days I got with my father. Like I once told William, "The cost of love is the risk of losing it." But it's always worth it. After all, in the end, what else is there?

My father willed everything to William and me. William was shrewd in business and today we own six car dealerships; three in Utah, two in Nevada, and one in Colorado. It's hard to believe I was once so poor. Now we have the chance to help and bless others. It's nice being on that side of the menu too.

Dylan graduated from Arizona State, where he met a lovely woman and was married shortly after graduating with an MBA. Today he owns a BMW and a Porsche dealership in Phoenix. He even likes the smell of new cars.

William and I have since retired. We have been traveling a lot. A year ago we took a vacation to Vietnam. It was a powerful experience for both of us. The "Hanoi Hilton," where William was held, was mostly demolished twenty years after the war, but not all of it. Today, the existing structure operates as a museum and memorial. Propaganda inside the museum shows pictures of happy inmates shooting pool and playing cards, and claims that the term *Hanoi Hilton* was coined by happy, well-cared-for inmates. William said little as we walked through the site.

Two days later, William took me to where Isaac fell, next to the waterfall. I was surprised that, after all these years, he could still find it, but I shouldn't have been. War is about logistics and how do you forget what is unforgettable? I was wearing Isaac's ring as I knelt on the ground and wept for my love and thanked him for my new love. How different it must have seemed to me than to William. To an outsider, the land was beautiful and lush and full of life. I suppose time has changed and healed the country, just as it has us.

William and I now spend our winters in Arizona, blessed with our three beautiful grandchildren. William is restoring my grandpa's old Fairlane with Seth, our oldest grandson. Life is good. God is good.

As I look back over that year it's amazing to me to see how so unexpectedly life can switch tracks to a new destination. But the complexity of those junctions are far too great to assign to the cogs and machinations of mere chance and circumstance.

Maybe that's why I've always thought of God less as an engineer than as an artist—one who uses our hopes, fears, dreams, and especially our tears, to paint on the canvas of our souls, rendering something beautiful. The hardest part, I suppose, is waiting to see what He's up to.

ACKNOWLEDGMENTS

I wish to thank my new editor, Lauren McKenna, for her clever insight, charming personality, and commitment to this book. *Noel Street* is better because of you. Also, a sincere thank-you to her amazing sidekick, Maggie Loughran, who always makes Lauren look good. Thank you to Jen Bergstrom and the whole Gallery team. I'm excited to be working with you.

As always, I'm grateful to my adorable and patient wife, Keri. Also to my agent, Laurie Liss; my assistant, Heather McVey, for her years of service; and Diane Glad, who retyped every correction I made.

ABOUT THE AUTHOR

Richard Paul Evans is the #1 bestselling author of *The Christmas Box*. Each of his more than thirty-five novels has been a *New York Times* bestseller. There are more than thirty-five million copies of his books in print worldwide, translated into more than twenty-four languages. He is the recipient of numerous awards, including the American Mothers Book Award, the Romantic Times Best Women's Novel of the Year Award, the German Audience Gold Award for Romance, five Religion Communicators Council Wilbur Awards, the Washington Times Humanitarian of the Century Award, and the Volunteers of America National Empathy Award. He lives in Salt Lake City, Utah, with his wife, Keri, not far from their five children and two grandchildren. You can learn more about Richard on Facebook at Facebook.com/RPEFans or visit his website at RichardPaulEvans.com.

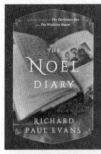
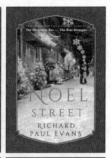
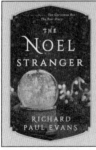
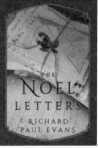

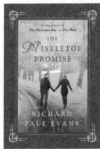

DON'T MISS A STEP IN THE UNFORGETTABLE JOURNEY...

The Broken Road

series

The Noel Stranger

Grace
The Gift
Finding Noel
The Sunflower
A Perfect Day
The Last Promise
The Christmas Box Miracle
The Carousel
The Looking Glass
The Locket
The Letter
Timepiece
The Christmas Box

For Children and Young Adults

The Dance
The Christmas Candle
The Spyglass
The Tower
The Light of Christmas
Michael Vey: The Prisoner of Cell 25
Michael Vey 2: Rise of the Elgen
Michael Vey 3: Battle of the Ampere
Michael Vey 4: Hunt for Jade Dragon
Michael Vey 5: Storm of Lightning
Michael Vey 6: Fall of Hades
Michael Vey 7: The Final Spark

✦ RICHARD PAUL EVANS ✦

The Noel Stranger

FROM THE NOEL COLLECTION

GALLERY BOOKS

NEW YORK   LONDON   TORONTO   SYDNEY   NEW DELHI

G

Gallery Books
An Imprint of Simon & Schuster, Inc.
1230 Avenue of the Americas
New York, NY 10020

This Gallery Books hardcover edition October 2020

GALLERY BOOKS and colophon are registered trademarks of Simon & Schuster, Inc.

For information about special discounts for bulk purchases, please contact Simon & Schuster Special Sales at 1-866-506-1949 or business@simonandschuster.com.

The Simon & Schuster Speakers Bureau can bring authors to your live event. For more information or to book an event, contact the Simon & Schuster Speakers Bureau at 1-866-248-3049 or visit our website at www.simonspeakers.com.

Manufactured in the United States of America

3   5   7   9   10   8   6   4   2

Library of Congress Cataloging-in-Publication Data has been applied for.

ISBN 978-1-5011-7205-2
ISBN 978-1-5011-7206-9 (ebook)

✦ To Keri 2.0 ✦

The Noel Stranger

CHAPTER

One

You might be wondering why I would let you, a complete stranger, read parts of my diary. Maybe it's the "bus-rider syndrome," in which people, for unknown reasons, share with total strangers the most intimate details of their lives. Maybe, but I think it's simpler than that. I think our desire to be understood is stronger than our fear of exposure.

—Maggie Walther's Diary

How did I get here?

I once heard someone describe her life as a car with four flat tires. I would be happy with that. If my life were a metaphorical car, it would be in much worse shape—wheels stolen, windshield smashed, and dirt poured into its gas tank. I'd say that the demolition of my life happened in a matter of months, but that's not really true. It had been happening for the last three years of my marriage. I was just oblivious.

You probably read about the horror of my life in the newspaper or somewhere online. It's one of those tragic stories that people love to wring their hands over and feign sympathy about as they lustfully share the sordid details—like describing a car accident they witnessed.

Before the truth popped out like a festering pustule (excuse the gross simile, it just seems fitting), my life seemed idyllic on the surface. I own a thriving—and exhausting—catering company called Just Desserts. (We do more than desserts. The woman I inherited the business from started by baking birthday and wedding cakes, and the name stuck.)

My husband of nine years, Clive, whom, by the way, I was madly in love with, was a partner in a prominent Salt Lake City law firm and a city councilman going on almost four years. I went through the whole campaign thing with him twice, speaking to women's groups, holding babies, the whole shebang. It wasn't really my thing, I've always been more of an introvert, but it was his and I loved him and believed in supporting my husband. Unlike me, Clive was a natural at public life. Everyone loved him. He had a way of making you feel like you were the most important person in the room. I think that's what initially drew my heart to him—the way he made me feel seen.

Less than a year ago, Clive's name had been placed on the short list of potential Salt Lake City mayoral candidates for next year's election. One newspaper poll even showed him leading, and lobbyists and politicos began circling him like bees at a picnic. At least they were. No one's calling now. That ship didn't sail, it sunk. Just like our marriage.

I've learned that the things that derail our lives are

usually the things that blindside us when we're worrying about something else—like stressing over being late to a hair appointment and then, on the way there, getting T-boned by a garbage truck running a red light.

My garbage truck came via a phone call at nine o'clock on a Tuesday morning. Clive was out of town. I had just gotten home from a Pilates class and was getting ready for work when the phone rang. The caller ID said *Deseret News*, the local newspaper. I assumed the call had something to do with our subscription or my catering business, as the paper would call every now and then for a food article. Last Halloween they had me do a bit on "Cooking for Ghouls," sharing my favorite chili and breadstick recipe.

I picked up the phone. "Hello?"

"Mrs. Walther?"

"Yes."

"I'm Karl Fahver, the political editor for the *Deseret News*. I'm calling to see if you'd like to comment on your husband's arrest this morning."

My heart stopped. "What are you talking about?"

"You didn't know that your husband was arrested this morning?"

"My husband's away on a business trip. I have no idea what you're talking about."

"I'm sorry, I assumed you knew. Your husband was arrested for bigamy."

"Bigamy? As in, more than one wife?"

"Yes, ma'am."

My mind spun like that beach-ball-looking thing on your computer when you're waiting for something to happen. Or maybe I was just in shock. "That's ridiculous. I'm his only wife. Are you sure you have the right person?"

The reporter hesitated. When he spoke again, there was a hint of sympathy in his voice. "According to the police report, your husband has a second family in Colorado."

Just then my call waiting beeped. It was Clive. "My husband's on the other line. I need to get this . . ."

"Mrs. Walther—"

I hung up, bringing up Clive's call. "Is it true?" I asked.

Clive didn't answer.

"Clive . . ."

"I'm sorry, Maggie. I wanted you to hear it from me."

"You wanted me to hear from you that you have another wife?" I started crying. "How could you do this?!"

Nothing.

"Answer me!"

"What do you want me to say, Maggie?"

"Say it's not true! Say, 'I'd never do this to the woman who supported me through everything.' How about, 'I'd never do this to you because I love you'?" There was another long pause. I couldn't stop crying. Finally, I said, "Say something, please."

"I'm sorry," he said. "I've got to go." He hung up.

I collapsed on the floor and sobbed.

According to the article in the afternoon's paper, my husband had another wife and two children in Thornton, Colorado. I saw a picture of the other woman. She was short, with a round face, a tattoo of a rose on her shoulder, and badly dyed blond hair.

After the story went viral, a malicious site popped up showing a picture of me next to the "other wife" and asking people to vote which one was hotter. There were more than twelve thousand votes. I won, 87 percent to 13 percent. I'm sorry I know that. It should have at least preserved my ego a little, but it only made me angrier. Clive could at least have had the decency to cheat on me with a swimsuit model—someone no one would really expect a normal woman to compete with. One that would have people saying, "I can see him doing that," instead of "His wife must have been awful to live with."

At the moment, Clive's out on bail, living with his parents in Heber, Utah. I doubt with his connections that he'll ever see the inside of a cell—unless he ends up with a judge he's crossed somewhere back—but either way, I'm feeling like I'm under house arrest, afraid to go out in public, even to shop for groceries. I'm afraid to see strangers gape at me.

The other day I went to the nearby food mart to pick up something to eat when I noticed a woman following me. At first I told myself that I was imagining things, until she followed me across seven rows at the supermarket, videoing me with her phone.

This too will pass, right? I know that pretty much all news is temporary. Scandals are like waves that crash on the beach, then quietly retreat in foam, but when it's about you, it seems like there is no other news. It feels like every spotlight is on you as the public watches from the gallery like voyeurs, their faces darkened and entertained by the drama of your life.

Obviously, I've thought this over too much. The thing is, I couldn't stop thinking about it. I'm just compulsive enough that I suppose I would have continued down my crazy spiral until I self-destructed or until something else unexpected turned up. Fortunately, it did. Actually, someone. A stranger. And he came at Christmas.

CHAPTER

Was I a fool to trust him? I suppose the last people to think themselves fools are fools.
                                        —*Maggie Walther's Diary*

WEDNESDAY, NOVEMBER 9

The story of my stranger began on a subfreezing November morning, the aftermath of a series of local blizzards. I was sitting alone near the window of the Grounds for Coffee. Not surprisingly, the coffee shop wasn't as busy as usual. The latest blizzard had dropped a blanket over the city, and the usual traffic warning went out: Don't leave the house unless necessary. I had no idea why Carina, my business assistant and best friend—my only friend—had been so insistent at meeting at the coffee shop this morning. She wouldn't take no for an answer, even though I'd said it at least four times. I hadn't left my house for nearly a week. I looked like it. No makeup. My unwashed, unbrushed hair was mostly concealed beneath a baseball cap.

The shop had its usual blend of clientele—as eclectic and caffeinated as their concoctions. I was the only one sitting alone, so I leafed through the newspaper to hide my awkwardness. I turned to the local section of the paper only to see a haggard-looking mug shot of Clive. It seemed that every time there was a discussion about the mayoral race or a vote of the city council, Clive's picture would be dragged up. The article du jour was about the woman the mayor had nominated to fill my husband's position.

Honestly, I couldn't tell you what's worse—the betrayal, the public humiliation, or the question that was on everyone's mind: *"How did you not know that your husband had another family?"*

They just didn't understand. Some people have husbands who come home from work, grab a beer, and watch TV all night. These people are not married to a politician or anyone in the public spotlight. Every night there's an event, an Elks club gathering or a women's political caucus. If I hadn't put my foot down, he'd have been gone every night and weekend.

Or maybe I really was just as dumb as everyone thought.

I knew he was cheating on me; I just thought it was with his career. Politics had always been his second wife. I mean, he didn't even have time for me. How could he possibly have time for another wife and family?

Looking back, I realized there were clues. My last birthday he gave me a leather miniskirt. When I looked surprised, he said, "But that's what you asked for." It wasn't something I had or ever would have asked for.

Another time, before going to bed, he called me Jen,

which, incidentally, is half the name of the other woman. Jennifer. It is also the name of one of the other council members, so it was easy for him to explain it away, and for me to brush it off. I just chalked it all up to his overtaxed brain and schedule. I wish I had been more suspicious. But then, there's a lot of things I wish I had done differently.

CHAPTER

Three

Carina thinks I need to change my environment to something more cheerful, like switching the song on the radio. To me it feels more like putting an ice cube in the microwave.

—*Maggie Walther's Diary*

Carina walked into the coffee shop about fifteen minutes late, escorted by a flurry of snow. She wore red leather gloves, a thick parka, and a red wool scarf with a matching beret strategically placed over her perfectly trimmed blond hair. She always dressed as if everyone was looking at her, and I suppose they were, probably *because* she dressed like everyone was looking at her. And she was pretty. Although she was seven years younger than me, people often said we looked alike, or asked if we were sisters. I doubt anyone would now. The contrast between our grooming made me feel self-conscious.

She looked around the room until she found me, then walked over, unpeeling her scarf as she walked. "Hi, love. Sorry I'm late. The roads were horrific." She leaned over and kissed me on the cheek. "I passed three accidents and at least a dozen cars off the road."

"I was almost one of them," I said.

"That's because my washing machine's bigger than your Fiat."

"No, that's *because* we should have stayed home."

"No," she said, unzipping her coat. "More time at home is the last thing you need right now." She sat down. "That's why I wanted to meet here. To get you out of your black hole of misery."

"Into the blinding bright world of misery?" I lifted the newspaper to show her Clive's picture.

"He looks wretched," she said. She looked me over. "Speaking of which, how much weight have you lost?"

"Nice segue."

"You look like a waif. You need to eat more. And you need to get out."

I collapsed back into my chair. "I'm too tired to get out."

"That's depression, honey. And you'll stay that way until you get out."

"I don't want to get out. I'm a pariah."

Carina touched her coffee cup. "I don't even know what that means."

"It means I'm an untouchable. A social leper."

Carina shook her head. "No, you're not."

"No one wants to be seen with me."

"I do."

"Besides you," I said. "And you're a poor judge of character."

"I am not."

I cocked my head to one side.

"Maybe in dating," she relented. "And marriage." Carina had been married twice, once to a man who had been married seven times before, the other to a guy who just left one day and never came back. She found out later that he was wanted for check fraud in eleven states. "You know what you need?"

"Cyanide pills?"

Carina frowned. "You need to get involved with something outside yourself. Like come back to work."

"I'm sorry," I said. "I'm not ready for that yet."

"Then at least change your environment. I drove by your house the other night and all the lights were out. It was only eight."

"You should have just rung the doorbell."

"I did." She raised three fingers. "Three times."

"I was sleeping. I've been sleeping weird hours lately. It's like my body doesn't know the difference between day and night. Did you know that during the winter months, beavers stay inside their lodges almost all the time? And since there are no light cues—like day or night—they develop their own circadian rhythm of twenty-nine-hour days."

Carina stared at me for a moment, then said, "I don't know if I'm more disturbed that you know this or that you're telling me this." Her eyes narrowed. "Why are you telling me this?"

"I saw it on a documentary . . ."

"While you were holed up in your lodge," she said.

"Yes, while I was holed up in my lodge. And I'm telling

you this because it resonated with me. My circadian rhythm is off. I get up in the middle of the night and can't sleep."

Her gaze intensified. "You're isolating. And identifying with beavers."

I frowned. "I know."

"Well, if you're not going to leave your home, at least bring some life into it."

"You want me to invite some other woodland creatures to join me?"

She grinned. "What I mean is that you need to shake things up. Right after my first divorce I read a book on breakups, and it suggested changing around your physical environment to help change your emotional environment. It was by Benjamin Hardy. It worked for me. Clean the house, buy new furniture, decorate. It's Christmas, put some lights up or something. Do you even have a Christmas tree?"

"Having a tree would mean the holidays are coming."

"The holidays *are* coming. Get a tree."

I took a sip of my coffee. "That's not going to happen."

"Why not?"

"To begin with, I don't feel *Christmasy*."

"Is that even a word?"

"It is now."

"Well, you don't feel *Christmasy* because you're not acting *Christmasy*. It's a verb, not a noun."

"Actually, it's an adjective."

"Don't get grammatical on me. Bottom line, you're alone. And loneliness is dangerous. Studies have shown it's more hazardous to your health than smoking or being over-weight. Especially during the holidays. There's a reason so many people commit suicide during the holidays."

"That's a myth," I said. "The suicide rate is highest in spring. It always has been."

She eyed me suspiciously. "How did you know that?"

"I'm not considering suicide, if that's what you're think-ing." She continued to look at me doubtfully and I threw one hand up. "You brought it up, not me."

Carina was quiet. After a moment she said, "Do you know the first thing you're supposed to do if you're lost in the woods?"

I looked at her blankly. "And you're mocking me about the beaver lodge?"

"There's a point to this."

"I'm dying to see where you're going with this."

"First thing you do, you build a fire. Do you know why?"

"To keep warm."

"No, to keep busy. To keep your mind from panicking. That's what you need."

"You think I should set fire to Clive's car?"

"That's what I'm talking about, Mag. No matter the con-versation, you bring it back to him like a magnet. You've got to get out of that. It's not about him, it's about you. You need to reclaim your life." Her voice softened. "Look, I understand why you want to isolate. I really do. But it's not the answer. You need to show Clive that he can't take away your life."

"He did take away my life."

"No, he took away your situation. You're still here. Life isn't through with you. You never know what's around the corner."

"That's what I'm afraid of."

She reached over and put her hand on mine. "This will pass, love. It's okay that you're lying low for now. No one can blame you for that. I just don't want to see this crush your spirit."

I looked down for a moment, then back up into Carina's sympathetic eyes. Tears suddenly filled my own, as the words I'd been thinking for weeks spilled out. "Why wasn't I enough for him?"

"No one could be enough for him," Carina said, sliding her chair closer. "Some people just have holes they can't fill. That's hard for you to understand because you're not that way. Clive was insatiable. He always wanted more. That's why he was always running for something bigger. He wanted more people to love him. He didn't understand that one person's love is better than a thousand people's approval."

I started crying more, and she put her arms around me. "Oh, honey. This will pass."

When I could speak I said, "Are you sure?"

"It will pass if you let it," she said. "Think about what I said about changing things up. I think it will help." She looked into my eyes. "Will you?"

I nodded.

She smiled. "Good girl. Now when are you coming back to work?"

CHAPTER

*Sometimes our past follows us like toilet paper
stuck to the heel of our shoe as we walk out of the
bathroom. And we're always the last one to see it.*
— *Maggie Walther's Diary*

I didn't have an answer for her question. I felt guilty leaving
Carina alone during the busiest time of the year. Ironically,
it's the exact same thing that had happened to me just before my company's previous owner passed the business on
to me.

But my absence from work was more than just isolation. It was confusion. The catering business, my broken
childhood, and Clive were all complexly tied together in
a knot. I felt like I was trying to find my way through a
confusing labyrinth that just kept taking me back to where
I had started.

Where I had started. I was born and raised in Ashland,
Oregon, just sixteen miles north of the California border.
It's a peculiar place. Today it's extremely liberal—so much
so that some of the neighboring communities refer to it
as "the People's Republic of Ashland." They'd probably
like to forget that their city fathers once held Klan pa-

rades downtown and advertised themselves as a haven for "American citizens—negroes and Japanese not welcome."

But times change and so do people and locales. The scenery is beautiful there, mostly woods and mountains. Sounds like an idyllic place for a little boy and girl to grow up. My childhood should have been idyllic, but it wasn't. My childhood was ugly.

If I had to sum up the reason for my pain in one word, I'd say, "My father." (Okay, two words.) My father never should have had children. Of course that means my brother and I wouldn't have been born, but sometimes I'm not sure that would have been such a bad thing.

My father never should have even gotten married. I don't know why he did. He was always cheating on my mother. I couldn't tell you how many times he cheated because I don't know if he ever wasn't. Sometimes there were fights; most of the time I just saw the pain and resignation on my mother's face. I could never understand why my mother didn't just leave. Eventually she did, just not the way I thought she would.

The end of their union came during my fourteenth year. My mother went in to one of those surgical centers for a routine colonoscopy. She developed complications and died. I still remember the look on the doctor's face when he told us. I didn't believe it until I saw her breathless body. I remember feeling angry at her for not taking me with her.

I've learned that everyone handles grief differently. My brother, Eric, just disappeared, first within himself, then, years later, physically. I don't know how my father handled the loss of his wife; the only emotion he ever shared was anger. I suspect that, among other things, he felt guilt. Maybe I just hope that he did, like a real human would. But I think he also recognized the opportunity—not that my mother kept him away from other women—but her presence kept other women away. At least the kind with a scrap of dignity. I could never figure out why my father wanted women so badly, then treated them so badly.

As far as our home life, my father pretty much just checked out. Six months after my mother's death, my father sued the doctor and clinic for malpractice and got all sorts of money. He bought himself a really big boat, the kind that could cross the ocean. I still had to beg him for grocery money.

I wanted to go to college, but I knew my father wouldn't pay for it. I asked him about it once and he said college was indoctrination, not education, and that he had already taught me all I needed to know about the world.

I learned young that whatever I wanted in life, I would have to get for myself. Fortunately, or unfortunately, I developed young, so I always looked older than I was. Everyone assumed I was twenty when I was barely fifteen. My first job was as a server at a local café. Every day old men hit on me. Looking back, I suppose they weren't really that old, probably in their thirties and forties, but they seemed ancient to me.

When I was a senior in high school, Eric ran away. He left me a note that read, "Good-bye, I'm sorry." That was it. No address, nothing. I didn't need to ask why. It was the same reason that I wanted to leave home, except my father was even worse to him than he was to me. It seemed to me that with Eric, my father was constantly trying to prove that he was the alpha dog.

Two weeks after I graduated from high school, I moved to Utah. It wasn't the kind of place I thought I'd end up. In fact, up until six months before moving there, I knew nothing about the place. It was just one of those peculiar twists of fate that pulls the seat out from under you.

One day I was talking to one of the truckers at the café—we had tons of them—who was hauling a load of lumber to his hometown of Salt Lake City. I asked him what Salt Lake City was like. He said he liked it. It was bigger than Ashland, smaller than Portland. He said there was the University of Utah, which would be cheap once I got residence, and in the meantime there was a lot of work there. The cost of living was low and the people pretty much left you alone, except the Mormons, who would probably bring me a loaf of home-baked bread and invite me to church. Best of all, it was seven hundred miles from my father.

With Eric gone, I didn't really have anything holding me in Ashland. I had a cute boyfriend, Carter, but I wasn't in love or anything, and even though he talked about marriage (which I always thought was a little bizarre for an eighteen-year-old), I knew he wasn't someone I wanted to spend the rest of my life with.

I wasn't afraid to leave home. After what I'd been

through, I don't think I was afraid of much. I was, by necessity, frugal, so between my waitressing and tips and the occasional babysitting, I'd saved about five thousand dollars, which my father never knew about. Even with all his money, I have no doubt that he would have cleaned me out if he did, then justify his action as another one of his life lessons.

About a month before graduation, I started looking around for someplace to live in Utah. I came across a want ad posted by a young woman looking for a roommate. Her name was Wendy Nielsen. She had just quit her job working for a catering company and even though her rent was only three hundred and seventy-five dollars a month, she couldn't afford it.

The place looked nice online. Then I asked her about work. I had some cooking experience at the restaurant and had done almost all the cooking at home, so I asked if there was an opening at the catering company she'd just left.

"There's always an opening," she replied. "The owner's a witch. She runs everyone off. She's like barely five-foot and she has a massive mole on her left cheek. Her name is Marge."

I hesitated a moment, then said, "She named her mole Marge?"

Wendy laughed so hard she had to run to the bathroom. We were friends before we even met.

Wendy was right about the catering job. They were hiring. Perpetually. Not only were the wages good—$18.50

an hour, which was more than double what I'd ever made before—but I also got tips. Sometimes big ones. And there were insurance benefits.

"It's not worth a hundred dollars an hour," Wendy told me. "It's psychological abuse. You'll end up paying more for a good therapist."

"Do they have mental health benefits?" I asked.

The thing was, I wasn't really afraid of anyone, and I needed better money than I was going to make waitressing. I figured I could do anything for a year. Catering certainly wasn't something I had planned on making a career.

Actually, at that point I had no idea what I was going to do with my life, as I had been more focused on what I didn't want it to be than what I wanted it to be. The job was just something I could do while I made up my mind.

It was also perfect timing for me, since I couldn't go to school until I had established residency and could apply for a grant. I was one of those kids in a bind: my father had too much money for me to get student aid, but he wasn't willing to give me any of it. I was stuck.

Wendy had understated the pay but not her former employer. Marge Watson burned through employees like cars burn through tires at the Indianapolis 500. She was professional enough to never scold an employee in front of a client, but that was about the extent of her self-discipline. She'd eat employees for breakfast. She was good at it, and since most of her employees were young kids who had never worked before, they never lasted long.

Her personality didn't faze me. Compared to my father,

she was a kitten. And unlike my father, she couldn't hit me—though Wendy told me that she did slap an employee once. The employee sued, and the slap ended up costing Marge thousands of dollars. She never hit anyone after that.

Still, I knew it was only a matter of time before she came after me, so I waited for my turn, not with fear but with curiosity. I wondered what I would do.

Outside of me and the revolving door of part-time employees, there were two Mexican women who also worked full time: Frida and Eiza. Marge wasn't nice to them either, but they never seemed to mind her rants. I wasn't sure if it was a cultural thing, if they needed the money too much, or if they just didn't really understand what she was saying, as neither of them spoke English very well.

Finally my day came. I had a confrontation with a trust-fund bridezilla who had had too much to drink and suddenly insisted that she had ordered a four-tier wedding cake instead of a three. I wasn't sure if she thought I was going to quickly bake her a new tier or what her endgame was, but I just brushed her off.

Then she shoved me. She shouldn't have done that. I threw her up against a wall and, with my forearm across her throat, said, "You touch me again and your wedding pictures will look like something out of a Stephen King movie."

When I let her go, she ran out crying. Of course the bride's mother went ballistic on Marge, who of course then came after me. Marge was blue in the face and yelled at me until I thought she might burst a blood vessel. I just looked at her, unaffected. I think she thought I would quit, like everyone else did, but I was going to make her fire me so I could collect unemployment if I had to.

Neither happened. When she finished her tirade, I said calmly, "You should try Prozac. And breath mints." Then I walked out the back door.

As I was about to get into my car, Marge poked her head out the door and shouted to me, "I am on Prozac. Don't be late Monday."

Marge never got mad at me after that. I was probably the first employee who had ever stood up to her and, in so doing, had earned her respect. It was almost like she was testing me— like at the end of the first Willy Wonka movie. The good one.

When I started, Just Desserts only did weddings and an occasional bar mitzvah. (Utah, due to its religious culture, has a myriad of the former and a dearth of the latter.) Then people began asking us to do their company parties and corporate catering. As we expanded, Marge taught me everything she knew about the trade.

After that first year, Marge offered me a sizable raise to delay college and work full time for the company. I'm not really sure why Marge started the company to begin with, other than she was fiercely independent and didn't like the idea of living in her husband's shadow. Her husband, Craig, was the CEO of a local plumbing supply company. I only met him a few times, but he was a good-looking, clean-cut man, always perfectly coiffed. One of those

shiny people like Clive. He and Marge were about as compatible as mayonnaise and maple syrup.

I have no idea what brought the two of them together.
He was soft-spoken, kind, and respectful, and Marge was
Marge. She treated him like dirt. I always felt sorry for
him.

Peculiarly, I had worked for Marge for more than a
year before I found out she had a daughter. Tabitha. Not
surprisingly, they didn't get along. From what I gathered,
Tabitha wanted to be a playwright and lived, with a credit
card from her father, in New York City, working backstage
on off-Broadway productions.

As time passed, I realized that I was Marge's only friend.
I also sensed that she was getting bored with the business,
as she gave me more and more responsibility until I was
pretty much running the place. (Kind of like what I was
presently doing with Carina.) After two more years Marge
doubled my salary and made me the chief operating officer, which meant I still did the same thing, I just got paid
for it.

Then, one snowy February morning, Marge called me
as I was getting ready for work. Her voice was hoarse and
a little stiffer than usual.

"Craig's gone," she said.

"Gone where?" I asked.

"He had a heart attack while he was shoveling the walk.
He's gone."

She was so stoic that I wasn't sure how to respond. "I'm
sorry."

"I won't be coming in," she said.

I didn't see her for almost nine weeks. Then, two weeks after my twenty-third birthday, Marge asked to meet me for lunch at her favorite restaurant, a local bistro run by German people who were as rude as she was.

I got to the restaurant a few minutes early. Marge still hadn't arrived, so the hostess sat me and brought me a drink. Ten minutes later Marge walked in. I almost didn't recognize her. I couldn't believe how much she had changed in just a short time. She'd already been skinny, but now she looked gaunt, her skin tight on her cheeks, which made her look old. Her hair had turned completely gray. I don't know if the stress of her husband's death had gotten to her or if she had just stopped coloring it. Maybe both.

"Have you ordered yet?" she asked, sitting down. I thought it was a strange thing to say to someone you hadn't seen in over two months.

"No. I was waiting for you."

"Who's your waitress?"

I pointed to a young, flaxen-haired woman setting drinks at another table. "Her."

"You," Marge shouted to the young woman. "We're ready to order now."

"I'll be right there," the waitress said, looking somewhere between annoyed and stunned. A moment later she walked over. "Are you ready to order?"

"I just told you we were," Marge said. "Now get out your little notepad there. We'll have the red hummus appetizer to share, then I'll have a bowl of the sweet potato soup, and tell the chef that if he puts too much turmeric in it this time, I'll make him eat it."

The server let out a short sigh, wrote down the order, then turned to me. "What can I get for you?"

"*May*," Marge interrupted. "What *may* I get for you. You're a professional, honey. If you're going to work with the public, you need to speak their language."

The woman flushed. By then I was not surprised by Marge's utter lack of social finesse, but I still felt bad for the young woman.

"What may I get for you?" she asked, noticeably softer.

"I'll have a spring salad, with the dressing on the side," I said. "Thank you."

She gathered our menus. "All right, I'll be right back with your appetizer."

After she was gone, Marge said, "I'm sorry I missed your birthday." That was one of the surprise quirks of Marge's personality. She kept track of all her employees' birthdays and, no matter how tenuous their employment, would commemorate them by coming in early to bake one of her raspberry almond cakes.

"It's okay. You've had a lot on your plate," I said.

She sighed deeply. "I didn't realize how heavy the grief would be." She seemed annoyed by this, as if her husband's death had been more of an inconvenience than she expected. "I've felt crazy."

"I thought the same thing when my mother died."

"I have a present for you." She reached into her purse and brought out an envelope, which she handed to me. I hoped there was money inside. There wasn't. There was only a birthday card with one of our business cards with my name on it. All the card said was *Happy Birthday*.

I didn't really understand why she was giving me one of my own business cards.

"Thank you," I said.

"You didn't read the card," she said.

"I read it."

"I meant the business card. Read it."

I looked back down and saw *Just Desserts. Maggie Walther. Owner.*

Owner. I looked up at her.

"I don't want to do this anymore," she said.

Her comment was a little odd since she really hadn't done anything with the business for months. "Do what?"

"The business. It's time I retired. I hate our clients and I have no desire to spend the rest of my life freezing my bones in Utah. I'm moving to Sun City, Arizona." I didn't know there was such a place but it sounded nice. "There's no one else who could run my business."

"What about Tabitha?"

"Oh, please."

"You could sell it," I said.

"To who? Some moron who would run it into the ground after I've put my best years into it? And then I'd have her calling me every time she had a problem. You know I don't need the money. Craig left me with more than I can spend. Besides, you're more a daughter than my own daughter."

It was the sweetest thing she had ever said to me. Maybe to anyone. "Thank you."

"You're the only thing that has made the last few years remotely tolerable."

"Thank you," I said again. "I'll miss you."

She said, "Yeah. Don't get sentimental on me. You know I hate that crap."

The waitress returned carrying our meals. She pretty much dropped the food on the table and ran. I watched in anticipation as Marge tried her soup. She took a second spoonful, so I knew we were safe. "When are you leaving?" I asked.

"I put the house up for sale last Monday. It's already under contract."

"You mean the kitchen?" I asked. Our company head-quarters was an old home that Marge had converted into a commercial kitchen and bakery. She usually just called it "the house."

"No, not the kitchen. You're going to need that. I meant my personal residence."

"That's fast," I said. "That's good."

"It means I sold too cheap." She shook her head. "What's done is done. The buyers want to close by April third, so I'm flying to Arizona tomorrow to find a place. I'll have Scott finish up the paperwork so we can legally transfer the company over before I leave. We'll need to transfer all the bank accounts into your name. I'll leave a cushion in there, but I doubt you'll need it. We have six thousand in receivables. There's at least fifty grand in equity on the kitchen."

"I'll pay you back when I can," I said.

"I don't want you paying me back. It's a signing bonus. We already have more than a hundred thousand in contracts. You'll do okay."

"I don't know what to say."

"Just eat your salad," she said.

I saw Marge only once after that. She died of cancer just eighteen weeks later. I found out later that she'd had stage four uterine cancer when she had turned over the business. She never even told me. She hated pity. There were only three of us at her funeral. Tabitha didn't even come.

CHAPTER

An anonymous woman posted her sympathy online for me, saying that she too had been "Clived." In spite of my pain, I almost laughed. You never want to live to see your name become a verb.

—Maggie Walther's Diary

I met Clive six months before I took over the company while we were catering a political soiree for the Salt Lake mayor's race. The event was held at the National Society of the Sons of Utah Pioneers convention hall. The room was filled with suits and pantsuits—ambitious political types. Clive was there, younger than most, yet swimming through the crowd as effortlessly as a koi in a backyard pond. He was already in his second year of law school and was clerking at the firm he would eventually become a partner at.

I thought he was handsome, though not in a way I was used to. Most of the guys I dated had long hair and tattoos. Clive looked perfectly arranged, from his flawlessly knotted tie to his expensive-looking shoes. His hair looked better cared for than mine. From my experience, those kinds of guys might give you a second look but never a second date. We shared eye contact as I came from the kitchen carrying a tray of hors d'oeuvres to the room.

He immediately took a step toward me. "I'll have one of those," he said, lifting a bacon-wrapped chestnut from my tray.

I might have been flirting. I don't remember. "Just one?"

"Let me see." He popped the morsel into his mouth, ate it, then took another. "Did you make these?"

"No."

"You just serve the food."

"No. I bake. I just made other things."

"What do you think of this party?"

"I'm working," I said.

"We all are," he replied. "The laughter is fake. Bunch of sycophants. Are you partisan?"

"No," I said. "I'm Pisces."

He burst out laughing. "That's the best thing I've heard all night. I'm a Leo. King of the jungle."

"Which jungle?"

"Whichever one will run when I roar," he said, a slight smile bending his mouth. "Pisces and Leo. We're compatible opposites."

"I need to get back to work," I said.

"What time do you get off work?"

"Long after the party is over."

"Is that a brush-off?"

"No. It's a fact."

"May I have your phone number?"

"You don't even know my name."

"That would be helpful," he said. "What's your name?"

"Maggie. What's yours?"

"Clive. Like Clive Davis."

"Your last name is Davis?"

"No. Clive Davis is a famous record producer."

"Never heard of him," I said.

"He signed the greats. Janis Joplin, Aerosmith, Billy Joel, Bruce Springsteen, the Grateful Dead."

"All before my time, but yes."

"Yes, you've heard of them?"

"Yes, you can have my phone number."

He pulled out his phone. "Go ahead."

"It's 555-2412."

"That's not a fake number, is it?"

"Do women often give you fake numbers?" He didn't answer. "If I didn't want you to call me, I'd tell you."

"That's refreshing," he said. He typed something into his phone. "I just texted you." I guessed he was testing me, waiting to see if something on me would buzz or ding. "Nothing."

"I'm not allowed to have my phone on while I work."

"That makes sense."

"I'm also not supposed to mingle with the guests. I've got to get back to work."

"I'll call you tomorrow."

"I hope you do."

He smiled and walked away, disappearing back into the crowd. I replenished the table. When I got back to the kitchen, Marge said, "Who was that man you were talking to?"

"No one."

"But you gave him your phone number."

"Yes."

"This is the last place I'd give anyone a phone number."

I should have listened to her. Clive called me early the next morning. I was still in bed. We hadn't left the party until midnight, and I hadn't gotten to bed until half past one.

"Hello," I said groggily.

"Rise and shine, princess," he said.

I rubbed my eyes. "Who is this?"

"Clive, from the party last night. May I take you to breakfast?"

"What time is it?"

"Seven."

"I was asleep. Who calls at seven?"

"Apparently I do. I couldn't get you off my mind."

"I don't know if I should be flattered or scared."

"I think you need more sleep," he said. "Tell you what, why don't I pick you up at noon and I'll take you to La Caille for brunch." La Caille was an expensive French restaurant tucked away in the canyons.

"Okay," I said.

"I'll see you then."

"Wait. You don't know where I live."

"Actually, I do. I'll see you at noon."

He hung up the phone.

How does he know where I live? I was too tired to think. I rolled over and went back to sleep.

Clive showed up on time. I had brunch with him, then dinner, then breakfast. We dated for only two months before he asked me to marry him. I said yes.

CHAPTER

Some days it's just best not to leave the bunker.
—Maggie Walther's Diary

On the drive home I thought about what Carina had said—at least when I wasn't worrying about sliding off the road and dying in a car accident. She was right. I knew that I needed to do something to get out of my funk. Or at least my bedroom. An undeniable part of me longed for normalcy. The idea of changing my environment and embracing Christmas made sense. The thing was, I loved Christmas. I always had.

This was one place where Clive and I were in sync. Clive was also big on Christmas. (Why can't I say *big* without thinking *bigamy?*) Typical Clive, he went overboard. Our house wasn't just dressed for the season, it was custom-decorated by the local commercial display company. I knew it had gotten too extreme when people began stopping in front of our house to take pictures. Our electric bill tripled during the season.

Every year got worse, and I fully expected our home to someday evolve into a Macy's-like Christmas attraction with window displays and long lines of spectators and pretzel carts.

All this attention to the season wasn't really for us. It was for Clive's schmoozers—my word, not his—who came to our parties. Clive was big on parties and he kept long lists of attendees, each carefully arranged and cross-checked against each other to keep the wrong people from attending the same party. He even invited his enemies to our parties, following the admonition to keep your friends close but your enemies closer.

With the exception of the other attorneys' wives, whom I superficially knew, I didn't know any of the people at the parties. Our home was basically another catering job, except I was also the hostess, smiling prettily as I told people where the bathrooms were, took their coats, and put coasters under their drinks.

In a moment of weakness, I had imagined what Clive's other wife's home looked like at Christmas. The thought of it made my stomach hurt.

When I got home, my front walk and driveway, like the rest of the world, were covered with snow. I pulled into my garage, grabbed a snow shovel, and spent the next hour shoveling the driveway and sidewalk until my back hurt.

As I was finishing up, it started to snow again. First in wispy, pretty flakes, then increasing in density until the sky seemed to be more snow than not. Within minutes the concrete I'd cleared was covered again. Defeated, I went back inside the house and curled up in bed. This was not a day to be out. The world had it in for me.

CHAPTER

Seven

The storm just keeps on coming—literally and figuratively.

—Maggie Walther's Diary

The storm got worse. Wondering if the world had slipped into an ice age that I hadn't been warned about, I actually turned on the local news. I say "actually" because it was the first time in a long time. For obvious reasons I had been avoiding the news, but I really wanted to see what they had to say about the weather. According to the annoyingly spunky weatherwoman, the storm wasn't slackening anytime soon. Worst case, it was supposed to shut down the city. I didn't really care. At least it made my isolation excusable.

After the news, I watched some show about a crazy woman who had killed her husband, then tried to dispose of the body by feeding it to her neighbor's pigs. That's the kind of mood I was in.

Around ten o'clock the power went out. I used my cell phone as a flashlight to walk around the house. I found some candles, which I lit in the kitchen. I hadn't eaten anything all day and I was feeling it. I made myself a turkey and cheddar cheese sandwich, which even by candle-light wasn't romantic in the least.

Then I just lay on the couch waiting for the lights to come back on. They didn't. After an hour the power was still out and though the house was warmed by natural gas, the heater's controls ran on electronics, so the house kept getting colder.

I raised a blind to look outside. Even though it was nearly midnight, it was eerily light out, as the blizzard-scape was illuminated by a full moon. The snow on the ground was already at least two feet deep.

I began to worry about the cold. One of the problems with isolation is that your imagination begins to create its own reality. I pictured myself being the subject of one of those stories the papers always run after a major storm, where a home's heat was shut off and the occupant is found, days later, frozen to death.

In the basement, we had an antique-looking wood-burning stove that we rarely used. Actually, never used. It had come with the house, and we had thought of it only as decoration: the polished copper firewood tub next to it had never been emptied of carefully stacked logs. Briefly, I wondered if the logs were still good or if they'd expired, which might have been the dumbest thing I'd ever thought—with the exception of believing that my husband loved only me.

I struggled with starting the fire for more than twenty minutes before shouting out, "I hate being alone!" I'm not entirely sure what being alone had to do with starting a fire, but my loneliness suddenly felt as heavy and cold as the air around me. I realized something. Marriage had changed me. I had once insisted on my alone time. Now I feared it.

As for the fire, I finally just filled the whole stove with newspapers, covered them with wood, then doused the whole thing in some lighter fluid I found in the garage. (Clive prided himself on being a barbecue "purist" and used one of those old charcoal-burning, wire-grilled barbecues.) The stove almost exploded, but the fire was going.

I got my pillow and a quilt from upstairs, then lay down on the couch in front of the crackling fire. As I watched the flickering flames, I remembered what Carina had said at the coffee shop about starting a fire when you're lost in the wilderness. I was lost in an emotional wilderness, and I needed all the help I could get.

CHAPTER

Eight

Why do I still miss him? Or is it just the myth of him that I miss? How much of each relationship is based on reality versus what we hope to believe about who the other person is?

—Maggie Walther's Diary

I woke sometime around three in the morning when the power came back on and the lights and television with it. I hadn't bothered to turn the lights on downstairs, so the room was lit only by the lamp in the stairwell and the glowing orange embers in the stove.

I went upstairs, blew out the candles, then turned off all the lights and the television. I checked the thermostat. The temperature had fallen to sixty-three degrees but the furnace had finally kicked on. I climbed in between the cold sheets of my bed and closed my eyes. As angry and betrayed as I felt about Clive, I missed him next to me—the warmth of his body, the soothing sound of his breathing. Three questions bounced around inside my skull, each taking its turn to inflict its pain like tag team wrestlers: *Why did he betray me? What's wrong with me? Why wasn't I enough?*

CHAPTER

*Lynch mobs never went away. They just migrated
to the Internet.*
                              —*Maggie Walther's Diary*

That night I had a peculiar dream. I was following Clive,
barefoot, through a snowy forest. I asked him where we
were going. "Nowhere," he replied. "Then why are we
walking?" I asked. He turned around. He was wearing a
mask. I asked him to take it off. He said, "Are you sure?" I
said yes. He lifted the mask. There was nothing there.

I woke, my heart pounding fiercely. The sun was pro-
jecting its bright rays through the partially open wooden
slats of my window blinds. I could hear the neighborhood
snowblower brigade, their machines' engines whining and
chugging beneath the weight of the night's snow. A reminder that outside my shuttered world, life was carrying
on as usual.

My body ached nearly as much as my heart. I forced
myself out of bed and walked over and lifted the blinds.
The light was intense, the morning sun reflecting off the
newly laid crystalline blanket. The sky was bright blue
and the storm was gone, but it had left behind nearly

thirty inches. My neighbor's Volkswagen, which had been parked in the street, looked more like an igloo than a car.

Now I really was snowed in and my back still ached from the few inches of snow I'd shoveled the night before. I didn't want to go out in public, but I needed to. I needed to prove to myself that the world wasn't laughing at me. I know that sounds paranoid, but there's a reason. After Clive's story broke, I made the mistake of reading the comments people posted online about the newspaper story. Many of them were directed at me, some mocking me, some blaming me. I was astounded to see such viciousness from people I didn't know and who didn't know me.

I once read that people, when cloaked in anonymity, would do things they wouldn't otherwise do—hence the invention of the masquerade party. When did society get so mean?

CHAPTER

Sometimes the simplicity of a kind act is inversely proportionate to the power of its effect.
　　　　　　　　　　　—Maggie Walther's Diary

I walked to my front door to see just how snowed in I was. As I opened the door, the freezing air on my face felt bracing. In the bright light, it took me a moment to understand what I was seeing. Someone had plowed my driveway, sidewalk, and walkway. On my doorstep was a red glass candle with a note taped to it. I stooped to pick it up.

> Dear Maggie,
> 　　My husband and I wanted you to know how sorry we are for what you are going through. You're in our prayers. Please let us know if there's anything we can do.
>
> 　　　　　　　　　　　Sincerely,
> 　　　　　　　　　　　Bryan and Leisa Stephens

Even though I'd lived across the street from them for more than three years, I hardly knew them. I saw them out walking their dog now and then—a miniature Maltese poodle—but our interactions had been scarcely more than a wave.

I looked across the street at their house. It looked dark. I wanted to show them my appreciation, so I decided to do what I did best. Bake. One of my most popular Christmas confections was thumbprint cookies—small, silver dollar–sized sugar cookies. I would press each with my thumb, then fill the indentation with a spoonful of jam.

I decided I should at least make myself presentable enough to not scare them. I showered, put on makeup, and did my hair. For the first time in weeks, I looked human again.

I went out to the kitchen and preset the oven, then started mixing ingredients. Thumbprint cookies are easy to make, a simple recipe of flour, baking powder, butter, sugar, eggs, and vanilla. Simple or not, I found myself enjoying the feeling of being absorbed in something other than my problems.

I scooped out balls of dough with a small ice cream scoop and pressed my thumb into each ball, flattening it and leaving an indentation, before adding the jam. After they baked, I filled a plate with the cookies, covered it with plastic wrap, and wrote a short note:

> Dear Bryan and Leisa,
>   Thank you for your thoughtfulness during this difficult time. It means more than you know.
>   Sincerely,
>   Maggie

I put my coat back on, walked across the street to their home, and pushed the doorbell. A moment later I heard footsteps, then the door unlocked. A dowdy middle-aged woman in a jumpsuit answered. "May I help you?"

Even though she didn't look familiar, I didn't know the Stephenses well enough to know if the woman was Leisa or not. I assumed she was. "Hi. I wanted to thank you for what you and your husband did for me this morning."

"I think you're mistaking me for my sister," she said.

"I'm sorry. Is Leisa or Bryan home?"

"They left half an hour ago."

The exchange felt awkward.

"Well, I brought them some cookies." I offered the plate. "They're still warm. I just wanted to say thank you. Bryan shoveled my driveway and walk."

"He would do that." She took the plate from me without looking at it.

"Do you expect them back soon?"

"Not until Thursday. They're going to be up in Logan a few days." Then, after a pause, she added, "Their son was killed yesterday in a snowmobiling accident."

The pronouncement stunned me. "I'm so sorry."

"It's a tragedy. He has four children, and his wife already suffers from depression."

I didn't know what to say. Finally, I said again, "I'm sorry."

"Who should I say came by?"

"I'm Maggie Walther," I said. "My name's on the note. I'll reach out next week."

She thanked me vicariously for the Stephenses and shut

the door. I turned and walked back to my house. I was moved by the couple's circumstance. As appreciative as I had already been for their kindness, now I was astounded. In the midst of such heartbreak, this good couple had reached out to me in my pain. For the first time in a long while, I felt hope in humanity.

CHAPTER

Eleven

I went to find a Christmas tree. I found something else.

—*Maggie Walther's Diary*

When I got home, I walked around the house opening the blinds, then turned on the radio. Not surprisingly, it was set to one of the local talk stations. I immediately started pushing other presets, stopping at a station playing Christmas music.

Christmas music has always been healing to me. I thought again of my good neighbors and their ability to transcend their grief. You don't find light looking in the dark, and consciously or not, for the last six months I had resigned myself to the dark, scurrying from light like a cockroach. I was ready to at least try to lift myself out of it. Maybe lifting the blinds had been a literal manifestation of that.

Burl Ives sang "Have a Holly, Jolly Christmas." I smiled, which was another groundbreaking achievement. When was the last time I'd smiled? Carina was right, I needed to change my environment. What would be more fitting than a Christmas tree?

I finished cleaning my kitchen, put on my long wool coat, and went out to my car. I drove to the Kroger's where I'd noticed a Christmas tree lot on the south corner of their parking lot.

In Salt Lake, like in most big cities, Christmas tree lots started springing up around November—usually in the corner of a mall or supermarket's parking lot. I remembered, as a girl, a place in Ashland where one of the Christmas tree lots had a fenced-in corral of Santa's reindeer. It was one of the few truly magical memories that had somehow survived the trauma of my childhood.

The traffic was light; it took me less than ten minutes to reach my destination. The Christmas tree lot was about a half-acre square and surrounded by a portable chain-link fence. Long rows of colorful Christmas lights hung over the lot, strung from white wooden posts that were wrapped with red ribbon—like peppermint sticks.

There was an aluminum-sided trailer parked near the lot's entrance with various-sized wreaths hanging from pegs on the front of it, all marked with price tags.

Music was playing from a PA system, but it wasn't Christmas music. It was seventies rock. "Take the Long Way Home" by Supertramp. *Who still listens to Supertramp?*

Business seemed light (who shops for a Christmas tree at three in the afternoon?), and there were only a few cars parked outside the fence.

I walked through the front entrance into the makeshift forest. There were four other customers inside the fenced area, an elderly couple and an older man with what was likely his grandson. A young, skinny man wearing a denim jacket over a hoodie passed by me dragging a tree toward the entrance. He was followed by the elderly couple.

"Can I help you with something?" he asked as he walked by.

"I'm looking for a tree," I said.

"Be right with you."

"I've got it, Shelby," another voice said.

I turned to see an attractive man walking toward me. He looked to be about my age, early thirties, with striking brown eyes beneath thick eyebrows. His hair was dark brown, short but combed back, half-hidden beneath a wool cap. His face was covered with a partial beard, kind of an extended goatee, though along his jawline it was not more than stubble, as if it had either just started to grow or he was trying to look like Hugh Jackman.

I had never seen Clive with facial hair. I'm not even sure he could grow a beard. Once when I'd suggested he attempt to grow one, he said, "No one trusts a politician with a beard." When I countered that Lincoln had had a beard, he replied, "Yeah, and look how that turned out."

Frankly, when it comes to facial hair and politicians, it's the mustache that should be feared. Stalin and Hitler had particularly memorable lip hair.

He smiled as he approached me. "Hi, I'm Andrew. May I help you?"

I felt butterflies. "Hi. I'm . . . I need a tree."

"I suspected that," he said with a half smile. "Not that I'm psychic."

I felt stupid. "I guess most people coming here want a tree."

"Unless they're lost," he said. "What kind of tree are you looking for?"

"Kind?"

"Most people have a favorite. It's usually what they grew up with. Norway spruce, Nordmann fir, blue spruce, Fraser fir, Douglas fir, lodgepole pine . . ."

The names were lost on me. I pointed to the one closest to me. "What kind of tree is that?"

"That's a Fraser fir."

"Is it good?"

"All the trees I sell are good."

"I mean, are some better than others?"

"That depends on what you're looking for. Like, do you want a tree with a nice smell or something that's a little lower-maintenance?"

"Lower-maintenance is good. I don't need anything dying on me," I added. "Enough has died in my life this year."

He looked at me empathetically and said, "Low maintenance. Then we'll stay away from this one." He stepped away from a nearly perfectly cone-shaped tree.

"But I liked that one," I said.

"You won't after you get it home. That's a Norway spruce. It's a pretty tree, but it has sharp needles, which it loses fairly fast. Unless you like vacuuming every day, but you said you wanted low maintenance."

"Definitely low maintenance," I said.

"How tall a tree were you thinking?"

"Just regular."

His brow fell. "Regular. How high is your ceiling?"

"I don't know. Normal."

He grinned lightly. "Regular and normal. Is your ceiling eight or nine feet?"

"I really don't know."

"What year was your house built?"

"What does that have to do with my tree?"

"Before 1995 most ceilings were eight feet. In the next decade, they changed to nine. Is it a new home?"

"It's an older house. I think it was built in the seventies."

"The golden years. So, you need a six-foot tree. You want to allow room for a star."

"I don't have a star."

"Or whatever. Not everyone puts a star on top of their tree. I've seen spires, cones, snowflakes. I've even seen a Death Star."

"I was just thinking how much I wanted a Death Star on my tree," I said sardonically.

"I might have a Yoda topper. Put me on a tree, you will."

I grimaced. "Was that your Yoda imitation?"

"Sadly," he replied.

"I want a tree that's sturdy," I said. "And cute. Not one of those asymmetrical ones. Something well-rounded."

"Cute, sturdy, six foot, and well-rounded. You're still describing a tree here?"

"Yes." I smiled, a surprising blush creeping down my neck. I pointed at a tree. "How about that one?"

He walked over to it. "This would be a good choice for you. It's a balsam fir. It's a classic tree with a nice scent and it doesn't lose its needles as fast as some of the others. Its only downside is that it's not great for heavy ornaments because its branches aren't real thick."

"I don't have heavy ornaments. How much is it?"

He pulled out a tape measure and measured the tree. "They're nine dollars a foot, so this is fifty-four dollars. I'll make it fifty even."

"Thank you," I said. "I'll take it."

He reached in to the tree's trunk and lifted it. I followed him as he carried my tree to a long worktable surrounded by piles of sawdust.

"I'm going to give it a fresh cut. That will help it live longer."

"I could use a fresh cut," I said beneath my breath. He furtively glanced over at me, then placed the tree up on the table with the tree's trunk hanging over the side. He donned plastic safety glasses, then fired up a chainsaw, its squeal drowning out all other sound. Cutting trees was something my father was always doing. I tried to imagine Clive holding a chainsaw, but I couldn't. His hands were too soft.

Andrew cut off the bottom three inches of the tree, then killed the chainsaw engine and brought the tree over to me. "She's ready to go."

"The tree is three inches shorter now," I observed.

"Yes?"

"That's like two dollars' worth of tree." I was only joking, but he didn't catch it.

"I'll make it forty-five," he said. "Do you need anything to go with it?"

"Like what?"

"Do you have a tree stand?"

"I think so. It's probably in our shed. If I can find it. I'm not sure where my husband—my *ex*-husband kept it."

He nodded calmly. "Well, you'll need one. If you want, I can get you one, then you can bring it back when you find yours."

"That works."

"What kind would you like?"

"Just pick one for me."

From the side of the trailer he lifted a large green stand that looked like an impaled plastic pail with aluminum pole legs. "I like these; they're big, but they hold a lot of water, so you can water every few days and not worry about it drying out. Do you need lights?"

"No. We've got a million of them. I mean, I do. Now." I sounded stupid.

"All right." He added up the amount on a tablet. "That will be fifty-five dollars with your discount. With tax, that's fifty-eight forty-three. The stand was ten."

"Thank you, but you don't really have to give me the discount. I was just kidding."

"It's done," he said. I pulled out my wallet and handed him my credit card. He ran it through a card reader, then handed me the iPad. "If you'll autograph that. You can use your finger to sign."

I signed it and handed it back.

"Thank you," he said. "You're parked out front?"

"Just outside your gate."

"If you'll take the tree stand, I'll carry the tree out for you."

I took the stand, which was heavier than I expected. He grabbed a ball of twine, got my tree, and followed me to my car. As I unlocked my front door, he stopped about ten feet behind me.

"That's your car?"

I was used to people taking jabs at the size of my vehicle. "Yes."

"It's a little . . . little."

"I prefer *fun-sized*. Besides, it gets forty miles to a gallon and I can park it anywhere."

"That's good," he said, "because parking it would be a lot safer than driving it. You could hit a squirrel and total it."

I bit back a smile. "Now you're mocking me."

"Mocking aside, tying the tree to your car isn't going to work real well. And by real well, I mean it's not going to work."

"Well, it's all I've got. Maybe I should have gone with one of those fake trees you can pull apart."

He shook his head. "Fake trees are for underachievers. Do you know anyone with a truck?"

"The FedEx guy."

A smile flitted across his face. "Where do you live?"

"About four miles from here. Over by the Target."

He glanced back at the lot. "We close at eight tonight. If you don't mind waiting, I can drive it over after we close. If that's not too late."

"How much will that be? To deliver it."

"A cup of coffee."

I liked the price. "Deal." I wrote down my address and handed it to him. "I will see you between eight and eight thirty. After that, I'm indisposed."

The corners of his mouth rose. "Then I'll try to be there before you're indisposed."

I got in my car, glanced at him in the rearview mirror, and pulled out onto the slushy street. I was glad he was coming to my house.

CHAPTER

Twelve

I invited a man over for coffee. His name is Andrew.
He is a pleasant stranger.

—*Maggie Walther's Diary*

Indisposed? Where did that come from? I'm not sure why I said that. It's not like I had plans. I supposed that I was protecting myself, but I wasn't sure from what.

I stopped at the grocery store on the way home and bought some coffee, chocolate biscotti, and a few other necessities I'd put off buying. Actually, I ended up with a cart full of groceries. I hadn't really been shopping in a while.

I went home and put everything away, then straightened up the house in anticipation of his arrival, even lighting the candle my neighbors had brought me. It made my front room smell like wassail.

I dragged an upholstered chair from the corner of the front room to make space for the tree, then went out to the garage to see if Clive had left our tree stand there. I couldn't find it, so I placed the new stand about where I figured the tree would go.

I thought about the man at the tree lot. Andrew. He was

beautiful, really. But especially his eyes. There was something mesmerizing about his eyes. They were clear but soulful, maybe even sad—an irony in light of his obvious sense of humor and contagious smile.

I made myself a vegetable omelet for dinner, started a fire in the front room's gas fireplace, then picked up a book and sat down on the couch to read as the grandfather clock in the foyer chimed six.

It was two hours past dark when a red truck with a yellow snowplow stopped in front of my home, backed up, and then pulled into my driveway. I could see Andrew inside. I opened the door and walked outside without my jacket, my arms crossed at my chest to keep myself warm. Andrew looked up at me, shut off his truck, and climbed out.

"You found me," I said, my breath freezing in a cloud in front of me.

"I'm glad you came out. I wasn't sure I had the right place. It's kind of hard finding addresses when the curbs and mailboxes are covered with snow." He walked around to the bed of his truck and dropped the gate. "Should I bring it in through the front door?"

"Yes. Do you need any help?"

"No, I've got it." He lifted the tree from the back of the truck and carried it up the walk to my front porch.

"Come on in," I said, stepping inside. "You can just put it there in the corner. Where I put the tree stand."

He stamped his feet on the mat. "I'm going to get your carpet wet. Should I take off my shoes?"

"You're okay," I said.

He carried the tree in, leaving a light trail of needles in his wake. He lifted the tree onto the stand's metal peg and moved it around until it fell into place. Then he stepped back to inspect it. "Perfect." He turned back to me. "It just needs some decorations."

"I can handle that. Thank you for bringing it. How much do I owe you?"

"I think I quoted you a cup of coffee."

I smiled. "Would you like to come into the kitchen while I make it?"

"Sure."

"This way." He followed me into the kitchen. "You can sit at the table."

He pulled out a chair and sat down. "You have a beautiful home."

"Thank you."

"How long have you lived here?"

"A little over three years. I'm going to miss it."

"You're moving?"

"Eventually. This house is too big for just me." I took the pot and poured two cups. "How do you like your coffee?"

"Cream and sugar."

"I've got half and half," I said.

"Even better."

I carried the cups over to the table. I retrieved a pint carton of half and half from the refrigerator and a tin can with sugar cubes from the cupboard next to it, then brought them over to the table and set them next to the cups. I sat down across from him.

"Thank you," he said.

"You're welcome. How often do you make deliveries?"

"Not often."

"Here's your sugar." I slid the tin can to him. "Then I'm lucky."

"Yes, you are." He lifted a sugar cube out of the can. "They're pink. And heart-shaped."

"I made them with rosewater. Then dyed them."

"You make your own sugar cubes?"

"Doesn't everybody?"

He laughed. "I don't even know anyone who uses them anymore." He lifted one between his thumb and forefinger. "These are . . . awesome. Definitely Martha Stewart."

"By awesome, do you mean an utter waste of time?"

He grinned. "They're art. No time creating art is wasted. They almost look too nice to use."

"They're not," I said.

He dropped two hearts into his cup.

"So, what do you do when you're not selling Christmas trees? Or is that a full-time gig?"

He smiled. "No, it's something I'm experimenting with. It's only ninety days out of the year. This is my entrepreneurial side. By profession I'm a financial consultant. Or was. I used to own an investment firm, but I let that go when I moved to Utah."

"Where did you come from?"

"Colorado."

My thoughts bounced immediately to Clive's extraneous Colorado family. I pushed the thought away.

"Why did you come to Utah?" I asked.

"A change of scenery," he said. "I had some bad things happen to my business, followed by a painful divorce."

"I'm sorry," I said. "We've got that in common. At least the divorce part. Where did you move from?"

"Just outside Denver. Thornton."

What are the chances? I thought. It was the same town where Clive's second family lived. I wondered over the vague possibility that he knew the woman. Again I pushed away the thought. "So how is the Christmas tree business?" I asked.

"It's all right. I'm not going to pay off the national debt with my profits, but I'll put a little away. Then onto the next thing."

"And what is that?"

"I'm not sure yet. I'm thinking of starting my firm up again."

"Is that difficult?"

"Yes. But I was pretty good at it. I had it up to thirty million before things went south."

I looked at him in surprise. "Thirty million . . . dollars?"

"If it were pesos, it wouldn't have been as impressive."

I sipped my coffee. "You said some bad things happened to your business."

"Horrible things," he said. "Nothing I'd want to ruin our time together sharing. What do you do?"

"I own a catering business."

"Which explains the fancy sugar cubes. What kind of catering?"

"Weddings, personal, corporate. An occasional movie production. Pretty much the whole gamut."

"You must be busy this time of year."

His words tweaked me a little with guilt, reminding me that Carina was working seventy-hour weeks. My absence was putting a lot of extra pressure on her. "We're swamped. Business is good."

"Good," he said. He finished his coffee.

"Would you like some more?"

"Thank you," he said, "but I'd better let you go; you said you were busy."

Disappointment washed over me. Still, he hadn't moved from his chair. "No worries. I'm okay on time. Thank you for bringing the tree. I wasn't even going to get one this year. I haven't been in a celebrating mood."

"I understand. I still don't have a tree myself."

"You sell them, but you don't have one?"

"You know how it is—the cobbler's children have no shoes. Besides, it's just me."

"It's just me too," I said.

"So what changed your mind about getting a tree?"

"A friend of mine. She thought it might help me emotionally to decorate for the season. You know, to get in the spirit of Christmas."

"Is it working?"

"Apparently. I'm not balled up in a fetal position somewhere."

He looked at me sympathetically. "Life can be hard. And the holidays seem to amplify whatever pain we're going through."

"They can," I said. I took a drink from my coffee, then suddenly blurted out, "So, you probably heard about my husband. It was all over the news."

He shook his head. "I'm sorry, I don't watch much news."

"Have you heard the name Clive Walther?"

"No. Should I have?"

"That's refreshing. You're probably the only one in Utah who hasn't heard of him."

"Well, I'm new here."

"Then I should probably tell you."

He looked at me for a moment, then asked, "Why?"

It was a good question. Here he'd sat down to enjoy some coffee and pleasant conversation, and now I was going to vomit all over him my tragic marriage.

"Is it something you want to talk about?"

I wasn't sure how to answer. It had practically become part of my introduction. *Hi, I'm Maggie Walther. My husband had another wife and family.*

"No," I said. "Not really."

"We don't need to talk about anything that brings you pain," he said, his eyes kind.

"Thank you."

The moment stretched awkwardly. I couldn't think of anything else to say. Finally, he said, "Well, I probably should go. I still need to count up the day's receipts."

"Of course," I said, silently berating myself over our conversation. "I didn't mean to keep you."

"I'm glad you did. I enjoyed talking. And the coffee."

He stood and we walked together to the front door, stopping on the threshold.

"Thank you for bringing my tree. It looks beautiful."

"A beautiful woman should have a beautiful tree," he said. The compliment was a little corny but still made me feel good. "Good night."

"Night," I said.

It was probably only fifteen degrees out, but I stood in the open doorway watching as he walked out to his truck and started it up. I waved and he waved back. Then he backed out of my driveway and I watched until he turned the corner and his taillights disappeared.

I hoped it wouldn't be the last time I saw him.

CHAPTER

Thirteen

I went back to get Christmas lights. No, actually, that was my excuse for going back to see Andrew. If you can't be honest in your own diary, you should be a novelist and get paid for writing fiction.

—*Maggie Walther's Diary*

FRIDAY, NOVEMBER 11

Two things were different the next morning. And, after the rut I'd been in, I figured anything different was good. First, the house smelled like pine. It smelled alive again.

Second, I couldn't get Andrew off my mind.

Yesterday had been a good day—the first in a very long string of bad ones. I had had two positive human interactions: first the Stephenses, then Andrew.

I decided to build on my momentum by decorating the tree. The Christmas baubles were in the downstairs storage room with the wrapping paper and Christmas books, but the Christmas lights were all back in the shed.

I looked outside the kitchen window over my backyard. Icicles hung from the garage and shed roof, some as thick as a cow shank. (I'm not sure why I used that simile. It was something my dad would have said.)

I hadn't braved my backyard since the first storm hit in mid-October. The snow level had only risen since then, piled more than three feet high in some places. From where I was, the shed looked a mile away, sealed by snow drifts halfway up the door. *It would take snow shoes just to get to it*, I thought. *And a pick to chip the ice and snow from the door. Maybe a flamethrower.* At least, that's what I told myself as I got in my car and drove back to the Christmas tree lot.

The truth was thinly veiled in my own mind. I knew why I was going. I wanted to see him again.

As I pulled into the Kroger's parking lot, I looked for his red truck but didn't see it. I parked near the entrance and walked in.

This time I was the only customer in the lot. There were two young men sitting on vinyl folding chairs next to a barrel with a fire inside, the flames occasionally rising above the barrel's rim. Both of them were vaping.

I recognized one of the men from the day before, the guy who had dragged a tree past me. His hair was tied up in a man bun.

When he saw me he pulled his earbuds out, set his vape down on a box near the chair, and walked up to me. "Hey. May I help you?"

"Is Andrew here?"

"No. The boss doesn't work weekends."

"Oh," I said. "Will he be back on Monday?"

"Sometimes Monday night. It depends when he gets

back in town. Tuesday morning for sure. He's on the schedule." He looked me over in a way that made me feel a little uncomfortable. I wasn't old enough to be his mother, but definitely a younger aunt.

"I'm Shel," he said, pushing his hands into his coat pockets. "You were here the other day."

"Yes. Andrew delivered a tree to my house."

"I gotcha," he said. "Is there a problem?"

"No problem."

"I'm in charge when the boss is gone. If you need something, I can help you."

"Thank you. I'm fine," I said. "I just needed to talk with Andrew."

"Cool," he said. "I gotcha. Tuesday morning's your best bet."

"Thanks," I said.

He walked back to his chair near the fire and lifted his vape to his lips. I was surprised at how disappointed I felt as I walked back to my car.

I started driving downtown to the bakery, an old house in the Sugar House area that had been converted to a kitchen and storefront. But, as my building came into sight, I changed my mind. Going in would unleash a multitude of questions and problems I wasn't up to confronting. I turned around and drove home, back to my isolation. At least, this time, I had something to look forward to.

CHAPTER

Fourteen

Did I ask him on a date? I think I did.
                                    —Maggie Walther's Diary

I got up early Tuesday morning thinking of Andrew, which, frankly, was a whole lot better than thinking of Clive or the drama surrounding him. I wondered if Andrew had even given a second thought to our visit. What if he hadn't? *What if he didn't even remember me?* The thought of that made me feel pathetic, but not enough to keep me from walking into the lot.

I spied Andrew almost immediately. He was standing near the east side of the lot, helping a family with two young children who were so bundled up for winter they looked like Easter eggs.

Andrew noticed me and, to my relief, waved me over.

When I got to him he turned from the family, who were still examining a tree. "Don't tell me your tree died already."

"No, it survived the weekend. But I can't get to my lights. You have Christmas lights, don't you?"

"More than you need," he said. "Let me finish up here and I'll help you."

As he went back to the family, I wandered around the

lot looking at the trees, hoping that I wouldn't see one I liked more than the one I had already bought. I was just that way.

Shelby again asked if he could help me. I told him I would wait.

Ten minutes later Andrew found me near the front of the lot. "Thanks again for the coffee the other night."

"Thanks again for bringing my tree," I replied.

"My pleasure," he said. "So, you've decided you need lights after all."

"Mine are buried in my shed. I couldn't get to them."

"Do you know what kind you want?"

"Pretty ones."

He smiled. "I have those. Come with me." I followed him over to the trailer that he used as an office. We stopped in front of an array of lights. "We've got five-millimeter LED lights on green wire, the M-six mini LED lights, the Icicle LED lights, and the C-nine ceramic warm light twinkle bulbs." He stood pleasantly close to me as he pointed out my different options. He smelled like pine and wood shavings.

"Whatever happened to just lights?" I asked.

"We live in a complicated world," he said.

"Which would you buy?"

"Do you know what color you want?"

"Something cheerful."

"Cheerful and pretty." He grabbed a box of lights. "I would recommend our five-millimeter multicolor LED color-morphing lights."

"That sounds exciting," I said.

"Breathtaking," he replied. "More fun than a Christmas tree owner should have. They're constantly changing colors, so with one hundred lights per strand, you never have the same tree twice."

"I'm not sure I could stand that much excitement."

"I'll tell you what. Take them home for a spin. If they're too much of a thrill, bring them back and I'll refund your money, no questions asked."

"Really? No questions?"

"Ne'er a one."

"All right. I'm sold. How many boxes of these miracle lights do I need?"

"The rule of thumb is about a hundred lights for every foot and a half of tree, so yours was six feet, minus the three inches I shorted you, that's about four hundred lights. Four strands."

"How much are they?"

"With the friends and family discount," he said, "just ten dollars a box. They're usually seventeen."

"Thank you," I said, handing him my credit card. "Does that include installation?" The words tumbled out of my mouth.

"No," he said. "That's extra."

"How much this time?"

He smiled, and my heart jumped. "Dinner."

I smiled back. "Dinner. It's a deal."

"Dinner it is." He ran my card and gave me a slip to sign. "When would you like me to come over?"

If I didn't want to look too eager, I completely blew it. "Is tonight too soon?"

"Tonight's good. My schedule is as open as a politician's mouth."

I don't think he had any idea how relevant his simile was to me. "Mine's pretty open too."

"I've got my other guy back, so I can leave a little early."

"What's a little early?"

"Around seven."

"Seven works. Do you like pasta?"

"I'm a quarter Italian. Pasta is my life force." He put the boxes of lights into a sack and stepped out of the trailer. "I'll carry the lights out to your car. They might fit."

"I don't know why everyone gives me grief about my car."

"Because they can." At the car he said, "Do you want them in the back?"

"The passenger seat is fine." I opened the door.

He reached over and set the boxes of lights on the seat, then stepped back. "Great. I'll see you tonight at seven."

"Great," I said back. I hesitated, then said, "Friday night was unexpected. I had a really good time talking to you. It's been a while . . ."

"I was thinking the same thing. I don't have any friends here, really. Just some employees who would rather be playing video games."

I wasn't sure what else to say. "Well, thank you. I'll see you tonight." I climbed inside my car and he shut the door.

"Ciao," he said.

I drove home. It was the happiest I'd felt in months.

CHAPTER

Fifteen

It feels good to be cooking again—figuratively as well as literally.

                                  —Maggie Walther's Diary

I stopped at the grocery store on the way home and bought everything I needed for dinner, then spent the rest of the afternoon cooking. It felt good to be in the kitchen again. Normalcy. I even made a tiramisu for dessert, one of Marge's recipes. I finished cooking around five. I took a quick nap, then freshened up and set the table.

Andrew arrived about five minutes before seven, carrying a brown paper bag. I opened the door as he walked up. "Come in."

"Thank you."

He stepped inside and pulled the bottle from the sack. "I brought some wine. Antinori Marchese. It's a Chianti."

"Thank you," I said. "I can't wait to try it."

"Whatever you're baking, it smells delicious."

"It's mushroom sausage ragù. And *arancini di riso*."

"Arancini di riso?"

"Little oranges. They're deep-fried rice balls full of meat and mozzarella."

"Shall we do the tree first or eat?"

"Definitely eat," I said. "I still need to boil the pasta. I wanted it fresh. In the meantime, I have antipasti."

He followed me back into the kitchen and I offered him a plate of salami, cheeses, and crackers with little pieces of honeycomb. He seemed pleased. "Where did you get this salami?"

"There's a little Italian deli not far from here. Granato's."

"I've driven by that," he said. "I've wanted to stop in but haven't yet. And the honeycomb?"

"The same. The deli owner keeps bees."

"I kept bees once. Like, ten years ago. I thought it might be therapeutic."

"Was it?"

"I learned there's nothing therapeutic about being swarmed by a thousand bees. It's what nightmares are made of."

I laughed. "Why did you think it would be therapeutic?"

"I read an article in the *New Yorker*. Some Madison Avenue executive was extolling the Zen-like experience of beekeeping. I fell for it. One of my employees at the time, Beatrice, had parents who were beekeepers, so she offered to help."

"Her parents kept bees and they named their daughter Beatrice?"

He nodded. "Unfortunately," he said. "I was out of town when my bees came in, so I asked my brother to pick them up without telling him what they were. He called me from the store, panicked. 'You didn't tell me I was getting bees.' I said,

'I know. I figured you might not do it if I told you.' When he tried to get out of it, I told him to quit being such a baby."

"So you shamed your brother into picking up your bees," I said.

"Basically. At least it worked. They came in a little plywood carton about the size of a shoebox. Most of it was screen and you could see the bees in a huge buzzing cluster inside. He was terrified.

"After I got back, Beatrice came over. We dressed up in our bee suits, then she helped me introduce the bees to the hive.

"I was surprised that they were so docile. My ego misread this to believe that I had some special power, like I was a bee whisperer or something. I even got brave enough to take off one of my gloves. Not a single sting. I told Beatrice that I thought the bees knew I meant them no harm and I probably wouldn't even need the suit in the future. She smiled and said, 'You might want to rethink that.'

"I asked her where the queen was, and she pointed to a matchbox-sized box connected to the top of the larger box. The little box was also mostly screen with a cork in one end. I said, 'We let her out last?' She said, 'No; if you let her out now, the bees will kill her. They have to get used to her smell.' Then she pulled out the cork and replaced it with one of those tiny marshmallows. She said, 'By the time she eats her way out, the bees will be used to her smell and accept her as queen.'

"We set the little box inside the hive, covered the hive with a cloth, and left. A week later I came back with my brother. He wanted to watch, but he kept his distance. I had told him how much the bees liked me and that I really didn't need the suit. I lifted the top of the hive and the bees went nuts. They swarmed me. I'm standing there covered with bees and screaming while my brother laughed and recorded it on his phone. He thought it was hilarious. So did the Internet. It went viral. It had like two hundred thousand views."

"Now I have to see that," I said.

"I made him take it down," he said. "I called Beatrice and asked why the change. At first she said, 'They're women, they get moody.' Then she laughed and said, 'When we introduced them to the hive, they didn't have anything to protect. When you went back, they had honeycomb, and babies, and a queen.'"

"So is that why you quit?" I asked.

"Actually, *they* quit me. One day I went out to the hive and they were gone. All five thousand of them. The queen left and took her friends with her. I took it personally. I mean, I introduced them, bought them a home, fed them, and they left me. I told myself it was them, not me."

I laughed. "Of course it was."

"Then after my wife left me, I figured it really was me."

He makes me happy, I thought. I cooked the pasta for a few more minutes, then fished out a noodle with a fork and tried it. "Al dente," I said. "It's ready." I poured the noodles into a colander, then put them in a bowl and brought them over to the table. After I sat down, Andrew opened the wine and poured our glasses.

"What should we toast?" he asked.

"You brought the wine. You decide."

He thought for a moment, then said, "How about loneliness."

"Loneliness?"

"If it wasn't for loneliness, you probably wouldn't have
asked me to stay for coffee."

"Well, if we're taking that route, then we should toast
my Fiat as well. Because if I was driving an SUV, there
would have been no reason for you to come over."

He smiled. "All right, to your Fiat. May it never encounter anything larger than itself."

"Amen," I said.

We clinked our glasses, then savored the wine. It was
delicious, fruity with a hint of chocolate and anise. Perfect
for the meal.

We ate a moment in silence. I'm not sure why, but I suddenly felt shy. I hadn't been on a first date in more than a
decade. *Was* this a first date?

"You're a good cook," he said, breaking the silence. "Of
course you are. You're a professional."

"Thank you."

"Do you like cooking? I mean, it's your business, which
means either you're living your passion or you're sick of it
by now."

"Yes," I said.

He smiled and nodded.

"Do you cook?" I asked.

"Some. Lately I eat out a lot, so this is especially nice."

"Do you always go by Andrew?" I asked. "Or do your
friends call you Andy?"

"Not if they want to remain friends."

I laughed.

"It's helpful, having a name that people want to abbreviate. People used to call my office and try to bypass my secretary by saying they were 'a friend of Andy's.' She'd say, 'If you were really a friend, you'd know he never goes by Andy. Good-bye.'"

"So it was like a secret password."

"Exactly. How about you? Is Maggie your name, or is it an abbreviation of Margaret?"

"Actually, neither," I said. "It's complicated. My real name is Agnetha."

"Agnetha. That sounds Norwegian. Is it a family name?"

"It's Swedish. And no, it's not family. My father was a fan of the Swedish band ABBA. Do you know ABBA?"

He nodded. "Agnetha was the cute blonde."

"My dad had a crush on her, so I got her name. Growing up in Oregon with the name Agnetha didn't work real well, so everyone started calling me Aggie. Then after I moved here, I learned that the Utah State sports teams are called the Aggies. After a year I got tired of being reminded that I shared the name with their blue bull mascot, so I added an M. Like I said, it was complicated."

"I've always thought of names as fluid," he said.

"Really?"

"Absolutely. I think everyone should have at least a couple of aliases."

"Do you?"

He looked at me with a peculiar grin. "Absolutely. So what should I call you?"

"Maggie," I said, glad that he asked the question.

"Maggie it is."

We quietly ate for a while, and then I said, "Do you mind my asking what happened to your marriage?"

"My marriage," he said with a sigh. "I guess she found out that I wasn't as great as she thought."

"She must have had unreasonably high expectations."

"Thank you," he said. "I tried to tell her that. She just wasn't having it."

I laughed. "I'm sorry."

"I should have seen it coming. You should never marry someone who is better-looking than you are. She was a full point and a half ahead of me on the Standard Attraction Scale."

"The Standard Attraction Scale? I didn't know there was such a thing."

"Oh, it's real. It was established by a grant from the Coco Chanel Looks Matter Foundation." I laughed again. He continued. "See, if I were smart, I'd get up and walk out that door right now, because you're at least a point and a quarter above me."

I grinned. "Only a point and a quarter? So you're saying your ex-wife was prettier than I am?"

He grimaced. "Yikes. I walked right into that one. And no, I may have exaggerated her a little."

I smiled at him. "You make me happy."

"At least I'm making someone happy. After she left me,

she married a rich guy who looked like a young George Clooney. She was always looking for the BBD."

"What's the BBD?"

"The bigger, better deal."

"Oh." I took a bite of pasta and followed it with a sip of wine. I thought Clive was my BBD. "For the record, I think you're better-looking than George Clooney."

"Now you've lost all credibility. But thank you for trying to flatter me."

"I'm not flattering. I meant it."

"Thank you," he said. "So what was your ex's Standard Attraction Score?"

"Clive, my ex, was handsome in a Ken doll sort of way, if that's what you're into."

"Is that what you're into?" he asked.

"I thought I was."

"And now?"

I grinned, swirling my wine in its glass. "Maybe clean-cut isn't the way to go."

He looked like he was thinking. "So if he's a Ken doll, what does that make me?"

"You're more like a G.I. Joe. The one with the beard."

"Nice," he said. "I had one of those when I was a boy. A G.I. Joe with lifelike hair. And kung fu grip."

"I've always wanted a man with kung fu grip."

Andrew laughed. "Speaking of martial arts, how long were you married?"

"Nine years. But I should have known it was doomed from our honeymoon."

"Why is that?"

"It was a train wreck. Clive wanted to take me to Taiwan, where he had served a church mission. I personally wanted something more romantic, but he was insistent.

"First, our flight out of San Francisco was canceled, so we ended up sitting in the airport for fourteen hours. Then we got rerouted to Japan, where we got stuck because a typhoon hit. We ended up waiting four days in a hotel in Tokyo, then flew back home because we were out of time and Clive was starting a new job. The fates were against us from the beginning."

"I can beat your honeymoon disaster," he said.

"You can beat a typhoon?"

He nodded. "Oh, yeah. Jamie and I had the worst honeymoon ever. In fact, it's so bad, someone could write a book about it."

"What kind of book?"

"A tragicomedy."

"This sounds interesting. Tell me."

"All right. So, Jamie's dream honeymoon was Bora Bora. You've seen the pictures—perfect Windex-blue water, white sand beaches, thatched huts."

"Which is what I wanted," I interjected.

He smiled. "Right. Well, I went one further and got us a place on a private island. To get there you had to go by boat."

"Sounds dreamy," I said.

"You would think," he replied. "As our boat approached the island, the first thing we saw was a woman standing on the dock wearing pink cowboy boots."

"Cowboy boots?"

"Pink ones. And nothing else."

"Oh, my."

"She was obviously some kind of model. I mean, she looked photoshopped. Then another nude model walked out. It turned out that I had booked the resort at the exact same time that *Playboy* magazine had planned their 'Girls of Bora Bora' issue. They took over the entire island. Every restaurant, every beach, no dress code. No shirts, no shoes, no problem."

"I'll bet you just hated that."

"Think about it," he said. "We're on our *honeymoon*. Jamie kept telling me she felt like chopped meat. So I'm dealing with massive insecurity and trying to pretend that I see nothing. We ended up spending almost all our time in our room, with Jamie looking at herself in the mirror and accusing me of looking at other women. After that, she didn't talk to me for days."

"You're right," I said. "You have the typhoon beat."

He took a drink of wine, then looked back at me. "May I ask you something about your divorce? You don't have to answer."

"I doubt it's something I haven't been asked before."

"I was just wondering if he filed for divorce or you did."

"I did. But it was because of something he did."

"He cheated?"

"I wish it were that simple. He took it to the next level. Are you sure you've never heard of my husband?"

He shook his head. "Clive Walther? I think I would remember that name."

"He didn't just have another woman, he had a whole other family in Colorado."

His brow furrowed. "Where in Colorado?"

"Thornton."

"My Thornton?" I nodded. He thought for a moment, then said, "Wait. He wasn't a politician—"

"He was a city councilman."

Andrew sighed. "I guess I did hear something about that. I'm so sorry."

"It's just so embarrassing."

"It is for him."

"It is for me too. People think I'm either a loser or stupid."

He looked at me quizzically. "What people?"

"You know." I flourished my hand through the air. "Them."

"You mean, the *public*?"

"Yes."

He set his napkin on the table. "You know public opinion is a vapor, right? Today's hero is tomorrow's loser and vice versa. And those who are shouting the loudest are usually those living the most desperate lives. They're just glad that someone came along who is having a worse week than they are.

"Second, the public has the attention span of a goldfish. I know what happened must seem like the end of the world to you, but that's because you're in the path of the storm. Trust me, they've already moved on to the next drama."

Oddly, it was the most comforting thing anyone had said to me yet. "I hope you're right."

He looked at me seriously. "I know I'm right. I've been there."

"You've been in the middle of a public scandal?"

He hesitated for a moment, then said, "Yes. But it was business-related, not family. I'm sorry that you had to share your heartbreak in the media. I think they forget that there are real people involved."

"Forget, or don't care?" I said.

"Maybe both," he said. "I'm sorry."

"This will pass," I said. "At least, that's what I keep telling myself."

Andrew frowned. "I'm sorry I brought it up. I'd like you to think of me as someone who makes you happy."

"You do make me happy."

"Good. No more talk of drama."

"I can do that," I replied.

We went back to eating. When he finished his pasta, he asked for more, which made me glad. As he was finishing I said, "I made tiramisu for dessert."

"I love tiramisu," he said.

"Good, because I made a whole pan, and I'm sending the leftovers home with you."

I got up and took our plates to the counter, cut us two rectangles of tiramisu, and brought them over to the table. He took a bite and said, "Perfect."

"Do you know what *tiramisu* means?"

"No idea."

"In Italian, *tira* means to lift or pick up, *mi* means me, and *su* means up. So it literally is a pick-me-up."

"Because of all the espresso in it."

"Exactly," I said. "The magic of caffeine."

"Now that I have all this caffeine in me," he said, "should we do the dishes?"

"I can handle them," I said.

"I know you can handle them, but should we do the dishes?"

"You're sure you have time?"

"I've got nothing but time."

"All right," I said, "you can help. You wash, I'll dry and put them away."

Andrew began clearing the table while I filled the sink with hot water. As I handed him a dish, he looked at my left hand. "Why are you still wearing your wedding ring?"

I shrugged. "I just never took it off." I glanced down at my ring, a simple white-gold band with a half-carat marquise diamond. "Maybe it's the same reason people wear cloves of garlic around their necks."

"Who wears cloves of garlic around their necks?"

"People who are afraid of vampires."

"Are you comparing men to vampires?"

"Some are," I said. "I've even met a few female vampires."

"I bet you have."

"The way I see it, everyone has good and bad in them. Some just have more of one than the other." I looked at him. "Unless they're bloodsucking vampires."

He nodded. "Unless they're bloodsucking vampires."

We both laughed. Then I looked into his eyes. "Are you a vampire?"

He met my gaze. "A real vampire would never answer that question in the affirmative. What do you think?"

I shook my head. "I think . . . you're sweet."

To my surprise, his mouth twisted in disappointment. "Sweet. Like a girlfriend is sweet?"

"There's nothing girlfriend about you," I said. As I looked at him I suddenly wanted him to kiss me. I hoped he was thinking the same. He smiled at me, handed me a plate, and said, "Last one. How about I finish drying and you put things away?"

I breathed out slowly. "It's a plan."

We finished up in the kitchen and went out to decorate the Christmas tree.

I said, "We put the lights on first?"

"Yes, but first we make sure the lights work."

"Good idea. The guy who sold them to me was kind of sketchy."

He grinned. "Yeah. I've never trusted drifters who work at Christmas tree lots."

He laid out the boxes, opened them, then carefully laid out the strands in neat rows. "Do you have an extension cord?"

"Yes. I'll get it."

"Maybe we should have some Christmas music. Set the mood."

"I can get that too." I walked down the hall to the closet and grabbed the extension cord. Then I found some instrumental Christmas music on my iPod and plugged it into my stereo in the kitchen. The comforting sound of music filled the house. I went back into the front room. The strands were all connected and laid out in order. I handed him the cord.

"Thank you." He plugged in the lights, and they flashed on. I had forgotten that they changed colors. "They work."

"They're pretty."

"That's what you asked for." He starting disconnecting the lights from each other.

"Why are you doing that?"

"Because they're easier to install if you break the tree up into quadrants."

"Do you start from the top or the bottom?"

"Always the top. Because if you get to the top and you have an extra yard of lights, what do you do?"

"You just wrap them around again."

He shook his head. "You are such a novice."

After we had wrapped the lights around the tree, he walked to the center of the room and looked at the tree, squinting.

"What are you doing?" I asked.

"I'm looking for dark holes."

"Why are you squinting?"

"That's the best way to find dark holes."

"You are hard-core," I said.

"No, I'm a professional."

It was after midnight when we finished decorating the tree. Then we sat down on the couch to admire our creation.

"There's something peaceful about a Christmas tree," I said. "When I was little, I would just lay there and look at the tree until I fell asleep in front of it."

He nodded slowly. "What was your childhood like?"

I groaned a little.

"It was bad?"

"Yeah. My father was interesting."

"Interesting unique, or interesting a living hell?"

"The latter, mostly. But he was definitely unique."

"Were you raised in Utah?"

"No. I'm from southern Oregon. A town called Ashland. You probably haven't heard of it."

"I've been there," he said.

"You've been to Ashland?"

"About six years ago I went with my brother to the Shakespeare Festival."

"Ashland's famous for that."

"What did your father do?"

"Pretty much everything. He was a jack-of-all-trades. He came to Oregon when he was nineteen to work in a lumber yard. He ended up owning a lot of land. More than six hundred acres. That was back when it was cheap and before the Californians started moving in," I said, imitating his drawl.

"Is your father still alive?"

"Yes."

"Do you see much of him?"

"I haven't seen him since my wedding. I was surprised that he even came to that."

"What about your mother?"

"She was wonderful. At least what I remember of her. She died when I was fourteen."

"I'm sorry," he said. "Did your father ever remarry?"

"About six years ago. He married a woman a few years younger than me. He made it a point to tell me that he redid his will so everything goes to her when he dies. He owns several millions of dollars' worth of land."

"So he's wealthy?"

"You wouldn't know it. He still lives in the log cabin he built forty years ago."

"He lives in a log cabin?"

"Well, it's not, like, Abraham Lincoln's place. It has plumbing, a Jacuzzi tub and sauna. It's almost three thousand square feet."

"Will he ever sell his land?"

"Not while he's living. It's his refuge. He's a . . . what's the word? Prepper? He has his own well, a shed full of dynamite, and an arsenal. He even makes his own shotgun shells." I groaned again. "He hates the world. And he hates that they're encroaching on him. Especially the environmentalists.

"Once he was clearing some trees on his property and his environmentalist neighbors called the police on him. As soon as the officer left, my father grabbed me and stomped over to their house. My dad's a big man, about six-foot-three, with an even bigger temper.

"In the old days he would have just called out the man—or dragged him out of his house—and beaten him up. But times have changed, and my father's smart enough to know it. He knew his neighbors would sue him, so he used a different strategy.

"He pounded so hard on the door that it shook. When the people came, they only opened the door enough to peer out. I remember how terrified they looked. They asked my dad what he wanted. He calmly said to them, 'You know, you live downwind of me. That eastern ocean wind flows down the mountain slopes like a rushing river.'

"The man said, 'How poetic. What's your point?'

"My father said, 'The next time you meddle in my affairs, I'm going to build a pig farm on the border of our property. Just right there, not twenty yards from your house. You snowflakes ever been to a pig farm?' The woman started making some clueless comment about being vegan and the horrors of the pig-slaughtering industry, and my father said, 'The smell carries for more than a mile, two on a windy day. In the summer it's so dank, you can taste the stink. Just twenty yards away, you're going to think you're living in a pigsty. Your food will taste like pig dung. That's not to mention the flies. The infestation will be biblical. Then I'll slaughter the pigs myself and leave them hanging on meat hooks by your fence. You won't be able to live here and you won't be able to sell your house. Hell, you won't be able to give it away.'

"The man said, 'You can't do that.' My father replied, 'Check the zoning, sweetie.' Then his wife said, 'You wouldn't dare.' My father laughed and said, 'Just try me, you liberal morons. Just try me.' Not surprisingly, they never called the police on him again."

"He sounds like an interesting man," Andrew said. "I'd like to meet him."

"No you wouldn't."

"But he was pretty shrewd."

"He could take care of himself. That's what he was best at." I frowned. "Sometimes I'm glad my mother died young so she didn't have to spend her life with him."

"How old were you when you left home?"

"Eighteen. I was waitressing and a driver told me about Utah. It sounded nice, so I moved here."

"Are you an only child?"

"No. I have a little brother. He's in Alaska working on an offshore oil rig."

"Do you see much of him?"

"No. Maybe every few years. He left five years after my mom died. I don't blame him. My father had registered him for the army so he could steal his girlfriend."

"Your father stole his own son's girlfriend?"

"He tried. That's how he was. After my mother died, he started dating girls from my high school. I'd be walking home from cheerleading and I'd see him drive by in his Porsche with one of my classmates. If it wasn't such a small town, he probably would have been in jail."

Andrew shook his head. "That's horrific."

"So that's how I ended up in Utah. I came here to go to

school, met the owner of a catering business, and ended up owning it."

"You've done well."

"The business does well. Not that I'm much help these days."

"So who runs it?"

"One of my employees. Actually, she's more of a friend than an employee. Her name's Carina. She's worked for me for over five years. When everything came down with Clive, I melted down, and she stepped in and took over. She's overwhelmed, but she doesn't complain." I suddenly yawned. "Sorry."

"It's late," he said.

"I'm okay," I said quickly. "You're the one with a job." I looked into his eyes. "Are you tired?"

"A little. But I don't want to go just yet."

This made me smile. I continued the conversation. "Are your parents still alive?"

"No. My parents died in a car accident when I was young. So my brother and I were raised by my aunt and uncle. They couldn't have children, so they adopted us."

"Are you close to your brother?"

"Very. Not physically, though. He's still in Colorado."

"How often do you see him?"

"Every chance I get."

I yawned again. Then Andrew yawned. We both laughed.

"I'll go," he said.

"All right."

He stood first, then reached down and helped me up from the couch. We walked to the door. "Thank you for dinner. And the conversation. It was delicious."

"Thank you for coming," I said.

He hesitated a moment, then said, "Can I be a little vulnerable with you?"

"Yes."

"After my divorce I told myself that I wouldn't get involved with anyone. But being with you has been nice." He looked vulnerable. Vulnerable and beautiful.

"I know what you mean. I thought it would be a cold day in hell before I spent time with a man."

He grinned. "It's been pretty cold."

"And I've been living in hell," I said. "So I guess it was time." We both smiled. "I guess I didn't realize how lonely I was." I looked into his eyes. "I needed someone kind in my life these days. This is unexpected and welcome."

"If it's okay with you, I'd like to see more of you."

"It's okay with me."

He touched my hair, gently brushing it back from my face. "Can I see you tomorrow?"

"I'd like that."

"What time?"

"Any time. All day if you like."

His smile broadened. "I'd love to, but I'm short on workers tomorrow. What if I came around five and took you to dinner?"

"That sounds nice."

"Do you like sushi?"

"Yes."

"I found a little place up on the Bench. Kobe." He just stood there. Then he leaned forward and lightly kissed me on the lips. I closed my eyes and drank it in. He straightened up. "Good night."

I touched his cheek longingly, then leaned forward and kissed him back. "Good night, Andrew."

He smiled, then turned and walked out the door. I watched him get into his truck, waved, then went inside. It was past two. In spite of the hour, it was the most awake I'd felt in months.

CHAPTER

Sixteen

*I saw Clive today. He asked something big of me.
(Bigamy. Yeah, I see it. Not funny.) I told him no,
but I felt so sorry for him that I could see myself
caving. Sometimes I don't know if I'm an angel or a
doormat.*

—*Maggie Walther's Diary*

I woke the next morning in a pleasant haze. Happiness. I hardly recognized it. It had been too long since I'd felt that way. My blissful state was interrupted by the phone.

"Did I wake you?" Carina asked.

"No, I was up. How was the party last night?" I'm sure the question surprised her. It was the first time I'd asked about work in weeks.

"It was crazy. They had double the number of guests than had RSVPed."

"They should know that no one in Utah RSVPs. What did you do?"

"Fortunately, we had three sheets of lemon bars and two sheets of éclairs for tonight's event. So we used them. The girls are at the house baking right now."

"I'm sorry I've just dropped this on you."

"Baptism by fire," she said. "It reminds me of how my dad taught me to swim by throwing me into the deep end of the pool."

"Sorry," I said again. "That wasn't my intent."

"I know," she said. She changed the subject. "I came by last night."

"Why didn't you come in?"

"Because there was a truck in the driveway."

"What time did you come by?"

"Around one thirty."

"Why were you driving by my house at one thirty?"

"Because I'm worried about you. I hate that you're all alone. But then I guess you're not."

"I had someone over."

"Who?"

"A guy I just met a few days ago."

"Does he have a name?"

"Andrew."

"You met him after we had coffee?"

"Yes."

"Where did you meet him?"

"Why do I feel like you're interrogating me?"

"Because I am."

"Fair enough. I met him while I was buying a Christmas tree—which, by the way, was your idea."

"Don't blame me . . ."

"I'm not blaming you, I'm giving you credit."

"When I said to change your environment, I meant get a tree, not the guy selling it."

"I thought you'd be happy I wasn't alone. Isn't that what you just said? You hated that I was alone?"

"I do," she said. "It's just that you've only been divorced a few months. You're vulnerable. Just three days ago you were swearing off men, and just like that you have a love interest?"

"I didn't say he was a love interest."

"He was at your house at one thirty."

"Actually, he was there until two," I said.

"Exactly. You're vulnerable. I don't want to see you taken advantage of. How well do you know this guy?"

"I know that he's kind. He's funny, in a subtle way, and he's a great conversationalist."

"How long has he been unemployed?"

"He's *not* unemployed."

"For the *moment*. He works at a Christmas tree lot. Seasonal work. How long was he unemployed before that?"

"He *owns* the Christmas tree lot," I said. "He's an entrepreneur."

"That's a French word for *slacker*."

"I'm an entrepreneur," I said. "He's not a slacker."

"Then why is he single?"

"I'm single, you're single; why would you ask that?"

"Because you and I are nuptial victims."

"So is he. He's divorced."

"How long?"

"I don't know. A few years."

"Where is he from?"

"Colorado. He's been in Utah just a few months. He

used to be a financial adviser in Denver. And he's gorgeous."

"Gorgeous?"

"Like, beautiful."

"Now we get to the core of the problem," she said. "Blinded by the hunk."

"I'm done with this conversation," I said.

"Just remember, honey. The nicer the package, the cheaper the gift."

"I am definitely done with this conversation."

"Love you, sweetie."

"Love you too. Have a good day."

In spite of my conversation with Carina, I felt happy all day in anticipation of seeing Andrew again. I didn't disagree with Carina that things were moving fast, warp speed, but after wandering through a desert, when you find water, you don't sip it.

I put on my favorite outfit, something I hadn't worn since before D-Day (Divorce Day). I also spent extra time on my makeup, even plucking my eyebrows, which shows I was motivated.

The clock moved slowly. At a quarter to five my doorbell rang, and my heart jumped a little. I was glad he was early. I quickly opened the door. Clive stood in the doorway.

"Sorry, I left my house key at the police station," he said. "You would think they'd make it a point to return your property."

"Otherwise you would have just walked in?" I asked. Clive didn't respond. "What are you doing here?"

"I need to talk with you."

"About what?"

"It's important."

"*Important?* Like our marriage wasn't?"

"Maggie, don't do this."

I shook my head as I stepped back from the door. "You have ten minutes. I need to be someplace."

"Where?"

"That's not any of your business. And the clock is ticking."

"I don't believe you're timing me." He walked past me to the kitchen. I followed him in as he opened the refrigerator. "Do you have anything to eat?"

"You have nine minutes. What do you want, Clive?"

He grabbed a pear out of the refrigerator, then sat down at the table, gesturing to a seat next to him. I leaned against the counter. "What is it, Clive?"

"I have a court date." He took a bite of the pear. "December fourteenth."

"Congratulations," I said sardonically. "And this has what to do with me?"

"I want you there. By my side."

"You want me to come to court with you?"

He took another bite. "Yes. To show support."

"Why would I do that?"

"To show the jury that I'm not such a bad guy."

"But you are."

"Am I? Wasn't I good to you? Weren't we happy?"

"I thought we were."

"If you think you're happy, you are." He looked at me. "Come on, Maggie. Just this one thing. It's important."

"Why don't you get your other wife to do it? I'm sure she'd be happy to take my place."

"For the record, Jennifer didn't know about you either," he said. "Look, I know I made a mistake."

"A mistake? Taking the wrong exit is a mistake. Taking a second wife is a bit more deliberate."

"Yes, I'm a broken man. I'm a sinner. Is that what you want to hear?"

"I want to hear you leaving my house."

He shook his head. "You mean, the house I bought?"

"The house *we* bought," I said.

He just looked at me. "You know, you used to be nice. You've changed."

"I wonder why."

He was quiet a moment, then said, "Maggie, I really need your help. I could end up in prison. Do this, and I'll make it up to you somehow."

"How?"

"I don't know. What do you want?"

"I want you to leave me out of this."

He sighed. "Mag, how does my going to jail serve the greater good? I know you're angry, but you still have a good heart. You don't want to be responsible for me going to jail."

"Now I'm responsible?" I groaned. "This is just like you, Clive. You're a master at turning things around. That's why you were such a good lawyer."

"Is that a compliment?"

I shook my head. Just then the doorbell rang.

"Expecting someone?" he asked.

"I have a date."

"A date?" He stood, taking his pear. "That didn't take long."

"You need to go."

He just looked at me, then said, "Think about it."

"I don't need to."

"Since when did you become so heartless?"

"If I were heartless, Clive, my heart wouldn't hurt so much."

"I never meant to hurt you."

"Well, you sure didn't mean *not* to."

He threw his hands up in mock surrender. "You're right. You're absolutely right. I never deserved you." He walked to the door, then turned back. "Just because I loved someone else doesn't mean that I ever stopped loving you. I didn't. I still love you. I never wanted the divorce. You know that."

"You had to divorce one of us."

"I don't know why I needed something more. It's something broken in me. I'm getting therapy."

There was a knock on the door.

"You need to leave, Clive."

He breathed out deeply. "Okay. I'll go."

I opened the door. Andrew stood in the doorway. The two men looked at each other.

"Be good to her," Clive said.

"I intend to," Andrew replied.

Clive turned back to me. "Think about it, Mag." He furtively glanced at Andrew, then walked past him to his car. He was driving a new Audi with the paper dealer plates still in the window.

I turned to Andrew. "I'm sorry. Come in."

Andrew stepped inside. "Clive?"

"In the flesh."

Andrew shut the door behind himself. "Are you okay?"

I wasn't sure how to answer. It had been such a shock seeing him. "I'm fine."

He just looked at me. "Are you sure?"

I began to tear up. I quickly brushed a tear from my cheek. "I don't know if I'm okay." The tears began to fall.

Andrew took my hand. "Come here." He led me over to the couch. We sat down next to each other, our knees touching. He looked into my face. "What did he want?"

"He . . ." I couldn't speak. I just started crying harder. Andrew put his arm around me and pulled me into him. I laid my face on his shoulder and sobbed. For nearly five minutes he just held me, gently running his hand over my back, saying softly, "You're going to be okay."

When I had gained some composure, I looked up into his face. "He wants me to be with him at his trial."

"Why would he ask that?"

"He thinks it will help with the jury."

"I'm sure it will. But why would he think he could ask that of you?"

"Because he knows I will. I always give in to him."

"You don't need to." He looked into my face. "Do you still love him?"

I swallowed. "I don't know. We were married nine years. Is it wrong if part of me still does?"

Andrew slowly shook his head. "There's nothing wrong with that. You're loyal, even if he wasn't. Just don't let him use that against you."

Why is he so kind to me? "Thank you."

He said tenderly, "I worry about you."

"I'm glad you worry about me."

He touched my face softly, stroking my cheek with the back of his hand. "You'll get through this. I promise. I'll help you."

I looked deeply into his eyes. "Will you?"

He nodded. "Yes." His face moved closer to mine, his eyes both wild and soft. I moved forward to meet him, our lips pressing together.

It was bliss, his soft lips and hard, whiskered face against my face. His love felt so sweet. I just wanted to bury all my pain in him. I wanted to escape in him. For the next several hours, I did just that. I couldn't believe what I'd done. I'd fallen in love.

CHAPTER

Seventeen

Andrew invited me on a trip to Mexico. It's just a
trip. Right? It's just a trip. Right.
                                    —*Maggie Walther's Diary*

I slept in the next morning. I woke hungry for a change.
Andrew and I had never gone out to dinner. Instead we had
talked until early in the morning. Actually, we had talked
and kissed.

My phone vibrated with a text. I rolled over and
grabbed it, hoping it was from him. It was. I had also
missed a phone call from Carina twenty minutes earlier.

ANDREW

Good morning, beautiful.

I texted back.

MAGGIE

Good morning, handsome. Just woke.

Someone kept me up late.

ANDREW

Who kept you up? Lol.

I thought you might sleep in. I have coffee/muffin
for you. Should I bring them?

MAGGIE

Bring you, please.

ANDREW

On my way.

I lay back in bed. My heart was so full of joy. How long
had it been since I'd felt such elation? Ten minutes later
my phone vibrated.

ANDREW

I'm at the door.

I pulled on a robe, walked out to the foyer, and opened
the door. Andrew was holding a cardboard coffee carrier
and a white bakery sack.

"Good morning, beautiful," he said. "May I come in?"

"Anytime," I said.

He stamped off his feet and stepped inside. We kissed, then he said, "Kitchen?"

"Yes, please."

I followed him. He set my coffee on the table along with the paper sack. "I brought muffins. I hope you like muffins."

"How did you know I was hungry?"

"We never went out to eat last night. I kind of felt bad about that."

"Did you hear me complaining?"

He smiled. "Honestly, I didn't feel too bad." He grabbed the sack. "I wasn't sure what kind of muffins you like, so I got almost every kind they had. Banana nut, oatmeal walnut, blueberry, and cinnamon apple. You don't have to eat them all."

"I'll restrain myself. I'll have the apple."

"It's yours," he said, handing me a muffin. "I'll have the blueberry."

We both sat down at the table. "What a nice surprise," I said. "It's almost breakfast in bed."

"That could be arranged," he said.

"So I was thinking, I could make dinner for us tonight. There's this Japanese roast chicken recipe I found. Does that sound good?"

His expression fell. "I can't tonight. I have to leave town."

My heart fell. "Oh. For long?"

"No, just the weekend. I've got to drive to Denver."

"Would you like some company? I don't have any plans."

"Not this time," he said. He must have read the disappointment on my face, because he added, "Maybe next time."

My offer had clearly surprised him. "Is there a next time?"

"I go every week. I have family there that I'm taking care of." He hesitated. "I'm really sorry. It's been this way since I came to Utah. It should only be a few more weeks."

"It's okay. You don't owe me anything."

"It's not about owing. I want to be with you." He just sat there looking at me. Reading me. "You still look upset."

"I'm sorry. I was just really looking forward to being with you. Last night was so . . ." I didn't finish.

"Amazing," he said. "I'm so sorry. But it's just a day. I'll be back by Saturday night. Then I'll be around for the week."

I think I probably still seemed upset, because he looked at me for a moment, then stood. "Come here."

"Where?"

He put out his hand. "Back to the couch."

"You sound like a psychiatrist."

"Exactly."

I stood and took his hand and we walked back out to the living room. We sat down next to each other on the couch. I draped my arms around him and we kissed. After we parted he said, "Where were we?"

"I was saying that I was looking forward to being with you. I couldn't tell you the last time I was that happy."

"And now I'm depriving you of it."

"Basically," I said, kissing him. We kissed for a couple of minutes, then I said, "You really want to go? And leave me?"

"No, I don't want to leave you. But I have to." He looked into my eyes. "Don't be blue."

"I'm always blue this time of the year. Why is that?" I said.

"I have no idea."

"You're not much of a psychiatrist."

"No. I'd be horrible at it. Why do you think you're blue this time of year?"

"I think I have that seasonal affect thing."

"SAD," he said. "Seasonal affective disease."

I laughed. "It's *disorder*, not *disease*."

"You're the one who called it a 'thing.'" He was quiet a moment, then said, "I have a solution, if you're interested."

"You have a solution for my SAD?"

"I do. It's called Los Cabos."

"Cabos? As in Mexico?"

He nodded. "A friend of mine has a condo there. There's no shortage of sun. We should go."

I leaned back to look at him. "Are you serious?"

"Yes. Have you ever been to Cabo San Lucas?"

"No. But I've seen pictures."

"This is the ideal time of the year to go. The weather is perfect and the condo has a perfect view of the ocean."

"You really are serious."

"I am. Is there a problem with that?"

"I barely know you."

"That's true for both of us. Which is why we'll have separate rooms."

"What about your Christmas tree lot?"

"It's November. Sheldon can run it."

"I thought his name was Shelby."

"Whatever," he said.

I laughed. "I can't believe you're serious." My mind reeled at the proposition. "I don't know."

"You said you could use some sun. And I'm betting you could use time out of Utah."

"Both true."

"So why not just say yes?"

"It's just so . . ."

"Spontaneous?"

"Yes. Pisces are not very spontaneous."

"But Pisces are fish and Cabo is on the sea, so it's kind of a natural."

"When would we go?"

"Let me check the flights." He looked at his phone. After some scrolling he said, "There's a direct flight from Salt Lake to Los Cabos Sunday morning."

"You mean Sunday, as in three days from now?"

He nodded. "I'll be back Saturday night. We could stay until Friday morning; that would give us six days."

I thought for a moment. "Wait—it's Thanksgiving that week."

His brow furrowed. "You have plans?"

"Just with Carina. And her parents."

He looked disappointed. "It was a nice thought."

"I could cancel," I said.

"I don't want to get you in trouble with your friend." He smiled. "Or, actually, I do."

"She'll understand. I already felt like a charity case. What about you? Don't you have plans?"

"No, it's just me. I usually spend Thanksgiving in Cabo. Spending Thanksgiving with you would be even better."

I wanted to go more than I could say. "It would be wonderful."

"So?"

"Let's do it," I blurted out.

He glanced down at his phone, then at me. "I'm going to book it. Are you sure?"

I took a deep breath. "Yes."

"And you have a passport?"

"Yes."

He smiled. "Good." He typed into his smartphone and looked up at me. "Done. We're going to Cabo."

"I can't believe I'm doing this. What do I bring? Besides my passport?"

"Just your clothes. Nothing you would wear in Utah right now. Swimsuit, nightwear, sunglasses. The condo has everything we need."

"And you're sure the condo's available?"

He smiled. "Positive."

CHAPTER

Eighteen

Carina's not happy about my impending trip. You would think that I had booked a seat on the Titanic.
—Maggie Walther's Diary

"What are you doing, girl?" I said to myself as Andrew drove away. I pulled up the weather app on my phone and typed in Los Cabos. It was sunny with a high of ninety-six degrees. *I know exactly what I'm doing. I'm going to Cabo San Lucas with a complete stranger I've fallen in love with.* A smile crossed my face. I was going to Cabo with a gorgeous stranger. It was the first time that I had something to look forward to in a long, long time.

I couldn't wait to tell someone, which, of course, meant Carina. I sat on the bed and called her. "Hi, doll."

She hesitated. "Maggie?"

"Yes?"

"Wow, I wasn't sure it was you. I haven't heard you this cheery since you found out that dark chocolate is good for you."

"Andrew just invited me to Cabo."

"The Christmas tree salesman?"

"The Christmas tree salesman," I said. "His friend has a

condo on the beach and he said we can use it. I checked the weather. It's like ninety-five degrees there today."

"You think that's a good idea?"

"I'll wear sunscreen."

"I meant going to Cabo with a stranger."

"He's not a stranger."

"Uh, he is, Maggie. You've known him like, a week?"

"Eight days," I said. "I'd known you for less than twenty minutes when I hired you. I'm not worried."

"Which is why I am."

"He's a gentleman, Carina. He assured me we'll be staying in separate rooms."

"What do you expect him to say? How do you know he's not dangerous? Mysterious past, just moved to town. A drifter working in a Christmas tree lot—"

"I'm going to pretend that you didn't just say that. He's not a drifter, Carina. He owns the Christmas tree lot. He's contracted with the store."

"Yeah, well, for all you know, he could be a serial killer."

"Now you're being crazy. Besides, he's too sweet."

"Serial killers are always sweet. It's how they lure their victims in."

"Now you're scaring me. Why can't you be happy for me? Last week you were complaining that I was isolating. Now I've found someone and you're unhappy about that."

"That's because it was just last week, Maggie. You don't really know this guy. It's too soon. I just don't want to see your heart getting broken again. You're so vulnerable right now. You're just way too trusting."

"I've never been too trusting."

"Your husband had another family."

I didn't answer. It stung.

"I'm sorry. I shouldn't have said that. I just mean, why don't you spend a little more time getting to know the guy before you run off to another country?"

"Because I like him. Besides, we've already bought the plane tickets."

"Whoa," she said. "You're really doing this. When are you going?"

"Sunday."

"Sunday? When are you coming back?"

I felt a little embarrassed. "We're coming back Friday."

"You're blowing me off for Thanksgiving?"

"I'm sorry. I felt like an imposition."

"Which you're not." She sighed. "All right. I guess I can forgive you. Just don't let him hold your passport. And I want to know the address of this condo."

"I'm telling myself that your paranoia is misguided love."

"It is love. And I want info in case you don't come back."

"If I don't come back," I said, "don't come looking for me."

CHAPTER

Nineteen

Today the Stephenses returned from burying
their son. How brightly some people shine in the
darkness of adversity.

—Maggie Walther's Diary

Saturday it was snowing again. Andrew called to make sure that I was okay, but, I think mostly to make sure that I hadn't backed out of our trip.

"Nope, you're stuck with me," I said. "Are you in Denver?"

"Yes. Just clearing out of my hotel."

"You don't stay with your family?"

He hesitated. "No, that wouldn't quite work."

"How long does it take to drive to Denver?"

"Driving the legal limit or my limit?"

"Your limit. If you have one."

"A little over seven hours."

"What time will you be home tonight?"

"That depends on the roads. Apparently there's a whiteout right now in Rock Springs. But the roads should be clear by the time I get there."

"It's snowing here too," I said. "You didn't stay very long."

"No. I've only got a small window to visit."

"What do you mean?" I asked.

"It's complicated," he said.

It snowed all day Saturday, which made me even more excited to go to Cabo. It also made me worry about Andrew's drive. I checked the weather in Rock Springs. It looked bad. I was hoping he would make it home in time to come over, but now I was worried he might not make it back at all. At best, he would make it home at two or three in the morning.

The day dragged on. One good thing: I went downstairs and ran on my treadmill. Outside of shoveling snow, I hadn't exercised for weeks. It felt good, though I was amazed at how quickly I was tired.

Around two, my neighbors, the Stephenses, came home. I saw them get out of their car and hold each other as they walked into their house. My heart hurt for them. I put down my book and went to the kitchen and baked them some more cookies. This time I made gingerbread cookies. They were still warm when I walked them over.

Mrs. Stephens answered the door. She recognized me. "How are you, dear?" she asked.

"I'm well," I said. "Thank you. I brought you some cookies."

She glanced at the plate I held. "But you already brought us some. They were a welcome treat to come home to."

"I wanted you to have fresh ones," I said. The truth

was, I was afraid that her sister had already eaten them all. "Your sister told me about your son. I'm very sorry."

She looked at me with gray, mournful eyes. "Thank you. He was our only son. A parent shouldn't have to outlive their child."

"I'm very sorry."

"We're grateful that we have the grandchildren. They're going to be moving in with us."

"It's good they have you," I said.

"It's good we have them," she replied. "Our son lives through them." We were both quiet a moment, then she asked, "And how are you doing?"

"I'm doing better. Your coming to help me made a big difference. I was having trouble getting out of the house."

"Well, with all this snow, it's hard for everyone to get out. We've had a lot of snow this year," she said. "I heard on the news it's one of the snowiest winters of the decade."

"I didn't mean the snow," I said. "I just didn't want to go out."

She looked at me thoughtfully, then said, "We were glad to help. If you ever need anything, just call."

"Thank you for being a good neighbor," I said. "Even when I haven't been one."

"You've been busy," she said kindly. "You're at a busy time of life."

"I suppose so."

"Have a nice Thanksgiving," she said. "And thank you again for the cookies. They look exquisite. Bryan will be delighted."

"My pleasure," I said.

I walked back home thinking I would like to be more like her.

I called Andrew around midnight to see if he'd made it back to Salt Lake. Far from it. He told me that the roads had been worse than anticipated and he had just passed Rock Springs, so he wouldn't be home until well past three. He said he'd still be at my house by ten. I told him to be careful.

I woke the next morning feeling anxious. Was it too soon? They say if you really want to get to know someone, you should travel with them. What if Carina was right and he was nothing like I thought he was? What if we didn't get along? I'd be stuck there with him and my flattened heart.

I pushed my worries from my mind. *It's just a trip*, I told myself. And, worst case, at least I'd be out of Utah and the cold. I should have left town long before then.

Anxious or not, I was happy to be leaving town.

CHAPTER

Twenty

They say that if you want to get to know someone,
travel with them. Do I really want to know him
that well?

                                    —Maggie Walther's Diary

Andrew pulled up to the house a few minutes before ten o'clock. I was sitting in the front room waiting for him. He got out of his truck wearing only a light denim jacket. I put on my ski parka, turned off the lights, and opened the door as he walked up to my porch.

"You're not going to need that coat in Cabo," he said. We kissed.

"I better not," I replied. "It's supposed to be in the nineties."

"I'm ready for it," he said. He opened his jacket. He had on a colorful Hawaiian shirt.

I locked my door. "I'll be ditching the coat the second we're on the plane."

Andrew grabbed my bag and we walked down to his truck. He opened the door for me, put our suitcases in the back seat, and walked around and got in.

Even with slushy roads, the drive to the airport took only a half hour. We parked in the long-term parking lot and Andrew carried both of our bags to the nearest shuttle stop.

There was one other person at the station—a man standing on the west side of the structure talking on his cell phone. He wore a herringbone peacoat, a long wool scarf wrapped around his neck, and one of those faux fur hats with flaps that fall down over the ears and ties under the chin. His nose was nearly as red as his scarf, and between talking he kept sneezing into a ratty tissue. I felt bad for him. I also kept my distance. I didn't want to get sick on my trip.

We had only been waiting for a few minutes when the shuttle arrived. Andrew grabbed both of our bags and carried them over. The shuttle bus was less than a quarter full, and there were two seats together near the back.

"You're quiet," he said, after we'd sat.

"I'm a little nervous," I said. "But I'm excited."

"When was the last time you took a vacation?"

"Like a real vacation, out of Utah?" I had to think. "About three and a half years ago. Clive went to New Orleans on business and I went with him."

"I love New Orleans," he said. "Best food in the world."

"I wouldn't know; I only had room service. I never left the hotel."

The shuttle dropped us off at the second terminal. The airport was slammed with pre-Thanksgiving traffic. We walked past most of the travelers to the priority access.

"I'll need your passport," Andrew said as we waited for an agent. I fished it out of my purse and handed it to him.

A few minutes later we checked our luggage and got our boarding passes. As Andrew turned from the counter, he said, "If you want, I can keep your passport with mine."

I remembered Carina's paranoid comment about holding my own passport and felt a wave of annoyance. "Thank you. I'd like that."

We still had an hour, so after passing through security, we stopped for coffee, then made our way to the D terminal. When we got to our gate, there was already a large crowd gathered around the entrance to the Jetway. We had been there for only a few minutes when the flight attendant called for boarding for those with premium seating.

"That's us," Andrew said.

"We're in first class?"

He handed me my boarding pass. "Life is too short for economy. You deserve a little pampering." Then he added, "Maybe a lot."

"I don't know if I deserve it, but I like it."

"You deserve it," he said.

I shed my jacket as we walked down the Jetway.

"Would you like the window or aisle?"

"I don't care."

"I'll let you take the window so you get a good view of Cabo."

The plane was crowded, but I wasn't. The only other time in my life that I had flown first class was seven years ago when Clive was meeting with a client in Pittsburgh, and since it was over a holiday, his client had offered to buy me a ticket as well.

"Did this cost a fortune?" I asked.

"About fifty Christmas trees. But you're worth it."

I settled back in the wide leather chair. "I like the way this trip is starting out."

"Good. It's just the prologue."

I took out my phone. "Here's something else I won't need." I shut it off. "I'm truly unplugged."

A minute later a flight attendant came by to ask if I wanted anything to drink. I ordered a cranberry juice with 7Up, then looked out the window. The snow was still falling and the plane's window was covered with slush.

"We'll probably have to deice the plane," Andrew said.

"How long does that take?"

"It depends on how many planes are ahead of us. Probably about fifteen minutes."

Andrew was right. The plane needed to be deiced. The process sounded like we were going through a car wash. When our plane finally lifted off, Andrew reached over and took my hand, then lay back in his seat. I liked it. I wondered if we would be holding hands on the way back.

CHAPTER

Twenty-One

Cabo is beautiful. My body and soul have gone from dismal cold to cheerful warm.

—Maggie Walther's Diary

The flight to Cabo took just under three hours. Andrew and I talked for most of the first hour while we ate breakfast. After our trays were cleared, Andrew read the *Wall Street Journal* while I reclined my seat and fell asleep. I woke as we began our descent and the flight attendants prepared the cabin for landing. Andrew had put a blanket over me. It made me happy.

I looked out over the blue sea churning with white foam against the rim of the peninsula. "It's beautiful," I said. I kissed Andrew on the cheek.

We landed a few minutes later. As I emerged from the plane, I was surprised by the intensity of the heat. Even without my coat I was overdressed. The air was warm and humid and smelled of flowery perfume. The landscape around the runways was rugged desert with the jagged silhouette of mountains rising in the distance.

We exited the plane from a mobile stairway attached

to the back of a truck, walking carefully down the rutted metal stairs and onto the hot tarmac below. Andrew paused near the base of the steps and took a deep breath. "It's good to be back."

"When was the last time you were here?" I asked.

"A year ago," he replied.

An airline employee directed us to immigration, which was located in a modern and air-conditioned building, and we claimed our bags. Several other flights had landed about the same time as ours, and there was a lengthy queue.

It took us half an hour to get through immigration. As we walked out into the main terminal, we were mobbed by English-speaking salesmen. Andrew just waved them off, saying, "*No estoy interesado, gracias.*"

"What are you saying?" I asked.

"I told them we're not interested."

"Are they taxi drivers?"

"No, they're selling time-shares."

We picked up our rental car, a cherry-red Mercedes convertible.

"Nice car," I said.

"I thought you'd like it."

"Is the condo far from here?"

"About a half hour. It's a nice drive."

We drove with the top down to the condo at Las Cascadas de Pedregal, a hillside community built along Pedregal beach. We drove past a security guard into a gated complex. The road was dark cobblestone and the grounds were carefully landscaped with exotic desert vegetation. I hadn't been expecting anything this nice.

"This is where we're staying?" I asked.

He nodded. "*Casa, dulce casa.*"

"It's ritzy."

"*Sí.*"

We parked our car in a reserved space in the parking terrace, carried our luggage inside the main building, and took an elevator to the third floor.

Standing in the doorway outside the condo, Andrew said, "It's going to be warm inside. We don't leave the air conditioner on. Electricity is too expensive." Andrew unlocked the door and opened it. There was an immediate loud beeping.

"Sorry, that's the alarm." He stepped over to a panel and dialed a number into it, then flipped on all the room's lights. A half-dozen white enamel ceiling fans began to turn. The far windows were concealed behind drawn drapes.

"Come in," he said. "I'll get the bags."

I stepped inside while Andrew retrieved our luggage. He shut the door and walked to the far side of the room, where he pushed a button on the wall. The drapes parted, revealing a large patio with a panoramic view of the Cabo San Lucas marina and bay.

I literally gasped. "Oh my."

He smiled. "Not bad, right?" He unlocked the glass doors and opened them. "Best view in Cabo."

I walked outside to the edge of the patio. "That is breathtaking."

"You're going to love the sunset," he said. "Then, after its gone, the city lights look like a little galaxy below us. Day or night, there's never a bad view."

The spacious patio had tile floors and a stainless-steel railing along the balcony. Waist-high, brightly colored pots spilled over with equally brilliant bougainvillea. The breeze from the ocean delivered a crisp, briny smell.

It was hard to believe that just six hours earlier I had been shivering beneath dark cloud cover. "What a beautiful day."

"It's always beautiful here," he said, walking up close to me. "That's Medano Beach below us. No SAD here." He looked at me, then added wryly, "Someday we'll find a cure for that."

"I think we just did," I said. I took his hand and looked up at him. "Thank you for bringing me here."

"Thank you for coming." We kissed, then he pulled back, his eyes excited. "Let me show you around."

Holding my hand, he led me back inside. There was an L-shaped suede leather sectional next to a long mahogany dining table.

The kitchen was new and modern, with granite countertops and backsplash and stainless steel appliances. There was original art on the wall—colorful, abstract pieces that chromatically popped from the textured, off-white walls and tan tiled floors.

"I thought we were going to be roughing it," I said. "This is nicer than my home."

"It's a nice little getaway," he said modestly. "They call

this area the Beverly Hills of Cabo. The villas around here sell for several million dollars."

"Your friend must be rich," I said. "How long has he owned this?"

"It's been about five years. It was one of the first condos purchased in the development, which is why it has the best views."

"It looks more like five weeks," I said. "It looks brand-new."

"Well, it only gets used a few weeks out of the year, so for all intents, it is." He grabbed my bag. "Your room is back here."

I followed him down a short hallway to a spacious room with a king-sized bed and an ivory-colored, tucked-leather headboard with mahogany trim. He walked to the side of the room and pulled back the drapes, exposing another gorgeous view of the harbor.

"This is the master suite. The bathroom's behind that door right there." He turned on the lights and I walked over and glanced inside. The bathroom was immaculate, with a tile and glass shower and dark cherrywood cabinets. The sinks were two alabaster bowls partially nestled into the counter with gold fixtures. I turned to him. "You should take this room."

"You're my guest," he said.

I walked around the room, then sat on the bed. It was firm but comfortable. I lay back, sinking into the lush padding.

"Passable?" he asked.

I almost laughed. "It's perfect." I sat back up. "Where's your room?"

"It's on the other side of the condo." He looked around. "I need to go to town for groceries. You're welcome to come with me or stay."

"I'll come," I said. "When are we going?"

"No rush. When you're ready. You need time to unpack and freshen up. I'll be out here when you're ready." He walked out of the room. I shut the door behind him, then undressed and got into the shower. I shampooed my hair with a sweet-smelling Mexican shampoo, then sat down on the floor of the shower and let the water wash over me.

Suddenly I began to cry without knowing why. Maybe it was a release, but I hadn't felt this free for as long as I could remember. There was no pain, no shame, no one—besides Andrew—who knew or even cared who I was. I was better than free. I was anonymous. I felt the shame wash off me like the foam running down my body and into the drain.

Best of all, I was with someone who cared about me. *Why did he care about me?* I couldn't remember the last time I had been that happy.

CHAPTER

Twenty-Two

*Andrew speaks nearly fluent Spanish. I keep being
reminded how false my first perceptions of him were.*
—Maggie Walther's Diary

I unpacked all my clothing into the room's empty armoire
drawers, then changed into something more appropriate for the Mexican heat—a bright-blue off-the-shoulder
romper with a tie at the waist.

I looked at myself in the mirror. It was the first time I
had worn the outfit and I thought I looked pretty cute,
even if I felt a little self-conscious. Normally I was more
conservative in my dress—not that I was prudish; rather, I
had just spent too much of my life being noticed by men.
But Andrew was different. I wanted him to notice me. I
hoped that he would think I looked cute too.

I pulled my hair back over my shoulders and walked
back out to the front room. Andrew was sitting on the
couch reading a business magazine, and he looked up as I
walked in. He stared at me for a moment and said, almost
reverently, *"Estás preciosa."*

I smiled. *"Gracias.* I think." I stepped closer, then spun a
little. "What do you think? You like this?"

"Yes. I especially like you in that."

Andrew had also changed his clothes. He was wearing shorts and had changed his Hawaiian shirt for a short-sleeved white linen shirt. He looked very handsome.

"Sorry I took so long," I said.

"There is no rushing in Cabo," he said. "In fact, I'm pretty sure there's an ordinance against it. I'm reminded of that every time I go into town." He stood. "Shall we go?"

We walked back down to our car and drove about three miles to where the seaside town sat below us. There was a white-sand beach lined with palm trees and saguaro cacti. In the distance, a cruise ship was anchored just outside the harbor. We pulled into the market's parking lot.

MERCADO ORGANICO

Between the two words was a colorful round sign that read:

CALIFORNIA RANCH MARKET
ENJOYING NATURAL AND ORGANIC FOOD

There were several well-used rattan tables and chairs in front of the building with menus on them, which I was glad for, since I hadn't eaten anything since breakfast on the plane. The store was well-stocked and air-conditioned. Most of the product packaging was in English, though there were products I'd never seen before, and the pricing was in both pesos and dollars. We purchased several cases of water, along with fresh fruit: mangoes, peaches, and some strange-looking produce I couldn't identify.

To my surprise, Andrew had a fairly lengthy dialogue in Spanish with the woman at the register ringing up our groceries. She put all our purchases in plastic sacks, and a lanky teenage boy took two of our three bags in his arms.

"How much Spanish do you speak?" I asked Andrew as we walked out of the store.

"Just a little," he said.

"You speak more than a little," I said. "How often do you come down here?"

"Not enough."

"Your friend doesn't use his condo very much?"

He shook his head. "No, he hasn't been here for several years."

"That's a shame," I said.

He nodded slowly. "More than you can imagine."

Andrew opened our car's trunk and the young man, who had followed us out, put the groceries inside. Then he just stood there.

"Does he want something?" I asked.

"Yes; it's different here than in America," Andrew said. "The baggers are volunteers. So we tip them." He took out his wallet and extracted a couple of dollar bills, which he handed to the boy. The boy said *gracias* and ran back to the store.

"They take American dollars?"

"They want American dollars," he said.

We walked back to the store and sat down at one of the

tables in front. "I took the liberty of ordering us something to eat," Andrew said.

A few moments later a young woman brought out two fruit drinks in tall, narrow glasses, a bowl of shrimp ceviche, and tortilla chips with a small bowl of guacamole. She said to Andrew, *"Aquí está. Ahorita regreso con su pedido completo."*

"Gracias," he replied.

Andrew handed me a drink.

I looked at him. "What is it?"

"Just try it," he said.

I took a sip. "This is yummy. Mango?"

"Mango and passion fruit." He took a drink from his own glass. "This is good. I didn't know passion fruit was a thing until I came here."

A moment later the young woman returned with a platter of lightly fried rolled tortillas with grated cheese melted on top.

"These are chile and cheese flautas," Andrew said. "You do like Mexican food, I hope."

I laughed. "Do I have a choice?"

"I'm sure we could find a nice Chinese restaurant somewhere."

We shared a caramel flan for dessert.

"I'm going to gain weight here," I said.

"I would hope so."

We went back in the store and picked up the bag of groceries that Andrew had left inside to keep cold, then we drove back to the condominium.

CHAPTER

Twenty-Three

*Tonight we ate dinner at a restaurant called Edith's.
I was serenaded by a mariachi band. This just
keeps getting better.*

—*Maggie Walther's Diary*

Back at the condo, Andrew said, "I need to take care of some business. It might take me a few hours. If you want, there's a swimming pool on the west side of the complex."

"Say no more," I said. "I didn't realize the Christmas tree business required so much tending."

He grinned. "It doesn't. I've got other irons in the fire."

As I started for my room, he said, "We have dinner reservations at six. We should leave around five thirty."

"That gives me four hours to burn."

"Speaking of which, there's sunscreen in your bathroom cabinet."

"That's not what I . . ." I smiled. "Thank you." I went to my room and changed into a bikini. When I walked out, Andrew was sitting at the couch working on his laptop. He looked up as I entered the room. "Wow."

"Yeah, right," I said. "If pasty white was—"

He held up his hand to stop me. "The proper response is, '*Gracias, Señor.*'"

I smiled. "*Gracias, Señor.*"

"*De nada.* Have fun."

The pool was luxurious and not at all crowded. If this were the antidote to SAD, I could totally overdose on it. The warm fresh air and cool water were emotionally and physically healing. I coated myself in tanning oil and lay out for half an hour before covering up. I was about as white as the snow I'd left behind and didn't want to ruin the trip with a sunburn. I sat under the shade of palm trees and read until four thirty, then went back to get ready for dinner.

When I got back to the condo, Andrew was on his cell phone. He waved at me.

I went to my room and showered, then did my hair and makeup. It was nice to have someone to look nice for. Back when I was married, I would laugh at Carina when she would rate her prospective dates on whether she would shave her legs for them or not. Now that I was single again, I understood that she wasn't joking.

Andrew was waiting for me when I walked back out. "You're going to love this place," he said. "It's called Edith's."

"I had an aunt named Edith."

"Was she Mexican?"

I smiled. "No. She was ornery."

Edith's restaurant was back down on Medano Beach not far from the market where we had shopped earlier. I could see why the restaurant was one of Andrew's favorites. The place looked like a Mexican fiesta. The layout was mostly open—a series of raised, thatched roofs surrounded, at least on the land side, by palm trees and bamboo and thick, snaking vines of bougainvillea.

The thatched roofs were hung with strings of colored glass and punched-tin lanterns and jeweled tin Moravian star pendant lights—the hodgepodge of fixtures hanging above the diners' heads like piñatas. Strings of icicle lights adorned the rim of the fronded canopies. The tablecloths were in bright colors ranging from fuchsia and orange to lime green and scarlet. Around the tables were wicker chairs draped with colorful Mexican blankets.

A trio featuring a violin, a guitar, and an acoustic bass moved throughout the restaurant serenading diners with lively traditional Mexican music, naturally blending in with the overall cacophony.

Adding to the dimmed, noisy atmosphere was a fair amount of fire, not just from the flickering tabletop candle centerpieces and sconces but from long streams of blue liquid fire poured from bottles and silver sauceboats.

"They're big on flambé here," Andrew said. "It's part of the festivities. If it burns, it earns."

"Did you just make that up?" I asked.

"I'm afraid so."

"It was clever."

"It's like the newspaper motto, If it bleeds, it leads."

I frowned. "I've done my share of bleeding in newspapers lately."

"We'll just leave that back in the land of cold," he replied.

Our hostess sat us in a section of the main canopy next to the central kitchen, an open, brick-walled edifice crowded with cooks wearing tall white toques.

"This place is fantastic," I said.

"You haven't tried their food," Andrew replied. "They're famous for their steaks, seafood, and desserts."

I opened the menu and gasped loudly.

Andrew laughed. "You saw the price."

"Shrimp is really seven hundred eighty-five dollars?"

"Pesos," he said.

"But there's a dollar sign."

"They use the same symbol for money. It's confusing, but you can usually figure it out. If it looks outrageously priced, it's pesos."

"How much is a peso worth?"

"Last I checked, about a nickel. So that shrimp dish is about forty dollars."

We decided to order several different plates and share. We had tuna carpaccio and cheese turnovers for appetizers followed by a "flirt" salad, which was made with honey, ginger, and hibiscus liqueur. The presentation of the food was as artistic as our surroundings.

Before we ordered our entrees, our waiter brought out a tray of uncooked meats to exhibit their evening's offerings. We ordered the grilled lobster, shrimp enchiladas, and chile rellenos.

"How long have you been coming here?" I asked.

"Since my first visit to Cabo, about eight years ago. I've eaten here every time since."

"Is Edith a real person?"

Andrew nodded. "She is. I actually met her on my first visit. Her story is amazing. She came to Cabo as a fifteen-year-old girl and got a job here as a waitress. Back then it had a different name, Esmerelda's by the Sea, something like that. Twenty years later she bought out the owner and renamed the restaurant after herself."

"That's a great success story."

"Kind of makes you happy, doesn't it?"

At Andrew's insistence (I didn't provide a whole lot of resistance) we ordered two desserts, the banana flambé and their house flan. While we were eating our dulce, the band made their way to our table.

"What can we play for your lovely lady?" the guitarist asked with a heavy accent.

"How about something romantic," Andrew said.

The guitarist raised his eyebrows. "Ah, you wish romantic. We will play 'Novia Mia.'"

"What does that mean?" I asked Andrew.

"It means my girlfriend," he said.

The trio began playing a lively song with the guitarist belting out the words over the restaurant's din, occasionally accompanied by the slightly out-of-tune, scratchy vocals of the other two band members. After the first stanza, Andrew started laughing.

"What is he saying?" I asked.

"He said, 'Your face is so pretty it will be my torment.'"

The men ended the song with a unified shout, sort of an *olé!* We both clapped. Andrew handed the guitarist a twenty-dollar bill and the men thanked him and moved on to a new table.

"That was fun," I said.

"It's true, you know."

"What's true?"

"Your face has tormented me since I met you."

"That doesn't sound like a compliment."

Andrew started laughing. "Sorry. You're right. Some things don't translate well."

We were in no hurry, so we didn't leave until we'd lingered over our coffees. As we walked into the condo I said, "What a day. It's hard to believe that it began in Utah."

"We're just warming up," Andrew said. "Literally. We've got a full day tomorrow, so we better get some rest."

"What are we doing?" I asked.

"We are going to the sea."

The sea sounded nice. "What time do we leave?"

"We have a boat to catch, so we should leave here by eight thirty."

I glanced down at my watch. "What time is it here?"

"Eleven. Los Cabos is on mountain time, same as home."

I leaned into him. "Good night."

"*Sueños dulces, Linda.* Sweet dreams."

I looked at him. "Did you just call me Linda?"

"*Linda* is Spanish for pretty," he said. "It wasn't a slip."

"Oh good. For a second I thought you were thinking of a previous Cabo guest."

He said, "You're the only woman I've ever brought here. Besides my ex-wife, of course."

"Of course," I echoed. We kissed. After we parted I said softly, "Maybe you could call me something other than Linda. I have an employee named Linda."

"I'll work on it," he said.

We kissed again, this time more passionately. Our kissing started to physically progress. Then he stepped back. "I need to stop."

"What makes you think I want to stop?" I said.

"It complicates things."

"Oh, that." I sighed. "Good night, handsome."

"Good night, Linda."

I smiled at him, then went to my room and got ready for bed. The blinds were still open, and I could see the city stretched out below me like a rhinestone blanket. I set my watch on the nightstand and climbed into bed. The sheets were fresh and sweet-smelling. I lay back and smiled. I had started the day anxious and cold and ended it happy and warm. I couldn't wait to see what tomorrow would bring.

CHAPTER

Twenty-Four

Something about him makes me throw caution to the wind. I hope the wind doesn't return as a tornado.

—Maggie Walther's Diary

I woke the next morning bathed in sunlight. It may have been the same sun as at home, but it definitely worked a lot harder here.

Andrew was already awake; I could hear him in the kitchen. I could also smell something cooking. I got up and put on my swimsuit and cover up, pulled my hair into a ponytail, then walked out.

Andrew was standing in front of the stove frying eggs in a skillet. He wore a blue-and-white swimsuit, water shoes, and a short-sleeved baby-blue linen shirt. He looked handsome. He always looked handsome.

"Good morning, *cariña*," he said.

I sidled up next to him. "Morning." We kissed. He handed me a cup of coffee. "Thank you," I said. "*Cariña?*"

"It means cute."

"My best friend's name is Carina, remember? She works for me too."

174

"Strike two," he said. "Linda and Carina. Maybe you should give me a list of your employees' names."

"I don't have that many. And I'm pretty sure Kylee and Nichelle aren't Spanish words."

"I'll keep working on it. How did you sleep?"

"Better than usual." I looked at the stove. "What are you making?"

"Huevos rancheros on corn tortillas. Do you like avocados?"

"I love avocados. Almost as much as I love a man who can cook."

"That's good," he said. "Because I am both."

"I have no idea what that means."

"Don't think too much about it." He lifted a fried egg and set it on the crisp tortilla layered with lettuce and refried beans. He dusted it with cilantro, then dropped on some jalapeños. "Those are to wake you up." He handed me the plate.

"I thought you said you didn't cook much."

"Not if I can avoid it," he said.

"You've even got the presentation down."

"I watch cooking shows when I'm bored." He brought over his own plate and a pitcher of guava juice.

"We're off to the sea today?"

"Yes. And beaches. You can only get to the best beaches by boat."

We finished eating and put our dishes in the sink. "Should we clean up?" I asked.

"No, Jazzy will be by to straighten up."

"Jazzy?"

"Sorry. Her real name is Jazmín. She cleans the condo when we're in town."

I went back to my room and got the canvas beach bag I'd brought, along with a book, my iPod, and a few other necessities. When I came back out, Andrew was standing by the door with a large backpack slung over his shoulder. "I've got sunscreen, oil, and towels. There are a few things we need to pick up at the grocery store."

We drove back down to the *mercado* and bought some bread, meat, and cheeses, along with two large bottles of water. We then walked down to the dock to the chartered tour boat, where Andrew was embraced by a short, barrel-chested man with a full beard and mustache and a T-shirt with a picture of David Bowie.

"Maggie, this is my friend, El Capitán."

"Hello," I said, shaking the man's hand. I glanced at Andrew. "You call him the captain?"

"After six years, that's the only name I have for him," Andrew said.

El Capitán gave us each a life jacket and snorkeling equipment, and then his assistant, a thin, ebony-haired teenage girl, gave a brief safety lecture in broken English. We boarded the boat along with three other couples—one Mexican, the other two American.

One of the American couples looked oddly mismatched. He was in his late fifties, obese and balding with dark sunglasses and a myriad of thick gold chains hanging around his neck and dangling down to his porch of a stomach. The woman was young, probably in her twenties, slim but curvaceous, perfectly tanned, and wearing a revealing string bikini. She had long blond hair, a full sleeve of tattoos on her arm, and massive diamond rings on most of her fingers, which perhaps explained the couple's attraction.

The craft we'd boarded was a long, canopied, glass-bottom boat with smooth, worn wooden benches along its sides. The boat's name was *ABBA*, which was not lost on either of us.

"Your dad would be a fan of this boat," Andrew said, after we'd settled into our seats.

"He would."

"Should I call you Agnetha?"

I grimaced. "No, please. Keep working on it."

Once we had boarded, El Capitán started the outboard engine, the crisp smell of gas and exhaust mixing with brine-scented sea air. The girl untied us from the dock, and we backed out of the slip into the harbor's waterway and headed out to sea.

Our first destination was Pelican Rock, where the boat stopped a hundred yards from shore and dropped floating diving flags. We snorkeled for about half an hour in calm turquoise water teeming with colorful, exotic fish.

The older man didn't leave the boat but his hot little woman did. (Do I sound catty?) I noticed that she swam unnecessarily close to Andrew, occasionally "accidentally" bumping into him. When she wasn't next to him, she looked like she was posing, even provocatively adjusting her swimsuit underwater where anyone with a mask could see. I did my best to focus on the sea life, but the blonde insisted on taking center stage.

After we were back on the boat, Andrew said, "Do you know what the most terrifying sea creature out here is?"

The blonde, I thought. "This sounds like a game show question," I said. "Sharks."

"Hammerhead sharks," the blonde said, inviting herself into our conversation.

"Squids," Andrew said. "Every year, the Humboldt squid comes to the Baja peninsula to feed. The fishermen call them *diablo rojo*, the red devil. They grow as long as nine feet and they've been known to grab people from the surface and pull them under."

"You're making this up," I said.

"Nope. I watched a documentary on it."

"I watch documentaries too," I said. "I saw one on beavers."

Andrew started laughing.

"I'm not kidding. I did."

"I . . ." He shook his head. "So the film crew sent a cameraman in the water at night wearing a Kevlar jacket."

"What's a Kevlar jacket?" the blonde asked. "Is that like a Gucci jacket?"

I barely suppressed my eye roll.

"It's a bulletproof vest," Andrew said. "And then they waited for the squid to come. The squid have the ability to change their color to match their surroundings, so they're virtually invisible until they're on you."

"Like a stealth squid," the blonde said.

"Exactly," Andrew said. "Only when they're in a feeding frenzy, they flash red and white. The squid attacked the diver and penetrated his vest with its beak."

"Squid have beaks?" I asked.

"Humboldt squid have very sharp beaks. They resemble a parrot's beak, except they're black and the force of their bite is more powerful than an African lion's. They can bite through metal. And their eight tentacles have more than a hundred suction cups, all lined with razor-sharp teeth."

"This is terrifying," the blonde said.

"To make it worse, the Humboldt travel in schools of more than a thousand squid. At night you can see hundreds of tentacles sticking up out of the water, like agave plants."

"What's an agave plant?" the blonde asked.

"It's a succulent," I said, reminding her of my presence. "With long, sharp, painful spines. You would not want to be stabbed by one." I noticed Andrew grin. "They use it to make tequila."

"I like tequila," she said, moving a little closer to Andrew. "I didn't know they made it from squids."

Andrew didn't bother to explain.

"Is this squid thing real?"

Andrew nodded. "Completely." Then he turned to me and held out his hand. "If my fingers are the legs, the beak is right here," he said, touching the center of his palm. "When they attack, they come at you like this." He put his hand in front of my face.

"This sounds like something you saw in a horror movie," I said.

"Just look at how much you learn being around me," Andrew replied.

"What are you talking about?" the blonde's sugar daddy asked, finally noticing how much attention his woman was giving to Andrew.

"Squids and agave plants," the blonde said.

"Agave," the man said. "That's what they make tequila from."

The blonde leaned toward Andrew. "That thing sounds like a monster."

"It gets worse," Andrew said. "The squid dragged the cameraman down nearly sixty feet before the rope he was tied to broke him free of the squid's grip. The squid was so strong that the diver dislocated his shoulder and his wrist was broken in five places. Had the beast gotten its beak around him, it could have amputated his hand."

"Thank you for not telling me any of this before we snorkeled," I said. "I'm not getting back in the water."

"You don't have to worry. The Humboldt only feed at night."

"That sounds like the name of a horror movie," the blonde said. She pressed her leg against Andrew's. *"They Only Feed at Night."*

She's talking about herself, I thought.

Andrew shifted away from her. "And they only live in deep waters," he said to me. "So you don't have to worry about them close to shore."

"I'm still staying on the beach," I said.

From Pelican Rock, our boat sailed to Land's End, the tip of the Baja peninsula, with a pungent ride past a sea lion colony, then on to El Arco de Cabo San Lucas, the famous stone arch.

"Every four years or so, the tide changes enough to create a walkway under the arch," Andrew said.

"Can we walk through it now?" I asked.

"No. Probably next year."

We stopped momentarily at the beach, where El Capitán made an announcement. "Friends, we are now going to Playa del Amor, also called Lovers' Beach. It is very nice sand and calm and good swimming. Next to it is Divorce Beach. It is not so calm, and it has dangerous rip currents. I recommend that you not swim there. Let that be a lesson to you."

Everyone laughed. "I've learned that lesson," I said.

Andrew nodded. "Ditto."

"I will pull the boat up on the shore, and you will exit from the front of the boat. The clock time is nearly eleven. I will be back to get you at the same place I drop you off at four o'clock. Remember, our boat is the *ABBA*. Please do not miss the boat or make your fellow passengers wait for you."

The boat pulled into the beach until its hull was on sand and we made our way out over the bow in single file. I made sure we disembarked after the blonde. I didn't want her following us.

The sand was immaculate, soft and warm, framed by

beautiful large rock formations that rose from the sand like sculptures.

Andrew carried our things over to a vacant space about thirty yards from the water, where we laid out our beach towels and rubbed each other down with sunscreen. We spent the next two hours at Lovers' Beach swimming and snorkeling, but as the crowds grew, we moved over toward the less populated Divorce Beach to sunbathe and eat our picnic lunch in privacy. We also ate ripe mangoes and drank passion fruit juice from local vendors. It was a lovely way to spend the day.

Our boat arrived back at Medano Beach as the sun began to set. The blonde and her man were waiting for us on the dock. They invited us up to their villa for drinks, which the woman pointed out on the mountain. Their villa was nearly half as large as the entire complex we were staying at. Andrew thanked them but politely declined their invitation, explaining that we were on our honeymoon.

"Congratulations," the man said. "I hope you remain on Lovers' Beach for as long as you can. Divorce Beach is expensive."

The blonde said nothing but looked at Andrew hungrily.

"Honeymoon?" I said as we walked away.

"I was just trying to refuse them politely," Andrew said.

We ate a simple dinner at a small bar called the Baja Cantina, where we had seafood chowder in sourdough bread bowls, coconut shrimp, and, my favorite, fish tacos.

It was dark when we arrived back at the condo. I was sunburned and tired but happy. The condo was cool and I was glad that the air conditioner had been left on.

I took a quick shower to get the salt and sand off my body, then met Andrew out on the patio. The moon glistened on the water like in a Van Gogh painting. The air was moist and comfortable.

"What's on the agenda for tomorrow?" I asked.

"I thought that after all the travel today, we'd take tomorrow easy. We'll sleep in, do some shopping in town, eat a nice lunch, and then, for after lunch, I made us a reservation at the Spa at Esperanza. It's one of Latin America's top spas."

"This just keeps getting better," I said.

"Even better than Utah?"

"Never heard of the place," I said.

He grinned. "Would you like a strawberry daiquiri?"

"Yes, please."

"I'll be right back."

He stood and walked into the kitchen while I just looked out over the city. About five minutes later he returned carrying two glasses with halved limes on the rims. He handed me one and sat down next to me.

"Thank you," I said. "I keep looking down at the water expecting to see a bunch of squid legs sticking out."

He laughed. "They're tentacles, not legs. And I'm sorry I told you about them. I didn't mean to ruin the water for you."

"Was that all true?"

"Every word of it."

"That blonde would have liked to pull you under."

He looked at me with an amused grin. "She was just being friendly."

I took a drink of my daiquiri, then said, "Yeah, right. If we'd been there much longer, she would have ended up in your lap. I wanted to clock her."

"I'm glad you didn't," Andrew said. "I think that guy she was with was in the Mafia." He took a small sip of his drink and set it down. "I like seeing you jealous."

"I'm not jealous," I said, sounding like a liar even to myself. "Maybe a little."

He lifted his drink. "You should try this. It's virgin."

"You're drinking a virgin daiquiri?"

He nodded.

"I noticed that you don't drink much."

"I used to. Especially whenever things went bad." He looked at me dolefully. "Back then, a lot of things were going bad."

"What kind of things?"

"Marriage. Family. Business. Pretty much everything that mattered."

"I'm sorry," I said. "But today was a perfect day. Thank you again for talking me into coming here."

"I knew it would be good for you to be here," he said. "And me."

"You know me," I said.

"I'd like to."

I looked out over the bay, then closed my eyes, feeling

the warm wind pressing against my face, brushing back my hair. I breathed it in and felt right with the world. After a few more minutes of silence I said, "It's been a long time since I've felt like this."

"How is that?"

"Happy." I looked into his eyes. Then the words came out. "In love."

He just looked at me. I suddenly felt awkward. "I'm sorry. I—"

"I feel the same," he said. "You just beat me to it."

His words sounded like joy. I set down my drink and nestled into him. We stayed that way for nearly an hour. Finally I said, "I'm tired. I guess I'll go to bed."

He kissed me on the forehead. "I'm going to sit out here a little longer. Good night."

"Night," I said.

We kissed and I got up and went to my room. As I lay in bed I couldn't believe that I had told him that I loved him. I hoped it wouldn't ruin our trip.

CHAPTER

Twenty-Five

When I first met Andrew, I took him for an attractive, simple man selling Christmas trees to keep the lights on. Not the case. He's attractive, but he's also smart, cosmopolitan, and possibly rich. He not only provided my plane ticket and accommodations, he's also paying for all my meals and activities. Today we went to the Spa at Esperanza. (I think I spelled that right.) It was a day of perfect pampering. It was the perfect everything.

—Maggie Walther's Diary

In spite of Andrew's invitation to sleep in, I woke early. Andrew must have been exhausted because I peeked into his room and he was sprawled out on top of his covers asleep and lightly snoring.

I put on my walking shorts and a tank top and went out walking, first around the complex, then all the way down to the edge of the beach and back. I passed a cactus garden with more than thirty different varieties of cacti. I had never realized how beautiful cacti were. I had just always thought of them as something painful to avoid. Maybe there's a metaphor there.

When I got back to the condo, Andrew was sitting outside on the patio drinking coffee.

He smiled when he saw me. "Where'd you go?"

"Just on a walk," I said. "I walked down to the beach and back."

"I was afraid you ran off with someone else."

I walked over, sat on his lap, and kissed him. "I like seeing you jealous too."

A half hour later we drove downtown and parked just a little east of the *mercado*. The area was crowded with tourists patronizing the area's street vendors, clothing shops, and restaurants. After we had walked around a while, we went to the flea market, which covered several acres and was filled with vendors hawking pottery, clothing, cheap jewelry, electronic gadgets, and all the usual touristy knickknacks. I didn't buy anything except a shaved ice and a hat, as the sun was frying me.

After the flea market we walked over by the marina and found a place to sit beneath the shade of a palm tree.

"There are so many boats," I said.

"I counted them all once," Andrew said. "Not that it means anything, since the number changes hourly. There were a hundred and forty-seven."

"What prompted you to count them?"

"My OCD. I'm always counting things. Maybe that's why I got into finance."

"Have you ever sailed?"

"I used to," he said. "A lot. Back when I had a boat."

"You owned a boat?"

He nodded, his expression looking slightly nostalgic. "A thirty-five footer. I called her *A Meeting*."

"*A Meeting?*"

"That way, when I was out playing and my clients called, my secretary could say, 'He's in *A Meeting* right now.'"

I grinned. "Brilliant."

"I loved that boat. I had to sell her when the business went down." He sighed. "I still dream of retiring in a little place on the sea with a fishing boat, just big enough to go in deep waters. Something about the size of Hemingway's boat."

"Hemingway the author?"

Andrew nodded. "Hemingway loved the sea. He had a thirty-eight-foot fishing boat called the *Pilar*, after his second wife's nickname. He was an avid, if unconventional, fisherman. They said that he took a tommy gun with him on his boat to shoot sharks if they tried to feed on his catch.

"Once he and a friend caught a thousand-pound marlin, the largest either of them had ever caught. As they tried to bring it in, sharks came after it. Hemingway got out his tommy gun and started blasting them, but his plan backfired. The shooting created so much blood and chum in the water that it drew hundreds of sharks in a feeding frenzy. They ended up with only half their prized catch.

"It ruined the men's friendship, since Hemingway's friend blamed his use of the gun for the loss of the biggest fish he'd ever caught. On the bright side, the world benefited, as it became the impetus for his book *The Old Man and the Sea.*"

"You are a surprising font of knowledge," I said.

"I read a lot," he said.

"I've always wondered what it is about men and boats."

"I've wondered too," he said. "Maybe we're just naturally wired with wanderlust, and the sea is our last viable frontier."

"Do you have wanderlust?"

He didn't look at me. "Sometimes I dream of disappearing," he said softly.

I looked back out over the marina. "My father's boat looked kind of like that one." I pointed to a sleek, twenty-plus-foot vessel in a slip across from us. "At least that's how I remember it. I only saw it once."

"Why is that?"

"It wasn't for us. He bought it with the insurance settlement after my mother died. I didn't see much of him after that."

For the next half hour we just watched the boats cruise in and out of the marina.

"Look at the size of that yacht right there," I said. "I wonder how much it cost."

"Probably a couple million," Andrew said. "There's money here." He pointed to a boat idling about a hundred yards from the dock. "See that yacht out there?"

"The one with sails or the huge black-and-gold one next to it?"

"The black-and-gold one next to it. My friend used to own it."

"It's giant. Your same friend who owns the condo?"

He nodded. "It's beautiful inside. I wish I could show it to you. It has marble countertops, hardwood floors, a formal dining room. It even has a dance floor."

"How much does a boat like that cost?"

Andrew smiled. "If you have to ask, you can't afford it."

"I already know I can't afford it."

"A little over three million."

"Your friend is very rich."

"He was," Andrew said. "Now he's just rich." He looked back out at the boat. "They changed its name. It used to be called *Seas the Day*."

"Carpe diem," I said.

"Except he spelled *seize* s-e-a-s."

"That's clever."

"He liked word plays. It was either that or *Nauti Buoy*, *naughty* spelled like *nautical, buoy* like an ocean *buoy*."

"Was he?"

"Was he what?"

"A naughty boy?"

"He was back then. Not so much these days."

"I'd like to meet him."

He turned to me. "I don't think I want you to meet him."

"Why is that?"

"He would like you."

I kissed him on the cheek. "You have nothing to worry about."

We ate lunch at a small seafood restaurant and pub on the marina, then walked around until it was time for our spa appointment.

The Spa at Esperanza lived up to its billing. After checking in, we spent the first half hour in their signature therapy pool, the Pasaje de Agua, for a water-passage purifying ritual, which basically involved moving back and forth from warm to cool water. We started in a warm-spring soaking pool, moved to the steam cave, then out to a cool waterfall rinse.

Afterward we donned thick terry-cloth bathrobes and sat in a quiet room until two therapists came for us. Andrew had booked us a treatment called "Romancing the Stone," which consisted of a deep heat stone massage followed by a private soaking tub, then scalp and foot massage. The whole treatment lasted three hours and I don't remember the last time that I felt so spoiled or relaxed. All my muscles felt like soft rubber.

As we exited the spa, I noticed the price tag on our treatment was nearly a thousand dollars each.

"What did you think of that?" Andrew asked as we walked out.

I sighed happily. "I think I just went to heaven."

"Glad to take you there," he said.

We ate dinner close to our condo at a restaurant called El Farallón at the Resort at Pedregal.

"What does *el Farallón* mean?" I asked.

"*Farallón* is a rocky outcrop."

The restaurant was built on a platform of rock jutting from the hillside. "Hence the name."

"Hence the name," he said.

I ordered carrot and coconut-milk soup with curry and

goat cheese, then we shared a lobster ceviche with grilled pineapple. For dinner I had sea bass with saffron rice and bell peppers, and grilled corn with epazote mayonnaise. For dessert we shared a tres leches cake with raspberries.

As in most Latin American restaurants, no one was in a hurry, so we ate and talked and laughed until past ten. I drank a little too much wine, so after dinner Andrew had to help me to the car, then up to our condo and my bed. I sat down on the bed and lifted my feet. "Please take off my shoes."

He knelt down and took them off. "Your feet are free," he said. He stood and sat on the bed next to me.

I leaned into him. "This has been the best day ever."

"At least until tomorrow," Andrew said.

"What are we doing tomorrow?"

"What would you like to do tomorrow?"

I touched my finger to his face, tracing the edge of his stubbled chin. "Be with you."

"That's a given. I was thinking that we might go for a drive to Todos Santos. It's a Mexican hamlet about an hour north of us. I think you'll like it. It has a unique charm."

"If all I wanted was a unique charm, I could just stay here with you."

"And they have great fish tacos," he said.

I couldn't believe how in love I was.

CHAPTER

Twenty-Six

Today we visited a lovely, quaint little town about an hour north called Todos Santos. Andrew took me to a remote beachfront house he's seriously considering buying to escape to. I would like someplace to escape to. Or maybe just some<u>one</u>.
                                        —*Maggie Walther's Diary*

We ate a quick breakfast of coffee and black sapote—an indigenous fruit that tastes like chocolate pudding—and baked breakfast rolls stuffed with ham, cheese, and chipotle.

We packed our swimsuits and towels, got in our car, and drove north to Pueblo Mágico Todos Santos. The Pueblo Mágico (Magic Town) title had been added a decade earlier by Mexico's Tourism Secretary to recognize it as a colonial town with historical relevance.

Andrew gave me a rundown of the town's history as we drove. Todos Santos was founded in the seventeen hundreds by Jesuit missionaries who came to establish a farming community with the intent of providing food for the nearby city of La Paz. The success of the community led to the founding of the Santa Rosa de las Palmas mission. Later, as its population grew, the town became a major sugarcane producer. It was also the site of the last battle of the Mexican-American War.

We drove north along Highway 19, a narrow, winding desert road that runs along the Pacific coast of Baja California Sur. The drive was pretty, with desert landscape, Joshua trees, and brightly colored flowers and cactus. There wasn't much traffic and Andrew and I talked the whole way.

"Todos has a town motto," Andrew said to me as the town came into view. "'Nothing bad ever happens here.'"

"I definitely should move here," I said.

"I'm seriously considering it," he said. "In the last few decades it's become an artist colony. Artists, writers, and musicians come here from all over. It's a little bit ironic: they came here because it was cheap and private, then their coming drew the public, making it not so cheap and private." He looked at me. "The tortured life of an artist."

"Are you an artist?" I asked.

"People used to say I was an artist with money," he said. "But what I really wanted to be was a novelist. That was the dream."

"What happened to your dream?"

"It got woken by the cold plunge of reality." He looked at me. "What about you? Any artistic pursuits outside the kitchen?"

"I've painted some."

"Are you good?"

"Do I still have a day job?"

His brow furrowed. "I don't know."

"You sound like Carina." As we drove into town, I said, "Deep inside, do you still have that dream of writing?"

He looked reflective. "I think I have stories to tell." He looked at me and smiled. "I don't know if anyone will want to read them, but I have them."

"I'll read them," I said.

"Good. I'll tell the publishers I have a reader."

The town of Todos Santos was old and picturesque. The mission church reminded me a little of the Alamo, at least the pictures I'd seen of it, and the cobblestone streets were overhung by colorful flags draped from the buildings that lined them.

The small town, like most tourist attractions, had an inordinate number of restaurants. Andrew called it a "foodie mecca," which was good because this week I was unleashing my inner foodie. I was definitely going to gain weight.

"One of the best places for lunch is a food truck run by two women friends," he told me as we walked toward town. "A few years ago *Condé Nast Traveler* did an article on them that made them world famous. One of the owners is a well-known Mexican actress and the other is a chef. They claim that their truck always has the freshest fish in town because the local fishermen are smitten with the women's beauty."

"We definitely need to eat there," I said.

"I've never been disappointed."

"With the food or the women?"

He smiled. "Either."

We found the food truck parked near the main park.

It was fittingly called La Chulita, which in Mexican slang roughly translates to "li'l sexy mama." One of the famed women was there, Daphne. She was pretty and dressed in retro clothing, her dark hair pinned up in a fifties-style hairdo. The truck specialized in ceviche; some claim it's the best in Mexico. We ordered two kinds: the first with clams, scallops, and marlin with corn, poblano chilies, and avocado; and the second with shrimp, mango, and pineapple. Both were excellent.

We spent the afternoon walking along the town's main thoroughfare, stopping in three different art galleries and two different bakeries.

"How did you find this place?" I asked, eating a sweet cream-cheese pastry.

"I read about it in a travel book," he said. "It was my third or fourth visit to Cabo. Sometimes the resort life gets a little staid. I came here by motorcycle."

"That sounds adventurous."

"Driving in Mexico is always adventurous," he said. "But back then, I was just trying to be a rebel."

"Were you?"

"Still am," he said. "I just need a cause."

Andrew continued to tell me about the places we walked by, usually in remarkable detail. Finally, I asked, "How do you know so much about this place?"

"I've thought about moving here."

"You were serious, then. About your dream of retiring on the sea?"

He nodded. "There's a little hacienda on the beach

just south of town. It even comes with a fishing boat. I've thought of buying it."

"With your Christmas tree profits."

He smiled. "Exactly."

"But if you bought it, you'd be down here—"

"That's the general idea."

"And I'd be up there. In the snow."

His brow furrowed. "That would be a problem." He looked at me. "But not one that would be hard to remedy."

I didn't know what to say to that. "I'd like to see your dream place."

"I'll take you by it on the way home."

We just wandered around the town until late afternoon, then Andrew took me to see the hacienda. There was nothing around it for miles. It was a charming little cottage painted coral pink with a large back porch for sitting and watching the sea. It was still for sale. The boat was gone.

"She must be out to sea," Andrew said.

"Who?" I asked.

"The boat. She's called *El Sueño*."

"What does that mean?"

He smiled. "The dream."

We started our journey back to Cabo with a side trip to Cerritos Beach, about ten miles south of Todos Santos. The road to Cerritos was a little rugged and a lot bumpy. Fortunately, Andrew not only knew the way but assured me that it was worth the rough ride.

It was. The beach was spectacular, and maybe it was the

hour, but it wasn't crowded like any of the other beaches we'd been to. There were only a few local surfers and some fishing boats in the distance.

"I think that's her," Andrew said, pointing out to the horizon. "*El Sueño*."

I changed into my bathing suit in the car and we went out for a swim. As the sun touched the horizon, Andrew laid out a towel and we sat on the beach and watched the sun set. For more than fifteen minutes neither of us spoke. It was too serene to ruin with words. When the sun was half drowned, Andrew put his arm around me. "I could do this every night. It never gets old."

Me too, I thought.

"It's Thanksgiving tomorrow," he said.

In the crush of our activity, I'd actually forgotten. "Do they celebrate Thanksgiving in Mexico?"

"Some do. It's a US holiday, but it's becoming more popular."

"Do we have plans?" I asked.

"I always have a plan," he said. "Not always a good one, but at least it's a plan."

"Are you going to tell me about it?"

"No."

I lay back onto his lap. "Okay."

We stayed nearly an hour after the sun was gone. We got back to the condo at around midnight and went straight to bed.

CHAPTER

Twenty-Seven

I've heard many people speak about putting the
"thanks" in Thankgiving, but today, Andrew
showed me how to put in the "giving."
  —Maggie Walther's Diary

"Good morning," Andrew said, pulling up the blinds in my room.

I opened my eyes to see him standing next to my bed, silhouetted by the morning sun.

"Good morning. What time is it?"

"Almost ten. I thought I'd better wake you." He walked over to the table and lifted a tray. "I brought you breakfast."

"You brought me breakfast in bed?"

"I'm sorry; you can have it in the kitchen if you like. Or on the patio."

"Don't apologize," I said, laughing. "No one's ever brought me breakfast in bed."

"It sounds great," he said, "but the truth is, it's hard to eat. I mean, you can't really move around, and you're worried about spilling your juice and coffee the whole time."

"That's what Clive always said. It was his excuse for not ever doing it."

Andrew had brought me a bowl of yogurt with raspberries and blueberries, sliced melon, and a unique pastry I'd never seen before. "What's this?"

"It's a *concha*," he said. "That's Spanish for seashell."

"It looks like a seashell."

"It's very popular here. It's like a cookie baked on top of cinnamon bread."

I took a bite. Not surprisingly, it was delicious.

"Happy Thanksgiving," he said.

"Happy Thanksgiving. You said we have plans?"

"I have a Thanksgiving tradition. I hope you don't mind me commandeering the day."

"You've commandeered every day since we got here," I said. "I'm not complaining."

"Good. Then as soon as you're ready, we'll go."

"Where are we going?"

"*A bendecir vidas*," he said, then walked out of the room.

I took a quick shower and dressed, then walked out to the kitchen. Andrew was on the couch reading a thriller.

"Let's go," he said.

"Where to?" I asked again. "In English this time, *por favor*."

"Back to the *mercado*."

"We're shopping for Thanksgiving?"

"Yes, we are."

"We should make a list," I said.

"I already have."

As we walked inside the *mercado*, the woman Andrew had spoken with on our first day embraced him. He followed her over to the register and she handed him a piece of paper that had handwriting on both sides. He examined the paper and then gave her a credit card, which I thought was curious, since we hadn't purchased anything yet.

After he signed the bill, she handed him a set of keys. Andrew turned to me. "We're done here."

"But we didn't buy anything yet."

"They took care of everything."

We walked out of the store. Instead of walking to our car, Andrew walked toward a small delivery truck with the name of the *mercado* printed on the side.

"We've changed vehicles," he said. "Hop in."

"We're taking a truck?"

"We need the space," he said. "And where we're going, the car would be an insult."

"Where are we going?"

A large smile crossed his face. "We're delivering Thanksgiving."

"To who?"

He held up the sheet of paper that the woman at the *mercado* had given him. "To the list."

We drove east, passing from the lush, gated communities and manicured yards of the tourist side of Los Cabos into a poor area of town, revealed in steadily declining buildings and neighborhoods.

The poor section of Los Cabos was only a few miles from the yachts, golf courses, and luxury resorts, but a universe away for the locals.

"This is San José del Cabo," Andrew said.

I looked around at the graffiti-strewn walls and abandoned buildings. It looked like a war zone. "Is it safe?"

"It's safe for us," he said. "The gangs usually leave American tourists alone. But especially us."

"The gangs know you?"

"It took a few years," he said.

He pulled the truck into a neighborhood that had all
the makings of a refugee camp. Dozens of poles stuck up
from the ground with electric cables crisscrossing in a nest
of wires.

"When they built the resorts, no one took time to plan
out where the workers would live, so these communities
sprouted up." He turned off the truck. "This is what a town
looks like without urban planning." He opened his door.
"Come on."

I met Andrew at the back of the truck as he opened
the cargo doors. The truck was stacked nearly to the top
with boxes, dozens of them. He pulled out a box that was
smaller than the rest. "I'll have you take that. It's for the
children."

I looked inside the box. It was filled with Hershey's
chocolate bars. Andrew grabbed one of the large boxes,
then shut the doors.

As we walked to the first home, the door opened and a
woman holding a baby emerged. *"Señor Colina, me da gusto a
verle. Pásele por favor."* She held the door open for us.

"She invited us in," Andrew said.

We walked inside. The home had dusty concrete floors
and painted plastered walls, though the paint had mostly

faded and much of the plaster had flaked off. On one side of the house was a kitchen and dining area with an old wooden table and a cupboard next to it. A wooden pallet fastened to the wall held aluminum pans hung from twisted, rusted wires. A blanket hung on the other side of the room as a partition, giving a scrap of privacy to the bedroom behind it, which had a single wide bed raised off the floor on cinderblocks. A naked lightbulb hung from the center of the room, its wires exposed.

In contrast to the concrete and plaster were colorful woven blankets and pictures hanging on the walls, bringing a sort of chromatic brilliance to the dusty room. The largest picture was an image of the Virgin Mary positioned next to a wooden cross icon with a crucified Jesus.

At the side of the room two dirty-faced children sat on a faded red couch next to a young girl who was nursing a baby. She looked too young to be a mother. The children's eyes were wide with excitement, and they sprang from the couch when they saw us.

Andrew set the box of food on the table, saying to the woman, "*¿Cómo está, Señora Abreyta?*"

"*Estamos bien. Mi hija ha regresado a vivir conmigo. Esta es su hija.*"

"*¿Ella es su nieta?*"

"*Sí.*"

"*Ella se parece a usted.*" Andrew said to me, "This is her granddaughter."

"*Bella,*" I said.

She smiled, then said in a thick accent, "Thank you."

The children were now standing in front of us, staring at the box I held.

"They remember that box from last year," Andrew said. "You can give them some chocolate."

I reached into the box and handed them each a chocolate bar. It might as well have been gold bullion for the excitement on their faces.

"*¡Gracias!*" they shouted. They ran back to the couch and peeled open their treats.

"*Que Dios le bendiga, Señor.*"

"*Ya lo hizo.*"

The woman kissed Andrew on the cheek, then she kissed me as well. "*Por favor comen con nosotros.*"

"*Gracias,*" Andrew said, "*pero no podemos. Tenemos que visitar a otros.*" He turned to me. "She's asking us to stay. They all will. We should go."

"*Cuidense mucho,*" he said to her and the rest of the family.

"*Adiós,*" I said.

I preceded him out, carrying the box of candy. As soon as I got in the truck, I began to cry.

Andrew climbed in the other side of the truck, buckled himself in, and looked over at me. "Are you okay?"

I turned back to him. "I can't believe I've felt so sorry for myself."

"One Thanksgiving I realized that the day had become meaningless to me. I was ungrateful and unhappy. That's when I realized that I was unhappy *because* I was ungrateful. That's when I started doing this. It benefits me more than them."

"How many years have you done this?"

"Six," he said. "A few years ago I missed a year. It's probably when I needed it the most." He marked the first name off the paper using a stub of a pencil. "One down."

"How did you get your list of people?"

"Rosa at the *mercado* helped me. When I first started, I asked her to put together a list of people who could use some help. The first year there were only three families."

"Your list has grown."

Andrew grinned. "Word gets out. It's hard to say no."

Andrew put the truck in gear and we drove just a few blocks to the next home. We spent the next two hours visiting homes, slowly depleting our truck of its contents. The homes were all different but, in one way, the same—humble, makeshift structures cobbled together with whatever materials their inhabitants could scavenge or afford at the time. As Andrew had predicted, every one of the families invited us to stay and eat with them, which Andrew politely declined.

As we neared the end of our deliveries, Andrew pulled the van into the middle of an open dirt lot. We were immediately surrounded by a group of tattooed, rough-looking youths. To my surprise, Andrew turned off the engine. He glanced over at me and said, "Don't be afraid. We're okay," then got out.

One of the larger and older youths approached him. To my surprise, he and Andrew embraced. Then, followed by the others, they walked around to the back of the truck. Soon several of the men walked past me, each carrying a box, going his own way. About five minutes later Andrew opened the driver's door. "That's the last of it."

"We're done?"

"Not quite," he said. He looked at me. "Are you okay?"

"Yeah. That just scared me a little."

"I wouldn't have put you in danger." He started up the truck. "We're going to have dinner with one of the families we left food with. It was the fourth home we stopped at. The Villaltas."

Andrew drove back to one of the neighborhoods where we'd started our distribution. We stopped in front of a house we'd already been to. Before we could get out of the truck, a short Mexican man emerged from the house. *"Bienvenido, amigo."*

Andrew quickly got out. *"Señor Villalta, regresamos."*

"Señor Colina, mi amigo, mucho gusto a verle de nuevo." The men embraced. Then he looked at me. *"Tiene una compañera. ¿Es su esposa?"*

"No. Solo una amiga."

As I got out of the truck, the man said to me. *"¿Habla español?"*

I turned to Andrew. "He wants to know if I speak Spanish?"

Andrew nodded. *"Un poco,"* he said to the man, which was a gross overstatement of my lingual abilities.

"Welcome, *Señorita*," he said in a thick accent. "My name *es* Ed-ward."

"It's nice to meet you," I said slowly.

He turned to Andrew and raised his eyebrows. *"Ella es muy bonita."*

Andrew nodded. *"Sí, ella es muy bonita."*

I understood that.

"Maggie," Andrew said, "there's a paper bag behind your seat, would you grab it?"

"Sí, Señor," I said, trying to be funny.

"¡Mira! Habla español!" the man said.

I grabbed the sack. It was heavy with a bottle inside. I followed the men into the house.

The inside of the home was slightly larger, though more narrow, than the first home we'd visited. The walls had also once been plastered and painted but the plaster had mostly chipped off, revealing the concrete walls underneath. Electrical wires hung along two of the walls, which they used to hang pictures, mostly older, photographic portraits of relatives and one large, colored poster of the pope. There was a rusted metal floor fan on the far side of the room next to one of the home's two clouded windows.

The main room's furniture consisted of a pair of couches set side by side and covered with bright blankets. I could see the two boxes of food we'd left earlier in the kitchen area, which was higher ceilinged than the rest of the house and had an exposed pitched roof of corrugated tin. It looked to be an addition to the house, as the plaster walls gave way to bare cinderblock.

Noticeably, they had an oven and a refrigerator. Both were smaller than anything I'd seen in the US, but a rare luxury among the houses we had visited. The smell of a baking turkey and ham filled the small room.

"Mag, I'll take that," Andrew said, reaching for the sack I held. I handed it to him.

"*¿Dondé está la Señora Villalta?*"Andrew asked.

"*Se fue a la tienda para comprarles un refresco.*"

"*Ustedes son muy amables. Muchas gracias, amigo.*"

Andrew turned to me. "I asked him where his wife was. He said she went to the store to get us sodas."

"She didn't need to do that," I said.

"It's important to them that they be good hosts." Andrew turned back to the man. "Then I can give this to you." Andrew slowly pulled an oval-shaped bottle of clear liquor from the sack.

The man looked at it in awe. "*¡Señor es un milagro! Muchísimas gracias!*"

"*De nada,*" Andrew said.

I smiled to see how happy the gift made our host. "What is that?"

"It's called sotol. It's a special liquor made from a desert plant like tequila, but it's especially potent. They say the first glass sharpens the senses, the second the conscience." Andrew handed the bottle to the man, who took it reverently. "It takes more than twelve years to mature, so it's expensive."

"How did you know he liked it?"

"When I first met him, he asked me if I had ever tried it. I had never even heard of it. He told me that it was the *néctar de los dioses.* Nectar of the Gods. He said that as a young man he had tried it once. He spoke of it like it was a lost love. I thought I'd make his dream come true."

Andrew turned back to the man. *"¿Y como está la familia?"*

I didn't know what Andrew had said, but the man's disposition abruptly changed. *"Estos son tiempos difíciles, amigo."*

"He said their family is going through a difficult time," Andrew said. *"¿Que pasó?"*

The man's face showed still more pain. *"Ángel se unió con una pandilla. Le dieron una coche y dinero. Le mataron por una pistola después de nueve días."* He pointed toward the door. *"Hace dos semanas que su hermana lo encontró tres calles por allá."*

Andrew embraced the man and said, *"Mis condolencias."*

I didn't know what was said, but tears fell down the man's cheeks. Andrew turned to me. To my surprise, his eyes were also wet. "A month ago their son joined a drug gang. He was killed nine days later. His sister found his body."

I looked at the man. "I am so sorry." I walked over and hugged him.

"Gracias, Señora."

He wiped his eyes with his sleeves, then said, *"No quitaré más de su visita. Estoy agradecido."*

A few minutes later Mrs. Villalta returned escorted by two teenage girls. She was carrying bottles of Jarritos soda. She was about the same build as her husband, short and broad, though lighter of complexion. The girls looked to be in their early teens.

"Señor Colina," she said, *"nos dió tanto este año."*

"¿Todavía está bien a cenar con usted?" Andrew asked.

"¡Sí! ¡Sí! Estamos listos!"

"She said, 'Let's eat.'"

Their table was set with the food we'd brought, as well as fresh tortillas and tamales. Their utensils were mismatched and the plates were small, battered aluminum pizza tins.

"Edward found these tins in a Dumpster behind a pizzeria where he was weeding," Andrew said to me. "Before that we used pieces of cardboard."

As we were sitting down, I asked, "Why does everyone call you Mr. Colina?"

"*Colina* means hill," Andrew said. "My last name."

"*Nuestro hogar es humilde,*" the man said to us.

"*No, no. Es un honor para nosotros,*" Andrew said. "He just told us his house is humble."

"*Oraremos,*" Mrs. Villalta said. She turned to me and said in English, "We pray."

I didn't understand anything she said, but she offered a lengthy and impassioned prayer and began crying just a few minutes in. After saying "Amen," everyone in the family crossed themselves and began to eat.

The turkey we'd brought them was large and would last them for several meals, which I wanted them to have, so in spite of our hosts' constant entreaties, I ate only a little.

"*Coma, coma,*" Mrs. Villalta said. "*Está delgada.*" She turned to Andrew to translate.

"She's telling you to eat," Andrew said. "She says you're too skinny."

"Tell her thank you," I said.

Andrew looked at me. "She didn't mean it as a compliment."

For dessert we had sweet cinnamon tamales wrapped in

corn husks. It was several hours before we left their home, the Villaltas doing all they could to extend our stay. As we drove away, I asked, "Why did she start crying during the prayer?"

"She was praying for her son's soul," Andrew said.

"I was sorry to hear about their son."

Andrew exhaled heavily. "It's a tragedy. The poverty is especially hard on them in Cabo. Poverty is hard anywhere, but here they can see the resorts and the wealthy foreigners' boats and cars, so they know what they're missing. Then they see the wealthy Mexican drug traffickers, and it seems like selling drugs is the only way out for them. It's especially sad, as I had just gotten Edward a good gardening job at the condominiums and things were looking up for their family. The young woman who cleans our place, Jazmín, is his niece."

We returned the truck to the *mercado*, then took a walk along the beach. I again took off my shoes. It would be my last chance to walk barefoot in the sand before returning to Utah. I felt sad at that thought. After a while Andrew turned to me. "I hope it was okay that we spent our Thanksgiving that way. I should have told you what I was up to."

"It was a privilege," I said. "I don't think I'll ever forget it."

"Hopefully it won't be your last time," he said.

I looked at him and smiled. "Hopefully."

"But it is exhausting."

"I was just thinking that I could use a nap," I said. "It's the tryptophan in the turkey. It's like a sleeping drug."

"I don't think you consumed enough of it to affect you," he said. "But I could use a nap."

We drove back to the condo. As we walked in, Andrew said, "Would you like to take a nap with me?"

"Yes."

I followed him into his room. It was the first time I'd actually been in it. It was not as large as mine but it was also nicely furnished, decorated with framed Mexican landscapes on the walls.

Andrew noticed me looking at them. "I bought those in Todos Santos."

"That's nice of you to buy art for your friend's condo," I said.

He smiled. "Least I could do."

I slipped off to my own room to brush my teeth and use the bathroom. When I came back, Andrew was lying on top of the sheets on the bed. I knelt on the side of the bed and crawled over to him, cuddling up against his chest. Without a word, he wrapped his arms around me, his chin against the crown of my head. I fell asleep to the sound of his heart beating.

CHAPTER

Twenty-Eight

*Have I ever been so in love? Has my heart ever been
in such peril?*
                                        —*Maggie Walther's Diary*

We slept until nearly six p.m. At least, I did. Andrew was already up. He woke me, gently shaking me. "We need to go in ten minutes," he whispered.

I rolled over. "Go?"

"We have dinner reservations."

I sat up, covering my mouth to yawn. "Where are we going?"

"I'm taking you to one of my favorite restaurants. It's called Sunset Mona Lisa."

"That sounds romantic."

"It's the perfect place to end our vacation."

End. The word sent a twinge of sadness through my heart. I never wanted this to end.

The restaurant, Sunset Mona Lisa, wasn't far from our condominium. We left our car with the valet and walked inside the building to check in, though the dining area was almost entirely outdoors—a series of terraced patios with wood-planked or tile inlaid floors, built around sapphire-blue pools and white-linen-draped tables and fire pits.

"You don't just walk into this restaurant," Andrew said, as we entered. "It's very popular. I booked it the same night you said you'd go. Luckily there was one last opening for two."

"So you had this up your sleeve the whole time."

"I don't like to leave things to chance."

The restaurant's maître d', a tall, handsome Mexican man, led us to our table near the edge of the lowest terrace. Our view overlooked the shore and the Pacific Ocean, which was now retreating with the sun.

Andrew tipped the man, then sat back in his chair looking very pleased. A pretty, older Mexican woman brought us our menus. *"Buenas tardes."*

"Buenas tardes," Andrew repeated. *"¿Qué tal?"*

"Muy bien." She looked at me, then said in clear English, "What may I bring you to drink?"

Andrew said to me, "May I order something for you?"

"Yes. Please."

"Please bring us each a glass of Dom Pérignon 2004."

"Muy bien. Are you ready to order?"

"We're still looking over our menus. In the meantime, would you bring us the calamari appetizer and the carpaccio?"

"Sí."

"Dom Pérignon?" I said after the woman left. "Champagne?"

"We're celebrating."

I smiled at him. "What are we celebrating?"

He pointed toward the west. "The sun. And you being in remission from SAD."

I gazed out over the horizon. "But our sun is leaving us."

"She'll be back tomorrow."

"And then we'll be leaving." I sighed. "I wonder what the weather's like at home."

"I'd rather not talk about going home yet."

"I'm sorry. What should we talk about?"

"How about the moment?" he said.

"We should toast that," I said. "It's a much better toast than loneliness."

"Or your car," Andrew added. He looked around. "This is considered one of the coolest restaurants in the world. I think the *New York Times* listed it as fifth coolest."

"I didn't know they ranked restaurants on the basis of cool."

"They do. It's part of the ambience rating."

"Is the food as good as the ambience?"

"I think so."

I lifted my menu. "What should I order?"

"I'd recommend the scallops or the lobster linguini, but I haven't had anything I didn't like."

A few moments later the waitress returned with our appetizers and drinks. I dove into the calamari. It was lightly fried and fresh.

"This is divine," I said.

"After I terrified you with stories of human-eating squid, I thought you might find it empowering to eat some."

I popped a ring into my mouth. "You're right. I do feel powerful."

He ate some himself, then said, "It couldn't get much fresher. They probably pulled it up just miles from here. I love calamari, but usually by the time it reaches Utah, it's turned to rubber. You might as well be eating elastic bands."

"I know," I said. "But this is amazing. And I love that they serve it with pecorino. It's one of my favorite cheeses."

"I keep forgetting that you're a professional foodie."

"I think I've tried it all."

"Which will only make you harder to please."

"I'm not hard to please," I said. "I'm just . . . discriminating."

"Hopefully we're still just talking about food."

I took a drink, then looked at him and smiled. "Maybe."

Our waitress returned a few minutes later to take our orders.

"Do you know what you'd like?" Andrew asked.

"I'll have the scallops," I said. "With the house salad."

"And I will have the lobster linguini," Andrew said.

We handed the woman our menus and she walked away.

"This restaurant was started thirty years ago by an Italian man. His name was Giorgio, so he named it Ristorante da Giorgio. Not especially original, but it was very popular until a hurricane hit in 1991 and wiped it out.

"The next year he sold what was left of it to a group of Italian businessmen, who rebuilt and renamed it. It's been the hot thing ever since." He looked at me. "So many schemes, so many people looking for the next thing." He took a drink of his champagne. "That's what makes the world go round."

"Speaking of schemes," I said, smiling, "have you decided what you're going to do after the Christmas season?"

"I have a few ideas. Like I said, I've always got a plan."

"In Utah?"

He was quiet a moment, then said, "I don't know. Some of that depends on my brother. We may go back into business together."

"Then you might move?"

"It's a possibility."

I must have looked sad because he said, "You could always come with me."

"I'll have to think on that."

"*Think* or *drink?*"

I laughed. "Both."

He was quiet for a moment, then said, "If you don't want to follow me, I could always just have two families."

My jaw dropped. "I can't believe you just said that."

"What? Too soon?" He started laughing. I hit him with my napkin, then started laughing myself. It was healing to laugh about it for a change.

An hour later, as the sun began to sink into the Pacific,

a loud gong sounded, followed by the bass tone of blowing conch shells. Before I could ask what was going on, Andrew said, "It's something they do every night. They say good night to the sun. It's their gimmick. That's where the restaurant got its name."

"That's cool," I said.

"Fifth coolest in the world," he replied.

After our meal we shared their specialty dessert, a *tartufo nero*—a decadent black truffle.

"Culinarily—" I started to say.

"Wait, is that a word?" Andrew asked.

"I just make up words sometimes," I said. "Culinarily, this may be the most unique Thanksgiving I've ever experienced. Except for the time my father cooked a raccoon for Thanksgiving dinner."

"You ate a raccoon?"

"My father lives by his own rule book."

"Clearly," Andrew said. His brow furrowed. "What does raccoon taste like?"

"Chicken, of course."

He laughed.

A minute later I said, "May I ask you something a little delicate?"

"I might not answer, but you can ask."

"Why do you love me?"

My question clearly surprised him. "So you're onto me."

"Well, if you were trying to hide it, you're not doing a very good job."

He breathed out slowly. "Well, I could tell you that I

think you're the most beautiful woman in the world, but that would be shallow, wouldn't it? And it wouldn't be completely true either."

"Then I'm not the most beautiful woman in the world?" I asked lightly.

"No, you are," he said, smiling, "but that's not the *complete* reason I've fallen for you." He paused and I sensed he was taking my question seriously. "When I was a young man, I was motivated by approbation. The prize. That's the message culture showers on us, men and women. It's in every television show, movie, magazine. Men marry for looks, women marry for situations, both equally exploitative."

"Like that couple on the boat the other day," I said.

He nodded. "Tragically, that's what motivated my first marriage. Jamie was beautiful on the outside. Stunning. The kind of beautiful that made men stop what they were doing and gawk at her, then glare at me in envy.

"I liked it, maybe even thrived on it. It was proof that I was winning. But the trophy was plastic. Beautiful on the outside but empty on the inside makes for a hollow life. It took me a few years and a lot of scars to get there, but I learned that what I really wanted was someone who was real. Someone with her own battle scars from fighting life. I had to lose a lot to get there, but I'm grateful for it. It's like the scales have fallen off my eyes. Now, there are a lot of beautiful women who look ugly to me."

"So that blonde on the boat didn't interest you at all," I teased.

He grinned. "I'm not a eunuch," he said. "There was a time when I would have eaten up her attention. But my marriage changed that. What I mostly saw was how she disrespected the man she was with. I suppose they were disrespecting each other. But I just don't have any interest in that game anymore." He looked into my eyes. "The first time I met you, I saw this beautiful, strong woman with vulnerability in her eyes. Someone who was doing her best to muddle through the storm. I was attracted to that."

"You saw all that the first time you met me?"

He nodded. "A soldier friend of mine who had seen heavy combat told me that he could spot another combat veteran a mile away. He said that once you've been in battle, you're different. I suppose it's like that in love as well."

"You've been in battle?"

"Unfortunately."

"I'm sorry."

"I was too. But I'm not now. It's what it took to bring me to this place."

"And where is that?"

"With you."

It was nearly midnight when we returned to the condo. Andrew walked me to my room, then turned to go. "Don't leave," I said.

He looked at me. "You know . . ."

"You don't need to say it," I said. "Just lie with me until I fall asleep. I don't want you to leave me."

He thought for a moment. "Okay."

"Just give me a minute." I went into my bathroom,

changed into a T-shirt and pajama shorts, then pulled down the covers and climbed onto the bed. Andrew took off his shirt and shoes, then lay down next to me. "Will you hold me?" I asked.

"Yes."

He lay back and I cuddled into him, my head against his bare chest, his strong arms wrapped around me. I felt so safe and happy and loved. "Never leave me," I said softly.

"Never," he said back.

The night faded into perfect fiction.

CHAPTER

Twenty-Nine

Love is just smoke and mirrors.
                              —Maggie Walther's Diary

I woke the next morning next to him. He was still asleep, his warm breath washing over me. I lay there, feeling him.

Before coming to Mexico I had wondered what awful thing I might discover about Andrew on this trip—which was more revealing of me than of him. What I'd discovered was that he was who he was. I still knew little of his past, but I knew his present. He was kind and vulnerable, honest and loving, not just to me but to others. No wonder the Mexican people loved him. No wonder I loved him.

I kissed his neck and he stirred a little. I looked up into his face and kissed him on the chin, then nestled back into him. I never wanted to leave this place—physically or emotionally.

"What time is it?" he asked softly.

"It's almost eight. What time do we have to leave?"

"Ten."

"I wish we didn't have to go."

"I think that every time I'm here," he said softly. "Not so much this time."

"How come?"

"This time, the best part is coming back with me."

I pressed my lips against his. Then I put my head on his chest and he pulled me in tight. "We have an hour," he said.

"An hour," I echoed.

I didn't fall back asleep. I didn't want to miss any of the moment. As I lay there I began thinking of the past year and this sudden juncture. Where would we go from here? I knew where I wanted to go. I wanted to join my life with his and fight life's battles together. That's what he said he was looking for. Is that really what he wanted?

I silenced my mind. There would be time to think about that later, and the clock was moving too fast as it was. It seemed like only minutes before he stirred, looking over at the clock next to the bed.

"Is it time?" I asked.

He kissed my forehead. "Yes."

I sighed heavily. "All good things must come to an end."

He rubbed his hand along my cheek. "Not all things." He kissed me and slowly sat up. "I'm going to shower." He got up, picked up his shirt and shoes, and walked out of my room.

I showered as well, then packed my things. I pulled my coat from the closet, a symbol of what I'd left behind and what I was returning to. Yet it didn't seem so awful now.

There was suddenly a warmth and strength inside me that felt greater than anything winter could throw at me.

My alarm clock said five minutes to ten. Time to go. I walked out into the living room. "I'm ready," I said.

Andrew was waiting for me on the sofa. "You're sure you didn't forget anything?"

"Pretty sure," I said. "If I did we'll just have to come back."

He smiled. Suddenly his expression changed. "I almost forgot our passports," he said, shaking his head. "That would have been bad. And I forgot to leave Jazmín a tip. Our passports are in that top drawer on the far right there," he said, pointing. "Next to the pantry. I put them under the papers so no one would find them. Would you grab them?"

"No problem," I said.

"I always leave Jazmín's tip in my top drawer, just to be safe." As he left the room, I went to the counter and opened the drawer. There was pile of official-looking papers inside. I rooted through them until I found our passports. As I brought them out, I noticed the top paper in the drawer. It had a graphic of an electric bolt and a green bar running across the top that read AVISO RECEIBO.

CFE Comisión Federal de Electricidad
Sr. Andrew Hill

The electric bill. I thought nothing of it as I shut the drawer. Then it struck me. It was addressed to Andrew

Hill. Why was the electric bill in Andrew's name? And if it was Andrew's condo, why would he lie about it?

An anxious chill ran up my spine. Was I being lied to again? I pushed the thought aside. *There's an explanation*, I told myself. Maybe he was just being modest.

After all the lies and deceit I'd been through with Clive, was I a fool not to worry? Why would he lie to me? Anxiety flooded in like groundwater.

Andrew walked back into the room, replacing his wallet to his back pocket. "Did you find them?"

I shut the drawer, feeling guilty, as if I'd been caught doing something I shouldn't have been doing. I held the passports up. "Right here."

"Good." He looked around, then breathed out. "Well, off we go. Back to the snow."

"I haven't even checked the weather," I said, trying to talk about something else besides what was on my mind.

"I did," he said. "It snowed twice while we were gone. At this rate, Salt Lake will be a glacier by the end of winter."

"We should stay here," I said. I think I meant it more than either of us suspected. Something told me that when this weekend was gone, it was really gone.

Andrew kissed me on the forehead. "We'll come back soon."

I closed my eyes as he kissed me. I know it was stupid—most fear usually is—but I just couldn't get the electric bill off my mind. *Why would he lie?*

CHAPTER

Thirty

*Before taking this trip, I was afraid that I would
come home with a man I no longer cared about.
Instead, I came home __without__ a man whom I care
too much about.*

—Maggie Walther's Diary

It was a longer ride to the airport than I remembered. Andrew and I hardly spoke, though he didn't seem bothered by my silence. He probably just thought I was quiet because we were going back home. I wished that were the case. It was true, of course, but the greater reason for my silence was the fear that had commandeered my thoughts. Several times I glanced over at Andrew and he suddenly looked like a stranger to me. I loved him. Why wasn't that enough? But I had loved Clive too. And trusted him. And where had that gotten me?

The trip had raised more questions than it answered. Andrew wasn't who I thought he was when we first met—a simple man in boots and worn Levis, working at a Christmas tree lot to keep the lights on. He had money, sophistication, intelligence, and a past whose surface I'd only begun to scratch. Who was he?

What seemed innocent before now scared me. Clive was about Clive. Our marriage was *The Clive Show*, and he had the spotlight and star billing while the rest of us were relegated to supporting roles or the studio audience. Personality-wise, Andrew was the polar opposite of Clive. He genuinely seemed more interested in me than in himself. At first I found this endearing. Now I was afraid that he was hiding something.

Or am I just being paranoid? If anyone had reason to be paranoid, it was me. I didn't even trust myself anymore. My husband had been able to keep another wife and family from me for three years. Clearly I was far more gullible than I ever dared believe.

My emotions blurred like the desert landscape around us, turning from fear to anger then to self-hate for undermining what seemed to be my greatest chance at happiness. This had been the perfect week. Andrew had been nothing but fun, generous, and loving. Why wasn't that enough?

We returned our car to the airport rental lot and took a shuttle to the terminal. The airport was insanely crowded with foreigners returning home from the holiday.

When it was our turn to check in, I followed Andrew up to the ticket counter, where he handed the gate agent—a mustached, ruddy-faced Mexican man—both of our passports. The badge on the man's chest read Javier de la Cruz.

The man opened the first passport, then glanced up at me. "Mrs. Walther?" he said in clear English.

I stepped forward. "I'm Mrs. Walther."

"Okay. Do you have luggage?"

"Yes," I said.

"Please put it here," he said, pointing to the opening next to his counter.

Andrew lifted my bag onto the scale while the agent printed out my boarding pass. He put a label on my bag and set it on the conveyer belt behind him.

Then Andrew set his own bag on the scale. "This is mine," he said.

The agent printed out another boarding pass, then slapped a label on Andrew's bag and also set it on the belt behind him.

"Here is your boarding pass, *Señora*," he said to me, handing me my ticket with my passport. "You will be departing from gate twelve." Then he turned to Andrew and did the same. "Here is your passport, *Señor*. You will be at gate seventeen."

I looked at Andrew. "Why are we at different gates?"

Andrew turned to me. "I'm sorry. I forgot to tell you, I'm flying straight to Denver. It was the only way I could stay here this long. I need to be in Denver tomorrow morning."

"To visit family," I said.

He looked at me peculiarly. "I told you I go to Denver every Saturday."

I don't know what it was, but this only added to my fear. My eyes began to well up. I turned and started walking toward security. Andrew came after me. "Maggie?" He grabbed my arm, then walked in front of me. "What's wrong?"

I looked at him, fighting to keep my composure. "Why didn't you tell me?"

"I'm sorry. I just forgot. It was an honest mistake." *Honest.* I suddenly hated that word. Andrew just looked at me with a concerned expression. "I don't understand. Why are you so upset?"

"I don't do well with secrets," I said.

Andrew's brow furrowed. "This wasn't a secret, Maggie. I just forgot to tell you. Do you think I'm hiding something?"

I took a deep breath, fighting back emotion. Then I looked at him. "I'm sorry. I'm just emotional. It's hard going home."

"I understand," he said. He took my hand. "We better get through security before we miss our flights."

We went through the security line, which even in priority took nearly thirty minutes. I tried to act calm, even though anxiety was building inside me like a pressure cooker. Why couldn't I shut it off?

When we got to my gate, Andrew said, "It looks like they've already started boarding." He breathed out slowly. "Look, I'm really sorry I didn't tell you, Maggie. I should have been more thoughtful." He took out his wallet. "You're going to need a ride home from the airport." He offered me a hundred-dollar bill. "That's for an Uber."

"I don't need money," I said. "I'll get a ride."

"Maggie, please."

I looked at him, unable to hold back the question that was haunting me. "Whose condo did we just stay in?"

He looked at me blankly. "Why are you asking me that?"

"The electric bill was in your name."

I could see that my question threw him. "Is that really why you're upset?"

"I don't do secrets," I said again.

He looked at me for a moment, then said, "Neither do I." He took a deep breath. "You better get on your flight." Even though he was upset, he kissed me on the cheek. "Remember I love you."

"I know," I said softly.

"I hope you do."

I didn't reply. He breathed out slowly. "Call me when you get home so I know you're safe." Then he turned and walked away. I watched him disappear into a river of humanity as a tear rolled down my cheek. He was the best thing that had happened to me in years. Maybe ever. And I had no idea who he really was.

I was a mess on the flight home. I kept bursting into tears. After my second breakdown, the elderly Mexican man sitting next to me asked if I were okay. I told him I was, then started crying again. He got a box of Kleenex from the flight attendant for me.

I thought of texting Carina for a ride home but I didn't want to explain my emotional state. I wasn't even sure that I could. After all he'd done, I felt so ungrateful. Still, as perfect as everything had been in Cabo, a part of me now wished that I hadn't gone. I just wanted to retreat to my house, lock my doors, and hibernate for the rest of the winter.

My Uber delivered me to my neighborhood around four in the afternoon. The city looked like Antarctica. We drove down a long white corridor, as the snowplows had left the road lined on both sides with snowdrifts nearly five feet high. Once inside, I left my bag in the kitchen and went straight to bed.

CHAPTER

Thirty-One

Am I protecting or sabotaging myself? I honestly don't know anymore. I feel like I don't know anything anymore—especially how much more of this I can take.

—Maggie Walther's Diary

I slept for a couple of hours, then woke and tossed and turned until around midnight, when I finally got up and took two Ambien with a glass of wine. I didn't wake until noon the next day.

I woke with a pounding headache. I looked at my clock, then got out of bed. I walked over to the window and opened the blinds. It was gray outside, the sun burning pale orange behind a thick curtain of clouds.

I felt like I was suffering from an emotional hangover. In the light of a new day I felt like a crazy woman—like the Clive-induced PTSD of the last year had left small land mines on my heart just waiting for someone to trigger them. Unfortunately, that someone had been Andrew. Why had I gotten so angry that he had to fly to Denver? Why would I accuse him of hiding something, when he had already told me that he went to Denver every week? And why was something as simple as an electric bill freaking me out? There could be a dozen plausible explanations. At least. Why couldn't I have just given him a little grace?

In the previous day's emotional state, I had forgotten to call Andrew to tell him I'd arrived home. My phone had been off since our flight to Cabo. I turned it back on, hoping that there was a message from Andrew. After all my drama, I doubted there would be, but I hoped.

Just seconds after turning my phone back on, it began beeping with voicemails and text messages. Carina alone had left three of the former and six of the latter. There were two voicemail messages from Clive as well. Then I saw the text message Andrew had sent late last night. I went directly to it.

ANDREW

I hope you got home safe.

Thank you again for such a beautiful time.

I hope you will forgive me for not telling you about my Denver flight. I'm back around six.

Would you like to get together?

I breathed out in relief. Then I typed back.

MAGGIE

I'm sorry I was so upset. Yes, I can't wait to see
you. I hope YOU will forgive me. Love, me

I felt both relief and shame. Relief that he hadn't given
up on me and shame that I had given him reason to. I
scrolled back on my phone to read my other texts. They
had started coming on Thursday.

CARINA

Happy Thanksgiving, doll. Hope you're having a
good time down south. P.S. I had to buy a dozen
new tablecloths. I'll explain later.

CARINA

Hi there. Call me when you can.

CLIVE

You there? I left you a voicemail.

CLIVE

Mag?

CARINA

Hey, doll. Are you back?

CARINA

Worried, please call.

CARINA

I thought you were coming back today. Please call. We need to talk. Important.

CARINA

Should I file a missing persons report?

I ignored Clive's pleas but listened to the last of Carina's voicemails. She sounded upset. "Honey, please call me as soon as you can. I have something important to tell you."

I immediately dialed her number. Carina answered on the first ring. "Finally," she said, making no attempt to conceal her exasperation. "Where in the world are you?"

"I'm home. I got back yesterday."

"Why didn't you call me? I've been worried out of my head. I probably left you a dozen messages."

"Nine," I said. "Sorry. I forgot that I turned my phone off. What's going on?"

"I need to talk to you."

"Yes?"

"In person. We need to talk in person."

"Why? Is it bad?"

She didn't answer, which I guess was an answer.

"So it's serious," I said.

"I think so."

I sighed. I really didn't need or want any more drama in my life. "All right," I said. "Where do you want to meet?"

"Coffee in twenty," she said.

"Give me forty. I just got up."

"Forty," she said. "Bye."

It took me a half hour to get ready. I felt heartsick knowing she had bad news. My mind ran the gamut of possible disasters, from finding out that a client was suing us to Carina quitting.

When I got to the coffee shop, Carina was sitting in a corner as far from humanity as possible. For once she looked unmade, her hair pulled back into a ponytail, her eyes, sans mascara, were rimmed with dark circles. Her appearance only added to my anxiety. She stood as I approached and hugged me. "I'm so glad you're back. I got you a grande. I hope that's okay."

"Thank you," I said, sitting down. "So, my heart's pounding out of my chest. What's so important?"

"How was your trip?" she asked.

"It was perfect."

"And Andrew?"

"He was perfect."

She looked more surprised than pleased. "Did he tell you much about himself? About his past?"

"A little. He was married before. He worked in finance but had some business problems just before he moved here from Colorado."

"Did he tell you why he had to move?"

"He didn't have to move," I said. "He said he had some business problems." Carina just shook her head. Her coyness made me angry.

"What is it you're dying to tell me?" I said.

Carina took in a deep breath, then reached into her purse. She brought out a sheet of paper and set it in front of me. It was a copy of a newspaper article she had printed off the Internet. The photograph accompanying the article froze my heart. It was a picture of Andrew being led away in handcuffs.

Denver Man Found Guilty in $32 Million Investment Fraud

Denver investment fund manager Aaron Hill was found guilty on six counts of investment fraud after transferring nearly $32 million in investors' funds into offshore bank accounts. Hill cooperated with security agents, who were able to locate and return all but $75,000 of the investors' capital. Hill was the CEO and founder of Hill & Associates, an investment company.

A federal judge ordered Hill to repay the debt and sentenced him to three and a half years in prison with parole eligibility in 24 months. Hill's sentence will begin on December 6. He will be incarcerated in the Englewood Federal Correctional Institution, a low-security facility for nonviolent offenders.

I looked up at Carina, my heart pounding wildly. "This man's name is Aaron."

"But's that him, right?"

I looked again at the picture. It was definitely Andrew. The article was dated December 3, 2014, almost two years earlier.

"He must have changed his name," Carina said.

"Where did you find this?"

"On the Internet. I googled him and this came up." She looked at me anxiously. "There's more."

She set down another paper.

Wife of Convicted Fund Manager Alleges Assault

Convicted fund manager Aaron Hill is being sued by his former wife for $2 million for assault and battery. Hill has recently been convicted of six counts of fraud after embezzling nearly $32 million from his firm's clients. Hill declined to comment, but his attorney said that his client denies the accusations and deserves his day in a court of law, rather than trial by misinformed public opinion.

I started to cry. Carina reached in her purse and brought out a tissue. "I'm so sorry, honey. I hate that I had to be the one to tell you. At least now you know why he's gone every weekend."

"What do you mean?"

"He probably has to go back to Colorado each week to check in with his parole officer."

I rested my head in my palm. Tears streamed down my cheek and fell to the table. Carina slid her chair over next to me. "I'm so sorry, honey."

"Every time I think I've found something I can trust, it's false. I thought Clive was the ideal husband. Now Andrew . . ."

"Aaron," Carina said.

"Whatever his name is," I snapped.

"It's okay, honey. You have every right to be angry."

"What am I doing to attract this?"

"It's not you." She rubbed my back. "It's not your fault. When do you see him next?"

"Tonight."

Carina's brow furrowed. "What are you going to do?"

"I don't know." I lifted the articles. "Can I take these?"

"Of course."

For a moment we were both silent. Then I said, "I've got to go."

"Call me tonight after you see him," Carina said. "Or whenever. Any time day or night. I'm here for you."

We hugged, then I followed her out of the cafe, holding back a torrent of emotions until I was in my own car. Then I leaned against the steering wheel and sobbed.

CHAPTER

Thirty-Two

I sent him away.

—*Maggie Walther's Diary*

I cried most of the afternoon. I didn't know what I should do. Should I confront him about what Carina had told me? Did I even have the strength to?

Andrew arrived a little after seven. He looked tired from travel but happy to see me. I'm pretty sure that I looked like emotional roadkill. I only partially opened the door.

"Hi," he said, his expression changing at seeing me.

I sniffed. "Hi."

"Are you all right?"

I shook my head.

"What's wrong?"

I swallowed. "I just don't feel well. It's been an awful day."

"Did something else happen?"

I didn't answer.

"Did I do something?" I still didn't answer. He looked at me for a moment, then said, "Do you want me to leave?"

I was seriously conflicted. I wanted him to comfort and

protect me from him. Finally I said, "That would probably be best."

"All right." He looked at me. "Are you sure that's all that's wrong?"

I hesitated for a second, then said, "Yes."

He looked at me doubtfully. "All right. I'll call you tomorrow. Good night."

He had started to step back when I said, "Where do you go every weekend?"

He looked at me for a moment. "You know where I go. Denver."

"Why?"

"To see my brother."

"Why?"

His eyes reflected his hurt. "Because it's the only time I can." Neither of us spoke for a moment, then he said, "I don't know what I've done to make you distrust me, but something's happened." His voice cracked a little. "Don't think this is easy for me either. Maggie, you're not the only one who has reason not to trust."

For a moment his words just hung in the air between us, then he looked as if he were going to say something but stopped himself. He just turned and walked away. Something in my heart told me to go after him, but I didn't. I went back to my room and cried.

The next three days passed in a lifeless funk. While the world around me glistened with holiday tinsel, my heart was as dark inside as I kept my house. I didn't even plug in my Christmas tree lights. The title of a book I'd read decades ago came to mind: *The Winter of Our Discontent*. That's what this felt like—the winter of my discontent. And it seemed like this winter would never end.

Andrew didn't call. Clive did. Three times. I didn't answer. I just wanted him to go away. Part of me blamed him for what had happened between Andrew and me. Had he not broken my trust, I wouldn't have been so untrusting. Or had he done me a favor? Like I said, I was conflicted. Then, late Monday, he texted me something cryptic.

CLIVE

It is what it is. Don't worry about coming to trial.

I almost called him back to see what he meant. I didn't have to. I found out soon enough.

CHAPTER

Thirty-Three

Someone threw a brick through my window. I'm afraid. What is wrong with people? Why can't they just live their own lives?

—Maggie Walther's Diary

My cell phone rang around six a.m. I rolled over and checked the caller ID before answering.

"Carina?"

"Are you up?" she asked.

"I am now."

"Have you seen today's paper?"

"I just woke."

"Clive had another family."

It took a moment for her words to gel. "What?"

"He had a third wife and three other children."

I was stunned. "Where?"

"Spanish Fork, Utah."

My already battered heart felt like it had just been delivered another sucker punch. More betrayal. More evidence of my stupidity. And still to come, more media circus. It was going to start all over again. Why wouldn't it end? I knew the answer. It wouldn't end until Clive stopped giving the media juicy things to report on. Or until it stopped selling newspapers.

"What are you going to do?" Carina asked.

"What is there to do?" I said. "Board up the windows for another storm."

Ironically, my words were answered by the crash of a breaking window.

"What was that?" Carina asked.

I pulled on my robe and ran into the front room. There was a large hole in my picture window, and my carpet was covered with shards of glass. In the center of my living room floor was a brick. It took me a moment to understand what I was seeing.

"Maggie? Are you okay?"

"Someone just threw a brick through my window. I need to call the police."

"Do you want me to come over?"

"I've got to go." I hung up and dialed 911. Then I sat down in my kitchen to wait for the police. How much worse was this going to get?

Ten minutes later my doorbell rang. It was a police officer. He looked boyish but was thickly built. I thought he appeared too young for the uniform.

"You called in a broken window?" he said.

"Yes."

"May I come in?"

"Yes."

I pulled open the door. He stepped inside and looked at the glass covering my carpeted floor. "I'm Officer Huber," he said. He walked over and examined the brick. "Is this what they threw through the window?"

No, I always keep a brick in the middle of my living room floor. "It would appear so," I said.

"Have you touched it?"

"No. That's where it was."

He took out a pad and wrote something down. "When did you notice the window was broken?"

"When I heard it," I said. "About fifteen minutes ago."

"So you were here when it happened?"

"I was in my bedroom."

"Did you hear a car or motorcycle drive away?"

"No. I only heard the window break."

"Is there any other damage to your property?"

"I don't know. I haven't been out. Not that I'm aware of."

"Do you have any surveillance cameras around the house?"

"No."

"How about your neighbors?"

"I wouldn't know."

He nodded. "I'll check with them, see if they saw anything." He again wrote something down. "Is there anyone you know of who is upset with you?"

"Not that I know of."

"A boyfriend or ex-husband. This kind of vandalism is usually perpetrated by someone the victim knows."

"They're both upset with me," I said, more to myself

than the officer. He looked at me with interest. "But they wouldn't do this."

He lifted his pad. "I'd better take their names."

"My husband was in the newspaper this morning. I think this may have something to do with him."

"Then you think he did it."

"No, I think someone who doesn't like him did it. He's a former city councilman. Clive Walther. He was arrested for bigamy."

"Councilman Walther," he said. "I know about his arrest." He again wrote something on his pad. "And this boyfriend?"

"He's not really a boyfriend. I don't want you contacting him. It would be embarrassing."

"You never know."

"He wouldn't do this. I don't want you contacting him."

A few minutes later there was another knock on the door. "That should be the detective," Officer Huber said. "May I let him in?"

"Yes."

He opened the door. A thin, bald man wearing an oversized down vest stepped inside my house. He held a camera in one hand and had a black, box-shaped bag hanging at his side.

"This is Mrs. Walther," Officer Huber said.

"I'm Detective Frederickson," he said to me. "I'm sorry this happened. I'm just going to take a few pictures for our records, then dust for fingerprints."

"Fine," I said, stepping back.

The detective walked over to the brick. "This is what was thrown through the window?"

"Yes."

"Have you touched it?"

"She hasn't," Officer Huber said.

"No," I said. "Can you take fingerprints off a brick?"

"Sometimes. Or DNA." He leaned over and took a picture of the brick, then stooped down and brushed it with powder.

I sat down on the couch and watched the police work as if I were watching a crime show on TV. My living room was as cold as my refrigerator and getting colder. I could see my breath.

"I'm going to talk to your neighbors," Officer Huber said. He pointed to the broken window. "You might want to hang something over that."

After he left, I asked the detective if I could hang something over the window.

"Just a minute," he replied. He took a few pictures of the window, then said, "Okay, I'm good."

I got some duct tape from the garage and a quilt from the hall closet and brought them into the living room. I tried to hang the quilt myself but failed.

"Excuse me; could you give me a hand?" I asked the detective.

He glanced up at me from the floor. "Sure thing."

He left his kit on the floor and came to the window. I got up on a chair and he held the quilt in place as I taped it around the sides of the window, darkening the room. I could still feel the cold coming through, but at least it was better than it was. I turned on the room light and started a fire in the fireplace.

The detective walked around my living room taking pictures for another few minutes, then said, "All right. I'm done here. Thank you."

"Thank you," I replied. I let him out the door.

Fifteen minutes later Officer Huber returned. I was in the kitchen making myself some toast when he knocked, then slightly opened the door. "Mrs. Walther?"

I walked back to the living room. "You can come in."

He stepped inside. "I visited with your neighbors. None of them saw anything or have functional surveillance cameras." He took a business card from his shirt pocket and wrote on it. "Here's my info and your case number for your insurance. You'll need it to file a homeowner's claim. What's the best number to reach you at?"

"My cell." I gave him my number.

"If I find anything, we'll give you a call."

"Do you think you will?"

He frowned. "We'll do our best. Have a good day."

He walked out. I went back to the kitchen to get my toast, which was now too cold to melt butter. I had just put it back in the toaster when there was another knock on my door.

"What did they forget now?" I said to myself. I walked back out and opened it. A young woman with a pixie cut stood on the doorstep.

"Hi, Mrs. Walther? I'm from the *Herald*. We received a report that someone threw a brick through your window. Is your husband Councilman Walther here?"

"No. And that's ex-councilman and ex-husband. He was removed from the council, and we're divorced."

She lifted her pad. "So you believe that this act of violence was directed at you?"

"Why would someone throw a brick through my window because my husband cheated on me?"

"I really don't know," she said.

"Neither do I. Good-bye." I shut the door with her still standing there. I went back to the kitchen. My toast was charred and smoking. I threw it away and started over. I was finally eating toast when the doorbell rang again.

I groaned. "Just leave me alone." I walked out and opened the door. An elderly man stood at my doorstep. It took me a moment to recognize him as my neighbor, Mr. Stephens. He had a roll of plastic tucked under one arm and a roll of duct tape in his hand.

"Mrs. Walther, I'm Bryan Stephens from across the street."

"Mr. Stephens," I said. "Please come in."

"Call me Bryan," he said as he stepped inside. "A police officer just came by to ask if we'd seen who threw a brick through your window."

"I'm sorry he disturbed you so early in the morning."

"It's no problem," he said. "I've always been an early riser. I was just having coffee and doing a crossword puzzle. Only thing the newspaper's any good for these days.

I'm sorry we couldn't be of assistance to the officer. But I figured you probably could use someone to patch your window." He looked over at the window. "I see you put a blanket up."

"It's all I had," I said. "It's not working too well."

"I've got this plastic painting tarp. It will seal up nicely until you can get someone to replace the glass. And it will still let some light into the room."

"Thank you," I said. "You're too kind."

"I'm just glad to still be of use."

"Do you need some help?"

"Nah, this is easy stuff."

He took off his shoes and laid the plastic roll on the floor. He pulled down my quilt and measured the window with a tape measure. Then he rolled out a long, rectangular piece of plastic and cut it with a razor knife.

Watching him work reminded me of my father. He was good with his hands and was always repairing things— something Clive never did. The truth was, Clive was domestically challenged. When we first got married, he'd call a plumber if the toilet got clogged. I had to show him how to use a plunger.

"May I get you some coffee?" I asked.

"That would be nice. Just black, please. Or maybe a couple spoonfuls of milk if you have it."

A few minutes later, when I brought out his coffee, my quilt was neatly folded on the couch and he had already taped the sides of the plastic to the window.

"This plastic is good material. I got it twelve years ago

when I was remodeling the basement. It's hard to find plastic this thick anymore. It's nearly twenty mils."

I had no idea what that meant but I nodded appreciatively. Then he precariously climbed up on a chair to seal the top of the window.

"You sure I can't do that?" I said.

"I've got it."

When he finished sealing the plastic, there was no more cold air coming through. I set down his coffee, then took his hand and helped him down from the chair.

"I'll take that coffee now."

"You've earned it," I said, handing him the cup. He sat down on the couch and sipped it. "This is good coffee."

"Thank you. It's a local roaster."

"I put your blanket right here." He patted the quilt.

"Thank you," I said. "You even folded it."

He took a few more sips, then looked at the window. "Yes, that's some quality Visqueen there. Like I said, it's good thick stuff. It's got an R-factor close to window glass, maybe even a four."

Again, I had no idea what he was talking about.

"Thank you," I said. "You're very kind."

"That's what neighbors are for," he replied. He took another sip of coffee. "Yes, that's a fine brew. You'll have to tell Leisa what kind it is when she brings your plates back. Those cookies you baked for us sure were tasty."

"I'm glad you liked them," I said. "I was so sorry to learn about your son."

His expression fell. He set down his coffee and said,

"That tape should hold a few weeks, but I wouldn't put off replacing the window too long." He stood. "I best get back to Leisa. She gets worried if I stay too long at a pretty girl's house. And she's got her own honey-do list I need to get started on." He put his hand through the roll of duct tape, lifted the roll of plastic, and walked to the door. "Have a good day," he said. "And have a happy holiday."

"To you too," I said. "And your wife."

"I'll pass on your sentiments."

I watched him carefully make his way down my icy walk. Then I shut the door behind him. *What a kind, broken man*, I thought.

CHAPTER

Thirty-Four

Once again, my life needs a reset button.
—Maggie Walther's Diary

I spent the rest of the day in bed reading, doing my best to escape the new reality I'd been tossed headlong into. I didn't know if I could go through this all over again. I didn't want to isolate myself anymore; I just wanted to run as far away as possible. I started thinking about moving out of state. Maybe I should have thought of it before; I just didn't know where I'd go. At first, all I could think of was Cabo, which only made me feel worse.

I considered going back to Ashland. I knew Ashland might be hell, but it was, at least, a hell I was familiar with. And, right now, it couldn't be as bad as Salt Lake. At least strangers in Ashland wouldn't pass any judgment on my life.

I hadn't seen my father for nine years—not since my wedding. I wondered what he was like now. I've seen men mellow as they age. I'm sure a psychiatrist would have had a field day with this, but I suppose some part of me still wanted to earn his approval. Or maybe the idea of going back was just another form of self-flagellation for all my poor decisions.

I wondered what my father would say if I came back. Most likely it would be some type of "I told you so." He wouldn't even have to say it: it would just shine from his eyes. He loved being proved right. He used to say, "I'm never wrong. It's the facts that get mixed up."

He had never liked Clive, though that didn't surprise me. Clive wasn't his type of man. In fact, he didn't consider him a man. My father called him "a slick-boy politician with a pretty mouth," which I'm sure was one of the worst insults Dad could think of. The morning of my wedding he said to me, "That pretty boy of yours needs to spend a week on the side of a mountain with me hunting bear. That'll grow him some chest hair."

My father was big on chest hair. When I was younger— before I physically matured—he was always saying things would "grow me chest hair." When I told him I didn't want chest hair, he just laughed. "Why not, you ain't got nothing else on it."

Was I really considering going back to that? Was I that desperate? It was like most of my life: my plans weren't about where I was going but about what I was running from. The cycle just continued. I was ready to give it all up—my home, my business, my life in Utah—just to escape the daily reminders of pain, reminders which had started with Clive but had since moved on to another man.

Andrew. Or Aaron, or whatever his name was. I couldn't stop thinking about him. It's easy to say that the pain of losing him was disproportionate to the time I had known him, but hearts don't always work like that. I have seen people walk away from fifty-year-old marriages without looking back, and I've seen hearts broken over week-long affairs. I had only known him for three weeks and my heart felt truly in peril. I had fallen in deep. Still, it was better to lose him now than later. I once heard it said that "It's best to dismiss bad love at the door, instead of after it has moved into the heart and unpacked all its suitcases." Why couldn't he just have been who I thought he was?

Around midnight, I made plans to return to Oregon. I had no idea how long I would stay. Maybe a day, maybe forever. The drive was a little over seven hundred miles, which I could do in twelve hours. If I left at eight a.m., I would get there a few hours after dark. I decided I would leave on Sunday morning.

CHAPTER

Thirty-Five

I've made a big mistake. Again. I'm getting good at it.

—Maggie Walther's Diary

I called Carina the next morning to tell her I was leaving.

"How long will you be gone?" she asked.

"I don't know yet."

"You're not talking about a permanent move . . ."

"I don't know yet."

"I don't want to talk about this. You can't leave."

"There's no reason for me to stay."

"No reason? Your home is here."

"It doesn't feel like home anymore."

"You have your business."

"You're already handling that."

She sounded exasperated. "What about your friends?"

"There's just you," I said.

"*Just?*" she repeated. "That was hurtful."

"You know I didn't mean it like that."

There was a long pause, then Carina's voice came in pained realization. "When are you leaving?"

"Sunday morning," I said.

"You're not even going to say good-bye?"

"I'll see you before I go. And I'll be back," I said. "There are things I'd need to do before I left for good. Business things. We'll have time together."

We were both silent for a moment, then Carina said, "I don't know what else to say. I understand why you want to leave. I couldn't go through what you're going through. I just think it's so wrong that you have to bear this."

"Life happens," I said. "By the way, I called Scott and told him to give you a Christmas bonus of all of November and December's profits."

"That's too much," Carina said.

"No. You earned it."

"Maggie?"

"Yes?"

"I hope you're not serious about staying in Oregon. You're not the only one short on friends."

We said good-bye and I went to shower. I was drying my hair when someone knocked on my door. (I don't know why almost no one used the doorbell. I'm not really complaining; it's just a mystery to me.) I quickly pulled on my jeans and sweater and walked out to the foyer, hoping it wasn't another reporter. I unbolted the door and opened it.

It was Andrew. He was wearing a leather jacket with a tweed scarf, his hands in his pockets. For a moment we just looked at each other.

"Hi," he said, his breath clouding before him.

"Hi," I returned softly.

He nervously cleared his throat. "I read about Clive in the paper. I just wanted to make sure you were all right."

I nodded. "I'm okay."

He sniffed. "Good. I just wanted to make sure."

"Do you want to come in?" I asked.

He looked at me cautiously. "You sure you want that?"

"No," I said. "Do you want to come in?"

He hesitated a moment, then stepped inside. Noticeably, he didn't hug or even touch me. I shut the door behind him. He looked over at my bandaged window. "The paper said someone threw a brick through your window."

I nodded. "Yeah. That was a nice addition to yesterday morning."

"You weren't hurt, were you?"

"No. Just frightened."

"I'm sorry. People are crazy."

"Would you like some coffee?" I asked.

"No, I was just dropping by on the way to work."

"I've missed you."

He looked like he didn't know how to respond. After our last encounter I'm certain he was confused.

"I've missed you too."

"I'll make us some coffee."

We went into the kitchen. Andrew sat down at the table. "Did they catch who threw the brick?"

"No. I doubt they will."

"Whoever did it must have thought that Clive was still living here."

"I assume so. I don't know why anyone would want to

throw a brick at me." I looked at him. "Except you. You probably want to throw a brick at me."

He didn't smile.

"That was a joke," I said.

He still didn't smile. I brought our coffee over and sat down. "The police asked me if I had an upset ex-husband or ex-boyfriend. I told him I had both. I wouldn't give him your name."

"Is that who I am? Your ex-boyfriend?"

I didn't know how to answer that. "I forgot your sugar." I got up, got the sugar tin, and carried it over to the table, then sat back down.

"Thank you," he said without looking at me. He took out two of my homemade sugar cubes and dropped them into his coffee. He drank for a moment in silence, then said, "What happened, Maggie? I don't know what's going on. I mean, you told me you loved me and now you won't talk to me."

"I know," I said softly. "It's complicated."

"I can do complicated. What I can't do is not knowing what I did wrong."

"You didn't do anything wrong," I said. I breathed out slowly. "I was afraid." I looked back up into his eyes. "I was afraid of getting hurt again. I've been hurt too much."

He gazed at me with a confused expression. "What made you think I would hurt you?"

"I don't know."

He leaned forward. "You can tell me."

I swallowed. "I'm afraid to tell you."

"What are you afraid of? Losing me? Because as things are, you already have."

Tears came to my eyes. Then I said, "Okay. I'll tell you."

He sat back in his chair.

I took a deep breath to compose myself. "It started the last day in Cabo when you sent me to get the passports. In that drawer, there was an electric bill with your name on it. I couldn't figure out why it was in your name. Then I wondered if it really was your condo and it made me think you were lying to me." I looked down. "It made me wonder what else you were hiding from me."

He thought for a moment. "And then I forgot to tell you about my flight to Denver." He took another swallow of coffee, then looked up at me and said, "The condo was part mine, once. Now it belongs to my brother."

"I should have just asked."

His expression didn't change. "There's more, isn't there?"

"Yes."

"Just tell me."

I felt like he was asking me to take a step off a very high cliff. I knew that once I was over the edge there was no turning back.

"Please," he said. "Give me a chance to explain."

I got up and walked to my room and retrieved the newspaper article that Carina had given me. I came back to the table and set it down in front of him.

He lifted the paper. He read through it, then set it back down. "I guess that explains it." He looked at me, his eyes dark and pained. "You think this is me?"

"It's your picture."

"Did you read the whole article?"

"Yes."

"Did you read the part that said his first chance at parole was in two years?" He pushed the article to me. "Look at the date of the article. It hasn't been two years yet. The man in the picture is still in prison." He sighed. "That's my brother. We're identical twins. He's being paroled in eight days. On the ninth."

For a moment I was speechless. "You're a twin?"

"Identical twins," he said.

How could I have been so stupid?

"Five years ago my brother and I started a business together. Hill Brothers Management. We were venture capitalists. We raised money for start-ups—risky, blue-sky opportunities. We were good at it, but Aaron was the brains behind it all. He had a sixth sense.

"Our first year in business we backed an investment that our investors weren't especially excited about—a little plastic gizmo that separates the wires on phone chargers. It did better than anyone expected. A lot better. Our client sold millions of them online at five dollars each. By the time everyone else started marketing their own version, he had sold more than twenty million units."

"I have one of those," I said.

"I know, I noticed it that night I brought your tree," he said. He settled a little in his chair. "We were riding pretty high. Everyone involved was making money. But some people can't leave well enough alone. Our investors got greedy, and since Aaron was making the most profit on these deals, they staged a coup and pushed him out of his own firm. Not both of us, just him."

"How could they do that?"

"It's complex," he said. "But the bottom line is, he was too trusting. It had never occurred to him that the people he had done the most for would be the first to turn on him."

His words made my stomach hurt. He could have been describing me.

"As if that wasn't bad enough, a week later he found out that his wife had been having an affair with one of the investors. Everyone he trusted had turned against him. Everyone.

"He was hurt, but he didn't quit. He started his own firm. Just him. With his record, investors threw money at him. But that's when things started to go wrong. Large amounts of money and a broken soul don't go well together. Things began to unravel. He started drinking heavily. Then, when his new projects weren't panning out, he started siphoning money to offshore accounts. He had moved over thirty million before he was caught."

"How was he caught?" I asked.

"He turned himself in. He didn't have the heart of a crook." He breathed out slowly. "His original company went under. That was no surprise. Aaron had always been the brains behind it. It had already started floundering soon after he left. Then, with all the media his trial generated, the Hill name wasn't just tarnished, it was poisoned.

That's why I left the state. There was nothing I could do there."

I sat quietly processing it all. "How is your brother doing?"

"About as well as you would expect for someone in prison. Thankfully it's not the usual correctional facility filled with violent offenders, but it's still prison . . ." He suddenly got emotional. "I'm all the family he has. The only time I'm allowed to see him is visiting hours Saturday morning. That's why I go back to Denver every week."

I looked at him. "I didn't know."

"You just needed to ask," he said quietly.

"I was just so afraid that I was being lied to. I was so stupid."

Andrew sat quietly thinking, then he said, "No. You're not stupid. You were right to protect yourself. You deserve the truth." He abruptly stood. "You were right, Maggie. This never could have worked." He walked to the door.

I was stunned. I got up and went after him, stopping him as he opened the door. "Andrew, I'm sorry. I know I screwed up. Please give me another chance. Please. I love you."

"You don't really know me."

"I do know you. I've seen your heart."

He looked at me with sad, vacant eyes, then took a deep breath. "What if I had been the one who stole the money? Knowing who I am now, would you have given me another chance? Could you have forgiven me?"

I thought for a moment, then said, "I don't know. But it wasn't you. It's not important."

His frown deepened. "It's more important than you think." He kissed me on the cheek, then turned and walked out the door. Now I was the one in the dark. Something told me I would never see him again.

CHAPTER

Thirty-Six

I wish I wasn't so good at getting in the way of my own happiness.

—Maggie Walther's Diary

Late afternoon the following day, Carina sat quietly at the kitchen table across from me. She had come directly to my home from catering a wedding rehearsal lunch and was still wearing her black serving tunic. The newspaper article lay on the table between us.

"So he's an identical twin," she finally said. "Do you believe him?"

Her question angered me. "Aaron Hill, his twin brother, is still in prison," I said. "It's public record. It's right there in the article. With all our genius, we somehow missed that little detail."

"All my genius," Carina said. "It's my fault."

"That's why Andrew goes back to Colorado every Saturday: to see his brother. He drives almost ten hours each way just to visit with his brother for a few minutes. I should have sainted him, not demonized him."

"You couldn't have known," Carina said.

"Yes, I could have. All I had to do was ask instead of jumping to the worst possible conclusion."

"Honey, after what you've been through, no one can blame you."

"I can," I said. "And I'm pretty sure that he does too. I don't think he's ever coming back. I've lost the best man I've ever known." Tears welled up in my eyes. "Maybe the best thing I've ever known."

"This is my fault," Carina said. "I should have just stayed out of it."

I put my head in my hands. When I could speak, I said, "What do I do?"

"You need to go to him."

"What if he won't see me?"

"I don't know. I guess we'll jump off that bridge when we come to it."

CHAPTER

Thirty-Seven

There is nothing more predictable than the law of the harvest. I'm reaping the pain of the hurt I've sowed.

—Maggie Walther's Diary

It was after dark on Friday night when I drove back to the Christmas tree lot. As much as I had replayed our conversation, I still really didn't know what I would say to him when I saw him. Truthfully, I think I would have said anything to make him like me again.

I had previously been to Andrew's lot only during the day; in the evening it was much busier than I had ever seen it. The parking lot was full, and I ended up parking at a drive-in across the street and walking over. The place looked different. The strands of Christmas lights that were strung above the lot were lit, and Christmas music played over a PA system. Everything felt more alive but me.

I looked up and down the rows of trees looking for Andrew. Twice my heart leapt when I thought I saw him, but both times it just turned out to be another customer.

I had walked the entire lot twice when I finally stopped Shelby, who was busy helping someone.

"Excuse me," I said.

"I'll be right with you, ma'am," Shelby said, then he recognized me. "Oh, hey. It's you." The woman he was helping glared at me as if I had just jumped a line.

"I'm looking for Andrew. Is he here?"

"Negatory. He never works weekends."

Of course, I thought. It was Friday. "So he'll be back Monday?"

"Ah, not sure about that." He shouted to someone I couldn't see. "Hey, Chris, when is the boss back?"

"Eighteenth," came the reply.

"Oh, gotcha, dude." He turned back to me. "Yeah, he's gonna be gone a while. Like until the eighteenth."

My heart fell. That was more than two weeks away.

"Excuse me," the customer said. "I'll take this tree."

"Gotcha," Shelby said without looking at her. He continued, "So, the boss was, like, kinda noncommittal, you know what I mean? He said, like, maybe the eighteenth, but then, like, maybe not. I think it depends on how things go down. I heard his brother's getting out of jail, and he's gonna spend some time with him, get him readjusted to life outside, you know what I mean?"

"I know what you mean," I said. I breathed out heavily. "All right. Would you please tell him I came by?"

"Gotcha," he said, then added, "I can go one better. If you give me your number, I'll text you when he's back."

I wasn't sure that he wasn't just trying to get my phone number, but it was worth the risk. I gave it to him and he dialed it into his phone. "Gotcha," he said, which by now I figured was his catchphrase. "Oh, wait. I need to put your name on this. What's your name?"

"It's Maggie," I said.

"I won't remember that. I'll just put Stacy's Mom. That's what Chris calls you. You know, like that song."

"Gotcha," I said. I walked back to my car, dragging my heart behind me.

CHAPTER

Thirty-Eight

Clive may have tied his noose with my heartstrings,
but that doesn't mean I have to attend the hanging.
                                    —Maggie Walther's Diary

The next two weeks were miserable. It snowed, of course. I had given up complaining about it. In a way, that was true about my life as well.

It literally took me most of a day to get up the nerve to call Andrew. He didn't answer, nor did he return my messages. I sent about a dozen texts before I accepted that I was just making myself look pathetic. For the first time, I was starting to believe that he really was done with me. I shouldn't have been surprised. That's what happens when you handle someone's heart carelessly.

On December ninth I thought about him all day. (Who am I kidding? I thought about him all day, every day.) According to our last conversation, that was the day his brother was to be paroled. I wondered what that would be like for him. I wondered if he had ever told his brother about me.

On the home front, I couldn't stand the isolation anymore and went back to work. Carina had done a good job taking care of the clients but not the business. It wasn't her fault. She had never been trained to run the place, nor did she have the authority to pay bills. Our Internet service had been canceled, and we were just two days away from the power company turning off the kitchen's electricity.

I worked at the bakery but none of the events. I still felt uncomfortable in public. Besides, there was enough to keep me busy with baking and preparation, let alone catching up with the business side of the company. I was glad when Carina stopped asking if I had heard from Andrew.

Tuesday night, the thirteenth, as I was getting ready for bed, Clive paid me a visit. He had probably lost twenty pounds, and his clothes, which looked like they hadn't been ironed in weeks, hung on him. He looked like an underfed scarecrow. In spite of everything, I felt sorry for him.

"May I come in?" he asked humbly.

"Yes." I stepped aside and he walked in. "Are you hungry?"

"No. You wouldn't have any vodka, would you?"

"I've got apple juice."

"Close enough," he said.

I poured him a glass of juice, and he sat down at the kitchen table. "In light of, recent revelations"—that was his way of saying the discovery of another wife without actually saying it—"the prosecution has decided to move the court date to January sixth."

"Have you pled yet?"

"My second arraignment was last week."

"What did you plead?"

"Same as the first time. Not guilty."

"But you are."

"It's a strategy. Once you plead guilty, you have no leverage." His eyes looked hollow. "With all the media attention, the prosecution is grandstanding. They're pushing to put me behind bars. I could do up to five years."

I looked at him sadly. "Are there more, Clive?"

"More women?"

I nodded. He looked down. "No other wives." Then he softly added, "There's a woman in San Diego. We weren't married . . ."

I shook my head in disbelief. "Why, Clive? We had such a good life. Why wasn't I enough?"

"I've been trying to figure that out myself. Yesterday, I read something on the mating rituals of primates. It said that once a male chimpanzee establishes his alpha position, he immediately starts collecting a harem. He can't help it. It's hardwired into the male's psyche for the protection and growth of the species."

"I wouldn't use that argument in court," I said.

He took a slow drink of juice, then rolled the cup between his hands as though he were thinking. He looked at me and asked, "Do you still love me?"

Sadly—or tellingly—I wondered if he had asked that to set me up for a request. Finally, I answered, "I loved the man I married. More than you know."

He looked like he didn't know what to do with that.

"Is that why you came, Clive? To ask me that?"

He scratched his forehead. "No. I came to tell you that I'm sorry. You were the best thing in my life. I didn't know it then, but I do now. It took me some time to figure that out. Too much time. A day late and a dollar short, right?"

"Nine years late," I said.

"Yeah." He stood. "At least." He exhaled. "I just wanted you to know that. Take care of yourself, Mag." He started toward the door, then stopped. "By the way, how's it going with that guy you're dating?"

I don't know why he asked me that. I don't know why I answered him. "He's gone."

"Is that your doing or his?"

"It was his."

"Then he's a fool."

"He's not a fool."

"Anyone who gives you up is a fool." He stepped outside, then turned back and said, "I've got someone coming to replace your window tomorrow afternoon. I hope that works for you."

"Thank you."

"Don't mention it." He turned and walked away.

C H A P T E R

Thirty-Nine

He came. <u>He.</u> I don't even know his name anymore.
—Maggie Walther's Diary

The next night there was an ambulance in the Stephenses' driveway. I walked out onto my front porch to see Mrs. Stephens being wheeled out on a gurney, with Mr. Stephens walking at her side.

It turned out that she had suffered a stroke. I planned to visit her in the hospital but never got the chance. She suffered a second stroke the next morning and passed away.

Saturday night I went to her viewing at a nearby Mormon chapel. Mr. Stephens was completely bereft, standing next to his wife's casket. He had lost the whole of his family in just one winter. I hated this winter.

In spite of his grief, Mr. Stephens seemed glad to see me. "First my son, then my wife," he said. "Leisa *was* my life. Why couldn't it have been me?"

We cried together. I think that's what love should be.

Every day I thought about Andrew. I kept hoping I would hear from him when he got back, if not sooner. The eighteenth came and went. I drove by the lot several times but didn't see his truck. I felt like a stalker. Maybe I *was* a stalker. Why couldn't I just accept that it was over? I guess because, for me, it wasn't over. I needed something more definite. I needed an axe to fall on something. Maybe my heart.

Around noon on the twentieth I received a text message from an unfamiliar number. All it said was,

555-5964

Boss is back

It was from Shelby. The hipster had actually come through. I drove immediately over to the Christmas tree lot. It was different from the last time I'd been there. The parking lot was nearly empty, and Andrew's truck sat up front near the trailer. I parked my little Fiat next to it, took a deep breath, said a mantra three times—*If you give fear legs, it will run away with your dreams*—and then walked into the lot.

There was only one customer, and Andrew was helping him at the trailer. I stood at a distance, waiting for him to leave. Then Andrew saw me. He glanced up at me, then turned away nearly as quickly.

He finished the transaction. As the customer was leaving, I walked up to him, our eyes locked on each other. When I got close, he said, "What do you want, Maggie?"

"You," I said.

He didn't say anything, which made my heart feel like a truck had parked on it. He just stood there.

"Wow," I said, more to myself than him, "you really are done with me." My eyes welled. I looked at him, fighting back the weight of his rejection. I finally said, "Before I go, would you do me just one kindness?"

"What's that?" he asked.

"Tell me that you don't have any feelings for me—that everything you once felt is gone." I wiped my cheek. "I need to hear it. It's the only way I can start to move on."

He looked down for a moment, then said, "I can't, Maggie. It wouldn't be true."

"Then why are you torturing me?"

His brow furrowed. "Why can't you see that I'm protecting you?"

"From what?"

"From *me*."

"I don't want to be protected from you. I don't care what you've done, or what your brother did. None of that matters to me."

He looked even more upset. Actually, he looked lost. He raked his hand through his hair. Then he said, "All right. I get off in an hour. We'll talk."

"Do you want me to wait?"

"No. I'll come over to your place."

"Thank you," I said softly.

"Don't thank me," he said.

I drove home with my chest aching. There was a fierce battle going on inside between fear and hope. I'm not sure which was more dangerous.

CHAPTER

Forty

*He came. He. I don't even know his name
anymore.*

—*Maggie Walther's Diary*

Andrew arrived at my house ninety minutes later, half an hour later than I'd expected. The extra thirty minutes felt like days. I wondered if he had changed his mind.

I met him at the door and let him in. This time he hugged me. I didn't know what kind of hug it was, one of love or condolence, but I wasn't picky. I was just glad to feel him. We sat down together on the couch—the same couch where he had comforted me and I had first fallen in love with him. Same couch, different world.

For a moment we sat in awkward silence, not sure how to begin. Then I said, "May I go first?"

He nodded.

My voice was soft and strained. I couldn't look at him as I spoke. "Andrew, I love you. I know I really screwed up and I don't deserve you, but I'm just hoping that you can somehow forgive me and give me a chance to show you how much I love you." A tear fell down my cheek. "My heart is broken." He still didn't speak. I looked up into his eyes. "Do you care that it's broken?"

His eyes welled up. Then he shook his head. "You're right, you don't deserve me. But not in the way you think." He gave a heavy sigh. "It's time you knew the truth." He pulled back slightly, squaring himself to me. "Of course I care that your heart's broken. My heart's broken too. But that doesn't change reality. What you need—what you really deserve—is the truth. And the truth is, you don't know who I am." He looked me in the eyes. "Maggie, I can't fake it anymore. I love you too much for that."

I took his hand. "I know who you are. You're the man who held me when my world was falling apart. You're the man who takes food to the poor. I know you. I know you're good and generous and kind. What more do I need to know?"

"A lot," he said softly.

"Tell me, then. What am I missing?"

He was quiet for a long time. Then he looked into my eyes and said, "Ask me my name."

I just looked at him.

"Ask me my name, Maggie."

I had no idea why he was asking me to do that, but something in the way he said it frightened me. I swallowed. "What is your name?"

"My name is Aaron Hill."

I just looked at him. "I don't understand."

"Andrew is my brother. I'm Aaron. I'm the one who stole millions of my clients' dollars. Not my brother."

"But your brother went to prison."

"I took the money, but my brother took the time. He went to prison in my place."

His words took a moment to sink in. "I don't believe you."

"You don't believe me, or you don't want to believe me?"

"Either."

"What would you have me do to convince you?"

"Tell me what happened."

He rubbed his chin. "All right." He took a moment to gather his thoughts. "I told you about the trial. It lasted almost two weeks. Most of it was technical, the state laying out exactly where the money had gone, how many illegal transactions had actually been made, all my criminal details. They didn't have to work for the information, since I provided them with most of it. You could say I helped build my gallows.

"It was the worst time of my life. It was as difficult as when my parents died. In some ways, worse. There was no shame with my parents' death.

"Every day I thought of taking my life. Several times I planned it out in detail. Every day I fought that battle by myself. I was completely alone. My friends, or at least the people I thought were my friends, deserted me. My cheating wife had already divorced me and was using my weakened position to make false accusations of abuse, hoping to take everything I had." He looked at me with despair. "Kick them when they're down, right?"

"What about your brother? Where was he?"

Aaron shook his head. "I hadn't seen Andrew since he helped boot me out of my own company."

"Your brother was involved with that?"

Aaron nodded slowly, and I could see that it still hurt him. "It couldn't have happened without him. Together we owned the majority of the stock. It wasn't his idea, but he made it possible. The truth is, the investors played him. But he went along." He slowly exhaled in anguish. "It's like I said: I was betrayed by *everyone*."

I just looked at him with pity.

"It was the morning of what was likely the last day of my trial. I had hardly slept, and when I got out of bed, I was so anxious that I threw up. I was literally counting down my last minutes of freedom, anticipating the fear and humiliation of life in prison. I can't begin to describe what that was like. I'd been on trial for almost two weeks by then, and all that was left were the attorneys' closing arguments and the jury's deliberation.

"The trial hadn't gone well." He smiled darkly. "That's an understatement. To begin with, I had already confessed to the crime, so I had no leverage. Nothing to bargain with."

I remembered what Clive told me the other evening about not pleading guilty.

"There was no doubt that I was going to prison. The only question was for how long. So there I was, numb and nauseated, my mind spinning like a top, wondering how long it would be before I saw my house again. I felt crazy, like I was losing my mind.

"Then, in the midst of that insane moment, Andrew walked into my house. Not exactly someone I wanted to see. Part of me wanted to punch him, but the fact was, I didn't have any fight left in me. I asked him if he'd come to gloat or to steal. He said he came to talk. I said there was nothing left to talk about and no time to do it. I told him my lawyer would be there any minute to take me to court. He said, 'I know. That's why I'm here.'

"I said, 'I'm going to prison, brother. I hope that makes you and your cronies happy.' I took out my wallet and offered him a hundred-dollar bill. 'Here, buy some champagne and have a toast on me. To your felon brother. May he rot in prison.'

"He just looked at me and said, 'You're not going to prison.'

"I said, 'You clearly haven't been following my trial.' Just then my lawyer honked his horn outside. I said, 'That's my ride. Lock up after yourself.'

"I started to leave, but he said, 'I've been following your trial, Aaron. You're not going to prison, because I am.' Then he set his driver's license and keys on my counter, along with a small leather book. 'I've put everything in order. These are the keys to my car and house. The house alarm number is the last four digits of your phone number. This notebook has every bank account, username, password, and code I have. It's all yours. There's a wall safe behind the floral painting in my bedroom. The combination to it is in the book. Inside the safe are keys to my safe deposit boxes and the Cabo condo. Everything else you can figure out.'

"'What are you doing?' I asked.

"He said, 'I'm taking your place. I'm going to leave with your lawyer, and you're going to take my car and drive to my home and start a new life with my name. Now give me your driver's license.'

"I couldn't believe what he was saying. I told him, 'You can't do this.'

"His eyes welled up. 'I *have* to do this,' he said. 'I helped them betray you. You never would have gotten caught up in any of this if it wasn't for what I let them do to you.'

"I said, 'I'm not going to let you.'

"He looked at me and said, 'I figured you would probably say that. So I'm going to lay out your options. You can give me your license and let me do this, or you can go to prison while I go home and wait for the verdict. If you're given anything besides probation, I'll blow my head off with that Smith & Wesson you gave me for my twenty-fifth birthday.' He stared me in the eye. 'Believe it or not, I actually do have a conscience. I can't live with what I've done. Guilt is its own kind of prison. It's what hell is made of.

"'Sorry to spring this on you, brother, but those are your options. You let me go to prison for a few years and attempt to make amends and assuage my guilt, or you go to prison with the knowledge that you killed your brother. That shouldn't be too hard a decision.' He held out his hand. 'Now hurry and give me your license. I'm assuming my lawyer charges by the hour.'

"I took out my wallet and gave him my driver's license. He said, 'You might as well give me the whole wallet, because after today, Aaron Hill doesn't exist outside of prison.'

"As I handed him my wallet, my cell phone rang. It was my lawyer. Andrew said, 'I should take that too.' He handed me his phone as he answered mine, saying he would be right out. Then he looked at me and said, 'I'm sorry for what I did to you. I hope this will help you forgive me.' He began to turn, then stopped and said, 'One more thing: I didn't know Scott was cheating with Jamie. I would have prevented that if I could have. I would have told you. I'm not that despicable.' I thanked him. He said, 'Thank you for letting me do this. I'll see you in a couple of years.' Then he put on his sunglasses, walked out of my house, and drove away with my attorney.

"I went down to the courthouse to watch the rest of the trial. It was maddening seeing the prosecution paint me as a monster and watching my brother take it. When the jury pronounced their verdict, Andrew didn't even flinch. After the gavel came down, my brother looked back and made eye contact with me. Then he nodded slightly and turned. The officer handcuffed him and took him away."

He took a deep breath. "My brother gave me his name. For the last two years I've lived as Andrew Hill." He looked at me. "He's out now. He's still in Colorado for the time being—but not as a convicted felon. I've given him his name back. He's Andrew again. And I'm Aaron, the ex-convict with a record."

I let the pronouncement settle. Then I said, "What if I told you that I love you no matter what you've done or what your name is?"

"I would say you're a fool." He leaned forward and kissed me on the cheek. "Good-bye, Maggie."

"Where are you going?"

"Someplace where bad things never happen."

CHAPTER

Forty-One

Today I had the most unexpected of visitors with the most unexpected of stories.
                              —*Maggie Walther's Diary*

The commercial world of Christmas kept me busy. There were parties everywhere, and my company catered more than its share of them—sometimes up to three events a day.

I had already abandoned my plans to go back home to Oregon, cataloging the idea in the "What was I thinking?" file. I suppose it's evidence of just how desperate I was to get away from my situation—like a coyote chewing off its leg to escape a trap.

I kept thinking how glad I would be when this year was over. These, no doubt, were days I would never forget, but I wanted to. Let's just say I was looking forward to looking back on them.

With all the business, I was able to keep myself distracted. I was grateful for that. But that's all it was: a distraction. You can throw a blanket over something you don't want to see, but it's still there.

I wondered where he was. I wondered how long it

would be before I stopped thinking about him every day and could let him go. Apparently, that's not what fate had in mind. My story still had one last twist.

It was a few days before Christmas. I had just returned home from catering a redneck wedding dinner that drew moments from *The Twilight Zone*—like when the drunk, obviously pregnant bride started yelling at her husband of six hours that he was ruining the day because he was more drunk than she was. Then one of the wedding guests loudly complained because we weren't serving fried chicken and corn on the cob. I told her that the bride hadn't ordered fried chicken and corn on the cob. The guest replied that that wasn't her problem and asked what I planned to do about it. I told her there was a KFC just a few blocks away and I'd be happy to draw her a map.

As I was pulling into my driveway, I noticed a red, expensive-looking sports car idling in front of my house. I'm not an expert on cars, but I'm pretty sure it was a Ferrari. I wondered who it belonged to and why it was parked in front of my house.

I pulled into the garage and shut the door behind me. Then, as I walked into my house, the doorbell rang. I walked to the front door. After the brick incident, I'd had a peephole installed by the same people who replaced my window. I looked through it to see who was there. It was Aaron.

I fumbled madly with the lock and dead bolt and swung open the door. The excitement on my face must have been pretty obvious, because the man raised a hand and said, "I'm not who you think I am."

I stopped, confused.

He stepped closer to me. "You're Maggie, right? I'm Aaron's brother, Andrew."

He looked exactly like his brother. He looked exactly like the man I loved.

"Come in," I said.

He stepped into my living room. Even his mannerisms were the same as Aaron's. I motioned to the couch. "Have a seat."

"Thank you."

I sat down in the armchair across from him. Andrew glanced at my Christmas tree and sat down. "Nice tree."

"Andrew and I . . ." I caught myself. "*Aaron* and I decorated it. It was from his Christmas tree lot."

"I thought it was a little strange that he got into that business. But if anyone can figure out how to make money selling Christmas trees, it's him."

Every time he looked at me I felt peculiar, as though it was him but also wasn't. It's like the time I made banana bread and someone had filled the sugar canister with salt. The bread looked the same, but it wasn't. Finally, I said, "I'm sorry, this is . . . surreal. You and your brother look exactly alike."

"Actually, I'm more buff than he is these days," Andrew said. "I've had more time to work out in the gym lately."

"Speaking of which," I said, "how are you?"

"I'm out," he said. "Out is good. Free is good."

"I can't believe you would do what you did for your brother."

"That's why I came to talk to you. If you knew how much he'd done for me, you wouldn't be surprised. He was always looking out for me. And being a twin added another dimension to that."

"What do you mean?"

"Like, when I was in middle school, I desperately wanted to play on the school basketball team. I wasn't a Jordan or a LeBron, but I had talent. I practiced every day to get ready for tryouts. The day tryouts began, some random kid at lunch thought it would be funny to drop a bowl of chili on my head. I broke his nose. Not surprisingly, I was sent to the principal's office. The principal assigned me detention every night after school for the next two weeks. I told him I had basketball tryouts. He said, 'You should have thought about that before you punched that boy.'

"There was nothing I could do about it. I could skip detention, but then I'd be suspended and wouldn't be allowed to play anyway.

"After school I went to the library for detention. When I arrived, Aaron was already there. He had checked in under my name. He just looked at me and nodded. I went to tryouts and made the team. I needed that right then, and Aaron knew it. He always had my back.

"Unfortunately—mostly for me—our genetic duplication only went as far as our appearance. Personality-wise, we were salt and pepper. He was the salt; I was the pepper. I was impetuous; he was methodical. I was careless; he was disciplined. I got in fights; Aaron talked people out of them.

"Mostly, he had more smarts than anyone I'd ever

known. He was the brains behind everything we did. I learned to just follow along, because he knew what he was doing; if I couldn't keep up, he would pick up the slack. I even got an MBA because he did. Except while he was at home studying, I'd be out partying.

"My last year I had a final in global economics. The class was a nightmare. The professor was one of those bitter, arrogant types who treated his students like dirt, then rationalized his cruelty as 'teaching moments.' I hated the guy almost as much as I hated the class. I just couldn't get into it. I didn't care enough to get into it.

"The day before the final, I took a practice exam to see how I would do. I failed it miserably. I knew I couldn't pass the test. And if I didn't pass it, I wouldn't graduate.

"That night, instead of studying, I went out and partied all night. I woke the next day at noon with a wicked hangover. Not that it would have made much of a difference, but by the time I remembered the exam, I had missed it.

"I was embarrassed to tell Aaron. I hated letting him down. A couple of hours later, when he got home, I said, 'I missed the test.' He handed me my student ID and said, 'No, you passed it. Now earn it.' That's the way it's always been.

"When we started our company, I knew I was just riding his coattails, but I was okay with that. I mean, it had always been that way, and it beat punching a clock somewhere. Besides, I was more social and Aaron was more focused on work, so it was kind of a symbiotic relationship. Aaron never once treated me like I was a burden.

"He would bring in these super-wealthy investors, the

kind of guys who could drop ten grand on a roulette wheel and not lose any sleep over it. Aaron took their money and made them richer. He was on fire, making all the right decisions, all the right acquisitions. He made just one mistake: he didn't take credit for what he did. He was too absorbed in succeeding to tell everyone about his success. I once had a professor tell me, 'In business, sometimes it's better to look good than to be good.' There may be some truth to that.

"So when the partners got greedy, they didn't know I wasn't making the same contribution Aaron was. Most of the time they didn't even know which of us was which. They just knew Aaron was taking the largest piece of the pie, and they wanted it.

"They couldn't make a move without me, since Aaron and I held the majority of the shares, but with my percentage, they could control everything. So they wined and dined me. They didn't tell me they wanted Aaron out; they just flattered me by saying I should be the managing partner and offered me a rock-star salary and full ownership of the condominium in Cabo San Lucas. The one you stayed at.

"The truth was, it wasn't the swag I fell for, it was their flattery. I wanted to believe that I was as good as my brother. I wanted to show Aaron that I was more than just his slacker twin.

"So, with my help, they took control. To my everlasting regret, they immediately pushed Aaron out of the company he had started." Andrew shook his head. "I'll never forget Aaron's face when they told him. We were all gathered around the conference room table, but it was like no one else was in the room, just him and me. The whole time, Aaron just stared at me in disbelief.

"The vultures did give me the raise they said they would; they just hadn't told me it would come from my brother's paycheck.

"Aaron was devastated. Of course he was. I had betrayed him. And if that wasn't bad enough, the next week his wife, Jamie, informed him that she had been having an affair with one of the investors and wanted a divorce. I think that's when he snapped. He had lost his company and his wife. But the biggest hurt, I think, still came from my betrayal.

"Broken or not, Aaron was no quitter. Within a month he had started a new firm. It had the same business model, the same plan; the only difference was him. He was drinking heavily. He wasn't careful. He wasn't confident. Then, when some of his early investments didn't pan out, he went off the rails.

"Rather than accept failure, he started taking his investors' money and hiding it. I don't know what his end game was—maybe he was planning to disappear off the grid—but we never found out. He couldn't go through with it.

"After he turned himself in, I watched him self-destruct. He had lost everything: his reputation, his company, his wife, his family—and, worst of all, his self-respect. Thankfully he cooperated with the authorities. That's why he got only a couple of years. A couple of years that I owed him."

I let the story sink in. My heart ached for Aaron and what he'd been through, but in light of our situation, it seemed moot. "Why are you telling me this? Aaron and I aren't together anymore."

"That's precisely why I'm telling you this. My brother visited me every week for those two years. Even after he moved to Utah. He would drive ten hours each way just so we could talk for an hour. I'd wait all week for that hour. It's what got me through.

"It didn't matter what we talked about. We'd usually start out discussing the latest headlines or sports, the Nuggets or Broncos, but we'd always end up talking business and some opportunities we could possibly pursue once I got out. Just like old times. Between the lines, he was assuring me that he had forgiven me. And he was leaving me with hope."

He smiled. "And then, one day, you entered the mix. After that, you were all he wanted to talk about. I was the one who suggested he take you to Cabo. When he came back from that trip, he told me he had found the woman he wanted to spend the rest of his life with."

"But then he left me."

"For a reason. It's because, in the same way he watched out for me, he was watching out for you. He doesn't want the woman he loves to live with a broken man. It's that simple. He left you because he loved you."

"That doesn't make sense."

"Maybe not to most people, but it does to him. Some people love for what they can get. A rare few, like Aaron, love for what they can give. The measure of love isn't how much you want someone. It's revealed in what you want *for* them. He wanted you to have something better than life with a felon."

"But he knew he was a felon when we met."

Andrew nodded. "I know. This is where it gets a bit hazy for me too. But I'm pretty sure that my release from prison complicated things. I think, on some subconscious level, he could function as Andrew. But after he gave me my name back, he was Aaron the disgraced businessman. Aaron the felon." He shook his head. "Names are powerful things."

I just sat there quietly thinking. Then I said, "What do you think I should do?"

"That depends on what you want. Do you know what you want?"

I nodded. "I want him."

He looked at me intensely. "Are you sure?"

"Absolutely."

"Then go get him."

"But I don't even know where he is."

A knowing smile crossed Andrew's face. "Of course you do."

CHAPTER

Forty-Two

Sometimes love requires us to leap and just hope
that there's someone there to catch us.
                              —*Maggie Walther's Diary*

My flight touched down in Los Cabos shortly before eleven on Christmas morning. I had hired an English-speaking Uber driver to take me to Todos Santos. He was a forty-year-old immigrant from Ukraine named Kostya, who claimed he spoke better English than Spanish.

I met my driver in the terminal. He was holding a piece of cardboard with my name written on it. He grabbed my bag, then asked me for the name of the hotel in Todos Santos I was staying at. I told him I didn't even have an address. We talked the whole ride about life in Mexico. He asked me how long I was staying. I told him I had no idea.

Kostya left the highway a few miles past the Todos Santos town sign. At my instruction, he turned down a short dirt road, then drove up onto the sandy beach. There was the house Aaron had shown me, except the For Sale sign was gone.

He drove to within thirty yards of the coral-pink structure and stopped. "Is this good, Mag-gie?"

"Yes. Thank you." I paid him in pesos I'd exchanged my dollars for at the airport. Then I gave him a hundred-dollar tip for Christmas. He was beyond happy. We got out of his car and he lifted my bag out of the trunk.

"Mag-gie, do you want me to wait?" he asked.

"Yes, please. I'd better make sure he's here."

The pink stucco home glowed brilliantly against the blue ocean backdrop. Palm trees surrounded the house; some of the shorter ones were wrapped with Christmas lights. A rope hammock had been tied between two of the trees. It rocked, unoccupied, in the wind.

As far as I could see, the only signs of occupancy were a motorcycle parked to the side of the house and clothes hanging on a line, rippling like flags in the ocean breeze. I recognized one of Aaron's shirts from our trip together.

I walked up onto the front porch and knocked on the door, but there was no answer. I tried the doorknob. It was unlocked, so I opened the door and looked inside. "Aaron?" The room inside was clean and spacious but showed no sign of anyone living there.

I walked around the side of the house. The back of the property was neatly landscaped with palm trees, cactus, and terra-cotta-potted kumquat trees set on beige slate pavers surrounding a bright-blue brick-and-mosaic-tile-lined swimming pool.

The property continued on about a hundred feet down to the ocean, with a wooden dock extending out over the water. A fishing boat was secured to the end of the dock. *What had he called it?* I couldn't remember its Spanish name, but I remembered the translation, because I remembered thinking, *How appropriate. The Dream.*

As I neared the dock, mixed with the sound of seagulls and crashing waves, I could hear music. Seventies music. Supertramp. "Goodbye Stranger." Aaron had to be there.

I turned and waved to Kostya, who was sitting on the hood of his car smoking a cigarette. He waved back, got into his car, and drove away.

Then I walked out onto the dock. In the distance, a line of pelicans roller-coastered past the beach. As I approached, I could see that a new name had been painted on the boat.

AGNETHA

Then I saw him. I'm not exactly sure what he was doing; he was facing the sea, kneeling on the boat's hull, sanding or polishing. He wasn't wearing a shirt or shoes, just a black, boxy bathing suit.

I had almost reached the end of the dock when he suddenly turned back as if he'd sensed someone's presence. For a moment he just looked at me. Then he tossed aside whatever was in his hand, jumped down onto the dock, and started toward me.

He was tan, his hair mussed as if it hadn't been combed for a while. I couldn't tell if he was more shocked or awed. When he got to me, he just said, "Hi."

"Hi," I said back.

"What are you doing here?"

"I came to wish you a merry Christmas."

"You could have just texted."

"You don't answer my texts. And besides, I had something to ask you."

"What's that?"

"At my house I said, 'What if I told you that I love you no matter what you've done or what your name is?' And you answered, 'I would say you're a fool.' Do you remember?"

He nodded. "It was something like that."

"It was exactly like that," I said. "I had a follow-up question."

"Okay."

"What do you have against fools?"

A large smile crossed his face.

"So here's the deal, Mr. Hill. I want you. I want to explore life with you. I want to experience life with you. I want to battle life with you." I lifted my arms and flexed. "I can do it. I'm pretty strong."

"I have no doubt," he said.

"So what will it be? Am I staying, or am I going back to Cabo tonight?"

"That depends on how long you were planning on staying."

Suddenly the lightness left my heart. I looked at him seriously and asked, "How long will you let me stay?"

His voice and demeanor also took on a more serious tone. He looked deep into my eyes. "How about forever?"

I just looked at him for a second, then rushed into him and we kissed. After we had kissed for a minute, I started laughing.

"What's so funny?" he asked, still trying to kiss me.

"It's good you said that."

"Why is that?"

"I already sent my car back."

Then we really kissed. Soulfully, passionately, joyfully. And the sea and beach and sun all witnessed and applauded our happiness in their own ways. Sometime later (a long time later) when we came up for air, I whispered, "I love you, Aaron Hill."

"I love you, Agnetha."

I smiled. "Merry Christmas, my stranger."

"Merry Christmas, my love," he whispered back. "Welcome to forever."

EPILOGUE

For far too long, all I saw was the night, forgetting that the sun must set if it is to rise again.
—Maggie Walther's Diary

Mi español está mejorándose. My Spanish is getting pretty good. At least I can order a coffee and concha and find a bathroom. What else really matters?

Aaron and I have breakfast or coffee every morning outside on the porch, with the cool Pacific breeze dancing in our hair. Sometimes I go out fishing with him, but not often. I'm still afraid to go into deep waters on account of his Humboldt squid story. One night at a Todos Santos pub a man lifted his shirt and showed us his scar from a Humboldt bite. It was horrific.

Aaron and I were married on November 10, 2017—a year to the day after we met at Aaron's Christmas tree lot. The marriage was performed by a local minister. I'd always wanted a beach wedding. Carina was my maid of honor. Andrew was Aaron's best man. I was hoping to hook the two of them up, but it just wasn't there. Sometimes the magic happens, sometimes it doesn't. There's no rhyme or reason to love.

Life is slower here. More deliberate. We have time together. We sleep in, make love, take long walks on the beach—pretty much all the things dreams are made of.

I gave Carina ownership of Just Desserts, passing it on just as Marge had done with me. But my entrepreneurial drive is still intact. I'm opening a bakery in town, and already have contracts with several local resorts.

Clive had his day in court. He was fined ten thousand dollars and ordered to perform two hundred hours of community service. No jail time. Some people thought he got off easy, but I don't. He was given a life sentence when he lost his dreams and political aspirations. And me.

Aaron continues to manage his investments, but lately, most of the time he works on his book. It's almost done. It's pretty good, really. It's about a twin who goes to prison for his brother. I'd always wondered how authors came up with their ideas.

I still slip up sometimes and call him Andrew. Whenever I do, he threatens to change his name to a glyph that has no pronunciation, like Prince did. I just tell him it will get in the way of his publishing career and maybe even our love life, and he quickly retreats.

We've continued the Thanksgiving tradition, though our list of recipients just keeps getting longer.

Andrew—the real Andrew—moved to Connecticut. He now has a fiancée. Her name is Emma. She's lovely. They visit often, though they usually stay in Andrew's condo in Cabo. Whenever they come, the brothers take a cooler with some fruit, a couple of six-packs, a loaf of bread, and a couple of chorizo sausages and go out on the *Agnetha*. What is it with men and boats?

Our love continues to grow. So does our happiness. That's how it's supposed to be, right? Our love is also growing in other ways: I'm five months pregnant with a little girl. We plan to name her Marissa, which means "of the sea." Marissa Hill. We still haven't decided whether we'll raise her here. I'll guess we'll see. We've got a few years before school starts.

Time rolls on. When I think back on all that happened that year, I'm still amazed that we survived it all. But that's what we do. That's what life and love require of us—to walk on in spite of the "slings and arrows of outrageous fortune," to walk on and hold to love. If we do that, we may suffer for a time, but we will not fail. In the end, love wins. It reminds me of a Mexican proverb that describes us perfectly: *Quisieron enterrarnos, pero se les olvidó que somos semillas*. It means, "They tried to bury us. They just didn't know we were seeds."

ACKNOWLEDGMENTS

I'd like to acknowledge and thank my Simon & Schuster friends, especially Carolyn Reidy and Jonathan Karp, for their continued friendship and support of my writing. To my new editor, Amar Deol, I look forward to working on more books with you. Continued love and appreciation to my agent, Laurie Liss, and my staff: Jenna Evans Welch, Barry Evans, Heather McVey, and Diane Glad. Also, to all my brothers in the Tribe of Kyngs.

Appreciation to award-winning producer Norman Stephens; it's been such a pleasure working with you on all those movies. (I'm so glad your wife found me.)

Most of all, to my sweet wife, Keri. This book is for you.

ABOUT THE AUTHOR

Richard Paul Evans is the #1 bestselling author of *The Christmas Box*. Each of his more than thirty-five novels has been a *New York Times* bestseller. There are more than thirty-five million copies of his books in print worldwide, translated into more than twenty-four languages. He is the recipient of numerous awards, including the American Mothers Book Award, the Romantic Times Best Women's Novel of the Year Award, the German Audience Gold Award for Romance, five Religion Communicators Council Wilbur Awards, the Washington Times Humanitarian of the Century Award, and the Volunteers of America National Empathy Award. He lives in Salt Lake City, Utah, with his wife, Keri, not far from their five children and two grandchildren. You can learn more about Richard on Facebook at Facebook.com /RPEFans or visit his website at RichardPaulEvans.com.

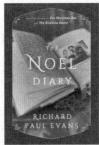
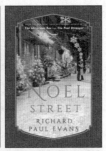
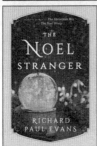

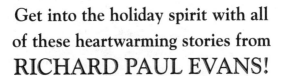

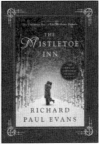

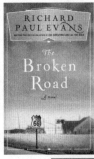 

The Noel Diary

The Noel Diary

FROM THE NOEL COLLECTION

GALLERY BOOKS

NEW YORK   LONDON   TORONTO   SYDNEY   NEW DELHI

G

Gallery Books
An Imprint of Simon & Schuster, Inc.
1230 Avenue of the Americas
New York, NY 10020

This Gallery Books hardcover edition October 2020

GALLERY BOOKS and colophon are registered trademarks of Simon & Schuster, Inc.

For information about special discounts for bulk purchases,
please contact Simon & Schuster Special Sales at
1-866-506-1949 or business@simonandschuster.com.

The Simon & Schuster Speakers Bureau can bring authors to your live event.
For more information or to book an event, contact the Simon & Schuster Speakers
Bureau at 1-866-248-3049 or visit our website at www.simonspeakers.com.

Manufactured in the United States of America

5   7   9   10   8   6   4

Library of Congress Cataloging-in-Publication Data has been applied for.

ISBN 978-1-5011-7203-8
ISBN 978-1-5011-7204-5 (ebook)

✦ *To Pam.* ✦
Wherever you are.

The Noel Diary

PROLOGUE

*M*ore than once, in the hazy dream-scape between slumber and consciousness, I've had a vision of a young woman with long black hair that glistens in the sun like obsidian. In this dream I am small next to her and she is holding me close to her breast, singing to me, looking lovingly into my face with her soft, almond-shaped eyes. It's always the same young woman I see. I don't know who she is or why she haunts the passages of my consciousness. I don't even know if she's real. But she feels real. And something inside of me longs for her. Whoever she is, she loves me. Or she did. And I love her.

This is the story of how I found that woman. And, on that journey, found love.

C H A P T E R

One

Wednesday, December 7

CHICAGO

The reporter from *USA Today* walked into the Dunkin'
Donuts looking harried and frazzled, which is to say, she
looked pretty much like everyone else in downtown Chicago. My publicist had arranged the interview for two
o'clock at the donut shop near Millennium Park. It was ten
minutes past the hour.

She looked around the room until she spotted me, then
hurried over. "Sorry I'm late, Mr. Churcher," she huffed,
dropping her bag on the empty chair between us. She
unpeeled the wool scarf that was wrapped around her
neck and chin. Her cheeks and nose were red from the
biting cold. "I should have taken the L. Finding parking in
downtown Chicago is almost as hard as finding an honest
politician in Chicago."

"No worries," I said. I looked her over. She looked

twenty-two or -three, twenty-five tops. They seemed younger every year. Or maybe I was just getting older. I sipped my coffee as she stripped off her outer winter shell.

"It's cold out there. I can see why they call it the Windy City."

"The name Windy City has nothing to do with the weather," I said. "The New York City editor of the *Sun* called it that because he thought the Chicagoans were braggarts."

"I didn't know that," she said.

"Would you like coffee?" I asked.

"No, thank you. I've wasted enough of your time already."

After grinding my way through more than five hundred press interviews I had learned to handle reporters with the same cautious approach one should take with stray dogs. They're probably safe but, for your own protection, assume that they'll bite. I also learned that saying "off the record" is tantamount to saying "Make sure your recorder's got batteries, baby, because this is the dirt you're looking for."

"How are you?" she said, looking more settled.

"Fine," I replied.

She pulled a hand recorder from her bag and set it on the table. "You don't mind if I record us, do you?"

They always asked this. I was always tempted to say no.

"No, you're good."

"Okay, then we'll get started." She pushed a button on

her recorder and a red light began to flash. "I'm interviewing bestselling author J. Churcher. This is for the Holiday Roundup edition." She looked at me. "Mr. Churcher. May I call you Jake?"

"Whatever you like."

"Jake, you have a new book out. It's still too new to have hit any lists, but I'm sure it will."

"I never take that for granted," I said. "But it's Wednesday. I'll find out about the list this afternoon."

"I'm sure you'll hit number one."

"Not likely, but we can hope."

"So what is this time of the year like for you?"

I took another drink of coffee, set down my cup, then gestured to the room. "It's just like this. A lot of travel. A lot of interviews. A lot of coffee. Sign a few books."

"You had a book signing last night in . . ."

"Naperville."

"Right. How did that go?"

"It went well."

"How many of your readers were there?"

"Five, six hundred. Kind of an average signing."

"How many cities was your tour?"

"I think twelve. New York, Boston, Cincinnati, Birmingham, Dallas . . . I don't remember the rest."

"You must be exhausted. When do you finish your tour?"

"This is my last stop. I fly home in four hours."

"Then you're headed back to Idaho?"

"Coeur d'Alene," I said, as if the city were a state unto itself. "I fly into Spokane."

"Home for the holidays. So what is Christmas like at the Churcher home?"

I hesitated. "You really want to know?"

"That's the focus of my story."

"Boring, mostly."

She laughed. "You spend it with family, friends . . ."

"No. I'm pretty much alone. I open presents from my agent and publisher, drink a couple spiked glasses of eggnog, then watch the football games I missed while I was on my book tour."

The reporter looked a little vexed. "Do you have any Christmas traditions?"

"Yeah. I just told you."

She looked a lot vexed. "What was Christmas like growing up? Any special memories that stand out?"

I exhaled slowly. "Define *special*."

"Is there a Christmas you'll never forget?"

I grinned darkly. "Oh, yeah."

"Can you tell me about it?"

"Trust me, you don't want to hear it."

"Try me."

"All right. Christmas afternoon. I was seven years old; my mother came into my bedroom to find me sitting on the floor playing with all my Christmas toys. She was apoplectic, screaming at me for making such a big mess. She made me go to the kitchen and bring back a heavy wooden mixing spoon. Then she pulled down my pants and beat me with it. It was like a demon had control of her. She didn't stop until the spoon broke.

"Then she filled a suitcase with my clothes, dragged me outside to the street, and told me to go find someplace else to live. I stood there for nearly three hours, shivering in the cold. I wasn't sure what was supposed to happen or how it was supposed to work. I figured that mothers must do this all the time to children they didn't want anymore. I wondered if maybe someone would just come along and take me.

"Finally, after three hours, more than an hour after the sun had set, freezing and hungry, I walked back to the house and knocked on the door. It took her about five minutes to answer. She opened the door and just stood there, staring at me. Then she asked, 'What do you want?'

"I said, 'If I'm good, can I come back and live here?'

"Without a word she turned and walked back into the house. But she didn't tell me to leave or slam the door in my face, which I took as permission to come back inside. I went to my room and crawled beneath my bed and fell asleep."

I looked at her. "How's that for a Christmas memory?"

She looked back at me with horror. "Okay. I think I've got what I need." She hurriedly shoved her things back into her bag and put on her coat. "Thank you. This will come out a week or so before Christmas." She walked back out into the cold.

My publicist is going to hate me, I thought.

✦

If you've read any of my books, you know me better by my nom de plume, J. Churcher. My full name is Jacob Christian Churcher. It was only as a teenager that I realized how weird my name was and wondered if, to my parents, it was some kind of joke, like the twisted people who name their children Ima Hogg or Robin Graves.

Christian Churcher. JC Churcher. The name seems even more ironic since my parents never took me to a church.

You would think that a writer of love stories would be good at romance. Not so. At least not in my case. Maybe it's a classic example of those who can't do, teach (or at least write about it), but at the age of thirty-four, all I had to my name was an unbroken string of failed relationships. Still I kept trying.

They say that only a fool keeps doing the same thing and expects a different result, and maybe I am that fool, but I think it's more complex than that. I feel more like there's something hardwired inside me to sabotage my relationships.

Or maybe it's just like the song says, I'm looking for love in all the wrong places. When I was just beginning my writing career, a veteran author gave me this sage advice: "Never date a reader." I ignored this advice over and over, meeting women at book signings and starting relationships that lasted about as long as the flavor in chewing gum.

The problem is, women read my books and fall in love with the supermen I create. If they can't find that kind of man in real life (good luck with that), they sometimes supplant him with me. These are the women I had been dating. And eventually they discover that I'm just as broken and flawed as every other man. Or in my case, maybe even more so.

There's a reason for that. The breaking of my world began while I was still young. Two things happened. My older brother died and my parents divorced. I was four years old—almost too young to remember. August 4, 1986. That's the day Charles died. Everything changed after that. My mother changed after that.

My mother, Ruth, struggled with mental illness. Of course, I didn't know that when I was young. For years I just thought that life was supposed to be a daily nightmare of beatings and neglect. When you're raised in an asylum, crazy is normal. It wasn't until I was a teenager that the scales fell from my eyes and I began to see the experiences of my life for what they really were—messed up beyond belief.

My mother wasn't always cruel. There were times that she was sweet and sensitive. They were rare, but those were the times I held on to. As I got older, those moments became rarer. Most of the time she was just absent.

She often had migraines and spent a lot of time in bed, in a dark room, with the phone off the hook, hiding from light and the world. I became abnormally independent for my age. I got my own meals, got myself off to school, washed my clothes in the bathtub if they had something on them.

When my mother took to bed I would go into her dark room to see how she was. She would often ask me to scratch her back. She had a pencil that she had taped two toothpicks to and I would run it up and down her back or neck or arms. Sometimes for hours. It was the only thing I did that made me feel that she loved or needed me. Sometimes she would say sweet things as I scratched her, something I craved like oxygen.

The isolation I lived in wasn't just at home. I mostly kept to myself at school as well. I was a loner—still am. Maybe it was because I always felt different than other kids my age. I was sullen and serious. People said I thought too much. Also, I didn't have time to make friends because I had to keep my mother alive. She was suicidal and more than once she involved me in her plans to die. Once she handed me a carving knife and an electric knife sharpener and asked me to sharpen the blade so she could slit her wrists.

Another time, when I was a little older, I came home from school to find a garden hose coming out of the car's exhaust pipe and clamped into the back window of the car, the rest of the car's windows rolled up completely. My mother was unconscious. I dragged her out and laid her on the concrete floor of the garage. She had a terrible head-ache but suffered nothing else. I suffered for years.

By the time I was thirteen I was already bigger than my

mother and she stopped beating me. I figured that it was either because I no longer cried when she did it or because I could have beaten her up. Not that I would have. In spite of all the violence I'd experienced, I wasn't a violent person. I detested violence. I still do.

Memories of my father are hazy at best. Most of what I knew about him came from what my mother told me, that he didn't care about me. As much as I had learned to discount what my mother said, there was no denying that my father was missing in action and, from what I could tell, had made no effort to be a part of my life. In a way I was even angrier with him than with my mother. Why hadn't he been there? What was his excuse? If he cared, how could he have left me in such a place?

My last day at home was remarkably anticlimactic. I was sixteen. One night I came home from my job at Taco Time and everything I owned was on the front lawn. Even my pillow. The house door was locked. I never even talked to my mother to find out what I'd done wrong this time. It didn't matter. Something inside me clicked. I knew the time had come for me to leave.

I picked up a few of my things from the lawn, then walked back to Taco Time. There was a girl I worked with there named Carly who was always nice to me. She was a little older than me and had a car, a two-tone black-and-tan Chevy Citation. I told her that my mother had kicked me out, and she said I could stay at her place until I found something else.

Carly had also been kicked out of her über-religious

house when her parents caught her drinking alcohol, and now she lived with her sister and brother-in-law, Candace and Tyson. I helped her clean up at work, then went home with her wondering if they'd really let me stay. Her brother-in-law was a massive, tattooed Samoan man. Tyson terrified me. He was the biggest man I had ever seen.

But I had nothing to fear. Tyson was as kind as he appeared intimidating. He had an infectious smile and a laugh that rumbled like thunder when he was especially amused. He was also a devout Christian who, along with Candace, attended a nondenominational Christian church. He also went to a weekly early-morning Bible study with a group of men. When he found out that my mother had thrown me out, he was indignant. He told me that I could stay with them for as long as I needed to get back on my feet. Considering my age and situation, it was a remarkably generous offer.

Their home was small, less than seven hundred square feet on the main floor, with an unfinished basement and a dated Pepto-Bismol pink–walled bathroom. They didn't have another bed, but they had an extra queen-size mattress that they set on the floor in the basement. Just like that I had a new home.

Candace worked during the day as a legal secretary. Tyson worked in sales at an international phone equipment company, which granted him the luxury of being home by five thirty. Almost every night after dinner he'd sit down with me and ask what was up.

It was nice having male company. I wasn't used to it, but it was nice. I think he liked it too since Candace had little interest in most of the things he liked: rugby, hellfire-hot chicken wings, and Harley-Davidson motorcycles.

Even though I had left home, I continued to go to school. Actually, Tyson and Candace insisted on it, but I would have anyway. It wasn't the same school I'd been going to. Not even the same school district. I liked my new school, especially English and creative writing. Much of the reason was my teacher—a pretty, fresh-from-college woman named Janene Diamond. You hear about students having crushes on their teachers: that was me. I don't know if Ms. Diamond had any idea of what was happening in my home life, but I think that she sensed it. Or maybe she had a crush on me too (something I fantasized about). Whatever the reason for it, she took a special interest in me and encouraged me. She told me that I was writing at a college level and had what it took to be a professional writer. It was foreign to me to have someone so positive about something I did. I would often stay after school and help her grade papers.

Writing always came naturally to me. It was like speaking, but easier. Actually, a lot easier. I felt awkward standing in front of a crowd of people; it made words and ideas just bounce uselessly around in my head like microwave popcorn.

I believe that, for the most part, we don't succeed in spite of our hardships but precisely because of them. I think it was the drama of my life that gave me my stories and empathy. I had always created a lot of fantasy in my head as a survival technique. I spent a lot of time in different mental worlds to escape the real one and all its pain.

Without telling me, Ms. Diamond entered one of my papers into a district creative writing competition. I won first place. Tyson, Candace, and Carly all came to see me get the award. They called me up onstage and I was given a plaque, a leather notebook, and a Cross pen and pencil set. They were the nicest things I had ever owned. They were also, aside from a cupcake I'd won in a second-grade spelling bee, the only things I had ever won.

A year and three weeks after I'd moved in with them, Tyson announced that his employer was transferring him to Spokane, Washington, and we'd be moving in two months, just after I graduated from school. *We* would be moving. There was never any question over whether I would go with them or not, as they had assumed it. By that point, we were family.

Ironically, it was Carly who remained behind. She had finished her freshman year at the University of Utah and decided to stay in Salt Lake with her friends. The four of us boxed up the house, then Tyson, Candace, and I filled up a U-Haul trailer and the back of his truck with everything they owned, said a tearful good-bye to Carly, and drove the seven hundred miles from Salt Lake to Spokane—Tyson and Candace in their truck, me in the used Toyota Corolla I had bought six months earlier.

It might seem a little odd that I never told my mother that I was moving out of state, but I had no reason to believe that she cared to know. She had made no effort to find me since she'd kicked me out. I guessed there was just no point to it. It would be like telling a homeless guy on the street what channel your favorite TV show was on. Pointless.

Just a week after we had settled in Spokane, I got a job as a pizza delivery guy at Caruso's Sandwich & Pizza Co. I made good money in tips and they were pretty easy about feeding us, so that was a big benefit. I'd usually bring home whatever unclaimed pizzas were left at the end of my shift, which Tyson would happily demolish by himself for a midnight snack.

As summer came to an end, I enrolled at Gonzaga University in their creative writing program. I got a grant and good grades. I liked the college life. It wasn't the college life you see on TV, with wild, beer-chugging fraternity parties and such. Mine was a pretty solitary deal, but it worked for me. I spent a lot of time in the library and I wrote a dozen or so short stories, several of which were published in *The Reflection*, the school's journal of art and literature. I also picked up a little side money writing for the school newspaper, *The Bulletin*.

For the first time in my life I knew what I wanted to do with my life. I wanted to be a writer. My ultimate dream was to write books and be a published author. One of my professors was a published author. He wasn't exactly famous, but he had a following. I couldn't imagine that life could be any better than that.

I graduated with a BA in literature at the age of twenty-three. During my final year of school, I got an internship with a Spokane company—Deaconess Healthcare—writing their weekly newsletter and online articles. I was hired full-time upon my graduation.

Financially, things were going the best they ever had in my life. That's when I finally moved out of Tyson and Candace's place. They never asked me to leave—in fact, they seemed a little upset that I was leaving—but after all they had done for me, I just didn't ever want to put them in a situation where they had to ask. Also, after years of trying, Candace was finally pregnant, and I figured that it was time they had their own life.

I moved into a small basement apartment just a half mile from where they lived. We still had dinner together at least once a week. And every now and then I'd bring Tyson a midnight pizza.

I dated a few girls, but nothing took. There was one benefit to my loneliness. Without a significant other in my life, I had most of my nights free. A year after my graduation I started writing my first book, a twisted tale about a broken family. I never showed it to anyone. I started my second book at the age of twenty-six. It was better than my first, but still nothing to brag about. I began wondering if I really had what it took to be a novelist.

Fortunately, my passion was stronger than my doubt. A year later I wrote my first *real* novel. I call it my first "real" novel because it was my first book that I felt was decent enough to let someone else read. It was called *The Long Way Home*. It was a story about a young man trying to find his mother. It wouldn't take Freud to connect the dots about where I drew my inspiration from.

After finishing the book, I made a few copies and began sharing it with people at work. One of my colleagues, Beth, had a cousin, Laurie, who was the co-owner of a literary agency in New York. After reading my book, and without my knowing it, Beth sent the manuscript I'd given her to Laurie. It was like the time Ms. Diamond had entered my writing into the district competition without telling me.

I'll never forget the day Laurie called me. Our conversation went like this:

Laurie: Mr. Churcher, this is Laurie Lord of Sterling Lord Literistic. How are you?

Me: Who is this?

Laurie: My name is Laurie Lord. I'm with the Sterling Lord literary agency in New York. You wrote *The Long Way Home*?

Me: Yes.

Laurie: It's a really beautiful book, Jacob. May I call you Jacob?

Me: Yes. How did you get my book?

Laurie: My cousin Beth sent it to me. Apparently you work with her.

Me: Beth Chamberlain?

Laurie: Yes. She didn't tell you that she was sending me your book?

Me: No . . .

Laurie: Well, she did. And it's terrific. I'd like to take it to publishers. I currently represent thirty-two authors, seven of whom are international bestselling authors. I'd like to make you number eight. If you're interested, I'd love to fly out to Spokane to meet you.

Me: Uh . . . sure.

Three days later I met Laurie Lord, the woman to whom I would soon be professionally married. I signed a contract with her firm and she went to work, distributing the manuscript to big-name publishers. Six publishers wanted the book and it went to auction, selling for a quarter-million-dollar advance, which, needless to say, is a ridiculously high amount for the first book from an unknown author.

Within a month, the film rights were picked up by a

major production studio. It was an exciting time. It was also a major paradigm shift for me. My life suddenly seemed charmed.

Literary lightning struck. My book was both a commercial and literary success. The reviewer from the *New York Times* gave my book a stellar review. It also received a starred review in *Publishers Weekly*, and even the notoriously snarky reviewer at *Kirkus* gave it a nod.

My publisher contracted me for another three novels and I quit my job at Deaconess to write full time. My writing career was now what a million would-be writers dreamt of. Every now and then I'd wonder if my mother had read my book.

My next contract was for more than four million dollars. My life changed after that. A year earlier, Candace had given birth to an eleven-pound three-ounce baby boy. (Yikes.) That Christmas, to show my gratitude for all Tyson and Candace had done, I paid off their home and bought Tyson the Harley-Davidson Fat Boy he coveted. It was great to be giving to them for a change. Candace kissed me, while Tyson tried—unsuccessfully—to hide his tears.

"It's too much, man," he said.

I hugged him. "No, it's not. You saved my life."

I bought a home in Coeur d'Alene, a peaceful resort town a half hour east of Spokane. The home was on the lake and beautiful but, as in all wealthy neighborhoods, isolated. More and more I felt the loneliness.

Before she overdosed, Janis Joplin said, "Onstage I make

love to twenty-five thousand people; and then go home alone." More times than not, I felt that way. Not that I hadn't had offers. I remember the first city I flew into, I was met by a beautiful media escort. When she checked me into the hotel, the clerk behind the counter asked, "How many keys do you need?"

"Just one," she said. "He's alone." Then she turned to me. "Unless you'd like me to spend the night."

I pretended that I hadn't heard her. "One key is good," I said.

That was my life. A million fans. One key. And all the while, somewhere in my heart, was this woman who still haunted my dreams. A woman as elusive as an angel. I once tried to catch her in my writing but she eluded me even there. The story wouldn't come. I felt like I was fictionalizing a nonfiction story.

My life fell into a routine as predictable as a Tokyo subway car. I wrote a book a year and traveled around the country with a first-class ticket for one, meeting readers, signing books, and talking to reporters.

Then one day, almost three weeks before Christmas, I got a phone call that changed everything.

CHAPTER

December 7

I was in the car on the way to O'Hare when my agent, Laurie, called. "Churcher, you still in Chicago?"

"I'm on my way to the airport."

"Lucky you. I know how you love to fly. How did your interview go with *USA Today*?"

"No idea."

"That sounds ominous."

"It was."

"I have no idea what you're talking about, so I'm just going to let it go. So, I have the *Times* list."

"And?"

"Congratulations. You're number three."

"Who's one and two?"

Laurie groaned. "Man, you're hard to please. It's Christmas and you're running with the big dogs, Churcher. King, Sparks, Patterson, Roberts, and Grisham all have books out. Be happy with three. Your sales are up again; it's good. You're only competing against yourself."

"Tell that to the other authors."

"Good-bye," she said, not hiding her annoyance. "Have a good flight. And congratulations, whether you'll take it or not. Call me when you're in a better mood. Wait, wait," she suddenly said. "One more thing. I know you don't like to fly, but—"

"No, I *don't like* brussels sprouts. I *abhor* flying."

"Unfortunately you live on the wrong side of the country. We need to plan your trip to New York. Your publisher wants to know what day we're meeting."

"I don't know. I'll call back after my anxiety meds kick in. Bye."

"Ciao. Call me later."

I was about to set down my phone when it rang again. I looked at the caller ID. It was an unknown number with an 801 area code, something I remembered from my childhood. Utah. Even after all these years, just seeing the area code raised my blood pressure.

"Hello?"

"Is this Mr. Jacob Churcher?" It was an unfamiliar voice.

"Who is this?" I asked curtly.

"Mr. Churcher, my name is Brad Campbell. I'm an attorney at Strang and Copeland in Salt Lake City."

I groaned. "Who's suing me now?"

"No one that I'm aware of. I'm calling because I'm the executor of your mother's will."

It took me a moment to understand what he was saying. "My mother's will?"

"Yes, sir."

"My mother's dead?"

Now there was hesitation on his line. "I'm sorry. You didn't know?"

"Not until now."

"She passed two weeks ago. I'm really sorry, I assumed you knew."

"No. I didn't."

"Is there anything you want to know about her death?"

"Not especially. She had a funeral?"

"Yes."

"What was that like?"

"It was small."

"I'm not surprised," I said.

The lawyer cleared his throat. "Like I said, the reason I called is because I'm the executor of your mother's will and she left you everything. The house, some money, everything."

I didn't speak for a moment, and the man asked, "Are you still there?"

"Sorry. This is just . . . unexpected." Entirely unexpected. Like catching a taxi after a Broadway show on a rainy night unexpected. It's not that I didn't expect that she would die someday. Rather, I had so completely blocked her from my mind that having her suddenly barge back into my life was an interruption of my regularly scheduled programming and as jarring as an ice bucket challenge.

"Sir?"

I exhaled. "Sorry. I guess I'll probably need to come down to Salt Lake."

"It would be a good idea to see the property for yourself. You live in Idaho, correct?"

"Yes, Coeur d'Alene. I'll need a key to the house."

"My office isn't far from your mother's home. If you like, I can meet you and bring a few documents for you to sign. When are you planning on coming down?"

"I don't know yet. I'll call in the next week and let you know."

"All right. On a personal note, I have one more question."

"Yes?"

"You're not *the* Jacob Churcher? The author?"

"Yes."

"My wife's a big fan. Would you mind autographing a few books when I meet with you?"

"No problem."

"Thank you. It will mean the world to her. I look forward to meeting you."

I hung up the phone. *My mother was dead.* I had no idea how to process that. How was I supposed to feel? It's hard to admit it, but the very first thought that came to my head, unbidden, was this: *Ding Dong, the Witch is dead.* I know it makes me sound unsympathetic, if not outright crazy, but that's what I thought. Because even though I hadn't seen her for almost twenty years, the world suddenly felt safer.

✦

I called Laurie back. "I need to delay New York."

"What's up?"

"I need to go to Utah."

"*The* Utah?"

"Is there more than one Utah?"

"What's in Utah? Besides your mother and a head of bad memories."

"My mother died."

There was a long pause. "I'm sorry. How do you feel about that?"

"I'm not sure yet. I'm still letting it sink in."

"You're going for the funeral?"

"No. That was last week. She died two weeks ago. I need to go down to settle the estate."

"You sure that's a good idea?"

"Is what a good idea?"

"Going back. I hate the idea of you stirring those ashes. You never know what kind of fire it might ignite."

"I'm not planning on making any fires. Unless it's to burn the place down. I think I'll leave Friday morning."

"How long will you be there?"

"Not sure. Probably a few days. Maybe three."

"Flying?"

"Of course not."

"Of course not," she repeated. "That would be too quick and easy."

"I'll need my car."

"There are such things as rental cars."

"I like my car."

"I know you like your car. Do you need me to come out?"

"No. Thank you, but I'm okay."

She sighed. "All right. I'm sorry. I hope everything turns out all right."

"It will be fine. I'm just going back to settle a few things."

"That's what I'm afraid of."

CHAPTER

Three

December 9

COEUR D'ALENE, IDAHO

Laurie was right. As I prepared to leave for Utah, I wasn't sure if going home really was such a good idea. I wasn't even sure why, after so many years, I had so hastily offered to go back. It must have been something deeply subconscious because, in my conscious mind, I couldn't make sense of it. Then, after I committed, it just came together. I think that at least half the things I do are done out of inertia. Maybe that's true for everyone.

The last time I'd driven the route from Coeur d'Alene to Salt Lake was fifteen years ago coming the opposite direction with Tyson and Candace. That trip had taken us almost fourteen hours, but I was pretty sure I could do it in ten. For one thing, I had a bigger bladder than Candace did. And second, Tyson, pulling a U-Haul trailer in his old truck, pretty much did the speed limit the whole way. This time I drove a turbo Porsche Cayenne, which is basically a rocket disguised as an SUV. I can't remember the last time I'd driven the speed limit.

I made myself toast and coffee, then left my home at around nine in the morning. I drove southeast through Butte, Montana, down I-15 to Idaho Falls and Pocatello, across the barren, snow-covered landscape of the Utah border, then two more hours down to Salt Lake City, arriving a little after dark. I had made the trip in a little over ten hours, with only a lunch stop in Butte and a gas stop in Pocatello, Idaho.

The city was decorated for the holidays and the trees in front of the Grand America Hotel were strung with twinkling white and gold lights. The roads were clear of snow but there were three- to four-foot-high snowbanks on both sides of the streets. The city's skyline was larger than I remembered. Salt Lake had grown in my absence, and living in the smaller towns of Spokane and Coeur d'Alene had changed my perspective. The traffic was surprisingly heavy for that time of night. I guessed that there was a basketball game.

I avoided the hotel's massive porte cochere and uniformed valets by parking my car beneath the hotel. I rarely used valet parking. I hated asking for my car when I needed it.

The Grand America was every bit as grand as the name

boasted. The lobby was spacious, with marble floors and hung with brightly colored Murano glass chandeliers. The interior of the hotel was also dressed for the holidays with lush garlands, wreaths, and lights.

As soon as I got to my room I called the attorney. Campbell. He answered on the first ring. We agreed to meet the next morning at ten at my mother's house.

I ordered dinner—a beet and strawberry salad and some salmon—and lay back on the luxurious bed. The hotel was as opulent as anywhere I'd stayed in my travels. I'd come a long way since the last time I'd been in Salt Lake, when I slept on a mattress in an unfinished basement.

I still wasn't sure what it was that had brought me back. It wasn't the will. I didn't need or want anything from my mother. I suppose it was because there was still something dark inside me—something painful, like a glass sliver working its way deeper and deeper into my soul. Something I instinctively knew wouldn't just go away if I ignored it.

No matter the reason, something told me that I needed to go back.

I didn't sleep well. I had bizarre dreams. One of them was of my mother in a wedding dress. I came out dressed as the groom. I woke soaked in sweat and had to lay a towel down on my bed, since I wasn't about to call housekeeping to change my sheets at two in the morning.

CHAPTER

Four

December 10

I woke well after sunrise. I went down to the hotel's fitness center and worked out, then came back to my room, showered, and dressed. There was a text message on my phone from Laurie.

Good luck today. ☺

I'm going to need it, I thought.

I skipped breakfast and headed down to my car. Today my Porsche was less car than time machine, transporting me back to a place that existed more in memory than reality.

I had a plethora of feelings as I neared the old house. Driving down the old streets was like listening to an old vinyl record on a phonograph, with all the scratches and crackles, the surface noise as much a part of the music as the songs.

I hadn't been back to the house since I'd left Utah. In fact, I hadn't even been back to Utah. It's not that I hadn't had the opportunity, but I didn't claim it. The local papers, the *Deseret News* and its nemesis, the *Salt Lake Tribune*, had both written articles on me calling me out as a son of Utah—a title I had, at the time, no interest in claiming. I had refused interviews with both papers and turned down book signing requests and lucrative appearance and speaking fees simply because the venue was in Utah.

Now I was going back, without pay, media, or fanfare, quietly, like a thief in the night. Or perhaps a better simile would be like a veteran soldier making a solitary return to the battlefield where he was wounded. My own Utah Beach.

The whole neighborhood was in decline. And it didn't look like gentrification was in the immediate future. Nearly every home displayed an American flag or a crimson *U* for the University of Utah. Most of the yards were surrounded by chain-link fences or snow-laden hedges. In many of the driveways were cars old enough to be collectibles likely still in the possession of the original owner. I thought I recognized a few cars from my childhood.

As I neared the house, I could feel my anxiety rising. Everywhere I looked there were memories—mostly pain-

ful ones. Like the old run-down home with the plastic fla-
mingos where a mean woman shouted at me almost every
day as I walked to school because she was afraid I might
walk on her lawn. Or the home two doors from it where I
came across an old man illegally burning leaves. When he
saw me, he blamed the fire on me and threatened to call
the police. Maybe it was because it was a poor area, but
it always seemed to me that there was a meanness to the
neighborhood.

As I got closer to my childhood home, I could see
the tall, twisting oak tree my brother, Charles, had been
climbing when he died. I was watching my brother
climb the tree when he accidentally grabbed on to a
live power line and was electrocuted. I heard a loud *zap*,
and then he fell to the ground a few yards from where I
was standing. I was the only witness to the tragedy and
ran home to get help. Even now I felt sick to see the
tree.

Finally I came to the house. Like the rest of the neighborhood, it too was in decline. The house was a simple
redbrick rambler with chipping white window frames
and a single three-windowed gable on top. The roof was
topped with more than a foot of snow and icicles draped
from the rain gutters all the way across the roofline. On
the south corner of the house was an icicle so large that it
formed a column from the ground up, as in a cave when a
stalactite meets a stalagmite.

Snow-covered concrete steps ascended to a small front

porch with a white, paneled front door behind an aluminum storm door.

Everything looked so much smaller than I remembered. I've heard that's the case when we return to the places of our youth. Maybe it's because we ourselves were so much smaller back then. Or maybe it's because our minds make things seem bigger than they really are, like the opposite of a car's rearview mirror.

The oversized mailbox was still there, coated in ice. As a small child, I always thought it was big enough to hold me. More than once, when I was six, I wondered what would happen if I put a stamp on myself and got inside. I suppose that's kind of telling in its own way.

The home's front yard was surrounded by overgrown hedges of pyracantha, their clusters of crimson berries brilliant against the snow.

There was a silver Mercedes-Benz coupe parked in front of the house with a couple inside. The man in the driver's seat glanced in his rearview mirror as I pulled up behind them. As I shut off my car, he got out of his and walked toward me. He was short with oily, neatly groomed hair. He wore a pink polo shirt, jeans, and loafers. I got out of my car to meet him.

"Mr. Churcher?" he said, reaching out his hand as he walked.

"You must be Brad Campbell," I said, shaking his hand.

"It's a pleasure meeting you," he said. He casually glanced at the house. "Does this bring back memories?"

I ignored the question. "Is that your wife in the car?"

"Yes," he said, looking slightly embarrassed. "Her name is Kathy. I'm sorry, she begged me to come. She was hoping to meet you."

"No problem. Tell her to come on out," I said.

Brad turned back to the car and waved. The door opened and his wife sprang from the passenger side like she was spring-loaded. She held a large canvas shopping bag that she lugged heavily at her side. She looked at me with an expression gravitating between fear and awe.

"Hi, Kathy," I said.

Kathy Campbell set her book bag on the frozen ground and reached out to me. "Mr. Churcher, you have no idea how excited I am to meet you."

Truth is, I had some idea. She was wearing mismatched athletic shoes. Or maybe that was a thing in Utah.

"Thank you," I said, taking her hands in mine. "I'm excited to meet you too."

"You're just saying that." She really looked like she might faint. "I'm sure you get sick of this, but would you mind signing a few of my books?"

"I'd be happy to."

"I brought a pen," she said. She handed me a felt-tip Sharpie pen, then stooped down and proceeded to lift the entire pile of books out of the bag. There were five in all, which she held in a column in front of her. "I have your other books too," she said. "I didn't want to burden you, so I just brought my favorites."

"Let's take them to the car," I said. I took the stack from her and set them on the trunk of the Mercedes and proceeded to sign them all.

After I'd finished she said, "Thank you so much. Can we have a picture together?"

"Of course," I said.

She lifted her phone. "Brad, come take our picture."

Brad looked embarrassed as he walked over. He took the phone and pointed it at us.

"Lift it higher," she said. "Always hold the camera higher. It hides the chin."

"I know, I know, honey." He snapped several pictures. "I got three of them."

Kathy stepped back. "Thank you so much, Mr. Churcher. My friends will be so jealous." She piled the books back into her bag and, with one last glance, returned to the car.

"I'm so sorry," Brad said, walking back up to me. "She's such a fan." He took a deep breath. "All righty, let's get this started." He reached into his front right pants pocket and brought out a metal ring with about a dozen keys on it. He went through the keys, detached one, and handed it to me. "Do you mind if I come in with you? I'd like to make sure things are in order."

"I don't mind." I turned back to the house and walked up the cracked, concrete walkway leading to the porch. "Careful, it's slick. I don't want you falling." I looked at him and smiled. "Actually, I don't want you suing me."

"I wouldn't," he said. "My wife would leave me if I did."

From the road, the brick house had appeared much the same as it was when I left it, though, like me, worn a bit and noticeably older. The inside, however, was a different story. I was shocked by what I saw.

The blinds were all drawn, but even in the dim lighting I could see that the room was crowded with junk. Actually, *crowded* isn't a strong enough adjective. It was overflowing. The room resembled a domestic landfill. Everywhere I looked there were piles of things, rising from the floor in dusty towers. I turned to Brad. "My mother was a hoarder?"

"That would definitely appear to be the case." He looked at me curiously. "She wasn't a hoarder when you lived here?"

"No. Almost the opposite." I found the light switch and turned it on. There were boxes stacked on boxes and newspapers everywhere, as well as bulging black plastic leaf bags. I couldn't tell what most of the things were, but some I could, such as open boxes of clothing, old paperback books—an entire pile dedicated to Harlequin romances—and stacks of VHS tapes. I lifted one. "VHS. Do you think she thought the medium was going to make a comeback?"

"This is probably why she never let me in," Brad said.

I looked around. "Doesn't look like she ever threw anything away." *Besides me*, I thought.

"Hoarding's an interesting behavior," he said.

I looked at him. "By 'interesting' do you mean bizarre?"

"It's a compulsion. All compulsions are bizarre."

"Look at this crap. This is its own kind of crazy."

"I had a lawsuit involving a hoarder once. A woman sued her own church over it. She had had knee replacement surgery, and while she was still in the hospital recovering, her Relief Society friends came in and cleaned her place. The woman kept everything. I mean, there was even a porcelain toilet in her front room.

"The women and other church volunteers filled two thirty-cubic-yard Dumpsters with her junk. After they finished, they steam-cleaned the carpets, even did some light painting.

"When the woman got home they were all there, excited to see the surprise on her face. She was surprised all right. She collapsed. She had a complete nervous breakdown and spent the next month in a psychiatric unit. She sued the church for three million dollars."

"What's a Relief Society?" I asked.

"It's a women's organization in the Mormon Church. The name sounds a little ironic in this case. It didn't bring the woman much relief."

"You represented the woman?"

"I represented the church."

"Did you win?"

He looked at me seriously. "I always win."

I walked farther into the mess. "It's cold. Think the gas company turned off the heat?"

"No. Utah law wouldn't allow it in the middle of winter." He pointed toward the near wall. "There's the thermostat."

I walked over to it. It was set at fifty-five degrees.

"Fifty-five," I said. "That would explain why it's cold." I turned the thermostat up to seventy-five. I could hear the heat kick on.

My mother had made a trail through the piles that wound its way through the house. Brad followed behind me as I found my way through the maze. It was like we were exploring an undiscovered landscape. We could have been carrying torches. Of course, if I'd had a torch, I would have been tempted to just toss it into the middle of the room and run.

"It smells terrible in here," I said. "Makes me think we should be wearing masks or something."

"We probably should. Hoarding creates all kinds of health risks. That's actually what I used to win the lawsuit against the hoarder woman. I argued that the woman had created a public biohazard as well as a fire hazard, and what the church people had done in cleaning it up was no different than shutting down a meth lab. She was endangering herself and the neighborhood."

"The jury bought it?"

"Yeah. Fortunately for us, she wasn't the most sympathetic individual. She kept calling the jury 'a bunch of idiots' and wanted the people who cleaned up her house to be put in prison for life."

I stepped farther into the room, to the edge of the living room, an ironic title, as nothing but mold was alive in this house. There were things I remembered from my youth. A quilted rendition of a Grandma Moses painting and a small resin replica of Rodin's *The Kiss*.

I remembered that there had once been a piano next to the fireplace. I honestly didn't know if it was still there, as all I could see was a mountain of boxes.

"I think there might be a piano under there," I said. "A Steinway. Her uncle left it to her."

"Steinway Model O, 1914. It's worth about forty grand."

I looked at him. "How did you know that?"

"It was in the will. It hasn't been played in twenty years. Maybe if you dig into the mountain you might find other treasures."

"Or I could just take a match to it."

He rested his hands on his hips. "You know, there are companies that specialize in hoarder cleanups. They come in and cart it all away. I could recommend one."

I kept looking through the piles. "Maybe. But not now. I want to go through it."

"Then perhaps I could recommend a Dumpster rental."

"That I could definitely use."

"Their number is 801-555-4589. I'll text it to you."

I looked at him quizzically. "Why would you have their number memorized?"

"They were called in to court as character witnesses in my hoarding case." He shrugged. "I remember numbers."

"Do you remember your wife is still sitting out in the car?"

"Yes, she's fine. She's rereading one of your books. There's not many authors she likes, so if there's nothing new, she just rereads yours. The funny thing is, she forgets how they end, so she enjoys it just as much as the first time. I swear the woman could plan her own surprise party."

I grinned. "I would appreciate the Dumpster."

"Let me call them for you. They owe me a favor. He glanced at his watch. "It's probably too late to have it delivered today and tomorrow's Sunday. I'll see if they can deliver it first thing Monday morning."

"Thank you," I said.

"You know, the house could be worse," he said.

"How could it be worse?"

"She could have had cats." He scratched his head, then said, "I'd better go. Call if you need anything."

"Do I need to sign any papers?"

"You will, but not yet. The will is still in probate. I filed it the day after your mother died; it will probably be another three or four weeks."

"So the house isn't mine yet," I said.

"No. But since there's no other caretaker, it's our firm's policy to contact the future owner so they can take care of the place before it's handed over. Before that we had a few homes burn down before we could deliver the title. What a legal mess that was."

"I see. Thank you."

"No, thank you. You made my wife's day, month,

and year." He grinned. "Heck, you made her life." He turned and knocked over a pile of boxes. "Sorry about that." He walked back out of the house, closing the front door behind him, leaving me alone in my mother's mess.

CHAPTER

I laid my coat over one of the cleaner piles, then began moving boxes away from the spot where I guessed the piano was. (Moving boxes around the living room was like one of those sliding tile puzzles where you slide one tile at a time to the open space and keep moving it around until you arrange a picture.) After I had moved an entire stack of boxes, my curiosity got the better of me and I opened the top one. It was filled with tattered *National Geographic* magazines.

I dug back into the mountain of junk. After moving the next pile, I uncovered the ebony leg of the piano bench. There were boxes on top of the bench as well as beneath it. I moved them back, then cleared the piano. My mother had set boxes and paper directly on the piano's keyboard. I uncovered it and pushed down on a key. Even with the lid shut and boxes piled on top of it, the sound of the piano resonated beautifully in the room.

I got up and walked into the kitchen. It was no cleaner than the living room and smelled worse. Ironically, the counters were covered mostly with bottles of cleaning solution, from what I could see, two or three of the same kinds, grease cutters, scrubbing pads, dishwashing soap.

There was a can of Lysol spray. I sprayed it, or at least tried to, but nothing came out. Apparently she had even kept empty cans. I opened the window a few inches to air out the room.

The small Formica-topped kitchen table was covered with stacks of plates and bowls as well as Tupperware containers and empty cottage cheese tubs. It was all baffling to me. She had lived alone and, to my knowledge, never had anyone over. Why would she need more than a few place settings?

Under the sink, I found an unopened box of plastic garbage bags. I took out a bag and began to fill it with everything that was unquestionably disposable, like a pile of Cool Whip container lids and a sizable collection of catsup and mustard packets from drive-in restaurants.

It took me about five hours to clean about half the kitchen. I had gathered the bags in a big pile outside the back door. I was covered with dust and grease.

The half of the kitchen I had cleaned revealed a long scratch on one of the cupboard drawers. That was my doing. I was only eight at the time. I had damaged the drawer when I tried to ride it down the stairs like a sled. Actually, I damaged more than the drawer: I also broke my arm. My mother no doubt would have beaten me had I not already been screaming in pain.

I felt a little like an archaeologist, digging through sedimentary layers, uncovering the past. But not someone else's past. My past. That's probably why I couldn't hire someone else to clean or just take a match to the place.

Maybe someday I would, at least figuratively, but only after I had found what I was looking for. I wasn't entirely sure what that was, but I was certain that there was something.

As I finished cleaning for the day, it was already dark outside and I realized that I hadn't eaten anything all day. There was food in the house, just nothing edible. I had opened the refrigerator and just as quickly shut it, the smell of curdled milk and mold-filled Tupperware containers was more than I could stomach.

I washed my hands and arms off in the sink, locked the back door, and, after taking one last look around, turned off the light and went out the front door. I stopped for sushi on the way back to my hotel. I hadn't even known what sushi was when I left Utah. I don't even know if there was a sushi restaurant back then.

That night I dreamt again of the young, dark-haired woman, only this time my dreams were especially lucid. These were the clearest dreams I had had of her so far. We were in my mom's kitchen. It was just the two of us and she was standing next to the sink. Something was wrong. She was bent over the sink throwing up. I was afraid that she was sick and might die. But then she looked back at me and smiled. "It's nothing," she said.

CHAPTER

December 11

I woke the next day to my phone ringing. The sun was streaming in through the windows. I rolled over to answer my phone. It was Laurie.

"Did I wake you?"

"No."

"Liar. How late were you up?"

"I don't know. I didn't sleep well."

"Sorry. I just called to see how things were going. Have you seen the house?"

"I saw it yesterday."

"How was it?"

"Interesting. There could be a book in this."

"I thought there might be."

"My mother was a hoarder."

"She was a mess, or she was a genuine hoarder, like on the reality show?"

"The latter. Every room was filled with junk."

"Was she a hoarder when you were little?"

"No. This is new to me."

"I read that hoarding can be a coping mechanism, triggered by a traumatic event. People hold on to things because it buffers them from the world and gives them a feeling of control."

"Trauma. Like my brother dying?"

"Yes, but you were with her after he died."

"More than ten years."

"So unless it was some crazy delayed response, something else must have happened." She sighed. "You're still sure that you don't want me to come out?"

"No. I've got this."

"All right. I'm around. I'm just cleaning the house this weekend."

"I'll send you some pictures of what real house cleaning looks like."

"I want to see those pictures," she said. "Good luck. Don't get trapped under anything. Oh, you're still at the Grand?"

"Yes."

"Try the eggs Benedict. It's out of this world."

"You've stayed here before?"

"I stay there every time I go to Utah. I have two authors there."

"Why haven't you ever told me?"

"Because it would be like telling John McCain you're planning a vacation to Vietnam."

"That was cold. Have a good day cleaning."

"You too. Talk to you tomorrow."

I hung up the phone, dialed room service, and ordered the eggs Benedict and an apple pastry with a glass of fresh orange juice. I was getting out of the shower when there was a knock on the door. I shrugged on one of the hotel's robes and opened the door. A woman stood next to a serving table covered in white linen.

"Good morning, Mr. Churcher," she said. "May I come in?"

"Please," I said, stepping back.

She pushed the table inside my room. "Where would you like to eat?"

"Over by the sofa," I said.

"How's your day so far?"

"Good," I said. "I just woke up."

She prepared the table for me, removing the cellophane from the top of the glass of orange juice and the metal lid from the eggs Benedict. I signed the check and she left the room.

Laurie was right. The dish was excellent. I finished eating, dressed, then headed out to face my mother's mess.

CHAPTER

Seven

It was a bright and clear morning, and the massive Wasatch mountains rose like great, landlocked icebergs. I had forgotten just how big the mountains were. And how ubiquitous. With the Wasatch Range in the east and the Oquirrh Mountains in the west, mountains surrounded the city like a fortress wall.

Salt Lake City is a religious city, and since it was the Sabbath there wasn't much traffic on the roads. I stopped at a Smith's Food King for bottled water, dishwashing gloves, a bucket, mop, cleaning rags, and several boxes of Lysol disinfectant. Then I drove through a Starbucks for a Venti caffè mocha before heading to the house.

The home was warm as I walked in, which was an improvement over yesterday, but the mess actually looked worse than I remembered—if that were even possible. I carried my coffee and my cleaning supplies to the kitchen and went to work. Inside one of the cupboards were boxes of Teenage Mutant Ninja Turtles cereal and Quisp, two cereals that were nearly as old as I was. I don't know what it is about old boxes of cereal, but frankly I felt nostalgic toward them. Maybe I had inherited some of my mother's hoarder instincts, but I couldn't throw them away. I finished wiping off the counter and was taking a sip of my coffee when I heard a voice.

"Hello."

I almost spit out my coffee as I spun around. An elderly woman stood in the kitchen entrance. She had whitish-gray hair and was slight of frame, though she wasn't stooped. Her eyes were clear and friendly.

"I'm sorry, I should have knocked, but honestly, after sixty years of just walking in, it didn't cross my mind." She looked around the kitchen with a slightly amused expression. "You're cleaning. This would have made your mother crazy." She turned back to me. "You're Jacob, aren't you?"

"Who are you?"

"You don't know?" she said. "I'm Elyse Foster. I live two houses down. I was your mother's friend."

Something about her claiming friendship with my mother bothered me. *My enemy's friend is my enemy?* What kind of a person would befriend my mother?

"I didn't know my mother had any friends."

"She didn't have many. How old are you now, Jacob? Thirty-four? Thirty-five?"

"Thirty-four," I said.

"Charles would have been thirty-eight."

The mention of my brother's name shocked me. "You knew my brother?"

"Honey, I knew both of you like you were my own." Her brow fell. "You really don't remember, do you?"

I shook my head. "No."

She stepped toward me. "I always said you'd be a lady-killer someday. You were such a beautiful boy. Big eyes. Big curly mop of hair. I was right. You're still beautiful."

I felt awkward with the compliment. "Thank you."

"You're writing books now."

I couldn't tell if it was a question or a statement. "Yes."

"I'm not surprised. You always had such an imagination." She looked around the kitchen. "It's always different after they leave, isn't it?"

"After who leaves?"

"The home's inhabitant. It's like the spirit leaves the house as well as the body." She looked at me with a sympathetic expression. "It must be difficult for you to be back after all these years."

"Very."

The moment fell into silence. After a minute I took a deep breath, then said, "Well, it's nice to meet you. I'll get back to work. I've got a lot to do."

She didn't move. "Don't be so dismissive of me, Jacob. You're not 'meeting' me. I'm a bigger part of your life than you know."

Her directness surprised me. I wasn't used to it. Once you become rich and famous, people don't talk to you that way. At least, not if they want something from you.

"And I know you have questions."

"How would you know that?"

"Because anyone in your situation would." Her voice suddenly lowered. "I may be your only witness."

I had no idea what to say to that so I didn't say anything. She broke the silence. "How long will you be in town?"

"I don't know yet. A few days."

"Are you staying here?"

"No. I'm staying downtown at the Grand America."

"The Grand," she said. "Used to just be the Little America down there and Hotel Utah. Now there's a Grand America." She smiled. "I'll come back later. Give you a little time to digest things. Welcome home, Jacob. It's good to see you again. I was hoping you'd come home."

"This isn't my home."

"No," she said, frowning. "I suspect not. Good-bye." She turned and started to walk away, then stopped in the middle of the front room and turned back. "You know what they say about truth, Jacob."

"What's that?"

"It will set you free." She turned and walked out of the house, gently closing the door behind her.

I went back to work, Elyse's comment replaying in my mind. *My only witness?*

I took a break for lunch at around two, driving to a hamburger joint called Arctic Circle. I used to eat there when I was a boy. They had foot-long hot dogs and brown toppers—vanilla ice-cream cones dipped in chocolate. Arctic Circle is a Utah-based hamburger chain and the inventor of Utah "fry sauce," a surprisingly tasty mixture of catsup and mayonnaise. When I was young there were two unique Utah hamburger chains, Arctic Circle and Dee's Drive-ins, which no longer existed. When I moved to Spokane there had been an Arctic Circle, but I had never gone there. I don't know why. Maybe because it reminded me of Utah.

After lunch I went back to work, finishing the kitchen at around seven. I had collected more than a dozen garbage sacks with junk and dragged them outside the back door with the others.

When I had finished mopping the floor and disinfecting the countertops and appliances, I sat down at the table and looked around the kitchen. There had been life here once. I remembered Charles asking for Mickey Mouse pancakes and my mother making them with chocolate chip eyes. It was nothing more than a snapshot of a memory, but it was significant. My mother was smiling.

CHAPTER

Eight

Monday

It was snowing the next morning. When I arrived back at the house, there was a large metal Dumpster in the driveway. Actually, it pretty much filled the driveway. I must have just missed the delivery because the truck's tire tracks were still fresh in the new snow.

I walked around to the back of the house, carried back thirteen garbage sacks, and threw them into the Dumpster. Then I unlocked the door and went back into the house.

The next room I decided to clean was my bedroom. It wasn't as bad as the kitchen. There were still the same four posters on the wall that I'd hung shortly before running away: a movie poster of *The Matrix*, one of Eminem, and two basketball posters, one of the Utah Jazz's Karl Malone, the other the famous Michael Jordan flying dunk poster.

I was surprised to see the posters still up. I guess I'd assumed that my mother would have torn them down along with any other reminder of me. But the room was mostly the way I remembered it, though back then it wasn't filled with boxes and strange junk like an old water cooler, a toy cotton candy machine, and about fifty empty plastic Coke bottles.

I had brought a Bluetooth speaker I could use to play music from my phone. Appropriately, I played my Red Hot Chili Peppers and Eminem, who had just hit it big about the time I left home.

Not only had my mother left my room exactly the way it was the last time I'd been there, but she had even made the bed and the drawers were filled with the clothes I had left on the front lawn the night I left home. It made no sense to me. Why would she have brought my things back into the house and put them away? Did she think I was coming back?

I was going through one of my drawers when the doorbell rang. I walked out and opened the front door. Brad Campbell stood on the porch. He was holding a tall Styrofoam cup that steamed in the winter air.

"Brad," I said. "Come in."

"Thank you," he replied, his breath freezing in front of him. He stepped inside. "I thought I'd drop by to see if they brought the Dumpster."

"It was here when I arrived. Your friends start early."

"They start work around five in the morning. There's less traffic to deal with." He handed me the cup. "I brought you a peppermint hot chocolate."

"Thank you."

He looked toward the kitchen. "Looks like you're making progress."

"It's coming along. Slowly. The kitchen took me all day yesterday."

He nodded. "It looks like a kitchen now." He put his hands in his pockets. "I'll let you get back to your cleaning. If you need anything, just call."

"I don't know what I'd need, but thanks."

"Don't mention it." He slightly nodded, then turned and walked out. I carried the bags from the room to the Dumpster, then came back inside, washed my hands, and drove again to Arctic Circle. I had their famous ranch burger with a raspberry shake, then went back to the house.

The hall outside my room was piled high with boxes. Since it was a main thoroughfare, it wasn't as cluttered as the other rooms, not that it really contained less junk, rather it was just slightly better organized.

I started going through the boxes. One of them contained all my schoolwork, from kindergarten to seventh grade. I was surprised that my mother had hung on to these things.

It took me about three hours to finish the hall. Almost all the boxes were filled with paper and documents of one kind or another. My mother had kept all her financial records and bills for the last fifteen years. The boxes were heavier than most of what I'd been carrying and, in spite of my daily appointment with an elliptical machine, I was a little winded after getting them all out to the Dumpster.

Next I started on the bathroom at the end of the hall. The bathroom was small and my mother had filled the tub with an eclectic pile of trash: unfinished knitting projects, two lampshades, and an old, rusted woman's bicycle with two flat tires and no seat. I had no idea what a bicycle was doing inside the bathtub, let alone the house, but I'd given up trying to make sense of the mess.

I was carrying the bicycle out of the bathroom when there was a knock at the door. I looked over to see the door open. Elyse Foster stepped in. She had snow on her hair and she was holding a cardboard box that looked too heavy for her to have carried through the snow.

"I couldn't imagine there would be anything to eat in the house, so I brought you some hot soup."

"Let me get that," I said, setting the bike down and taking the box from her. "Come in."

She stepped farther inside the room. "I made you tomato soup. You always liked tomato soup. You liked to crumble saltines in it."

"I still do," I said. "It embarrasses my agent when we're in a fancy New York restaurant. Old habits." She followed me into the kitchen and I set the box down.

"I put some crackers in there. Also some buttered rolls and a piece of chocolate cake."

"You didn't have to go to all that trouble."

"It was no trouble. Now sit down and eat. You haven't left the house since noon, you must be hungry."

I wondered how she knew I hadn't left the house since then. I got two bowls down from the cupboard. "There's enough here for two," I said.

"I've already eaten," she said. "I didn't want to force my company on you."

I came back to the table, unscrewed the lid from her thermos, and poured the soup into the bowl. "You're not forcing anything. Have a seat."

"Thank you." She sat down across from me and began unwrapping the crackers. She set them in front of me. "It's already looking much better in here. How is it going?"

"It's a lot of work."

"It ought to be. It took her more than fifteen years to compile it." She looked around and her expression grew more somber. "These walls hold a lot of pain."

"*These* walls hold a lot of pain," I said, setting my hand over my chest.

"I know. I'm sorry."

I looked at her. "You said something yesterday, about being my only witness."

"Yes?"

"What did you mean by that?"

"I meant that I'm the only one who knew you before the change."

"The *change*? You mean before I became famous?"

She shook her head. "No. Your mother's change. She

wasn't always the way you remember her. After Charles died, she changed."

"I was only four when he died."

"I know. I doubt you remember much of your mother before that."

I thought over what she'd said. "You said that you thought I would have questions."

"I think anyone in your situation would." Her face looked heavy with concern. "You don't know how I've worried about you over the years. Your mother was so sick. I'm so happy to see that you've done well in life."

I frowned. "I'm not doing as well as you think," I said. "That's why I write."

She nodded slowly. "I know. I've read your books."

I looked at her with surprise. "You have?"

"That's how I've kept track of you. I recognize many of the places and people you've drawn from. You've even put me in a few of your books, whether you know it or not."

I looked at her intensely. "How well did you know me?"

"You really don't remember," she said sadly.

"I'm sorry, I don't."

"Well, I shouldn't be too surprised. The mind blocks out painful times. I used to have those little Brach's chocolate stars. You would come over and ask for one of those almost every day."

"I remember those. That was you?"

"For years I took you whenever your mother had a migraine. When my nephew stayed with me, I would take you for days at a time. Anything I could do to get you out of that house."

Memories suddenly flooded in. There was a boy I would play with from time to time. He didn't live in my neighborhood, his aunt did. Sometimes we would go on adventures in the backyard, playing explorers or pirates; other times we would go to his aunt's house and play games. It was like we played alone, but together. But even he stopped coming around by the time I turned seven or eight.

"His name was Nick," I said.

"Then you remember him."

"You were his aunt."

She nodded. "He came to stay with me every summer until you were seven. His father was military and was transferred to Germany. You stopped playing at my house after that. That's probably why you don't remember."

"I always wondered why he stopped coming."

"Your mother became more secluded after that. I didn't see you as much."

"You knew my father . . ."

"Yes. I knew Scott well."

It was strange hearing him called by his name. "All I knew about my father is that he abandoned me."

Her brow fell and she shook her head. "No. That's not true. At least not completely."

"What do you mean, *completely*?"

"He left you, but it wasn't his choice. After your brother died, your mother stayed in her bedroom for nearly a year.

She withdrew from everyone. Your father felt guilty for your brother's death, and that was a pretty big club she had to beat him with."

"Why would he feel guilty?"

"From what I understand, he was supposed to be with him when it happened. Your mother blamed him for Charles's death. I think he was so grief-stricken, he blamed himself. She withdrew all love from him. After two years, he couldn't take it anymore. So they divorced."

She looked at me somberly. "You have to understand that your father wasn't doing well. He'd lost a son too. Only he carried the guilt with it. I'm not saying it's an excuse, but it's a reason."

"I never saw him again."

"Until just recently, neither had I. He never came back."

"Then he did abandon me."

She nodded sympathetically. "In a way."

Hearing her say that angered me. "*In a way?* He left and never came back."

She looked at me stoically. "If you want to see it that black and white, it's up to you. But life is more complicated than that. Motive matters. It wasn't what he wanted. And it wasn't his idea. Haven't you ever done something you thought was so bad that you lost faith in yourself?"

"I never had faith in myself to begin with."

"You must have had some faith in yourself." She looked down for a moment, then said, "Let me tell you something about blame. My brother took his own life thirty-six years ago.

"He was a very smart and successful obstetrician. He was delivering a baby when something went wrong. Both the baby and mother died. There was nothing he could do. Still, the woman's husband filed a malpractice lawsuit against him. It didn't matter that my brother was found innocent or that all his colleagues stood behind him." She looked into my eyes. "Do you know what group of people are most likely to commit suicide?"

I wasn't sure if it was a rhetorical question or she expected an answer. After a moment I ventured, "Teenage boys?"

"Doctors in malpractice lawsuits," she said. "It's because the very core of their identity is called into question. Whether they're guilty or not makes almost no difference. That's just the way we're wired.

"In a way, that was your father. It doesn't matter that your father was trying to help someone in need. It doesn't matter that your brother's death was an accident that could have happened even if he'd been home. He wasn't there and your brother died. That kind of thinking can ruin a person." She let out a long, slow breath. "I talk too much. And you haven't eaten your soup. It's probably cold by now."

"I'll heat it up in the microwave." I looked into the old woman's eyes. She looked tired. "Thank you for sharing."

"Considering the topic, I won't say it was a pleasure. But it is good to talk to you after all these years. I really have worried about you." She stood. "I'm so pleased that you became a good man."

"What makes you think I'm good?" I asked cynically.

She didn't answer. "I'll pick up my thermos later. Good night." She slowly made her way through the mess back to the door.

I put my bowl in the microwave and tried to start it but nothing happened. The microwave didn't work. I took my soup back out and ate it cool with broken crackers. As I sat there eating, I replayed our conversation. For the first time since I could remember, I wanted to see my father.

I finished the soup, then went back to the bathroom, finished cleaning up, and carried all the bags out to the Dumpster. It was snowing as I left the house—not much, just a few errant flakes here and there—but it looked pretty.

On the way to the hotel I stopped at a grocery store and picked up some more bottled water and trash bags, then drove back downtown. When I walked into my room, the message light on my phone was flashing. It was the front desk wanting to know if I was planning on extending my stay. I had already stayed longer than I had planned. I was starting to get the feeling that it might be a lot longer.

CHAPTER

December 13

I could tell something was different the moment I woke. Even in my room there was a peculiar stillness. I checked the clock. It was eight o'clock, but it was dark for the hour. I climbed out of bed and walked over to the window and parted the curtain. There was a blizzard outside. A complete whiteout.

From my eleventh-floor vantage point I could see Fifth South, the main thoroughfare to I-15. The street was invisible, completely covered with snow. Only a few intrepid drivers were on the road, crawling along at just five or ten miles per hour and still occasionally fishtailing. A block east I could see flashing police lights where two cars had crashed at the State Street intersection.

As I stood there my phone rang. It was Laurie.

"You didn't call," she said.

"When?"

"Sunday morning. You said you were going to call me tomorrow, aka, the day before yesterday."

"Sorry. I got busy. What's up?"

"How's the weather?"

"It's a blizzard."

"I saw that on my weather app. Did you finish cleaning?"

"No. It's going to take a while."

"How long is a while?"

"I don't know."

"Well, please find out—we've got work to do."

"I'll call you when I know."

She sighed. "All right. Be careful out there. Ciao."

I went back to the window and looked out. It's not often you see a city frozen. Then I got dressed and went down to the fitness center, where I worked out for several hours. Not surprisingly, the exercise room was slammed, everyone held prisoner by the weather.

By the time I got back to my room, the blizzard had lightened to a mild snowfall. Yellow snowplows with flashing orange lights looked like Tonka trucks below me. They were out in force, scraping the downtown streets, a mechanical salt spreader tossing salt behind them like rice at a wedding.

There were already significantly more cars on the road than there had been before. Salt Lakers are used to snow, and weather that would render a Floridian housebound barely warrants a sweater along the Wasatch Front. Utahans, like most people who live in cold climates, take a curious pride in that.

I took a shower and ordered room service. I should have ordered before my shower, because there was an hour wait for food, since no one was leaving the hotel to eat.

I turned on my laptop and pulled up the book I was currently working on, but couldn't get into it. I had written only a few hundred words when room service knocked on my door. The woman pushing the tray looked harried. "Busy?" I asked rhetorically.

"A bit more than usual," she said. "The blizzard's kept everyone inside."

I signed the bill, and she ran off.

It was almost noon when I finished breakfast. I looked out the window again and the snow had completely stopped. I knew that the freeway and downtown streets would be cleared before the suburbs, so there was no sense trying to go out to my mother's house just yet. I had another idea. I grabbed my coat and went down to the concierge counter in the hotel lobby.

"Could you call me a cab?"

The young woman behind the counter replied in a British accent. "You can catch one outside, sir. They queue near the front."

"Thank you." I walked out the gilded revolving door. A

young man in a hunter-green jacket and top hat nodded to me.

"May I help you, sir?"

"I'd like a cab."

"Yes, sir." He lifted a whistle and blew. An oxblood-red taxi pulled up. "There you go, sir," the young man said, opening the back door for me. I handed him a five-dollar bill and climbed in.

"Where to?" the driver asked.

"The Salt Lake cemetery," I replied.

The driver pulled out of the hotel's large circular drive-way onto Second West. The traffic was still light as we wound our way through the downtown streets.

"That was some blizzard this morning," the driver said. "Shut us down for a while."

"I'm surprised at how quickly it stopped and everyone got back to business."

"That's the weather in Salt Lake, you know. It's the lake effect. You don't like it, wait a few minutes." He glanced back at me in his mirror. "Can't guarantee the roads will be clear at the cemetery."

"I'll take my chances."

About ten minutes later we pulled into the diagonally faced gates of the old cemetery. I could see that the roads had been freshly plowed.

"Whereabouts in the cemetery are we headed?" the driver asked. "It's a big cemetery. Here's some trivia for you: it's the largest city-operated cemetery in the country."

"Do you know where Lester Wire was buried?"

"Lester Wire?"

"The inventor of the traffic light."

"Hmm. No, but I can look it up." He pulled over to the side of the narrow, snow-banked road and consulted his smartphone. "Lester Farnsworth Wire. Inventor of the electric traffic light. It says here he picked red and green colors because it was Christmas and he had electric Christmas lights available." He set down his phone. "He's up on the northeast side." He pulled back onto the street. "And now I'll know who to cuss out when I hit three traffic lights in a row." He glanced back at me. "He a relative of yours?"

"No. My brother is buried near him."

"Gotcha."

We wound through the labyrinthine roads of the cemetery until we came to a vertical concrete monument and the driver stopped.

LESTER FARNSWORTH WIRE

SEPTEMBER 3, 1887–APRIL 14, 1958

INVENTOR

ELECTRIC TRAFFIC LIGHT

"There's your man. Or at least his grave."

"I'll just be a few minutes," I said. I climbed out of the

car. Even though we had only driven ten minutes from the hotel, we were higher in altitude and the temperature had dropped. I shivered as I pulled my coat tighter around me.

My brother was buried twenty steps to the right of a ten-foot obelisk with a cement ball on top. His headstone was level with the ground and subsequently buried in snow. I walked to the grave, felt the stone out with the tip of my shoe, then knelt down and cleared the snow from the marker's granite face.

I had been to this spot more times than I could remember. Enough that even after all these years I could find it covered in the snow. The tradition must have started early, as I had a vague memory of my father and mother lighting a sparkler and sticking it into the ground on Charles's birthday. After my parents divorced, my mother and I went alone. Three times a year. On Charles's birthday, on Christmas, and in August on the anniversary of his death.

But now it had been seventeen years. I stood up and looked down at the marker.

"You shouldn't have gone, Charles. Wherever you went, I hope you had a better time than I did."

I looked at the grave for a few minutes, then felt suddenly curious whether my mother's grave was next to his. I took a few steps through the snow, about five or six feet east of my brother's stone, until I felt another gravestone. I pushed the snow off with my foot, exposing the top of the marker.

RUTH CAROLE CHURCHER

REST IN PEACE

I sighed. Then I walked back to the taxi and climbed back in. "Back to the hotel," I said.

I must have looked different, because the driver didn't say a word the whole way back.

I didn't return to my room. Instead, I went from the cab down to the parking garage and got in my car. I waited a few minutes for it to warm up, then I drove out to my mother's house.

The south end of the Salt Lake Valley had gotten even more snow than downtown, and from what I could tell, my mother's neighborhood had been deluged with more than thirty inches. The entire place looked like an ice village, and cars looked more like igloos than automobiles.

A plow had been by, so the road was like a roofless tunnel with five-foot snowbanks towering on both sides. Those unfortunate souls who had left their cars parked in the street found the driver's side of their vehicles piled with snow up to their roofs.

I parked in front of my mother's house. I had to climb over a large snowbank to get into the yard.

It was already twilight when I arrived, and much of the home was obscured in shadow. As I neared the walkway I found footsteps leading up to the front door. They were recent enough to still be distinguishable: small, feminine-sized, with a small heel. I wondered if Elyse had tried to make her way over, but I decided that was unlikely. She would have seen that my car wasn't here. Besides, for an elderly woman, walking through this snow and ice was just begging for a broken hip. Still, I couldn't think of anyone else who would have come by in this weather.

I unlocked the front door and went inside. I flipped on the lights and walked over to the thermostat. I turned it up to seventy-five, turned on the music on my phone, and went to work on the space I'd dreaded most of all—the front room.

As I worked, I thought of Charles, the day he died, as well as all the times I went with my mother to the cemetery. I never knew how she would react. Sometimes she would fall to her knees and wail. Other times she would just stare angrily at the ground. Those were the times that frightened me the most. I never knew what Charles Day would bring.

I worked for about five hours, calling it quits a little after ten. I had managed to completely uncover the piano, which was my goal for the evening. I wiped off the bench with a damp cloth, took off my gloves, and sat down. I began to play. The piano was out of tune, but not horribly.

My mother had made me take piano lessons until I left the piano along with my home. With the exception of a few parties, I hadn't played for years. It was one of the things I had left behind, I think, because it didn't belong to me. Charles had wanted to play the piano. And a year after his death, the charge was given to me. I never wanted to learn to play and I hated every minute of practicing. Still, it was part of my past. It was part of me. And in spite of my resistance, I had been good once.

I began to play Simon and Garfunkel's "The Sounds of Silence." I remember one night my mother coming into the front room and sitting down while I played it. After I finished, she said softly, "Play it again."

It was the last song I learned, which is probably why I still remembered it. Or maybe it was because it was one of the saddest pieces of music ever written.

As I finished playing the song, tears were falling down my cheeks. For the first time since I'd heard the news of my mother's death, I felt loss. I pounded on the keys, then laid my head against the fallboard and wept. The thing is, I wasn't sure what I was feeling loss for. Maybe my mother. Maybe the loss of the mother I'd never had. Maybe my childhood. Maybe just everything.

As I sat there I remembered something. I got on the floor and slid my head under the seat. It was still there. Charles had written on it in black marker:

Charles Churchers piano

Five years later I had written beneath it:

You can have it

I stood back up, closed the lid on the piano, then locked up the house and drove back to the hotel.

C H A P T E R

December 14

I woke the next morning around nine. On my way back to the hotel I had decided to keep the piano, so I looked on the Internet for a piano mover. The first two balked when I told them I wanted it delivered to Coeur d'Alene. The third was glad for the work.

I left the hotel early. The day was beautiful, the sky as blue as a Tahitian lagoon. I stopped at the Starbucks drive-through for a Venti coffee and blueberry scone, then drove to the house.

For the first time since I'd come to Salt Lake, the old neighborhood looked alive. People were out shoveling their walks or pushing snow blowers with great white arches spraying from their machines. One man was brushing snow off his car with a push broom.

The footprints I had seen on the walkway the day before were now iced over, preserved like winter fossils. I went into the house and went back to work in the front room. Now that I had exposed the carpet in places, I remembered it, an avocado-green shag that was outdated long before I was born. They say that if you wait long enough, everything comes back in style, but I think you might have to wait a few centuries for the avocado love affair to rekindle.

Several hours after I started cleaning, I came across boxes with Christmas ornaments and decorations that had been magical to me as a kid. The boxes still contained magic. Instead of pushing them out to the Dumpster, I opened them up, carefully unwrapping each treasure. One box contained old holiday records, a collection as eclectic as the season itself. Vince Guaraldi's *A Charlie Brown Christmas*, Kenny G's *Miracles*, Bing Crosby's *White Christmas*, the Carpenters' *Christmas Portrait*, *A Fresh Aire Christmas*, Nat King Cole's *The Christmas Song*, *The Perry Como Christmas Album*, Herb Alpert's *Christmas Album*.

I kept digging through the pile until I found what I was looking for—my mother's record player. It had been decades since I had used one. I had seen the old vinyl records coming back in vogue at the bookstores I signed in. I had even been tempted to buy a few albums; I just never got around to it.

I brushed the dust off the record player and plugged it into the wall. The tan, felt-covered turntable began spinning. I checked to make sure that the speed was set at 33 rpm, something I have no idea how I remembered, then I took the *Charlie Brown Christmas* album from the sleeve and put it on the player. Counting down the songs by the grooves in the record, I gently set the needle at track four, "Linus and Lucy." As the familiar strains of the song started, a smile crossed my face. Even in the worst of times, there had always been something healing about the music of Christmas.

Later that afternoon my phone rang. It was Laurie. I turned the record player down and answered.

"What's up?"

"You're number four," she said.

"I'm number four what?"

She paused. "You're kidding, right? Your book, dummy."

I had completely forgotten about the list. "Wow. It's already Wednesday."

"Yes, it's Wednesday, there's a new list, and you're fourth on it."

"Great," I said.

"What's going on?"

"I'm cleaning."

"I know you're cleaning, but what have you done with my author? You practically took my head off last week when I told you that you were three. It took me a half hour today to get up the courage to call you. I was prepared to talk you down from the ledge. I was going to tell you that the only reason you dropped a spot is that three more big books came out, including a Danielle Steele."

"No worries," I said.

"You're freaking me out." Pause. "Is that . . . Christmas music I hear playing?"

"Yes."

"So are you done out there?"

"Almost," I said.

"What does that mean?"

"*Almost* means very nearly, about, roughly . . ."

"I know what the word means. I want to know what it means in your specific circumstance."

"I only have the front room to finish, then I'm done. The piano movers come Friday to get the piano."

"You're keeping it."

"Yes," I said. "It's a Steinway."

"Do you even know anyone who plays the piano?"

"I play the piano."

"Another secret emerges from the past. So you meet the movers on Friday, then you fly home?"

"I drive home," I said.

She groaned. "I forgot you drove. Your publisher's driving me crazy about the next contract. I was going to try to talk you into flying to New York before going home. I guess that won't work."

"I can fly out from Spokane. I'll just need a few days to collect myself."

"Then I'll give them a definite *maybe* for next week," she said. "So back to you. How are you?"

"Good."

"Find anything interesting?"

"I found a lot of interesting things."

"Have you found what you're looking for?"

"It would help if I knew what I'm looking for. But no. Not really. Maybe there's nothing to find."

"All right," she said. "Don't forget me."

"Never. Ciao."

"Ciao."

I set my phone on the piano bench, then turned the Christmas music back up. I began listening through the Christmas albums. I was listening to Karen Carpenter belt out "The Christmas Song" ("Chestnuts roasting on an open fire . . .") when I heard a knock at the door. I turned down the music, walked over, and answered it.

I was expecting to see Elyse. Instead, it was a young woman. She looked about my age, maybe a few years younger. She was pretty. She had almond-shaped eyes and dark-umber hair that tumbled out beneath a wine-colored knit cap. She wore a long scarf and mittens that matched the cap. Something about her looked familiar.

"I'm sorry to bother you," she said in an uneasy voice. "But is this the Churcher residence?"

"Yes. What can I do for you?"

She looked at me anxiously. I couldn't tell if she was shivering from nerves or the cold. Actually, I had seen this kind of behavior before at book signings and I figured I had a fan. I wondered how she had found out I was there.

"Are you Jacob Churcher?"

Definitely a fan, I thought. "Yes."

"Ruth Carole Churcher was your mother?"

"Yes."

"Good," she said. "My name is Rachel Garner. I . . ." She hesitated. "I'm sorry, I'm a little flustered. I've been trying for so long to catch someone here, I really wasn't expecting anyone to answer."

I looked at her quizzically. "Who are you looking for?"

"I'm looking for my mother. Has your family lived in this house for thirty years?"

"More than thirty-five," I said. "I was born here."

She nodded. "Would you know if a young woman lived here about thirty years ago? She was pregnant?"

"A pregnant woman?" I said. "No."

She looked down, clearly upset. "Is it possible that you don't remember?"

"I would have been four, but it seems like the kind of thing I'd remember. Or know."

She looked even more upset. Actually, she looked heartbroken.

"Here, come inside," I said. "It's cold."

"Thank you."

She stepped inside the house, and I closed the door behind her. I could tell from her expression that the state of the room surprised her.

"I know, it's crazy in here," I said. "I didn't know that my mother was a hoarder. I'm just cleaning up the mess. I'd offer you a seat, but . . ." I gestured to the pile of boxes that hid the sofa. "But that's the seat."

"That's okay," she said. "I don't mind standing. Thank you for talking to me. I know it's a difficult time for you."

"Difficult?"

Her forehead furrowed. "I'm sorry, didn't your mother just pass away?"

"Yes. Of course," I said, feeling embarrassed that I wasn't experiencing the usual grief.

"I'm sorry," she said again.

"We weren't close."

"Then I'm sorry for that too," she said. She rubbed her hands together. "It's so cold in Salt Lake."

"You're not from around here?"

"No. I live in St. George. Are you from here?"

"I was born here, but I live in Coeur d'Alene."

She just looked at me sadly.

"May I take your coat?"

"Yes. Thank you."

I helped her off with her coat, then took it over to the piano bench, one of the few clean surfaces in the room. "Did you come by yesterday?" I asked, thinking of the footprint I'd seen in the snow.

She nodded. "In the afternoon. I thought I'd try again after that storm."

"How did you know my mother died?"

"A few weeks ago I saw the obituary in the newspaper, and I thought that maybe someone might be here and I could find some answers."

There was something about the way she said this that

stoked my interest. Maybe it was her vulnerability. Or maybe it was her beauty.

"I've got the kitchen cleaned up. We can sit in there." I led her there and pulled out a chair at the table, then sat down across from her. "It's Rachel?"

"Yes, Rachel."

"Why did you think your mother was here?"

"I was told that she might have been living here when I was born."

"Are you sure you have the right place?"

"I'm pretty sure. Scott and Ruth Churcher?"

"Those are my parents' names."

"I think my mother—my birth mother—lived with them. I was adopted as a baby, and a few years ago I decided to try to find out more about her, to try to find her. I went to the state but my adoption records were sealed. They sent a letter to her to see if she would be interested in meeting me, but she never even replied. I don't know if she's still alive or if she just doesn't want to have anything to do with me.

"Then, about four years ago, a friend introduced me to her new boyfriend. He worked in the state records department. I asked him if there was anything he could do to help me and he said he would look into it. He called me a few days later. He told me what I already knew, that the record was sealed. He said that he couldn't give me that information or else he could lose his job and face prosecution as well as a civil lawsuit. I figured that I was just out of luck. Then he told me something I didn't know. He said that my birth mother was only seventeen when she gave birth and wasn't married. He said that the record showed that my mother had come to live with a family with the last name Churcher. I think her family may have sent her away when they found out she was pregnant."

I looked at her curiously. "What year was that?"

"I was born in 1986."

I thought for a moment, then said, "I was only three or four years old. It's possible I could have forgotten. It was also a very traumatic time. It was the year my brother died."

"I'm sorry."

"Do you know your mother's name?"

She frowned. "No."

"No, of course you don't," I said. "My mother would have known. It's too bad you didn't come here before she died."

"Actually, I did. I came here at least a dozen times and rang the doorbell, but no one would ever answer. I could usually tell that someone was inside, but . . ." She sighed. "I even tracked down the phone number and called, but no one answered that either."

I wasn't surprised my mother hadn't answered the phone. She rarely did when I lived with her, and it appeared that she had become even more of a recluse in her last days.

"When I came across the obituary for your mother, I figured that if there was family, they might be here."

"And you might find someone who knew about your mother."

She nodded. "I was hoping."

I took a deep breath. "I'm sorry. I wish I could help you."

Her eyes welled up with tears. She looked down for moment, then said, "Do you have any siblings or relatives who might know anything?"

"I only had my brother. And my mother was an only child."

"What about your father?"

"That's another dead end. I don't have any contact with him. I don't even know where he lives."

She wiped a tear from her cheek. "I'm sorry." I could tell she was becoming more emotional, as her eyes welled still more. Suddenly she started to stand. "I've wasted enough of your time. I'm sorry to bother you."

"Wait," I said, a thought occurring to me. "There's an elderly woman who came by to visit. She was my mother's best friend. She's lived in the neighborhood longer than I've been alive. She ought to know. She just lives a couple houses from here."

Her face lit up. "Could you ask her?"

"We can go ask her right now."

"Thank you."

I helped her back on with her coat, then got my own and we walked out.

"Watch your step," I said. "It's pretty icy."

"I know. I fell trying to get over that snowbank. I'm glad no one was watching."

We walked down the drive and I helped her over the bank, then straddled it myself to get over. We crossed the street and walked up to Elyse's front door. I rang the doorbell. I could hear a chime inside, but no one came. Then Rachel knocked with her gloved hand.

I looked at her and laughed. "That was about as loud as a kitten falling onto a pillow."

"Nice use of simile," she said.

"It's my job. I'm a writer." I rang the doorbell again, then pounded on the door. Nothing.

"What kind of writer?" she asked.

"Books. Mostly."

"That's cool," she said. "Can you make a living doing that?"

I smiled. "Some do. I get by."

"I admire people who throw caution to the wind to pursue their dreams."

"Throwing it every day," I said. It pleased me that she didn't know who I was.

"Look," she said, returning to the matter at hand. "There's just one set of tire tracks in the driveway. She must have left."

"Good deduction," I said. "Let's go back."

We walked back across the street. Once we were inside the house, I took off my coat and said, "I'll tell you what. Give me your phone number and I'll call you once I talk to her."

"Thank you. Do you have something to write on?"

"I'll put it in my phone." I input her number, then

said, "You mentioned that you wouldn't be up here that long . . ."

She frowned. "No. I've got to get back to St. George by Saturday."

"Work?"

"No. I'm kind of between jobs."

"What do you do?"

"I *was* a dental assistant, but my boss retired. I don't think I'll have much trouble finding work, but I thought, as long as I'm free, I'd look again. But it's bugging my fiancé. He thinks I'm crazy."

Hearing that she had a fiancé bothered me. "Your fiancé?"

"Yes. Brandon. We finally set a wedding date for next April, so he's nervous that I'm not working enough and saving money right now."

I just nodded.

"The truth is, he thinks this whole thing is a waste of time."

"What 'whole thing'?"

"Looking for my mother. He says, 'So you find her, then what? It's not like you can change anything. What are you even going to say? Hi, I'm the baby you didn't want.' He's just practical that way."

Practical wasn't the word that came to mind. "What would you say to her?"

"I don't know. I think in the moment I'll know. Her eyes met mine, and I couldn't believe how beautiful she looked. "That probably sounds dumb to you."

"No," I said. "I understand why you need to find her. It's the same reason millions of people do their genealogy. They're looking for clues to who they are. It's the same reason I'm cleaning my mother's house."

Her expression relaxed. "Thank you for understanding. I was beginning to feel like I was crazy."

"I'm sorry your fiancé makes you feel that way. It's not right." I breathed out heavily. "Well, I better get back to cleaning."

Her eyes panned the room. "Do you want some help?"

I looked at her with surprise. "You're offering to help me clean this dump?"

She shrugged. "Why not? I have to go right now, but I have nothing tomorrow. And when your neighbor gets home, we can talk to her."

I wasn't sure why she was offering, but I liked the idea of having her around.

"I'd be a fool to pass that up."

She smiled. "Tomorrow it is. What time do we start?"

"I usually get here in the morning around ten."

"I'll be here," she said. She smiled at me. "I'd better go." I followed her to the door and opened it for her. She looked into my eyes. She looked vulnerable again. "Thank you for caring. I don't know why you do, but thank you."

"It's my pleasure. I look forward to seeing you tomorrow."

"Me too. Bye."

She carefully walked down the snowy walkway, awkwardly climbing over the snowbank. I watched from the doorway as she got to her car. Before climbing in, she looked back once more. She smiled and waved to me. I waved back. There was something about her that was different from any woman I'd ever met. Something about her felt like home.

CHAPTER

Eleven

The things my mother kept were inexplicable. Old dishes, pots, unfinished crocheting projects, stacks of every magazine you could think of, paperback books (none of mine), eight-tracks, a porcelain hula dancer. The place was like a flea market on crack.

I learned things about my mother that I hadn't known. For one thing, she had a Troll Doll collection unlike anything I had ever seen. It took up three boxes. The trolls were in mint condition and I didn't feel good about throwing them away, so I stacked them up in the hallway to give to charity.

I hadn't eaten lunch and was about to go out to get dinner when there was again a knock at the door. This time it was Elyse. Again she had brought food. "I brought you some dinner," she said.

"Come in," I said, stepping back.

She walked directly to the kitchen and set the food on the table. "I just came from a funeral. When you get to my age, it's pretty much the main social activity. I helped make supper for the family. The usual funeral fare: fried chicken, funeral potatoes, green Jell-O with grated carrots, strawberry salad, and potato rolls. The rolls just came from the store, so they're nothing to write home about."

"Funeral potatoes?" I asked.

"I know, it's a ghastly name," she said. "Sounds like you're eating something from a casket. But they are delicious."

"Now I'm really intrigued. What are they?"

"Nothing fancy. It's a Mormon dish. Basically they're hash browns mixed with cream of chicken soup with cheese and cornflakes on top."

"Cornflakes?"

"Cornflakes," she said. She looked around the room. "You're making progress."

"Slowly. The front room is more work than I expected."

"You could fill a Dumpster just with that."

"I did find an old record player and some records."

She smiled. "That's exciting. Finding old music is like running into an old friend, isn't it?"

I nodded. "I like that. Do you mind if I eat?"

"No. That's why I brought it."

I got a plate and silverware, dished up some food, and brought it over to the table. "Did you want anything?"

"Heavens no. I've been pilfering calories all day."

"Well, thank you for thinking of me."

She waited until I sat down, then said, "How's it coming?"

"It's taking longer than I thought it would."

"I know. When you said you would only be a few days, I wondered if you knew what you'd gotten yourself into."

I lifted a full fork. "Funeral potatoes?"

"Funeral potatoes," she confirmed.

I took a bite. They were good. "Well, at least I don't have to do anything with the yard."

"Until the last few years you wouldn't have had to. Your mother spent a lot of time gardening. I think it was her therapy. Her yard was beautiful. That was before she stopped going outside. After that . . ." She didn't finish.

"The pyracantha bushes are out of control."

"The red berries do look pretty against the white snow, though, don't they? In the spring the birds get drunk on them."

"Birds get drunk?"

"They roll around like sailors on a weekend pass. It's kind of funny to watch," she said. "And in the summer, the berries are always good for the bees when the flowers start to dry out."

"My mother once sent me out to pick pyracantha berries to make them into jelly," I said. "I don't know if it was intentional or not, but she didn't bother to tell me that the berries were poisonous. Fortunately, they were bitter and didn't taste good, so I only ate a handful and ended up throwing them up."

Elyse frowned. "I'm sure it wasn't intentional," she said softly. "I've made jelly with those berries before. If you prepare it right and you add enough sugar, it tastes like apple jelly and you cook the toxins out. Of course anything is palatable with enough sugar."

"Speaking of palatable, this is all delicious."

"I'm glad you like it. I forgot to mention, there's a piece

of apple pie in there. I wrapped it in foil. I had to stash away a piece for you or else it would have been eaten. I guess funerals make people hungry."

I was really surprised at her consideration. "I love apple pie. Thank you again for thinking of me."

"My pleasure," she said. "So you came over to the house earlier."

I looked up. "How did you know that?"

"We have neighbors with too much time on their hands. They said you were with a young lady."

"Yes, I was."

"You don't need surveillance cameras when you've got neighbors like mine. If you had driven to my house, they would have given me the license plate number. Did you need something?"

"I had a question for you. I don't know if you would remember, but when I was little, did we have a young pregnant woman live with us?"

Her brow furrowed. "A pregnant woman? No." She slowly shook her head. "I could always be wrong, but it was always just the four of you." Her answer made me sad. "Why do you ask?"

"The young woman I was with, she came by to see if anyone remembered her mother living here. She said she thought her mother had lived here when she was pregnant with her."

Suddenly Elyse's expression changed. "Come to think of it, there was a young woman staying with you for a short while. She was pretty, had dark, almost black hair. I think she came a few months before your brother passed."

"Why was she living with us?"

"I don't know. It may be that her family was very religious and embarrassed. That used to happen a lot in my day. She stayed until she gave birth, then left a short time after that without her baby. She never came back. I don't know how I could have forgotten that, except it was such a difficult time, with your brother passing."

"Do you remember her name?"

Again her brow furrowed, then she said, "No. It was too long ago. I didn't ever really see much of her. She didn't go out much, or it was after dark when she did, like she was hiding. I usually just saw her when she would answer the door. She helped out around the house, did dishes and cooked meals. Looked after you." She looked at me. "Your father would know. Is it important?"

"It is to my friend."

"You could always just give your father a call."

It was strange to think of that possibility. In the alienation of my youth he had always seemed to me like a mythical creature.

"I haven't talked to him since he left. I don't even know where he lives."

"He lives in Mesa, Arizona. It's a suburb of Phoenix."

"I've been there," I said. "Several times. On book tour. There's a famous bookstore near there in Scottsdale—The Poisoned Pen." I wondered how close I had unknowingly come to my father's house.

"I have his contact information," Elyse said. "I spoke with him at your mother's funeral. He gave me his phone number. He also asked me to contact him if I saw you."

I don't know what surprised me more, that he went to my mother's funeral or that he asked about me. "Did you?"

"Not yet. I thought I'd talk to you first."

"May I have that number?"

"Of course. I don't have my phone with me, but if you give me your phone number, I will call you with the number when I get back to the house. It's one of those new smartphones. I know there's a way to share things, but I don't know how to do it. I'll just call you with it."

"I'll write down my number," I said. I walked over to the cupboard and found a pen I had left in there and wrote down my cell phone number. "Here you go," I said, handing it to her.

She looked at it and smiled. "Jacob Churcher's personal phone number. Think I could sell this on eBay?"

I smiled back. "If you can get anything out of that, you're welcome to it."

She laughed. "You're still delightful. Well, I best be getting back. I've been on my feet all day and I need to get them up."

I stood with her and walked her to the door. "Thank you for dinner," I said. "And for the information."

"You're very welcome. Have you ever wondered if people come into our lives for a reason?"

"I can't say that I have," I said.

"Well, you might just give it a thought." She turned and walked out the door. I shut the door behind her.

My mind was reeling. How could I not have remembered Rachel's mother? Then again, I was young and I had other things to worry about. Then a thought struck me. *Could she have been the woman I was dreaming about? Was that why Rachel seemed so familiar?*

After I finished eating, I cleaned the dishes and went back into the front room to decide whether or not I wanted to dive back into the mess or just call it a night. I received a text from Elyse with my father's contact info.

As I looked at the address, I had a strong desire to see him. I played around with the idea of driving to Arizona as I drove back to my hotel.

That night I dreamt of the woman again. Only this time the dream was more real than ever. I could feel her soft hands on my face. Her lips, kissing my cheek. I was crying. I don't know why, but I was. And she was gently telling me that everything would be okay.

CHAPTER

Twelve

December 15

I woke excited to tell Rachel what I'd found out about her mother. At least I think it was that. It had been a while since I'd looked forward to seeing any woman, engaged or not.

I got to the house early, even though I'd stopped and picked up a couple of lattes. As I pulled up, Rachel's red Honda Accord was already there, idling in front of the mailbox. When she saw me she turned off her car and got out. She was also carrying coffee cups. She laughed when she saw me. "Looks like we'll be well caffeinated."

We made our way into the house and took our beverages into the kitchen.

"I didn't know what you liked to drink," Rachel said, taking off her jacket. She was dressed in denim jeans and a black V-necked tee that accentuated her petite yet curvaceous form. "So I got you something sweet, their signature hot chocolate, and something bitter, the caffè misto. You pick first. I can go either way."

"Sweet or bitter. That ought to be an easy choice." I took the caffè. As I looked at her, I thought she was even more gorgeous than I remembered. "I got us a couple of pumpkin spice lattes."

"Perfect. We can drink them all. Then work much faster."

"Before we start, I need to tell you something. You'd better sit down."

"That is so cliché," she said, sitting down. She looked anxious. "Is it something bad? Did I do something wrong?"

I thought her second question was kind of telling. "No. I have good news. The elderly lady I told you about remembered your mother."

Rachel screamed. Then she came around the table and hugged me. When we parted, she looked me in the eyes. "What did she say?"

"She said a few months before my brother died, there was a young pregnant woman who came to stay with us."

"Did she know her name?"

"No," I said. "I'm sorry."

The excitement left her face. "Then I still have nothing."

"But she said my father would."

"You said that's a dead end."

"It was. But she gave me my father's contact information. He lives in Mesa, Arizona." I took a deep breath. "I'm thinking of driving to Arizona," I said. "Maybe it's time I confronted him. I'll ask him about your mother as well."

"Thank you." She looked down a moment, then blurted out, "May I go with you?"

I looked at her in surprise. "You want to go with me to Arizona?"

"I'd like to talk to your father in person."

"Will your fiancé be okay with that?"

She frowned. "Yeah, I'll need to talk to him about it. He won't be happy."

"You've been looking for your mother for half your life. Why wouldn't he be happy for you?"

"Because I told him that I would be back by today. He's not exactly spontaneous. And he has a work social he wanted me to help cook for." She breathed out in exasperation. "I'll talk to him. In the meantime, we have a lot of work to do. Come on." She grabbed a coffee and took it into the front room.

The room looked less daunting with someone helping me. A few minutes after we started working, Rachel said, "That is such a beautiful piano. Is it really a Steinway?"

I nodded. "It's a pearl in this oyster. My mother's uncle left it to her when he died. I was really young when she got it, so I don't remember life without it."

"Can you play it?"

"A little," I said. "I used to be pretty good."

"Play me something."

"All right." I sat down on the bench and began to play James Taylor's "Fire and Rain." When I finished, I turned around on the bench. "Well?"

"That was beautiful," she said. "I love that song."

"Me too. It has soul."

"Like you," she said.

We went back to work.

I came across three boxes filled with piano music, most of which I remembered. I dusted off the boxes and stacked them by the piano to send home with the instrument.

I found some more vinyl albums of my parents that I had grown up with. The soundtracks to *South Pacific* and *Camelot*, Herb Alpert's *Whipped Cream and Other Delights;* the picture of the girl on the cover had wrought havoc on my potent teenage male hormones. I lifted the Herb Alpert album to show Rachel. "Ever seen this? The cover is pretty iconic."

She shook her head. "She's pretty. Can we play it?"

"Yes we can." I put on the album, and the sound of brass filled the room.

"This music makes me happy," she said.

I looked at the simple joy on her face and also smiled.

Around one, Rachel drove to a nearby deli to get us something for lunch. I was able to fill three more trash bags by the time she got back. I saw her walking up to the door and I opened it for her.

"Thank you," she said, walking in. She carried the food to the kitchen table. "Sorry that took so long. There was a long line. I also got us a couple of Cokes," she said, handing me a bottle.

RICHARD PAUL EVANS

We sat down at the table. When I looked up, Rachel had her head bowed in prayer. A moment later she looked up and smiled at me.

"Do you always pray?" I asked.

"I always give thanks," she said.

I couldn't remember the last time I'd prayed.

We both started eating. A minute later Rachel said, "So, I called Brandon while I was waiting in line at the deli."

"And?"

"He wasn't happy." She groaned lightly. "Actually, that's putting it mildly. He was livid. He tried to talk me out of it."

"Because of me?"

"No. He didn't want me to be gone any longer. And he was worried about the cost of gas."

"He was worried about the gas money but not about you driving to Arizona with another man?"

She looked at me sheepishly. "I didn't tell him about you."

"Okay, so he was worried about gas money but not about you driving *alone* to another state."

"He cares," she said. "Men just aren't expressive like that."

"Don't pin that on us," I said. "Most men are highly protective."

"If it was you, would you have been upset?"

"If it was me, I would have gone with you."

She breathed out softly. "Well, we're going. I'll deal with the fallout later. I shouldn't have called him. It's easier to ask forgiveness than permission." She frowned. "The thing is, I'm really easy for him to manipulate, because I feel guilty a lot. I feel guilty about everything. It's like this crushing weight on me. I can't even take the last cookie on the plate without feeling guilty." She shook her head. "Brandon doesn't feel guilt very much. I once asked him why he didn't feel guilty like I did and he just laughed."

"Are you sure you want to go?"

"I feel like I need to. And I feel like I can't let him stop me from doing this. If I missed this opportunity, I might not forgive myself. I might not forgive *him*. I can't be sure that I wouldn't always resent him. And that wouldn't be good for our marriage."

"No, it wouldn't," I said. "So, it will take about nine hours from here. If we leave by noon, we could make it by night."

"We could leave earlier."

"I would, except I can't leave until after the piano movers come; but we'll leave right after."

"Okay," she said. "I'll be packed."

By six o'clock we had cleared out more than half the room. We stopped at my mother's doll collection, about six boxes filled with American Girl dolls and accessories. I don't know when she had started purchasing them, but since she'd only had boys, they were clearly just for her. Rachel said that if I was planning on throwing the dolls away, she wanted them.

We were both getting tired and hungry, so I locked up the house and took Rachel to dinner at an Italian restaurant I'd driven past a few times. I guessed that the restaurant must have been pretty good since the parking lot and dining room were always full.

The hostess led us to a small, candlelit table in the corner of the room. I slid out the chair for Rachel, then sat down across from her. She looked a little anxious.

"Are you okay?" I asked.

"I'm fine," she said. As she looked at the menu, she looked even more upset.

"Are you sure you're okay?"

She nodded unconvincingly.

"Is it that you're uncomfortable being out with me in public?"

CHAPTER

Thirteen

She set down her menu. "No. Otherwise, I never would have offered to go on a road trip with a complete stranger."

"I'm not a *complete* stranger."

She grinned. "You're not?"

"For the sake of argument, do we ever really know anyone?"

She laughed. "Now you're going existential on me. You and I don't have history."

"But we just sorted through decades of history together."

"That's true."

"And we both like James Taylor."

"Yes. That is telling."

"Then what are you worried about?"

"Actually, it's just that this place is too expensive. We can go somewhere else."

"No, no. It looks good."

"We'll go Dutch."

"I can afford it," I said.

"I just don't want to take advantage of your kindness."

"That's refreshing."

"What?"

"Someone who doesn't want to take advantage of me."

She paused for a moment. "I think people like you probably get taken advantage of pretty often."

"People like me?" I said.

"Kind people."

I took a deep breath. "Maybe I am a complete stranger."

She smiled, then lifted her menu, pausing a moment to look over it. "Have you ever had—I can't pronounce it—gu-no-chee?"

"It's pronounced *nyok-ee*. The *chi* is pronounced hard, like *k*. It comes from the Italian word *nocchio*, which literally means a knot in wood."

"So, it's hard to pronounce, but is it good?"

"It usually is. American restaurants don't always get it right."

"I'll take my chances. What are you having?"

"I think I'll have the spaghetti vongole, that's spaghetti with clams. I'd recommend the Chianti to go with your meal."

"Are you trying to impress me?"

I set down the menu. "Yes. Is it working?"

"I'm very impressed. I'm just a small-town girl. The Pasta Factory in St. George is the best Italian in our area."

Just then the waiter came up to our table with water and bread. After we had ordered, I said, "So, tell me about yourself."

"What would you like to know?"

"All of it." I meant it. I wanted to know everything I could about this woman.

"Okay. So where do I start?"

"At the beginning," I said. "Then go through the middle and end at the end."

She smiled. "Like I said, I live just a little northwest of St. George in Ivins. Have you heard of Ivins?"

"No."

"It's just a little place. My parents moved there twenty-five years ago. It's beautiful, with the red rock and Snow Canyon, but when we moved there, it was mostly just poor people and farmers. We were sort of poor. I'm sure my parents moved there because it was cheap and isolated.

"It's changed. Now there's a lot of money coming in and big developments growing all around us. We used to be out in the middle of nowhere; now we're in a subdivision with big homes. Most of their garages are bigger than our house. The old people got pushed out and the new people moved in.

"My father grumbles about it a lot. What really gets him is that it's becoming kind of an artist enclave. 'Educated idiots,' he calls them. I bought him a bumper sticker that read *I lived in Ivins before Ivins was cool*. He never put it on his car."

I grinned. "Do you have siblings?"

"No. I'm an only child. My parents are older. They're retired now, in their late seventies. They were unable to have children, so it wasn't until they were in their forties that they adopted me. I was adopted at birth. My parents are pretty tight-lipped anyway, but they kept the whole thing secret, so I didn't even know until I was sixteen that I was adopted. I suspected it before then, but I didn't ask."

"Why did you suspect it?"

"We don't look much alike. Mostly my eyes . . ."

"You have beautiful eyes," I said.

She smiled shyly. "Thank you. You're embarrassing me. But thank you."

"You're welcome."

She seemed a little flustered. "I was saying, I don't look like them, but more telling than that was our personalities. I don't know how much is nature versus nurture, but in the personality department, I'm completely different from my parents. I'm kind of a free spirit and they're hyper religious. Like, my mother could have been a nun and my dad is practically ascetic."

"That must have been difficult for you, growing up that way."

"I disappoint them a lot. I suppose that's where the guilt thing comes in. Even my name."

"Rachel's a pretty name," I said.

"They named me Rachel because it's a Bible name. It means ewe. A female sheep. I was named after an animal."

I laughed. "Animal or not, it's still a pretty name."

"Thank you. They named me that because of the Bible verse in Matthew that said God will put the sheep on the right and the goats on the left."

"I'm a goat," I said.

"Well, if I'm a sheep, I'm the black one. When I was fourteen, I was with some friends in the St. George Mall when a man handed me his business card and asked if I would be interested in modeling, like in magazines or TV commercials. I was really excited. But when I showed my mother the man's card, she went crazy. She said that I needed to repent and that vanity was of the devil and all models are going to hell."

"That might be true," I said.

She looked at me, unsure if I was being serious or not.

"I was joking," I said. "But I've dated a few models . . ."

She grinned. "Then you should know."

I laughed. "I should know *better*, that is. When did you find out you were adopted?"

"When I was sixteen, a friend at school asked me how old I was when I was adopted. I said, 'I'm not adopted.' She just looked at me like I was crazy. She said, 'Really? Are you sure?' That night I asked my parents. They didn't have to say a thing. I knew immediately from their reactions that I was. I asked them why they hadn't told me sooner and my mother said that they were waiting until I was older, because they were afraid that I might feel different or unwanted by my birth mother."

"Is that why you started looking for your birth parents?"

"Not really. I asked my parents about them, but they said it was a sealed adoption and that even they didn't know who the mother was. They said that they knew the woman wasn't married and that the father wasn't any part of the deal." Rachel grinned. "I mean, he had to be *some* part of the deal. It's not like I was an immaculate conception."

"Not likely," I said.

I looked at her for a moment, then said, "Why do you want to find her?"

"*There's* a question," she said. "I don't know if I could put words to it. It's like finding yourself." She looked at me. "What about your mother? You said you weren't close."

"No. I moved out of her house when I was sixteen. This is the first time I've been back since then."

"You didn't see your mother before she died?"

"No."

"Do you wish you had?"

I thought over the question. "I don't know. Part of me does. Part of me wishes I could see her and she'd apologize. But more likely than not I just would have been disappointed again. She probably would have asked me who I was."

"I'm sorry."

I sighed. "It's nothing. I mean, it is, but it's history now."

"So why go through the house if all there is is pain?"

"I'm still looking for clues."

"Clues to what?"

I looked at her thoughtfully. "There's something I haven't told you about. For years I've had these dreams of me as a child and a woman holding me, loving me. I've wondered who she was or whether she even existed." I swallowed. "Now I'm wondering if she was your mother."

Just then the waiter walked up to the table carrying a tray. "Gnocchi with sage butter." He set the plate down in front of Rachel. "And the spaghetti vongole for you." He set another plate in front of me.

He turned to Rachel. "Would you like some Parmesan cheese on that?"

"Yes, please." He grated cheese on top of it.

"There you go. Can I get you anything else?"

"Could you get me a glass of Chianti?" I said.

"Absolutely."

He walked away.

"Buon appetito," I said.

We ate for a moment in silence. Rachel spoke first. "This is really good. Do you want to try some?"

"Please."

She speared a couple of dumplings and held her fork out for me to eat. I ate them off the fork. "Those are good. Would you like to try mine?"

She looked at it a moment, then said, "I'm not a big oyster fan."

"They're not oysters, they're clams," I said.

"To-may-to, to-maw-to," she replied.

"Then I'll keep my shellfish to myself." I looked at her and added, *"Shellfishly."*

She laughed. "That was an awful pun."

"That's the nature of a pun—the more awful the better. Bad enough and it's good."

"You almost turned the corner on that one," she said. "I can see why you're a writer."

The waiter set the glass of wine on the table. "There you are, sir."

"Thank you."

He walked away. I took a sip, then set down my glass. "Do you like wine?"

"I've never tried it."

"You've never tasted wine?"

"No. I told you, my parents were . . . strict. Alcohol was forbidden."

"But you must have had opportunities. When they weren't around?"

"I tried beer at my high school graduation party," she said.

"You are definitely going to hell."

She laughed. "It *tasted* like hell. I didn't like it."

"It's an acquired taste. Like . . . clams."

"And oysters."

"And oysters. What do they say, it was a brave man who first ate an oyster."

"How do you know it wasn't a brave woman?"

"Because women have more sense than that." I took another bite of my pasta, then said, "Tell me about Braydon."

"Brandon."

"Sorry. Do your parents approve of Brandon?"

"Approve? I think they like him more than they like me."

"Why is that?"

"He's just like them. He's kind of . . . severe." She looked at me. "I shouldn't have said that. He's a good guy."

"What does he do?"

"He works for a sporting supply company."

"He's a jock?"

She burst out laughing. "No. He's a bookkeeper. He weighs almost the same as I do. Unfortunately, his job doesn't pay much, which is why he's so upset about me not working. But someday he wants to open his own store."

"A sporting store?"

"No. A video-game store. He plays a lot of video games. That's his release."

"And you?"

"I don't like video games."

I laughed. "I meant, what about *your* career."

"I like being a dental assistant. Someday I want to be a mother. Does that sound unambitious?"

"The world needs more good mothers."

"How about you?" she asked.

"I'd make a terrible mother."

She laughed. "I meant your career. I know you're a writer. Is that how you make your living, or do you have side gigs as well?"

I hid my smile. "Well, I used to work for a healthcare company, writing newsletters and press releases. But now I sell enough books to keep a roof over my head."

She nodded. "I wish I could do something creative for a living. But I'd first have to have some creativity." She ate a little, then said, "Before I go back home, I need to do some Christmas shopping. There are so many great stores in Salt Lake. How about you? Have you finished your Christmas shopping?"

"I haven't even started yet. I'll probably do some shopping when I go back to New York."

"Why are you going to New York?"

"To meet with my . . ." I stopped. "My friend."

"Oh." She looked at me. "A woman friend?"

I thought I detected a note of jealousy in her voice. Maybe I was just being hopeful. "You could say that."

There was a brief, awkward pause. "I've never been to New York City," she said wistfully.

"It's a great city. Especially at Christmastime. It's

crowded, but it has an energy you won't find anywhere else." Then I added, "Except maybe in Ivins."

"Yeah, right. I've always wanted to see New York. I'd probably just get lost."

"You just need the right guide," I said.

"Like you?"

I smiled. "Exactly like me."

We finished eating around ten. The restaurant was trying to close down and I could tell they were eager for us to leave. Especially when they started mopping the floor next to us. Finally we drove back to the house. I pulled up behind Rachel's car and turned off the ignition. Rachel turned to me. "That was a really good restaurant." She grinned. "Even if they tried to throw us out."

"The company wasn't bad either."

She smiled.

"Thanks for all your help today," I said.

"It was my pleasure."

"When I decided to come down, I didn't plan on having company. You are . . . enjoyable."

"Enjoyable?"

"Today wasn't miserable."

"*Miserable* is a long way from enjoyable."

"Exactly," I said.

She laughed. "About tomorrow. Are you sure it's okay if I go with you?"

"Of course it's okay with me. Like I said, I like your company. Are you having second thoughts?"

"No. I just wish I could be more straightforward with Brandon without him getting so angry about everything." She looked at me. "How about you? Are you worried about seeing your father?"

"A little. I really don't know how it will go. I guess I'll find out."

"When do the piano movers come?"

"They're supposed to be there at eleven. But I'm going over earlier. I wanted to get some more done before they get there."

"Name the time," she said.

"Is eight too early?"

"Eight it is."

"I'll bring the coffee," I said. "And some muffins?"

"I love muffins. Thank you. Good night."

"Good night," I said.

She leaned forward as if to kiss me, then stopped. Even in the limited light I could see her blush. "I'm so sorry, I don't know why I did that."

"It's just habit," I said. "No worries."

"Sorry. I'll see you at eight." She looked flustered as she got out and walked to her car. She looked back and smiled before climbing in. I lightly waved to her. She started her car, then did a U-turn in the road and drove away.

As I watched her go, I was definitely feeling something for her. Wrong or not, I wished that we had kissed.

CHAPTER

Fourteen

December 16

I woke early. Too early. A quarter to five. It had been a restless night. My mind was too active, spinning like a roulette wheel, the ball occasionally dropping on different topics of intrigue: encountering my father, my mother, the house, Rachel's mother, and Rachel.

A half hour later I gave up on sleep and went downstairs to the fitness center and ran on the treadmill for an hour, then went back to my room and packed for our trip. An hour later I left for the house.

I stopped at a Starbucks for coffee and blueberry muffins. Even though I was twenty minutes early, Rachel was already there at the house, smoke rising from her car's tailpipe.

She smiled at me as I walked toward her carrying our coffee and muffins. "Good morning," she said. "How did you sleep?"

"Awful. I had strange dreams."

"About what?"

"Things." I handed her a coffee, and she took a sip.

"I'm sorry," she said again. "I had strange dreams too. Only mine were nice."

"About what?"

"Things," she said, with a curious smile on her face. She turned and walked ahead of me through the snow to the front porch. When we reached the front door, I handed Rachel my cup, took the house key from my pocket, unlocked the door, and opened it. I followed her inside.

The room was warm, and I could hear the sound of the furnace blowing. I turned on the lights, then walked over and opened the blinds.

"It doesn't smell as bad as it did yesterday," Rachel said behind me.

"The magic of Lysol."

"And we have a full three hours before the movers get here. We might actually finish." She set her coffee down on a cleared end table. "So, after dinner, I went back to my hotel and decided to see if I could find your books on Amazon."

"And?"

"I found five of them, all major bestsellers, with thousands and thousands of fans. Then I looked up your Facebook page. You have like a million followers. I was so embarrassed."

"Why?"

"I kept asking how you made a living. You didn't tell

me you were a famous author and have sold millions of books."

"If you have to tell people you're famous, you're not."

She laughed. "You could have told me."

"Why? So you could act differently?"

"No. Because it's who you are."

"No, it's not really who I am. It's my image. You've seen more of who I am digging through this junk than my readers will ever know."

She nodded. "I believe that."

"It's nice to not have to be author Jacob Churcher, just Jacob."

"I understand that," she said. "I'm sorry. I hope I didn't ruin anything."

"We'll be okay," I said, smiling. "We've got enough ground beneath us."

"You mean because I liked you *before* I found out you were famous?"

I liked the comment. "Something like that."

"Well, how about, I'll still like you *even though* you're famous."

"So that's how it is," I said.

She smiled. "Yep. That's how it is. Your fifteen minutes of fame are over. Now get back to work."

I grinned. "Now you sound like my agent."

I was sitting on the ground in front of the piano bench going through a box of Christmas decorations when

Rachel said, "I think you're going to want to see this." I looked over. She was holding an open box.

"What is it?"

She handed me the box. "It's a diary."

I took the box from her. Inside was a leather book about the size of one of my paperback novels. The word DIARY was embossed in gold into its leather face. I opened it up. The lined paper was old and the handwriting that covered it was graceful and feminine and mostly in red ink. I started to read.

June 11, 1986

Dear Diary,

I've started this new diary, since I'm starting a new life. I'm afraid to say that nothing will be the same after today. I'm leaving home tomorrow morning. I don't know when I'll be back, or if they'll even let me back. My parents are sending me away to Salt Lake City to have my baby. The woman who is facilitating my stay says that I would usually first meet the people I'll be staying with, but my parents are rushing this because my mother says I'm beginning to show, even though I'm only eleven weeks along. Last night at dinner my parents argued over whether they should tell people that I went to live at my aunt's house or went away to a special school. They chose the latter alibi, as family members would see through the other. It's the story I've been told to stick to. They're ashamed

*of me. And I have this baby that I'm bringing into
the world in shame. I'm so sorry, little one. I still
haven't heard from Peter. I miss him.*

Noel

"Noel," I said. I looked up at Rachel. "I think your mother's name was Noel. I think this is your mother's diary."

Rachel stood. "It's my mother's?" She practically ran back over to my side. "Her name is Noel?"

There were three photographs inside the book. I lifted them out. The first was a picture of my family. My mother, father, Charles, and me. I looked like I was about four, so it must have been fairly close to the time my brother died. My parents looked so young. I was sitting on my mother's lap. She looked different than I remembered her. Besides being noticeably younger, there was light in her eyes. My parents were smiling. It seemed so foreign to me.

The next picture was of a young man. He looked about nineteen or twenty. He was sitting on a motorcycle. He had long, black hair and wore a leather bomber jacket. He had a look of confidence in his eyes.

"I wonder who that is," I said.

I lifted the next picture and froze. It was *her*. The woman in my dreams. She was real, right there in color. She was in the photograph with my father. He was standing in the kitchen about to blow out the candles on a birthday cake. To his side sat a young woman with a slightly protruding stomach. She was holding me on her lap.

Rachel gasped. "That's her. That's my mother . . ."

I handed her the picture.

"Oh my . . ." Her eyes welled up. She covered her mouth with her hand. Then she began to cry.

I let her cry for a moment, then put my arm around her. "Are you okay?"

"I can't believe I'm finally seeing her. I look like her." She held the picture in front of her face like it was a mirror. She looked stunned.

"You have the same facial features."

She wiped more tears away. "I can't believe this." Then she leaned her face into my shoulder and just broke down crying. I put my arms around her, gently rubbing my hand over her back to comfort her. She kept saying over and over, "She's real. She's real."

I shuffled back to the second picture. "I wonder if that's your father."

She took the picture from me and just stared at it. Then she turned it over. Scrawled on the back in the same handwriting as the diary was one word:

Peter

I held up the photo and looked at Rachel. "There's a resemblance," I said.

More tears welled up in her eyes. When she could speak, she said, "I have to see her. I have so many questions."

I took a deep breath. "Now I know why you looked so familiar to me the first time I met you. Your mother is the girl in my dreams."

CHAPTER

Fifteen

The woman in my dreams existed. In a way, Rachel and I were having the same experience: both of us had wondered for most of our lives about the same woman, then suddenly there she was, captured on film. It was surreal—like seeing a picture of Bigfoot or the Loch Ness Monster.

I started to read Noel's diary out loud.

June 18, 1986

Dear Diary,

The home I have been sent to belongs to a family named the Churchers. It's small but comfortable. They're nice. The man, Scott, is a social worker, which is why I was sent here. He's kind. The woman, Ruth, is polite to me but quiet. I don't know if she really wants me in the house. They have two young boys: a very active eight-year-old named Charles, and a sweet little four-year-old named Jacob. His middle name is Christian. Christian Churcher. I think that's kind of cute. He's adorable and immediately took to me. I think we will be good friends. Still no word from Peter. Where is he?

Noel

I looked over at Rachel, who sat rapt, clearly eager to hear more. I turned the page.

June 25, 1986

Dear Diary,

Peter is gone. I called my friend Diane. She saw him with another girl. Rebecca. I feel like the victim of a hit-and-run. How could he do this? He said he loved me. Of course he did. He wanted me.

I just finished the first trimester of my pregnancy. Time is moving very slowly. I have very strange cravings. The other day I wanted to eat the dust on the windowsill. I feel like I'm losing my mind. Not all is bad. I was in my room crying, and little Jacob walked up to me. He laid his forehead against mine. It's like he knows I'm hurting. He just stood there. I took him in my arms, and he nestled into me. It's almost like he came at this time to show me the potential joy of motherhood.

Noel

As a writer, I found it surreal to be reading about myself in the third person, like a character in someone else's story. Yet the truth of what I was reading resonated like a thinly veiled memory.

There was a knock at the door. I looked out the window and saw a large white truck with a picture of a piano keyboard running the length of its trailer. I handed the journal to Rachel.

"Looks like the piano movers are here," I said. I got up and walked over to the door and opened it. A broad Polynesian man stood on the front porch. He wore a black beanie, a hoodie, and leather gloves. His breath froze in the air in front of him. "We're here for the piano."

"It's right in here. Come in."

He stepped inside the room. "That's a big one," he said. "Steinway. Nice." He stepped back out the door and waved at the truck. The truck's driver pulled forward out into the road, then backed up to the end of the driveway. Then, gathering a little speed, the truck broke through the tall bank of snow into the driveway, stopping about ten feet before the Dumpster. The driver shut down the truck.

"Grab a snow shovel," the man on my porch shouted to the driver as he climbed out.

"Sorry," I said. "I should have shoveled, but I don't have one. I don't live here. We're just cleaning up."

"No worries, man."

It took the piano movers about an hour to wrap the piano in cellophane and padding, attach it to a gurney, carry it outside, and load it into their truck. I gave them my home address and the number of my housekeeper, Lilia, to call when they reached the city. Then I called her and arranged for her to prepare a place for the piano in my living room and to meet the movers at the house and let them in.

After they were gone, I looked back at Rachel. "Ready to go?"

She hadn't stopped reading from the journal. "Can I bring this with us?"

"Of course."

She tucked the diary carefully under her arm.

I turned off the kitchen lights and locked the back door, then turned down the thermostat. As I walked back into the front room, someone knocked at the door. I opened it to see Elyse standing in the cold. She wore a long, red wool coat and boots.

"I'm glad I caught you," she said. "I saw the moving truck."

"They were just taking the piano. I'm having them deliver it to my home."

She stopped and looked at Rachel. "We haven't met."

"I'm Rachel Garner."

Elyse extended her hand. "I'm Elyse Foster. I live just two doors east from here, but I think you've been to my house."

"Yes, ma'am."

"I remember your mother being beautiful too."

"You remember my mother?"

"Only a little. She wasn't here long, and it was a very long time ago."

"Come in," I said.

"Thank you." She smiled a little as she walked over to the couch. "I always liked this couch." She looked at me. "When I saw the moving truck pulling out, I was afraid that you might be leaving today."

"Actually, I am."

Her face fell. "Are you going back home?"

"No. I'm driving to Phoenix to see my father."

"Oh." She looked thoughtful. "He'll be very happy to see you."

"I hope so."

"I know he will."

"How do you know that?"

"Because he told me that he was very disappointed that you weren't at the funeral." She forced a smile. "So do you know what you're going to say when you meet him?"

"No idea. I've got the drive time to figure that out." I looked at Rachel. "I know that I plan to ask him how to find Rachel's mother."

"He might know that," she said, glancing at Rachel.

"So do you have any advice?" I asked. "For how I should approach my father?"

She thought for a moment, then said, "With grace."

I looked at her quizzically. "You think he deserves it?"

"If he deserved it, it wouldn't be grace, now would it?" She looked at me. "It's easy to see how things should have gone after the fact. He didn't know how your mother was. She didn't turn the way she did until several years after he was gone. He never would have allowed it."

"You know that?"

"I knew him. He was very protective of you boys. That's why he was so broken by Charles's death." She sighed. "Well, I better not keep you any longer. Do you plan to come back here before you go home?"

"Yes. I still have some legal work."

"Very good. Then please stop by and let me know how

everything goes. I'll pray that it all goes well and you find what you're looking for."

"Thank you."

She looked past me to Rachel. "Good luck to you, dear. And Merry Christmas."

"Thank you. Merry Christmas to you too."

She turned and walked out the door. I helped Elyse down the stairs, then went back inside where Rachel was sitting on the sofa.

"What do you think?" I asked.

"She's nice. It's just weird thinking that she's seen my mother. It's like these people who have near-death experiences and come back and say they've seen God."

"I'm pretty sure that your mother's not God."

"No. But they do have something in common."

"What's that?"

"I've never seen either of them."

CHAPTER

Sixteen

Dear Diary,

I'm having a little morning sickness. Actually, a lot. I throw up a lot. It's been three weeks, and I haven't heard from my parents. I know that I've messed up, but why are they not even talking to me? Then again, based on our last conversations, maybe this is a good thing.

Noel

I took Rachel's suitcase from her car and put it in mine, and then we drove separately downtown to the Grand America. We switched cars so I could park hers below in the parking garage. Then I took the elevator up to meet Rachel.

She was standing in the middle of the spacious lobby next to a massive display of flowers, looking at all the Christmas decorations. A young woman was near the back of the lobby playing "Greensleeves" on a harp. "This is a really nice hotel," Rachel said. "Do you always stay here?"

"I haven't been to Utah since I was a teenager. It didn't even exist then," I said.

"Their Christmas decorations are beautiful."

"Down that corridor there are window displays and a massive gingerbread house. Maybe when we get back we can look at the decorations."

She smiled. "I'd like that."

"It's a date," I said.

She looked at me.

"Well, not really a date. More like an appointment."

"Appointment sounds cold," she said. "How about an engagement?"

I grinned. "No, you already have one of those. Let's stick with date. As in a platonic hookup."

"You're the wordsmith."

"Should we get some lunch before we leave or should we just grab something on the way?"

"Let's get something on our way," she said. "We should try to make it before dark."

We walked outside and the valet handed me the key to my car. "Let's get out of here."

The I-15 southbound on-ramp was only a few blocks from the hotel. We drove south through the Salt Lake valley into Utah County through Provo, almost a hundred miles before we stopped at the town of Nephi for gas. We hadn't talked much, as Rachel had been reading from her mother's diary most of the way, and I didn't want to interrupt her.

After filling the car with gas, I went inside the mart and bought a couple of energy shots and beer nuts, then went back to the car. "It's past two. Let's get some lunch," I said. "What sounds good?"

"I don't care," Rachel said. All around the gas station were the typical fast-food joints. Almost adjoining the gas station was an independent restaurant. "What about that place? J. C. Mickelson's?"

"Cars in the parking lot," I said. "Must be good."

"It's got your initials," she said. "Maybe that's a good sign."

Inside, the restaurant looked as homegrown as it sounded. There were model trains that drove around on a suspended track that ran the perimeter of the restaurant.

I ordered a French dip sandwich with a baked potato and an Arnold Palmer to drink. Rachel ordered soup and salad with a homemade scone served with honey butter, which started a brief conversation on the true definition of scone. What is called a scone in Utah is really just deep-fried bread dough—what they call elephant ears in the South or fry bread, skillet bread, or sopaipillas in most other places. Whatever you call them, two came with Rachel's soup and we shared them.

It was a quarter past three before we were on the road again. Our route took us south on I-15 until about twelve miles past Beaver (where a billboard advertised the best-tasting water in America), east on I-20 through Bear Valley to I-89, then south down past the turnoffs for Bryce Canyon and Zion National Park, through Kanab, then east and across the border into Page, Arizona, where we stopped for gas. It was past eight o'clock, so we got some dinner. Actually, it was seven o'clock since we had gained an hour crossing the border.

We stopped at a small Mexican restaurant before continuing south on 89 through the Navajo Indian Reservation to Flagstaff.

Even though Flagstaff was only a little more than two hours outside of Phoenix, I decided that it was still too far to drive. It was already past one. Rachel had been asleep for several hours, and the kick from the energy shots I'd downed had faded.

I stopped at the first hotel I came to—a Holiday Inn. Rachel woke as I parked underneath the hotel's lighted front entrance. She looked cute, her hair slightly mussed and her eyes heavy with sleep.

"Are we here?" Her voice was scratchy. Morning voice.

"We're in Flagstaff," I said. "I'm too tired to drive."

I opened my door. "Just stay here. I'll make sure they have rooms." I got out of the car and walked inside. The front desk was abandoned and I had to ring a bell for service. Almost immediately a weary-looking clerk walked out to greet me. His eyes were bloodshot and he looked like I had woken him. "May I help you?"

"Do you have two rooms available?"

"Sure. King or queen?"

"Doesn't matter. Just as long as it's quiet."

"It's quiet."

I gave him my credit card and ID, and he produced two plastic keys for me.

"Thank you." I walked out and got back in the car. "They have rooms." I parked the car and got our two suitcases from the backseat. Rachel was practically sleepwalking. Actually, she was acting drunk.

"Come on." I led her to the elevator that we took to the second floor. Our first room was just two down from the elevator: 211. I set down the luggage and opened the door, turning on the lights. "Here you go. Get some rest."

"Where are you staying?" she asked groggily.

"I'm just next door."

"We could have shared a room," she said, almost slurring her words. "Saved money."

"It's okay," I said. I led her inside the room. There were two queen beds. I helped her over to the far bed, then knelt down and took off her shoes.

She smiled. "You're really nice. Have I told you you're really nice?"

"You just did," I said. I pulled down the sheets on her bed. "There you go."

"I wish you could stay."

I grinned. "It's a good thing you don't drink," I said. "Good night." I leaned forward and kissed her forehead. She wrapped her arms around me. "Thank you." She kissed my cheek, then lingered, her arms still around me.

"C'mon, sweetie," I said. "It's time for bed." I put my hands on her arms and lightly pushed back. "Now go back to sleep."

She giggled. "I need to brush my teeth."

"Your suitcase is right here. I'm just next door. Call me when you wake in the morning. Good night."

"Good night, handsome."

"Good night." As I stepped out of her room, I hoped that she wouldn't remember anything she'd said. From what I knew of her I was certain she'd be embarrassed and feel guilty. I went into my own room, took off my shoes, and fell back onto the bed. I fell asleep with my clothes on, on top of the covers.

CHAPTER

Seventeen

July 9, 1986

Dear Diary,

   My body is changing. I have what they call the pregnancy mask, though it really just looks like I need to wash my face. The skin is also darkening around my nipples and belly button. Mrs. Churcher is keeping me very busy helping her clean the house and watch the boys. Fortunately it's not a big house, and I like the boys. Charles is very bright. He asks me questions about my pregnancy, some not appropriate. I don't tell his mother. Mrs. Churcher leaves the house a lot with her friends. Mr. Churcher is very kind. I'm anxious around men right now. I've been abandoned by all the men in my life. I feel like Fantine in <u>Les Misérables</u>. But I must admit that Mr. Churcher is nicer to me than the women in my life.

Noel

DECEMBER 17

I had a bizarre dream again. One I remembered and woke hoping wasn't real. Or a harbinger of things to come. It was of my dream girl again, only this time every time I reached out to her, my father stood in front of her, blocking my view of her. She was reaching out to me.

I woke the next morning to the sun streaming into my room. It took me a moment to realize where I was. I sat up, rubbed my eyes, and yawned, then stood and walked over to the window. Even though we were in Arizona, there was still snow on the ground. Flagstaff is one of the only large cities in Arizona that has four seasons.

I knew this about Flagstaff as I had once done research on the city. One of my characters was driving Route 66. The famous road passes directly through Flagstaff, which not only averages a hundred inches of snow a year but is also the highest point on the route.

I looked over at the clock. It was almost nine. I wasn't surprised that I'd slept so late. I had gotten up the day before at five a.m. and not gone to bed until one forty a.m. Just then my cell phone rang. It was Laurie. I sat up in bed and answered.

"Are you home?"

"No. I'm in Arizona."

Long pause. "What are you doing in Arizona?"

"Warming up."

"You could just put on a sweater for that. You drove, no doubt."

"Of course I did."

"May I ask why you're in Arizona?"

"I'm looking for my father."

She let out a soft sigh. "And when were you going to tell me this?"

"When I got around to it," I said.

"You are such a pain."

"I do my best. And that's why my books sell. It's all that pain I share. It's schadenfreude."

"Schadenfreude," she echoed. I could envision her rolling her eyes.

"I need you to do something for me," I said.

"Name it."

"I need you to book a couple of rooms at the Phoenician."

"This close to Christmas, you know they're going to be sold out."

"I know. That's why I'm asking you to do it. You can work magic."

She groaned. "The things I do for you."

"That's why I love you. Let me know when you've got it."

She groaned. "Ciao."

"Bye." I hung up, then dialed Rachel's room. She answered on the first ring.

"There you are," she said brightly.

"You were supposed to call me."

"I know. I didn't want to wake you. You needed the sleep. How long have you been up?"

"I just woke up," I said. "How about you?"

"I've been up about an hour. I've been getting ready."

"I still need to shower. I'll be ready in a half hour. I'll knock on your door when I'm done."

"See you then."

I showered and dressed, wearing lighter clothes than the day before. It wouldn't be short-sleeve weather, but compared to Utah, it was a heat wave. As I walked out my door, Rachel emerged from her room pulling her bag.

"Good morning," I said.

"Hi," she said softly, parting her hair from her face. "They have a complimentary breakfast downstairs."

"Good. I need a coffee. Or two."

I grabbed her bag and we took the stairs down to the main floor. The dining area was in a small room at the side of the lobby. I got some scrambled egg concoction with parsley flakes, croutons, and Swiss cheese, while Rachel got a bowl of oatmeal and English muffins, which she spread thickly with orange marmalade. With the exception of an old man watching CNN, we were the only ones in the dining room.

After we started eating, Rachel said, "What time did we get here last night?"

"It was a little after one thirty."

"Oh," she said. She hesitated, then went back to eating her oatmeal.

I watched her spoon a few bites, then asked, "Are you okay?"

She looked up anxiously. "Did I embarrass myself last night?"

"No."

"I don't believe you."

"You were a little . . . affectionate."

She groaned. "I'm so sorry. I get crazy at night."

"Best time to get crazy," I said.

"I've always been that way. When I get really sleepy, it's like I turn into a completely different person; half the time I don't even remember what I say. Please don't tell anyone."

I cocked my head. "Who exactly would I tell? Oh, wait. I could call your fiancé."

"That would not go over well."

"Or I could just put it in a book."

"You wouldn't dare."

"You have no idea what I would dare."

She looked at me like she wasn't sure if I was being serious or not. "You wouldn't, would you?"

"No. That's the best way to get sued." I changed the subject. "So, I had a freaky dream last night. It was your mother again, only this time my father stood in front of her, like he was trying to shield her from me."

"You don't think he would try to keep us from her."

"I have no idea."

"My mother aside, you must have a lot of things you want to talk to him about."

"The only thing I want to know is why he abandoned me in an abusive home and never came back."

"Maybe he was abusive too."

I took a sip of my coffee. "Maybe. I don't have any recollection of that. But maybe. Neglect is abuse too." I suddenly smiled darkly. "Maybe it's like 'A Boy Named Sue.'"

Rachel looked at me quizzically. "What's that?"

"Really, you've never heard of it?"

She shook her head.

"It's an old Johnny Cash song. A father names his boy Sue before leaving him with nothing. Going through life with a girl's name makes him learn how to fight and defend himself. When he's older he decides that when he finds his father, he's going to kill him. Instead, the father tells him that he knew he wasn't going to be around, so he gave him that name to make him tough."

"That doesn't make sense. He gave him a girl's name to make him tough?"

"Yeah. So when he finds his father, they have a big fight and the son finally wins and he's about to kill his father when his father says something like, 'You ought to thank me, before I die, For the gravel in your guts and the spit in your eye.'"

"Why didn't he just change his name?"

I grinned. "Then there wouldn't be a song."

She took a bite of her muffin, then said, "Why do we always take the hard way?"

My phone vibrated. I looked down. Laurie had texted me.

> Could only get one room—a suite with two beds.
> Under your name. You owe me big time, Mr. Big
> Time author. ☺

I looked back up.

"Who's that?"

"My agent. I asked her to book us some rooms."

"Really? She'll do that for you?"

"She does whatever it takes."

"Whatever it takes to do what?"

"To keep me happy."

"That must be nice."

I looked at my watch. "It's about ten thirty. If we leave now, that would put us in Scottsdale around one."

"Scottsdale?"

"Laurie booked us rooms at the Phoenician Resort. Actually, she booked us one room. A suite. She had to pull strings to get it. Are you okay with sharing a room, or should we try to find something else?"

"It's okay," she said. "I trust you."

I grinned. "After last night, the real question is, Do I trust you?"

She rubbed her forehead. "I'm so embarrassed. Please let me live this down."

I laughed. "I won't bring it up again."

"Thank you."

"So, we check into the hotel, have lunch. That would put us at around three."

"How far is Mesa from Scottsdale?"

"It's only about twenty minutes. I think I'd rather wait until evening to drop by, so we have a little time to kill."

"We could stop in Sedona," Rachel said. "It's only an

hour from here. I've always wanted to see it. And they say it has good energy. It's the vortexes or something."

"I could use good energy."

"Like your energy shots?"

"I'll take it however I can get it."

CHAPTER

Eighteen

July 16, 1986

Dear Diary,

Today Jacob called me Mommy. I know little kids sometimes accidentally call their teachers Mommy, so it's no big deal. Unfortunately it was in front of Mrs. Churcher. She wasn't very happy about that. Life goes on. I keep getting bigger. Next week, my friend Diane is going to drive down from Logan to see me. I'm lonely. It's strange to say that when there's another human inside me. I wonder what he or she is like. I wonder if we'll be friends someday. I wonder if she'll ever forgive me.

Noel

I checked us out of the hotel, carried both of our bags out to the car, and we drove out of town. In Flagstaff the freeway changed from Interstate 89 to Interstate 17 and we continued south, dropping in altitude as well as latitude.

After a few miles of comfortable silence Rachel turned to me. "Is it hard writing romances?"

"I don't really write romances. I write love stories."

"What's the difference?"

"Love stories are more universal."

"What does that mean?"

"They're about more than boy meets girl. The stories have universal themes that everyone can relate to."

"Everyone can relate to romance."

I looked at her. "Can they?"

She bit her lip. "Maybe not."

"Also, in a love story, the endings vary. Did you see the movie *Titanic*?"

"Yes."

"Love story. Rose falls in love with Jack, the standard rich girl/poor boy scenario, but in the end, the boat sinks and Jack drowns."

"Yeah, that kind of sucked."

I laughed. "Romances are more formulaic. Boy meets girl, boy loses girl, boy and girl end up together. Think Cinderella. The prince dances with Cinderella at the ball, Cinderella runs off at midnight, the prince tracks down Cinderella with the glass slipper she left behind. Cinderella ditches her ugly stepsisters, and she and the prince live happily ever after."

"Do they always live happily ever after?"

"They do in the romance genre. In love stories, it depends."

"On what?"

I grinned. "Whether or not there's a sequel."

When we passed the first sign for Sedona, Rachel said, "Have you heard that song 'There Is No Arizona'?"

"Who sings it?"

"Jamie O'Neal."

"Don't know her."

"Really? You've never heard it?"

"Don't give me grief. You've never heard of 'A Boy Named Sue,' and Johnny Cash is definitely more famous than this O'Neal woman." I looked over. "So, what's it about?"

"It's about a woman whose man goes to Arizona and tells her that he'll send for her after he gets things in order. He keeps sending her postcards, but he was really just lying about the whole thing. In the end she concludes that there's no Arizona."

"Hence the title. That's tragic."

"Very. Definitely not a romance."

"Not much of a love story either," I said. I glanced over. "Why did you think of that?"

"The chorus goes, 'There is no Arizona, no painted desert, no Sedona.'"

"Ms. O'Neal was wrong," I said. "I just saw a sign."

By the time we reached Sedona, there was no trace of winter. Ahead of us, jagged red sandstone formations jutted up from the stubbled Sonoran Desert plains.

Our entire side trip lasted less than four hours. We drove downtown and walked through the Main Street District full of sidewalk cafés, art galleries, jewelry stores, and tourist shops selling T-shirts and Sedona memorabilia.

After that we drove up to the chapel of the Holy Cross,

which looked out over the valley. Most of the people inside the church were foreigners. In spite of Sedona's reputation as a New Age mecca, it is actually a religious town and there are myriad churches scattered around the natural rock cathedrals.

We could have easily spent more time sightseeing, but I was beginning to feel like I was avoiding something, which, no doubt, I was. I'm a savant at finding distractions when something's uncomfortable. It's amazing how many distractions arise when I'm not in the mood to write.

We finally headed back to I-17 and drove the remaining couple of hours to Scottsdale. The temperature in Phoenix was pleasant, hovering in the low seventies. Rachel was glad for the warmth, as she wasn't as used to the cold as I was. St. George, which is near her home, is among the warmest parts of Utah and never really gets very cold. It's the place where Salt Lakers go to golf in the winter or escape the gray-brown air of Salt Lake's frequent inversions.

The Phoenician is a green napkin on the dusty stone lap of Camelback Mountain. As we drove down the immaculate palm-tree-lined streets and well-groomed greens of the resort, Rachel looked around in wonder. "This is really nice," she said. "It must cost a fortune to stay here."

"It's not cheap," I said. "Especially this time of the year."

"We could have stayed somewhere less expensive."

"We could have, but I'm still trying to impress you."

She smiled. "It's still working."

We drove past the hotel's main entrance to the upper property—the luxury Canyon Suites. I suppose that I was showing off a little. Or a lot. Two young men wearing matching uniforms of hunter-green shorts, caps, and smock-like blouses met us beneath the portico. One of them took my car while the other put our luggage on a cart and wheeled it inside.

Rachel and I went inside the beautiful, marble-floored lobby and checked in at a desk with an attractive older woman. As the woman handed us our room keys, she said, "Welcome to the Canyons, Mr. Churcher. Forgive me for gushing, but I'm a big fan of your work. I hope you and Mrs. Churcher enjoy your stay with us. If there's anything I can do to make your stay more pleasant, please don't hesitate to call me."

I was about to correct her on our matrimonial state, but Rachel spoke first. "Thank you, Claire. We're looking forward to our honeymoon."

"Forgive me," she replied. "I wasn't told that it was your honeymoon. Congratulations. I'll have a bottle of champagne sent to your room."

"Thank you," I said, standing.

As we walked away from the desk, I said, "Our honeymoon?"

Rachel smiled. "Just protecting your reputation, Mr. Churcher. Don't want your fans to get the wrong impression."

I nodded. "That was thoughtful of you. And we got a bottle of champagne out of it."

We followed the bellboy with our luggage rack down the soft carpeted corridor about a hundred feet to our room. I unlocked the door and the bellboy brought in our suitcases.

The suite was spacious and beautiful, and as Rachel walked in, her eyes grew wide with wonder. She walked over to a double glass door that led to a wide patio that overlooked the golf course. Outside our window was a colorful cactus garden. "What a view." She walked around the rest of the suite, disappearing into another room. After the bellboy left, I turned up the air-conditioning. "What do you think?"

Rachel walked back into the room. "So this is how the other two percent live."

I sat back on the couch. "I could still try to book us something on Airbnb."

"No, I'm good," she said. "This room is really, really big."

"It's eighteen hundred square feet. It's bigger than my mother's house. Of course, I usually just get the one bedroom."

"Then you've been here before?"

"Many times. Phoenix has some classic bookstores I come to for book signings. There's the Changing Hands Bookstore in Tempe and The Poisoned Pen in Scottsdale."

"What an amazing life you have," she said.

"An amazingly lonely one," I replied. "Once I came here

in the dead of summer. It was a hundred and seventeen degrees."

"That sounds awful."

"At first I thought the same thing. But actually it turned out quite nice. Hardly anyone was here and I pretty much had the pool and service to myself. Speaking of which, I was thinking we should have lunch by the pool."

"Should I put on my swimsuit?"

"If you want to swim."

"I'll be right back."

A few minutes later she returned in a bright-red halter-top tankini. She had a beautiful figure, which she modestly covered. She looked at me as if awaiting my approval. I was speechless.

"So? Do you like it?"

"Wow."

"Wow?"

"It's beautiful." I looked into her eyes. "You're beautiful."

She looked at me doubtfully, then down at her suit. "It's not too . . . risqué?"

"Maybe for the nineteen hundreds," I said.

"I'm sorry, I'm just self-conscious."

"With a body like yours, most of the women I've dated would wear as little as they could get away with."

"Well, that wouldn't be me." She glanced at herself in the mirror. "It's the suit. It's flattering."

"That's like saying the *Mona Lisa* has a nice frame."

She laughed. "Stop it." She looked at me and said, "Brandon thinks it's too immodest."

"That suit?"

She nodded. "I wore it once, then put it away. Sometimes I think he'd have me wear a burka if he could."

"That would be putting a candle under a bushel," I said.

She laughed again. "Are you putting on your suit?"

"Ugh," I said. I wasn't dying to expose my physique. "Yes. But I'm warning you, I have an author's body."

"You have a nice body."

"Now you've really lost all credibility. Give me a moment."

I went into the bathroom and slipped into my black Tommy Bahamas swimsuit and a Green Day T-shirt, then came back out.

"All right. Let's go."

The Canyon had its own palm-tree-lined pool surrounded by luxurious wooden lounge chairs and amber-colored cabanas. There were several dozen people outside but no children, so the pool area was quiet. We sat down at a table near the pool and a server approached us.

"Good afternoon. Will you be dining?"

"Yes," I said.

He handed us lunch menus. "Can I get you something to drink?"

"I'll have a Diet Coke with lime, and she would like . . ." I glanced over at Rachel.

She looked up at the server. "I'd like a pineapple juice with a splash of cranberry juice."

"With vodka?"

She looked surprised by the question. "No, sir."

"One virgin sea breeze and a Diet Coke."

He returned a few moments later with our drinks and took our orders. I ordered a Mediterranean chicken wrap. Rachel ordered the chicken and kale Caesar salad.

As we ate, we talked about the resort and Arizona's climate, comparing it to Rachel's home in St. George. It was tempting to avoid thinking about the reason we'd come to Phoenix. Especially since every time I did, I was filled with anxiety.

Had I been too rash in coming? Was I only here for Rachel? I had no idea how my father would respond to the meeting. I wasn't even sure how I'd respond. Elyse had said that he wanted to see me, but why? Was he regretful and trying to make amends? Or was this one of those cliché cases where the parent returns after their child makes it big? What if he asked me for money? Or a kidney? You can see why I didn't want to think about it.

Peculiarly, Rachel didn't bring it up either, though I think she might have sensed my reticence and was waiting for me to broach the subject. After a while she went for a swim, first dipping her feet into the water, then sliding in off the edge. The pool was about four feet deep, shallow enough for her to stand and talk to me.

"This is perfect. Come in."

I smiled at her. "I'm good."

"I know you're good. Come in."

"I can't. I just ate. You shouldn't swim for at least a half hour after you eat."

"That's a myth. If you cramp up, I'll save you. I promise."

I grinned. "All right. I've run out of excuses. But don't look as I take off my shirt. The glare might blind you."

"I have been warned," she said.

I took off my shirt and got in the pool. She was right, the water did feel great. Rachel leaned back against the side of the pool, resting her arms on the cement ledge. "Do you remember what we were talking about this morning, at breakfast?"

"You mean . . ." I hesitated bringing it up. "How you were acting last night."

She frowned. "You said you wouldn't bring that up again."

"I didn't. I thought you were."

"I won't ever bring that up."

"All right, so what were we talking about?"

"We were talking about that 'Boy Named Sue' song. And I asked 'Why do we always take the hard way?'"

"I remember."

"I've been thinking about that. And I think I figured out why. It's because we don't believe that we're worthy of happiness. Or love." She looked me in the eyes, then said, "At least, that's what I was thinking."

"I understand that," I said. "I've always believed that we don't choose the life we want. We choose the life we think we deserve. We self-sabotage as a way to punish ourselves."

"Why would we punish ourselves?" Rachel asked. "Doesn't the world punish us enough?"

I frowned. "Why wouldn't we? We live in a world that's always making us work for love. It's cause and effect. That's the story of my childhood. If I can be good enough, maybe my mother will love me.

"The problem is, somewhere along the way you figure out that you can't ever be good enough. It finally just got to be too much for me. You hit this point where you just want to scream, 'Love me for who I am or get out of my life.'

"I think that's why I was never interested in religion. Everyone I talked to about religion basically said I'd have to work really hard to earn God's love. I spent half my life working just to get my mother's love and it didn't work.

"Some would give me this explanation that we were really just finding our way back to God. The way I see it, it's like this: Would you take a kid, drop him off in the middle of China, then say, 'I'm going to disappear now. It's your job to find your way back to me. There will be thousands of people giving you different directions and different maps and you'll never really know if the one you choose is right. But if you screw up, you can't come back home.' I know what it is to be kicked out of your home by the ones you love and not know why. If that's God, an omnipotent version of my mother, I want no part of him."

Rachel looked at me thoughtfully. "I told you that my parents were really strict. They're highly legalistic in their approach to God. In their minds, God is like a cosmic traffic cop. For every action there must be an equal and opposite reaction. If you make a mistake, you must be punished. Which is why they've always been highly punitive. I can't tell you how many times they beat me. What made it worse is they would express their love to me as they did it. It was pretty messed up."

"Your parents beat you?"

"Frequently. And with holy intent, sometimes even quoting the Bible as they did. Proverbs thirteen twenty-four: 'He who withholds his rod hates his son.' Proverbs twenty-three fourteen: 'Thou shalt beat him with the rod, and shalt deliver his soul from Sheol.' They got it all in writing."

"I'm sorry."

"Yeah. Me too. But the thing is, I think Proverbs was just King Solomon's parenting style. And wise or not, his son, Rehoboam, who took his place, was a vicious, cruel leader whom everyone hated and was almost killed by his own people. So what Solomon indirectly was saying was, 'My parenting advice stinks, and if you want a kid like mine, raise him the way I did.'"

I laughed. "How do you know so much about the Bible?"

"My family studied the Bible every day before school."

"I'm impressed."

"Don't be," she said. "They made me. So at first I just accepted their twist on everything. Then, as I got older, I realized that they were adding their own interpretations and personalities to their teachings, so I started studying not to please them but to figure out the truth of what was written in the Bible. I started asking questions."

"How did that go?"

"They saw it as rebellion. Like most people, they were more interested in protecting their beliefs than learning the truth. I kept seeing these contradictions in what I read and what they believed. When I was sixteen I asked them what grace meant, and my father said, 'Grace means that after you do everything you can possibly do, then, and only then, is God's grace sufficient to save you.' I walked away despairing. I thought, That's impossible. No one can do *all* they can do. Because you can always pray for one more second or give one more dollar to the poor or read one more word in the Bible. You can always do more. And everyone screws up sometime and that alone means you haven't done all you could have done."

She breathed out in exasperation. "I've seen people spend their entire lives chasing their spiritual tails and end up nothing but exhausted. People who believe in a traffic-cop God end up either full of shame or full of delusional self-righteousness. I think that sums up my parents. Both of those things. If you were to ask them if they were good, they would say no. But if you were to ask them if they were sinners, they would be offended.

"The hard part is that even though you know it's not right, once that mind-set is programmed into you, good luck getting it out. Because it feels like you are constantly rebelling against what's right even if you know it's not right." She squinted at me. "Am I making any sense?"

I nodded. "More than I've heard in a long time," I said.

"And you're making an absentee father sound better and better."

"It's not better. It's just different. It's like saying which is better, abuse or neglect. Like you said, they're both forms of abuse. It's just that one is passive."

I thought over her comment, then looked down at my watch. "Speaking of neglect, it's past five. We better go."

We climbed out of the pool, dried ourselves off, and walked back to our suite. I changed back into my clothes in the bathroom while Rachel did the same in the master bedroom.

Preparing to see my father, I had one of those "first day at school" moments where I wondered what I should wear. I told myself that it didn't matter and put on a T-shirt and khaki shorts and tennis shoes with no socks and went out to get my car. If he didn't want to see me in a T-shirt, why would he want to see me in an Armani jacket?

The valet brought up my car and handed me the keys. "Have a good evening."

"Thank you."

I had already opened the door for Rachel, and she climbed in next to me.

"Are you ready?" she asked.

"No. Are you?"

"Nope. Let's go."

I smiled. I loved this woman's spirit.

C H A P T E R

Nineteen

July 23, 1986

Dear Diary,

Tomorrow is the 24th—that's Pioneer Day here in Utah. We're all going to the Salt Lake County Fair and a rodeo. I'm very excited about that. I haven't been out much. We have rodeos up in Logan. They're always fun to watch. My stomach just keeps growing. I have some pain down my leg. Mrs. Churcher says that it's my sciatic nerve and is no big deal. It will go away. I'm glad for that. Having a baby is a big commitment. Not something you think about when some boy is taking your clothes off. I wonder if I'll ever see Peter again or what I'll say to him if I do. It will probably never happen. That's okay—I have a boyfriend. His name is Jacob, and he loves me more than any boy has ever loved a girl. He told me so.

Noel

I programmed my father's address into my phone and Rachel and I set off.

The drive from Scottsdale to Mesa took us only twenty-five minutes. Fortunately it was a Saturday; otherwise we would have hit rush-hour traffic. We drove south on the 101 to US 60, where we drove east to the South Gilbert Road exit, then north on Gilbert to Broadway. There we turned east, driving a short distance to Twenty-Fifth Street and then south a block to Calypso Avenue and my father's neighborhood.

It was a simple, middle-class suburb with smallish homes. I found the address painted in black and white on the curb. Number 2412.

The home was one of the older ones—a bland, chiffon-yellow stucco rambler with a two-car garage and a terra-cotta tiled roof. The front yard was austere, landscaped all in red lava rock with a small cactus garden in the center. Near the home's front door was a large clay pot with a small lemon tree, which looked slightly at odds with the Christmas wreath hanging on the door. I pulled the car up to the curb.

"That's the place," I said.

"It looks nice," Rachel said. "Simple."

I glanced over at her. "What do you think? Ready to meet this guy?"

"I don't think I should go with you. I will if you want me to, but it's a big moment. Me being there might just confuse things."

I thought for a moment, then said, "You're probably right. If things go well, I'll come get you."

"Good luck," she said. "I'll say a prayer for you."

I got out of the car and walked up to the door, looking

for any sign of life. There was a folded copy of the *Arizona Republic* newspaper on the front porch near the door.

I rang the doorbell and a dog inside the house started barking. A small dog with a yappy bark.

I heard footsteps and the door opened. A woman, tall and thin with slightly graying hair, opened the door. She had kind eyes.

"May I help you?" she asked gently.

"I'm here to see Scott Churcher."

"Scott's not here right now. May I help you?"

"Do you know when he'll be back?"

She looked at me for a moment, then said, "You're Jacob."

I looked at her quizzically. "How did you know?"

"You look like Scott. Will you come in?"

"Thank you, but I have someone in the car. When do you expect him?"

"He's in Tucson today, but he'll be back tomorrow afternoon. Is that all right?"

"That's fine," I said.

"I'll let him know that you came by. What time should I tell him you'll be here?"

"What time do you expect him back?"

"Three. But if he knows you're here, he'll be back earlier."

"Three is fine," I said. "I'll come back then."

"Would you like to leave your phone number?"

"No."

"All right," she said kindly. "We'll see you tomorrow."

As I started to turn, she said, "Jacob."

I turned back. "Yes?"

"Thank you for coming by. He'll be very happy to see you."

I nodded slightly, then went back to the car.

CHAPTER

Twenty

July 30, 1986

Dear Diary,

I didn't get to go to the rodeo. It wasn't the Churchers' fault. My father called and asked if they were going anywhere for the 24th. When Scott told him we were going to the rodeo, my dad said I must not go, since they knew a lot of people were going there from Logan. I don't think my parents really care about me. All they care about is how they look to the neighbors they go to church with. I once read this in the Bible—something like, they are like sepulchres, white and shiny on the outside but filled with dead men's bones. That's my parents, all right. Their life is a lie. I would rather live an honest life than an admired lie. Besides, no one ever is really happy for people who are having only good things happen. They resent them because behind their own masks they are hurting too.

I spend a lot of time snuggling with little Jacob. He's my buddy. I love Charles too, but he's not close to me the way Jacob is. He used to like it when I read to him, but now he just reads to himself. I

*think he resents me because he wants his mother,
and since I came she hasn't given the boys much
attention. I think maybe she was tired before and
is now enjoying her freedom. My mother sent me a
letter. I haven't opened it.*

Noel

I climbed back into the car. Rachel looked at me with anticipation. "Was he there?"

"No. He's in Tucson. He gets back tomorrow afternoon."

"Are we coming back?"

I started the car. "Yes." I pulled away from the curb, eager to leave the house. I didn't speak, and about five minutes later Rachel asked, "Are you okay?"

I just looked ahead. "I don't know."

"Are we going back to the hotel?"

I glanced over at her. "Yes. Unless there's someplace else you'd like to go."

"No. Would you like to go for a walk when we get back?"

I didn't answer immediately. "We'll see."

Twenty minutes later we pulled into the resort. The valet opened the door for Rachel as I got out. I handed him the keys.

"It's such a nice night," Rachel said. "How about that walk?"

"Are you trying to keep me busy?"

"Yes."

"Okay." I turned to the valet, who was just about to get in my car. "Where's a good place to hike?"

"There's a good trail to Camelback, but you're a little too late for that for tonight. This trail right here leads around the property and past the cactus garden. It's a nice walk."

"Thank you," I said.

"If you do Camelback, be sure to take a lot of water with you."

"Thank you."

We walked up on the trail, which led us down to the main resort. The path was beautiful and along it were myriad species of cacti and large magenta hedges of bougainvillea. The foliage was pretty but most of it was prickly, which reminded me of many of the women I had dated recently.

Rachel was a little quiet, no doubt because I was. We walked about fifty yards in silence before she asked again, "Are you okay?"

I looked down. "I'm not sure what I am. I'm sorry, I guess I'm spinning out a little."

"It's okay. I can't imagine how hard this must be."

We kept walking. We were near the golf course when Rachel's phone rang. "I'm sorry, I forgot to turn it off." She looked at the screen, then answered it. "Hi."

A male voice began shouting. I couldn't make out the words, just the angry, nasal tone of the assault.

"I'm sorry, I . . ." Shouting. "I forgot . . . I'm sorry . . ." Shouting. "I'm really sorry." More shouting. Her eyes began to well up. "I know. I'm sorry. Please forgive me." Another burst. "I—I—" Gasp. "I'm sorry, he wasn't there. I'm sorry." The voice settled some. "Okay. I'll try. Call me later. I love you too. Bye."

She hung up the phone, then turned away from me. "Are you okay?" I asked.

"I'm sorry . . ."

"You don't need to say you're sorry to me."

"I'm sorry." She shook her head. It was like she had been so conditioned to apologize for herself that she couldn't do otherwise.

"Do you know how many times you just told him you were sorry?"

She suddenly looked angry. "Why? Were you counting?"

I just looked at her. "I wasn't insulting you. I just wanted to point out . . ." I sighed. "Is that how he always talks to you?"

She didn't answer.

"It's not respectful. It's not a healthy way to have a relationship."

"You're giving me relationship advice now? How's all that wisdom working for you?"

Her words stung. I just looked at her, momentarily dumbstruck. Then I breathed out. "Sorry. It's none of my business." I turned to walk away.

I had taken a dozen steps when she called after me. "Jacob."

I turned back. She walked up to me.

There were tears in her eyes. "I'm sorry." She put her arms around me. "Please forgive me. I didn't mean that. I'm just upset."

After a moment I said, "All right. Let's go back to the hotel."

She wiped her eyes. "I need some time alone."

I looked at her, then nodded. "I'll be back in the room." I reached in my pocket and brought out a plastic keycard. "Here's the key. Be safe." I leaned forward and kissed her on the forehead. Then I turned and walked back down the path toward the hotel.

I was still hurting when I got back to the suite. What she said had pierced. The truth always hurts, right? But my pain wasn't just from her attack. I was angry at Rachel's fiancé. And I was angry at her for allowing herself to be treated so poorly.

As I thought it over, I realized I was also angry at myself. I was angry because I was falling for her. I was falling for a woman who was engaged to another man. No, I wasn't falling. I *had* fallen. I had already hit the water. I was drenched.

And to make it worse, she was with someone who I didn't think deserved her. Not that I really knew that; I'd never met him and no doubt my judgment, as a matter of self-interest, would be skewed. But I knew for certain that

I never would have talked to her the way he just had. The more I thought about it, the more I realized that I needed to tell her how I felt.

I got a mini bottle of Jack Daniel's out of the refrigerator, poured it into a glass with a Coke and ice, and took a drink. After a few sips my thoughts changed. *What was I thinking?* This woman was getting married. She had already ordered the flowers and booked the reception center. I had only known her for a few days. I ran a great risk in telling her. She would shut me out. No, it was better to just follow the plan.

I grabbed the remote, then sat back in an armchair and turned on the television. The Arizona Cardinals were playing the Denver Broncos. I watched for a few minutes, not that I cared about either team; I really just needed a distraction while I drank.

After a second drink, I remembered Noel's diary. Rachel had left it on the nightstand next to her bed. I picked it up, then turned off the television and took off my shoes and lay across my bed.

August 6, 1986

Dear Diary,

Something horrible beyond words happened. While I was at the doctor's, Charles climbed a tree and grabbed on to a power line. He was electrocuted. Little Jacob was with him. He ran back home and got his mother. When I got home the

ambulance was still at the house, but no one was
moving quickly. When I got close I saw his little
body covered by the sheet. I confess, my first fear
was that it was my little Jacob. I felt guilty about
that. I don't know what will happen with me.
Maybe they will send me to another home. Not my
home. That would never happen. I still haven't read
the letter from my mother. I don't know if I ever will.
There is so much pain in this world.

Noel

August 13, 1986

Dear Diary,

    I am halfway through my pregnancy. It's
hard to even think of me or my baby at this time.
Charles's funeral was last Thursday. It was the
saddest thing I've ever seen. When they shut the lid
on the coffin, Mrs. Churcher fell on the ground and
wailed. I worry for her. She has not stopped crying.
She doesn't eat. She stays in her bed all day with
the light out. She has told me at least five times
that she wants to die. One time she asked me to
bring her sleeping pills. When I came in she yelled
at me because she wanted the whole bottle. I just
left her room. I knew she wouldn't come out. She
never comes out.

Noel

August 20, 1986

Dear Diary,

Things here are not getting worse or better. The world is stuck in a hopeless limbo. There is a darkness that pervades everything. Through it all, it's as if they've forgotten that they still have a son. My poor little Jacob. He clings to me all the time now. I hold him. He kisses me at night when I put him to bed. I am all he has, mostly. Mr. and Mrs. Churcher got into a big fight. I heard something break. Mr. Churcher came out of the room. He looked at me, and I could see his pain.

I finally opened the letter my mother wrote me. I wish I hadn't. She told me that I was such a disappointment to the family, and that she has racked her brain trying to figure out where she had gone wrong. Then God told her the truth. She hadn't gone wrong—I had. She was relieved of her guilt and is now worried about my soul. She said I was a chewed piece of gum and no one would want me. I wish she would worry less about my soul and more about me. Or even the baby she pretends doesn't exist. I wish I had never opened the letter. I wish I had never been born. Then I wouldn't be the cause of so much trouble.

Noel

August 27, 1986

Dear Diary,

I am having a little girl. A sweet little girl. It's hard for me not to name her. Before I came here, my father told me not to name my baby. He said it would make it much harder when I gave my baby up. Then he told me that when he was little he lived on a farm and they raised pigs. He named one of the pigs Wilbur after the pig in <u>Charlotte's Web</u>. Then they slaughtered Wilbur for Christmas dinner. He said it was his worst Christmas ever. I think that was the worst story ever. Did he really compare my baby to a pig?

I'm not going to name her.

Noel

It was dark outside when I heard the doorknob turn and the door open. I looked at my watch. It was a quarter past nine. I walked out to the foyer. Rachel was letting herself in, trying to be quiet about it.

"Hi."

She turned to me. "Oh, hi. I thought you might be in bed already."

"No. I'm a night owl."

She walked up to me. "I'm so ashamed about what I said to you. I don't know where that came from. I'm just such an emotional mess. I'm getting married in four months. I shouldn't have come. It was selfish of me."

I looked at her, disappointed in the conclusion she'd arrived at. "Taking care of yourself isn't selfish. Especially when others aren't."

She forced a smile, though her eyes still looked dull and puffy. "It's been a long day. I'm going to take a shower and go to bed. Thank you for this lovely room." She kissed me on the cheek. "Good night." Then she walked into her room and shut and locked her door, leaving my heart and mind still reeling. Mostly my heart.

My heart hurt. I was in love. And I was stupid to let my guard down. *When had my feelings crossed that line?* I went to my room and lay back on the bed. Laurie was right. I never should have stirred the ashes.

CHAPTER

Twenty-One

September 3, 1986

Dear Diary,

   I know I wrote that I wouldn't give my baby a name, but I can't help it. I know that it won't even keep. I'm calling her Angela. Like an angel. That's what she is. And if she's born on Christmas like I was, she'll be a Christmas Angel. This was a pretty good week. Nothing big or important happened. Maybe that's why it was a good week. The weather is getting colder. No matter the weather, I think this is going to be a long, long winter.

Noel

September 17, 1986

Dear Diary,

   Looking through a <u>National Geographic</u> magazine at the doctor's office, I saw a picture of a boa constrictor that had swallowed a pig whole, and I thought, <u>That looks just like me</u>. Well, without the scales and fangs. I'm huge. Someone in *the doctor's office asked me if my husband wanted a boy or a girl. I told her that he was fine with either. I feel so alone. I'm so tempted to reach out to Peter, but I won't. I've made enough mistakes in my life. If he loves me, he'll come back to me. If he doesn't love me, why would I want him to?*

Noel

DECEMBER 18

I woke early the next morning. Rachel was still sleeping, so I wrote her a note, then put on my bathing suit and went out to the pool. I was still hurting from the night before. I was seething with jealousy and there was no reason for me to believe that she would leave him. Part of me didn't even want to see her.

There were only a handful of guests in the pool area and only one other person actually in the pool.

I jumped in and started swimming laps. About a half hour later I noticed that Rachel had come out. She waved at me. I swam over to the side of the pool. She looked like she felt better than she had the night before. She looked lighter.

"Don't wear yourself out," she said, crouching down near the edge of the pool. "I was thinking, since we have the time, maybe we should hike Camelback. Want to? The concierge says it takes about two hours each way. She gave me a map."

"I'm game," I said. I got out and went back to the room

and got dressed. As I walked out of the bathroom, Rachel was sitting on the couch.

"How are you feeling today?" I asked.

She looked at me with soft eyes. "I still feel bad about my behavior last night. You've been nothing but good to me." She shook her head. "It was the guilt. And I took it out on you."

"We don't need to talk about it," I said. "I understand."

She smiled a half smile. "At least one of us does."

I took her hand to pull her up from the couch. "Let's go climb the mountain." I lifted her.

After she was standing, she still clung to my hand. She smiled awkwardly, then let go. "Sorry."

We stopped at a sundries shop in the resort for lip balm, sunscreen, and water. I bought myself a hat and Rachel a bandana, which I helped her wrap around her head. She looked really cute.

We parked near the base of the mountain and took the Cholla Trail to the summit. The trail was well marked and the landscape was rugged and beautiful with saguaro cacti popping up around the mountain.

We made it to the craggy summit in a little more than an hour and a half. We had a 365-degree view of Phoenix, a checkered grid of dusty green flora, red tile roofs, and blue swimming pools. From this vantage, Phoenix looked like anything but Christmas. There was a nice, steady breeze, and I sat down on a flat, wide rock to take it in.

There were others on the summit, at least a dozen or more hikers, and they were generous with their water.

One man had carried a dozen bottles up just to hand out along the way. He told me that just two months earlier a man from France had died of sunstroke near the summit. He hadn't thought to bring any water with him.

Rachel walked around the summit and, not surprisingly, several men flirted with her. She was laughing with them, innocently, but it still felt like little pinpricks on my heart. I kept waiting for her to come sit by me but she never did. Finally I got up. "We better go back down."

"Wait," she said, walking over. "I want to get a picture of us."

She beckoned one of the flirting men over to take her phone. Clearly a body builder, he was wearing a tank top that exposed muscular arms the size of my thighs. He switched her phone to take a selfie. "Sorry," he said. "Got a picture of me. You can keep it, no charge."

Rachel slid up next to me on the rock. "Okay, do it right this time," she said. Even though she had apologized about last night, I still felt cautious and was being less physical with her. Or maybe she was being less physical with me and I was reacting cautiously. Either way, our pose looked anything but natural. Finally she leaned back against me and said in a tone that could have been flippant or earnest—I couldn't discern which—"It's okay if you act like you like me."

Without saying anything I put my arm around her. Rachel made the man take about a dozen pictures. She thanked him, then sat back down on the rock next to me and offered me a bottle of water. "Have some water."

"I'm okay."

"Drink," she said. "That's an order."

I took the bottle and drank half of it, then handed it back. "Happy?"

"Why wouldn't I be happy?" she said, standing. "I'm with you." She took my hand. "Let's go."

* * *

It was almost one when we got back to the hotel. I took a quick shower, then went out to the suite's living room. Rachel was waiting for me. We walked out to the front. I had called for my car and it was parked next to the valet desk.

"Do you need me to look up the address again?" Rachel asked.

"No. I've got it."

I pulled out of the resort's parking lot, and we headed off for Mesa.

It was Sunday and the Phoenix traffic was considerably lighter than it had been the day before. We arrived at my father's house ten minutes early. This time a white Subaru Impreza was parked in the driveway.

"Nervous?" Rachel asked.

I looked at her and forced a smile. "Why would I be nervous?"

She looked at me sympathetically. "What are you most nervous about?"

"I don't know. I mean, why am I even here?"

"The same reason I'm looking for my mother. You want to know yourself."

"I'm not him."

"No, but he's part of you."

I took a deep breath. "All right. Let's get this over with." I looked at her. "You're okay waiting in the car? I may be a while."

"That's all right. If you're long, I'll go for a walk."

"I'll leave the keys."

She grinned. "You mean, just in case we need to make a quick getaway."

I grinned back. "Exactly."

I opened my door. I walked up to the front of the house. The front door opened before I could ring the bell. My father stood in the doorway. I knew it was him instantly. He was still handsome, though he was completely bald. Actually, he had no facial hair, including eyebrows and eyelashes. My mind was flooded with a myriad of thoughts. *Cancer. Was he dying? Was this why he was so eager to see me? Deathbed repentance?*

Other than his lack of hair he looked healthy. He had bright eyes and a slight paunch of a stomach that comfortably filled out his khaki slacks and the short-sleeved Tommy Bahamas Hawaiian shirt he was wearing. For a moment neither of us spoke. Then his eyes welled. "Jacob."

I swallowed, my feelings spinning around like a wheel of fortune, waiting to land on something. "Scott."

We just stood there, neither of us sure what to do next. His wife, or at least the woman I'd spoken with the day before, walked up behind him. She was smiling. "Scott, why don't you ask your son in?"

It was like he had suddenly woken from a trance. "Of course. Come in. Please."

"Thank you." I stepped inside. The house was cool and bright inside. Skylights allowed the sun in and the interior design was modern and clean.

"Can I get you something to drink?" Scott said.

"Sure. I'll have a beer if you have one."

"I'll get it," the woman said.

"This is my wife, Gretchen," Scott said.

"We met yesterday," I said.

"It's good to see you again," she said. She turned to Scott. "Did you want something to drink?"

"Please," he said. "A beer too." He turned back to me. "So, have a seat." He gestured to a couch, a light-gray sectional with chrome legs and bright-crimson accent pillows. On one of the side tables was an eight-by-ten framed photograph of my father and me. We were standing on the porch of my childhood home, me in a coat and hat, my father holding my hand.

Lying on the glass coffee table in front of us, next to a porcelain figurine of Santa Claus, was a hardcover copy of my latest book. I guessed he had put it there so I would see it. Probably the photograph as well.

I sat down, and he sat close to me in a matching chaise. His eyes were still red. I could tell that he felt awkward, but I could also tell that he was glad to see me.

Still, neither of us knew what to say. It's not like there's some approved script for this. I thought, *It's a shame I haven't written about something like this in one of my books. At least I'd have something to fall back on.*

Scott was the first to bridge the gap. "So, what brings you to Phoenix?"

"You," I said.

He just nodded.

"How have you been?" I asked.

"I'm okay." He gestured to his head. "Lost all my hair."

"Cancer?"

"Yeah. Testicular. That chemo took all my hair."

"Did it help?"

"The doctors think they got it all. Old age aside, I feel pretty good."

"That's good," I said.

His head bobbed a little in agreement. "So, you live in Coeur d'Alene?"

"How did you know?"

He gestured to my book. "It's in the back of your book." He smiled. "I've read your books. All of them. They're excellent. You certainly didn't get that talent from me."

Gretchen walked in with two mugs filled with a dark amber beer. "This is Scott's favorite."

"Thank you," I said.

"Thank you, honey," Scott said.

After she left, I took a drink and said, "You always keep my book on the table?"

He grinned. "I put it out because you were coming."

"Honesty," I said, nodding. "And the picture of me?"

"No, that's always been there. Has since we moved here twenty years ago."

I let that sink in. "So, what are you doing now for work?"

"I'm semiretired, but I still do a little in social work. I'm a consultant. I work with hospitals and their mental health workers. I was in Tucson yesterday. It keeps me busy. And you? Book writing keep you busy?"

"Book writing, promoting, all the junk that comes with it."

"It sounds exciting."

"It has its moments."

The moment fell into silence. We both took another drink. Then Scott leaned back in his chair. "Thank you for coming. When Gretchen told me that you had come by, well, I didn't get much sleep last night. I was hoping to see you at your mother's funeral. I wasn't surprised that I didn't, but I was hoping. I hear she left you the house."

"I've been cleaning it."

He looked at me curiously. "Why?"

"Because it's a mess. She was a hoarder."

"I know; I meant, why you? You're an important man. You could hire someone to do that."

"I guess I thought I'd dig through the relics myself. Maybe answer some questions."

"I can see it being cathartic," he said. "Has it helped?"

I took a drink, then set the mug down on the napkin. "Not really. But maybe it's good to confront the pain."

He nodded knowingly. "Would you like to ask me any-thing?"

I looked at him for a moment. Then the words just shot out of my mouth, the verbal equivalent of projectile vom-iting. "Yeah. Why did you leave me there?"

The words hung like smoke in the air between us. He looked down and his face fell with sorrow. He took a drink, wiped his mouth, then took another. Then he looked at me with red eyes. "Because I was stupid. At the time, I thought it was for the best." He exhaled. "The road to hell is paved with good intentions, right?"

He shook his head. "The thing is, I was a mess myself. Ruth blamed me for Charles's death. I blamed myself as well. I felt like I had already taken one son from her. I couldn't take another child from her. Not that the state would have let me anyway. Men don't often end up with the children, I knew that."

He breathed out slowly. "When I first told her that I wanted a divorce and I wanted to take you with me, she said to me, 'You want to take another child from me? You want to kill him too?'"

I swallowed.

"I couldn't do it. I had no right to do it. I had visitation rights, but I didn't take them. Not that I didn't want them— I desperately missed you—but because I had lost the ability to see you. I was so filled with grief and guilt that I did the worst thing I could do. I started drinking." He looked at me. "Long story short, four years later, I cleaned up. I re-married and went back into the field.

"I desperately wanted to see you, but it had been so long by then that I couldn't see how to do it without causing you pain." He looked me in the eyes. "In my profession I'd counseled clients who suddenly had a parent come back into their lives, and sometimes it just really messed with them. It caused them more pain, not less. It just didn't seem fair to put you through that. I didn't feel I had the right to."

His expression grew still more serious. "You have to understand that I honestly didn't know about Ruth's condition. I had no idea what she was doing to you. Years later, when I found out that she might be abusive, I contacted a lawyer about getting custody of you. I even called my old friends at DCFS to see if I could pull some strings. Then I called her. I told her that I was going to take you. That was a mistake. She freaked out. The next time I called, you were gone. You had run away."

"I didn't run away," I said. "She kicked me out. I came home one day and everything I owned was in the yard."

"I'm so sorry," he said, shaking his head. "Even when I tried to help, I failed you." Suddenly his eyes filled with tears. "I'm so sorry I wasn't stronger. I know, at this point, that saying I'm sorry is absurd. Way too little, way too late." He looked again into my eyes as a tear fell down his cheek. "I don't expect you to forgive me. I don't expect anything from you. But for what it's worth, I really am sorry."

His apology washed over me without effect. The moment fell into deep silence.

After a few moments he said, "I tried to find you, you know. I never forgot about you. I just thought I was doing the right thing. From where I was coming from, it made sense. Ruth had always been a good mother. She was a better mother than I was a father. She was a good person. At least when I knew her.

"And she loved you both. Losing Charles was the most difficult thing she had ever gone through. I could understand her turning on me—I guess she needed someone to blame—but I never imagined that she would turn on you."

He breathed out heavily. "In hindsight, I wish I had stayed with her. For both of your sakes. But hindsight's always twenty-twenty, isn't it?"

In spite of my pain, I slowly nodded. Then I looked into his eyes. "I hated you."

"I would expect that," he said softly. "You have every reason to hate me. I failed you. And I can't give you back what you lost." He grimaced and wiped his eyes. Then he looked back up at me. "If there's anything I can do for you now, I'll do it." His eyes welled up again. "Even if you tell me to stay out of your life."

The moment again fell into silence. My father had poured out everything he had, and now it was my turn to respond. My mind reeled. I wasn't sure what I had expected in coming back to see him, but it wasn't this. I realized that there was some part of me that had hoped he would attempt to justify his actions, giving me justification for my hatred and anger. But he hadn't. He was humble and self-deprecating. He had thrown himself under the proverbial bus.

As I sat there, Elyse's words about truth came back to me. In less than an hour, my perspective on the world, past, present, and future, had changed. In all honesty, had I been in his position, I might have done the exact same thing he had. I could fault his failure—even his wisdom—but not his heart. He had clearly suffered deeply for his mistakes. He was still suffering. I felt no reason to add to his pain. Again Elyse's words came to me: *Grace. Grace.*

As I looked at him, he seemed different to me. It was like looking in a mirror. We were the same person, in the same place, seeking the same thing—peace and reconciliation with the past. There was no point in dragging this into the future.

"There is something you can do," I finally said.

"Anything," he replied.

"There's someone I want you to meet. She's outside in the car."

CHAPTER

Twenty-Two

Dear Diary,

My baby was hiccuping today. It's so strange to think that she has a life of her own. I wish I could be in there with her, where no one could see me. Today Jacob asked me if I had ever been to the moon. I said, "No." He said, "I have." I said, "What was it like?" He said, "Charles was there."

I love that little boy.

Noel

Scott looked at Rachel curiously as I led her into the house.

"This is Rachel," I said.

He offered his hand. "It's nice to meet you."

"Thank you. Likewise."

"Please sit."

Rachel and I sat down on the couch. Scott sat back in the chaise. "So, are you two . . . married?"

"No," I said. "Rachel's a friend."

"Sorry. You make a good couple."

Rachel smiled. "You're not the first to think that."

"Can I get you a drink?"

"I'm okay," she said.

"Jacob said you had something to ask me."

"Yes." She glanced at me, then back at my father. "Did you have a young woman living with you about the time you lost Charles?"

My father just stared at her for a moment, then said, "That's why you look so familiar. You look exactly like your mother."

Rachel took a sharp breath. I reached over and squeezed her hand.

"The answer to your question is yes. She was a young lady named Noel Ellis. She was from Logan, Utah. She was almost three months pregnant when she came to live with us."

I glanced over at Rachel. She was nearly shaking. "Do you know where she lives now?"

"It's been a little while. After she got married, she moved to Provo. We lost touch after that, but up to that point she would call fairly regularly."

"Why?" I asked.

My father looked at me. "Because of you, I think. She loved you. Of course I was still around at the time, but she had seen how hard your mother was taking things. I think she had better intuition than I did."

"If she got married, her last name changed," Rachel said.

"Right," Scott said. "She married a guy named King. I think his first name was Keith. Maybe Kevin." He leaned back in his chair and finished his drink. Then he said,

"Noel King. Unless she got divorced and moved out of state, it shouldn't be hard to find her."

"Thank you so much," Rachel said.

"I'm glad to help."

Just then Gretchen walked in. "Hi, I'm feeling left out." She walked up to me. "Welcome home, Jacob."

"Thank you," I said.

She turned to Rachel. "And what is your name, dear?"

"Rachel," she said. "It's nice to meet you."

"And?" she said, wagging her finger between us. "You two are . . ."

"Just friends," Rachel said, a little too quickly.

My heart panged a little.

"Oh," Gretchen replied. "Pity. You look so cute together."

"That's what I said," Scott said. "I just didn't use the word *cute*."

Gretchen smiled. "Well, food is almost ready. I'm broiling salmon and I'm told that I'm quite good at it, so if you would like to eat with us, we would be delighted."

I looked at Rachel.

"I love salmon," she said.

"Love to," I said.

"Wonderful. Rachel, would you like to come into the kitchen while I finish? I could use some girl talk."

"Of course," she said, standing.

After they left, I looked at my father. "Gretchen seems nice."

"She's a really fine woman." Then he looked down. "I'm

a lucky man, Jacob. I've married two fine women in my life. I'm grateful for both of them."

I looked at him quizzically. "Even after all Mom did?"

"What she did?" he repeated gently. "She gave me love. She gave me you." His eyes welled. "You should know, I wept at her funeral. But she died long before that. I knew the woman she was, Jacob. And I still love that woman. I always will." He shook his head. "She had my sympathy, even my pity for what she became, but not my disdain. She deserves that respect." Then he looked at me again. "She gave me you and Charles. What more could I ask for?"

CHAPTER

Twenty-Three

I was glad that I had said yes to the dinner invitation, not just because the food was remarkable but because Gretchen had undoubtedly spent the better part of the day in the kitchen preparing for us with little more than a slim hope that we might dine with them.

We started off our meal with a light arugula and avocado salad, followed by salmon with glazed sweet carrots, garlic green beans, and crispy roasted new potatoes. For dessert we had something Gretchen called a strawberry cool brûlée, which was something like a crème brûlée but without the cooking or caramelized sugar on top.

After we ate, we sat around the table and talked. Scott brought out wine, a four-year-old bottle of Rioja Blanco he had been saving for a special occasion. It paired perfectly with the dinner. Even Rachel had a little. She didn't have much, just a glass, but it seemed to immediately affect her.

Rachel said to Gretchen, "I don't really drink. Actually, I never drink."

"You shouldn't have much, then," Gretchen said.

"I'll just have a little more," she replied.

My father filled her cup half-full. "There you go, dear."

"Thank you." She turned to me. "I'm such a lush."

We all laughed.

It was a pleasant evening, and, frankly, not at all how I'd expected it to go. As the evening waned, my father said, "You need to tell me something. Even though, technically, you did live in the same house, you never met. So how did the two of you hook up?"

Rachel looked at me and smiled widely. "It was my fault. I kept coming to the house to see if I could find someone to tell me about my mother. One day I came by and there was Jacob. It was . . . fortuitous."

"It was fortuitous," I said. "That was a good day."

Rachel smiled. "For both of us."

I cleared my throat. "Rachel's engaged."

Gretchen turned to her. "Oh? Who's the lucky man?"

"His name is Brandon," Rachel said. "He's from St. George. He's an accountant."

"Well, Brandon must be an amazing guy," my father said. "Not just because Jacob is tough competition, but because you are definitely a catch."

"You're embarrassing me," Rachel said, smiling. Then she said to me, "Do you think I'm a catch?"

"Of course I do."

She looked at me with a peculiar expression. Scott and Gretchen must have noticed it as well, because no one spoke for a moment. Then Gretchen said, "Would anyone like some coffee? I have decaf."

"No, thank you," Rachel said.

"Thank you," I said. "But it's been a long day. We should probably get back to the hotel."

"It's been more than a long day. It's been a really good day."

"Hear, hear," I said, lifting my glass.

At the front door Scott said to me, "Thank you. For giving me a chance."

I nodded slowly. "Thank you for the truth. And what you gave Rachel."

"It was my pleasure."

"I'm curious. What you told us about Rachel's mother— are you supposed to share that information?"

He shook his head. "No. That was not kosher."

"Can you get in trouble with the state?"

He shrugged. "I suppose."

"But still you shared it."

"I had just told you that if there was *anything* I could do for you, I would do it. That was no time to renege on an offer. So, you asked who she was, I told you."

"Thank you. You have no idea how much this means to her."

"You have no idea how much this means to *me*. I'm just glad I was around for it."

"Me too," I said.

He suddenly sighed. In a softer voice he said, "Tell Rachel not to get her hopes too high."

"Why is that?"

"Noel's parents went to such great lengths to hide her pregnancy that they probably wanted it kept secret. It's possible that when she married, she never told her husband that she'd had a child. It wouldn't be the first time I'd run across that in marriage counseling."

I nodded thoughtfully. "I'll tell her. Thank you."

"When can I see you again?" he asked.

"You name the time."

"You're the busy one. You say when, and we'll be there. Gretchen and I like to drive. I've never been big on flying."

I nodded. "So that's where I got it."

CHAPTER

Twenty-Four

October 29, 1986

Dear Diary,

Two days ago I thought I was going into labor. Mr. Churcher had to come home from work and drive me and Jacob to the hospital. They said it was false labor, something called Braxton Hicks. (Of course it was named after a man. Like he ever had it.) I wouldn't want a false labor named after me. I was sorry to inconvenience Mr. Churcher. Little Jacob was so confused. He didn't like it when they took me back into the checkup room and wouldn't let him go with me. He started crying. He didn't even want to be with his father. He wanted me.

Noel

Rachel was the happiest I'd seen her since we'd met. The night air was cool, so I opened the car's front windows a few inches to bring in fresh air. As we drove back to our hotel, I said, "What a night. I thought it was going to be awful. Instead, it was perfect."

"He was so happy to see you," she said. Then she added,

"I'm happy to see you." I glanced over at her and she suddenly laughed. "I feel so good."

"It's the wine," I said.

"I might have to do this more."

"Yeah. Well, not tonight."

"How come?"

"Because you've had enough."

As we neared the resort Rachel became less talkative and I wondered if the alcohol was making her sleepy. I handed my keys to the valet, then took Rachel by the arm and walked into the hotel.

As we walked down the long corridor to our suite, she laid her head on my shoulder. I put my arm around her. We walked inside our room, then Rachel turned to me, a soft smile warming her face. "Thank you for helping me find my mother."

"You're welcome," I said. "We helped each other."

She looked into my eyes. "Did you mean what you said?"

"What did I say?"

"Do you really think I'm a catch?"

"Yes. You are. Not just because you're insanely beautiful but because you're a really good person. You're very sweet."

She giggled. "I am sweet," she said, touching my chest with her finger. "Do you like me?"

"Of course."

"I don't think Brandon likes me. I think he wants to marry me, but I think he would change a lot of things about me if he could. I think he's going to put a leash on me."

I chuckled. "He'd be a fool to do so. And you have definitely had too much to drink."

"I only had a little."

"I know. But for you a little is a lot."

Her eyes softened with a childlike vulnerability. "Do you love me?"

The question had more power than she could have known. My heart throbbed in my chest. I looked into her eyes. "Yes."

"I love you too. I love you more than anyone I've ever known." Then she leaned into me and we kissed. Softly at first, then with growing passion and power. After a couple of minutes she stepped back from me and grabbed my hand. "Come here." She led me into her bedroom and we both fell over on the bed. We drew together like magnets, her soft, full lips dissolving into mine. Then she reached over and began to undress me. I took her hands and stopped her.

"No," I said, sitting up. "We can't do this."

"Of course we can," she said breathlessly. "I want to do this."

"No. You'll hate me tomorrow. You're engaged to another man."

"I don't want to be engaged anymore."

"You're in no condition to decide that right now. I'm not going to lose you by taking advantage of you."

She started to cry. "You won't lose me."

"Yes, I will. Your guilt will eat you alive. You won't want it to, but it will."

Her wet eyes pleaded with me. "But don't you want me?"

"More than I've ever wanted anyone." I kissed her again. Then, with our eyes still locked on each other, I stood. "We'll talk in the morning, Rachel. We'll make plans in the morning."

I didn't just walk out of her room, I walked out of the suite. I took a brief walk around the property to cool myself off. I was pretty sure that I wanted her more than she wanted me. But I was also sure that I wanted her for more than just one night. And after her last meltdown, it was clear to me that her guilt was bigger than she could handle.

Later that night, as I lay in bed, the quote from Hamlet came to mind: "Thus conscience does make cowards of us all."

CHAPTER

Twenty-Five

November 25, 1986

Dear Diary,

I've missed a few weeks of writing. I just didn't feel like writing anything. I had nothing new. Thanksgiving is this Thursday. No one has said a word about it. I know Mrs. Churcher won't do anything. Even though I'm tired, I told Mr. Churcher that I would be happy to make the Thanksgiving meal. He said that would be nice. I'll take Jacob shopping with me tomorrow. I don't know how to make pumpkin pie, but I think it will be easy. One pie will be enough for us. My mother is very good at baking pies. She'll make apple, mincemeat, pumpkin, and cherry. There will be a big turkey. The whole family and Aunt Genielle and her two hundred children will be there. I miss my family. I wonder if they'll talk about me at dinner and ask how I'm doing at school. My mom will say, Oh, you know Noel, she always gets good grades.

I don't think anyone around here is very grateful for anything these days. If a meteor came down and landed on this house, everyone would probably

be better off. Except Jacob. If a meteor came down, I
would put my body over his and try to shield him.
I would give my life for this little boy. What am I
thankful for this Thanksgiving? I'm thankful for
him.

Noel

DECEMBER 19

I woke the next morning with a light hangover. I had slept in a little. It was almost nine. Hangover or not, a big smile crossed my face. I felt like I'd just won the lottery. Rachel wanted me too.

I pulled on some shorts and a T-shirt, then walked to her room. At first I slowly opened the door, trying not to let in too much light. To my surprise, the room was filled with light. The blinds were open and the room was empty.

"Rachel?"

She probably just went out for a walk, I thought. I walked into her bedroom. "Rachel." I checked her bathroom. Her suitcase was gone. Everything was gone. She was gone.

I walked back out to the front of the suite. On the counter next to the door was a note.

> *Dear Jacob,*
>
> *I woke in the middle of the night feeling dark and heartsick. Most of all, ashamed. What am I doing here, sharing a room with another man? What kind of woman sneaks off on a trip with another man,*

*then tries to seduce him? I am so, so ashamed. I tried
to tell myself that last night was an accident, that
it was the wine, but I know the truth. I didn't need
to see your father. There's nothing he could tell me
that you couldn't have relayed to me. The truth is, I
wanted to go with you because I wanted to be with
you. And that's wrong. It's wrong that I like that you
get jealous of Brandon. It's wrong that I'd rather be
with you than him. Most of all, it's wrong that after
all of Brandon's trust in me, I chose to cheat on him.*

*Last night you told me that you loved me because
I was a really good person. Obviously, I'm not. I
want to be. But I'm not. You deserve a good woman.
You did the right thing last night. I didn't. I'm not
the woman I thought I was. Thank you for respecting
me enough to not make my sin worse. Please forgive
me. I will never stop thinking of you. With love
always,*

Rachel

*P.S. Thank you for letting me read my mother's
journal. I wanted to take it with me, but it's not
mine. I realize that she belongs to you too.*

I put the note back down on the counter, then kicked
the cupboard door beneath it.

CHAPTER

Twenty-Six

November 27, 1986

Dear Diary,

Thanksgiving was actually nice. Even Mrs. Churcher came out for a little while. She had some turkey and stuffing and mashed potatoes. She thanked me, then went back into her bedroom. Mr. Churcher was in pain. I could see it. After dinner I went to do the dishes, and he came in to help me. He was standing next to me, and I could see that he was crying. I put my arms around him, and he laid his head on my shoulder and cried hard. I suppose it would have looked very weird, but grief isn't a beauty pageant. Jacob grabbed onto my leg. (I think he may have been jealous.) I've wondered where God has been in all this, but maybe I was supposed to come to this home at this time, because some days I feel like I'm the only thing holding it together. As I put Jacob to bed, he asked me why we had a Thanksgiving. I told him about the Pilgrims, then said, We do it so we can remember what we have to be thankful for. He asked me what thankful was. I said, Thankful is what we are glad we have. And he

said, I'm thankful for you. I almost started crying.
But then he said, And whipped cream. I kissed him
and laughed.

On the pregnancy front, my baby dropped.
And my boobs are getting big and heavy. I feel like
someone has commandeered my body. Oh, wait,
someone did.

Noel

It was time to go home. Not just back to Salt Lake, but really home. Back to Coeur d'Alene.

The traffic out of town was miserable. Actually the whole drive back to Salt Lake was miserable. Almost as bad as flying. In fact, worse, since I could sedate myself on a plane trip and driving lasted ten times longer. I was tempted to abandon my car in Phoenix and catch the next flight out to Salt Lake.

Driving the same route back that we'd come down on was like watching a rerun of a canceled show. I could practically hear Rachel's voice the whole way. *This is where Rachel said this. This is where Rachel laughed about that.* It was miserable. And the most despairing part was that life wasn't going to stop being miserable anytime soon. Because the woman I had fallen in love with was going to marry a manipulative little man out of guilt or duty or religious obligation and be miserable for the rest of her life. And I was going to think about her for the rest of my life and hurt for her.

My heart hadn't hurt this badly for many years.

Laurie called as I was passing through Panguitch, a small town in southern Utah.

"Where are you?"

"I'm driving home," I said.

"Home to Coeur d'Alene?"

"No. Salt Lake."

"You don't sound well."

"What do I sound like?"

"You sound angry. Like you're about to go on a shooting spree."

"I'm thinking about it."

"So things didn't go well with your father."

"No, things went better than expected. But I lost Rachel."

"Who's Rachel?"

I hesitated. "She's no one."

Laurie knew better than to ask. "I'm really sorry. Is there anything I can do?"

"No. I just need space."

"You got it. Just drive safe. Be safe. And let me know when you're back in Coeur d'Alene. Otherwise you can call anytime. I'm here for you."

"Thank you."

"Bye. Kisses. Take care of yourself."

"Bye."

I drove fast. In fact, I made it back to the Grand America Hotel before nine p.m. It was cold and bleak in Salt Lake, which pretty much matched my temperament. I didn't know what to do. Actually, I did. I needed to go back home, get good and drunk for a week, then get on with my life, hoping that the embers of my feelings for Rachel would soon grow cold.

In spite of my decision, I still had things to do in Salt Lake. I needed to sign papers with Brad so we could list the house. And then I was going to see my dream lady. I planned to do both as soon as possible, then retreat to my previous, lonely life.

As I got in bed I thought, *At least there's probably a book in this.*

CHAPTER

Twenty-Seven

December 3, 1986

Dear Diary,

This morning I helped Jacob write his Christmas list to Santa. He asked me what I was getting. I said, A baby. He said, That's like Jesus. He was a Christmas present too. I don't know how he came up with that. No one here talks about Jesus. Then he said, Jesus got golden franks for Christmas. What is your baby getting? It came out without thinking. I said, A new mother. Jacob asked me why I was crying.

Noel

DECEMBER 20

I woke at nine fifteen, just missing a phone call. I rolled over and checked my phone. It was Brad Campbell. I called him back.

"Churcher," he said. "How are you?"

"Good."

"I dropped by the house on Sunday but you weren't there."

"I was in Phoenix."

"Lucky you. I could use a respite from this weather. Maybe I'll find an excuse to fly to Phoenix. Or St. George."

His mention of St. George brought Rachel to mind. And pain. "Do you have some papers for me?"

"Yes I do. I can bring them by your hotel if you like."

"That would be great."

"Do you have time for lunch? The Grand has a nice restaurant."

"Sure," I said. "A late lunch."

"How late?"

I thought about it. "Two. I'm checking out today."

"Two o'clock is good for me. Headed home, huh?"

"I've got just one more thing to do before I leave."

"Well, it's been nice having you here. I hope it was a memorable visit."

"It was definitely that," I said. "I'll see you at two."

I skipped working out and breakfast, opting instead for a protein bar, then took a shower. I sat on the floor of the shower and let the water cascade around me. *What had I done wrong?* I had tried to do the right thing. The hard thing. And it had blown up on me. Then again, maybe there was no way for things to work out. Had I not done the right thing, I couldn't imagine how great her guilt would be.

I kept checking my phone, hoping that she had called, but she hadn't. She wasn't going to call.

I left my bags at the bell stand and met Brad at the hotel's Garden Café. Shortly after our food arrived, Brad asked, "So what are your plans with the house?"

"I'm just going to sell it," I said.

"Do you need a real estate agent? A local one?"

"That would help. Do you know a good one?"

"I know a few. They'll take good care of you." He lifted his leather portfolio. "I brought the documents." He laid a stack of papers on the table next to my food. Each of the papers had various Post-it arrow flags directing me where to sign.

"I don't have a pen," I said.

"You can have mine." He handed me a black resin pen inscribed with the name of his firm.

I signed all the documents, then handed the papers back to him.

"Thank you, sir. And that concludes our official business together. If you ever need a lawyer, you know where to find me."

"It's already in my phone," I said, then lifted his pen. "And it's right here."

"Just don't lose that pen," he said.

I reached for the check, and he put his hand on it. "I've got it. Business expense."

"Thank you for lunch. Actually, thank you for everything. Especially for taking care of my mother during her last days."

He looked at me with a peculiarly satisfied smile. "You did get a lot done, didn't you?"

We said good-bye and I drove my car up to the front doors and had the bell captain bring out my luggage. I opened the tailgate and he put my suitcase in the back. I unzipped the suitcase and took out the leather diary. Then I slammed the tailgate shut and handed the bell captain a ten-dollar tip. He thanked me. "Come back soon," he said.

"Not likely," I replied. "Have a good day."

I climbed into my car, turned the radio on to Christmas music, then rolled out of the hotel's circular drive and headed south to find Noel.

With a name like Noel King, she wasn't hard to track down. There were only two Noel Kings in the United States, and only one in Utah.

She no longer lived in Provo. Since her marriage, she had moved nine miles south to a small town called Spanish Fork. It was fifty-two miles south on I-15 from downtown Salt Lake, less than an hour away. Ironically, Rachel and I had driven past the town on our way to Phoenix.

Spanish Fork is a small town of about thirty-five thousand people. It wasn't difficult finding the King home. Besides living in my dreams for the last thirty-plus years, Noel King lived on a real street wonderfully called Wolf Hollow Drive, just south of the town's Centennial Park, which was sandwiched between the town's only cemetery and their only junior high.

The house was even smaller than my mother's, a box-shaped tiled home with a steeply pitched roof and a long front porch.

There was as much snow on the ground here as there was in Salt Lake, but the driveway was shoveled clean and dry, as was the walkway and sidewalk in front of the house.

The house was decorated for Christmas with multicolored lights strung across the length of the house and, in the front yard, an almost life-sized nine-piece model of the nativity in faded plastic. There was Joseph and Mary kneeling next to a manger with baby Jesus. There were three Wise Men, a shepherd, and a camel and donkey. It was an ambitious display for such a small yard.

I was parked across the street and still admiring the crèche when a utility van pulled into the home's driveway. The van was wrapped with a cartoon picture of a man wearing a crown and holding an orange pipe wrench like a scepter. To the side of the cartoon were the words

KEVIN KING PLUMBING

THE PLUMBER KING FOR YOUR CASTLE'S
ROOTER AND PLUMBING NEEDS

A heavyset man in Levi's and a striped denim shirt got out of the van and walked in the side door of the home.

"My angel's married to the king of plumbing," I said.

I grabbed the diary, got out of the car, and walked up the concrete path to the front door, which was adorned with a large pine-needle wreath with red ribbon and gold and blue baubles. There was a piece of electrical tape over the doorbell, so I knocked. A few minutes later the man I'd just seen enter the home opened the door. He was plump and red-faced with a five-o'clock shadow. There was a label sewn on his shirt that read KEVIN.

The first thing he said was, "That your Porsche parked across the street?"

I glanced furtively back at my car. "Yes."

"One of them Porsche SUVs. I tell ya, they'll make an SUV outta just about anything these days. Wouldn't surprise me a bit to see a Rolls SUV. So what that set you back, fifty, sixty grand?"

"It's the Turbo S, so it was about one sixty."

I thought his jaw would drop off. "Holy Mother of . . . You must be made of money, sir. I'm clearly in the wrong business. What is it that you do?"

"I write books. Novels."

"I'm gonna have to try my hand at writing books one of these days. I got stories, I tell ya. The things I seen in houses. Turn your skin blue. So what brings you by today?"

"I'm looking for Noel King. I'm guessing she's your wife."

"What you want with my wife? Never mind, you can have her. I'll trade you straight up for the Porsche." He laughed at himself. "No? I didn't think so. I'll call her." He turned around. "No-el. Someone's at the door for ya." He turned back to me. "We don't get many strangers

coming around here, just your usual alarm or water puri-
fier salesmen, but last few days we're two for two. Got
you today and a young woman last night."

Rachel.

"A young woman came by yesterday?"

"Pretty gal. Just a little mixed up. I figured she was probably smokin' some of that Colorado."

"Why is that?"

"Well, to begin with, she asked my wife if she had a
child thirty years ago. I told her that she wasn't even married back then. Noel felt bad for the young lady. She told
her that she was sorry, but she must be mistaken."

I recalled the warning my father had given me as I left
his house. "What did the young woman do?"

"She got all teary-eyed and just looked at my wife for
the longest time. It was kind of uncomfortable. Then she
walked away. Funny thing, she actually did look a lot like
my wife. At least the way she looked in her younger years.
Almost could have been twins. Sure shook up the missus,
though. She cried all night."

"You're sure she wasn't her daughter?"

The man looked at me as if I were dumb as a brick. He
crossed his arms at his chest. "Course I'm sure. I've been
married to her for twenty-seven years. I think I would've
known if I got her pregnant. Heck, Noel can't even have
children."

"You don't have children?"

"I just said that. She can't have children. She's barren."

"She's barren," I said.

He grinned. "Well, I assure you, the plumbing's all workin' in this house. And I know plumbing."

I hid my growing annoyance. "You are the king of plumbing."

He laughed.

I heard approaching footsteps as a woman walked up behind the man. My chest froze. It was her. My dream woman in flesh and blood. She looked younger than I had expected. In fact, she was still recognizable from the photograph I'd found in the diary. She still looked pretty.

For years I had wondered what this moment, if it ever came, would be like. I had thought it might be like meeting a favorite actor or rock star. But it wasn't like that at all. Sure, it was surreal in its own way. But it wasn't uncomfortable. I guess it was because she didn't seem like a stranger to me. How could she? She had been with me for all these years.

She looked at me with a peculiar expression, and I wondered if some part of her recognized me as well. Unfortunately, her husband didn't leave but stood there like a curious child not wanting to be left out.

"May I help you?" she asked kindly.

"You're Noel Ellis?"

"Ellis was my maiden name," she said with a guarded smile. "And you are?"

I reached out my hand, my eyes locked on hers. "My name is Jacob Christian Churcher."

She responded as if electricity had shot through me and shocked her. She dropped my hand. She looked afraid.

"I'm sorry," she stammered. "Do I know you?"

I glanced over at the plumber, then back at her. I pitied her that even now she felt that she had to live her life as a lie. "Actually, you probably don't remember me," I lied for her sake. "But you were briefly friends with my parents. I just wanted to tell you that my mother, Ruth Churcher, passed away."

She swallowed. "I'm sorry to hear that," she said. "And your father?"

"He's still alive," I said. "He's doing well."

"Well, give him my condolences, please."

"Of course." For a moment I just looked at her. I was certain that she knew who I was. And I was pretty sure that she knew that I knew that she knew who I was. So there we were, playing out a charade like actors on a front-porch stage with a one-plumber audience fueling the sham. I suddenly detested the man.

"All right," I finally said. "That's all I wanted to say. By the way, you should know something about that baby girl who was born in my parents' house. They named her Rachel. She's a good woman with a good heart. Just like her mother. Her mother would be proud of her." I looked into her eyes. "I just thought you might want to know that."

Her eyes welled up. The plumber looked at me like I was speaking Chinese, but Noel was clearly fighting her emotions, which still escaped in tears.

"Have a good day."

Noel wiped her eyes. "Good-bye," she said softly.

I was turning to go when suddenly something clicked inside me. Something angry and strong. Something unwilling to let the evil of the past win. I turned back around.

"Noel."

She looked intently into my eyes. "Yes?"

"There's something I need to tell you."

She looked at me expectantly.

"For almost as long as I can remember, I've dreamed of a lovely young woman who held me when my world was falling apart. She was the one woman who loved a scared little boy even when her own world was crashing down around her. That woman in my dreams held me in the dark when I was afraid. She kept me company when I was alone. And she loved me when I believed that I was unlovable."

My eyes suddenly welled up. "She was the best woman I have ever known. And I don't care if the world made her live a lie, but the truth of who she is is far too great to be put down by its shame and deceit. I love that woman with all my heart. And I told myself that if I ever saw her again, she would know that."

I lifted the diary. "This is yours, Noel. It belongs to you, not them. Not to the lie. You wrote in here that you would rather live an honest life than an admired one. You deserve both. It's your life, not theirs. It's your right to claim it." I offered her the book. "It's time to let go of the shame and walk free. The truth will set you free."

The moment was frozen. The plumber was utterly dumbstruck. But I saw something light in her eyes. Maybe it was courage. Maybe it was indignation. Maybe it was just exhaustion, but she reached down and took the diary. *Her* diary. Then she looked back up at me and said, "My dear, darling Jacob. My sweet Jacob." Tears fell down her face. "You have no idea how much I've worried about you." She moved forward and threw her arms around me. She cried for several minutes. Then, when she could speak, she said, "Please, Jacob. Rachel was here. Can you help me find my baby?"

CHAPTER

Twenty-Eight

Dear Diary,

*Around me people are counting down the days
until Christmas. I'm counting down the days until
I give birth. Last night, Mr. Churcher, Jacob, and I
watched <u>A Christmas Carol</u> on television. The one
with George C. Scott. I feel like the young Ebenezer
Scrooge, sent away to boarding school. My parents
haven't reached out to me once. They're religious
but not godly. Their religion is nothing more than
an idol of their own making, an image. A façade. I
used to be afraid that they wouldn't let me come
back home. Now I have no desire to ever live under
the same roof with them again.*

Noel

Noel and I talked openly for the next hour. Kevin came
and went, baffled by what was happening and totally clueless as to how to respond. I told her about how I had come
down from Coeur d'Alene after my mother's death and
found Rachel or, more correctly, how she had found me.

Noel said that she had driven by the old house a few

Ivins's climate, like St. George's, is typical of the desert southwest and significantly warmer than the rest of the state.

I took the St. George off-ramp at about a quarter to ten and drove west in the darkness toward Ivins, arriving just a few minutes past the hour. To me the landscape looked more like Sedona than Salt Lake. It took me just twenty minutes to find Rachel's home.

As she had told me, the home was older than those around it and, not surprisingly, more conservative in design and landscaping. It was one floor with a tan stucco exterior. The yard was all gravel rock and surrounded by a red cinder-block fence on both sides.

Even though it was only a little past ten, the house was dark, the only illumination being a single porch light and the ankle-high solar lights lining the walkway. I could see inside the house through a large picture window that had neither blinds nor curtains. Fortunately, Rachel's car was parked in the driveway.

I walked up to the house and knocked on the door. Twice. The second time I knocked, a hall light turned on. Then I heard footsteps shuffle up to the door. There was a short pause, followed by the sliding of a dead bolt. Then two more lights came on over the porch and the door opened to reveal an elderly man in a thick, umber terry-cloth robe. He was shorter than me, bald, with wire-rimmed glasses resting on the bridge of a sizable beak, and dark, bushy eyebrows that seemed as wild as an overgrown bush. All he needed was a pitchfork and he could stand in for the old man in *American Gothic*.

He pointedly glanced down at his watch, then said gruffly, "What do you need?"

"I'm here to see Rachel."

"Who are you?"

"I'm a friend of Rachel's."

He didn't flinch. "Rachel's already in bed."

"Sorry, I'm from Coeur d'Alene. It's an hour earlier there."

He didn't find my insight amusing.

"Sir, I just drove down from Salt Lake to see your daughter."

"Well, you're just going to have to drive back."

"I thought she was exaggerating," I muttered to myself.

"Excuse me?"

Just then I heard Rachel's voice. "Dad, who is it?"

He glanced over his shoulder, then back at me. I shrugged. "Sorry. Looks like I woke the baby."

Rachel walked up behind him. She froze when she saw me.

"He says he knows you," the old man said.

"He's a friend."

I looked at her.

"This is Jacob," she said softly.

"The guy?"

I looked at her. "The *guy*?"

"I need to talk to him," she said.

He looked at me with disdain, then said beneath his breath, "'As the dog returns to his vomit.'"

I looked him in the eyes. "Did you just call me a dog and your daughter vomit?"

Again, not amused. He turned and shuffled away.

I turned to Rachel. "The *guy*?"

"What are you doing here, Jacob?"

"The question is, what are you doing here?"

"I live here."

"You live here, or you're *incarcerated* here?"

She didn't answer.

"I saw your mother," I said.

Anger crossed her face. "So did I. She didn't know me."

"I know, she told me. She was sorry. It broke her heart."

"Yeah? Well, it broke my heart too. Do you know what it feels like to have your own mother reject you?"

"Yes. Actually, I do."

She paused. Then she said more softly, "At least my *warden* of a father isn't throwing me away like I was disposable."

"She was a scared teenager, Rachel. Tell me that life hasn't ever made you do something you didn't want to."

She took a deep breath, then exhaled slowly. "What do you want, Jacob?"

"You know what I want."

"And that is?"

"You left without saying good-bye."

"I said good-bye in the note."

"Now that's where I'm confused, because I write things all the time that people twist and manipulate, but when I tell someone that I love them more than anyone I've ever known and that I don't think my fiancé—"

"I'm engaged, Jacob."

"—I don't think my fiancé really likes me—"

"I was drunk."

"Sometimes it takes a little alcohol to be honest."

"I'm engaged."

"Engaged or not, I know the truth. So do you. You don't want to be with him. You want to be with me. And I want to be with you."

She started crying.

"Am I wrong?"

She just kept crying. When she could speak, she said, "What I want doesn't matter."

I looked at her in astonishment. "Then what does?"

"Doing what's *right*."

"And marrying someone you don't want to marry is right?"

She didn't answer.

"Come on, honey," I said gently. "I love you. I'll treat you the way you deserve to be treated."

Again she didn't answer. Finally, I said, "All right. Answer me this, and I'll leave you alone. If you hadn't already told him yes three years ago, would you still answer yes now?"

She just looked at me. After a long silence I said, "There's your answer."

"I didn't answer."

"If you have to think about whether you want to marry someone after being engaged for three years, you have your answer."

Her eyes again filled with tears. "I made a commitment."

"No, you made a commitment to make a commitment."

"It's the same thing!"

"No, it's not. If you were married, I wouldn't be standing here, and you know it. You know I would respect that."

She started crying harder.

"Rachel . . ."

Suddenly she shouted, "Yes!"

I looked at her. "What?"

"Yes. I would still say yes to him."

She looked as surprised by what she'd said as I was. I was breathless. She might as well have hit me in the stomach with a Louisville Slugger. After a moment I exhaled slowly. "Okay," I said softly. "Okay." The pain of her rejection jolted my entire body. It was like I was that child again, standing by the side of the road with my suitcase. I wanted to vomit.

Rachel looked at me, trembling. "Jacob . . ."

I couldn't look at her. I was unable to speak.

"Jacob."

I looked up at her slowly. "I'm sorry. I'll go."

I turned and slowly walked back to my car. Rachel was still standing in the doorway wiping her eyes as I backed out of the driveway.

In spite of the hour, I drove all the way back to Salt Lake City. When I got back to my mother's house, it was almost three in the morning.

CHAPTER

Thirty

December 24, 1986

Dear Diary,

Today is my birthday. I turn eighteen today. No
one here knows. Those who do know—my parents
and Peter—don't care. I told little Jacob. Only
Jacob. He smiled. It's Christmas Eve. I read tonight
about Mary. The story is different to me this
year, because I'm also with child. I'm also about
to give birth among strangers. And they too will
take my child from me. I'm not comparing myself
with her—I'm too much a sinner. I'm comparing
my pain. I hurt so much. And this home I'm in,
my sweet Jacob—what will become of him? Mrs.
Churcher is not well. She doesn't come out of her
room anymore except at night. She's grown so thin.
I don't know who will take care of Jacob now. I'm
praying that his father will be what his son needs,
because Ruth is gone. Maybe I shouldn't judge her.
But I too am losing my baby—though my baby
will still be out there, with someone else watching
her grow up.

Noel

DECEMBER 21

I woke with the sun streaming in through my bedroom window, striping my face with light. I had gone to sleep in my bed. My childhood bed. It was appropriate. I hurt then too.

I realized that I had woken because someone was knocking at the door. I just lay there for a while. Then, when the pounding didn't stop, I got up, pulled on my pants and shirt, and walked barefoot out to the front room and opened the door.

Elyse stood on the porch, shivering a little in the cold. She held a small brown sack. I must have looked as bad as I felt because she studied me with obvious concern. "Are you okay?"

"Yeah. I just got up."

"I read you writers keep strange hours. It's past noon."

"It was a long night." I rubbed my eyes. "I got in around three."

"From Arizona?"

"No. Ivins." I looked at her. "Do you want to come in?"

"Please."

She walked inside, panning the room as she did. "It looks nice in here."

"Thanks." I motioned to the couch. "Have a seat."

"Thank you." She sat down on one end of the couch. I sat down in the middle.

"I was glad to see your car here this morning. I was afraid you'd gone home and I would never see you again."

"I'm leaving this afternoon. But I wouldn't have left without saying good-bye."

"That makes me glad." She looked around. "You really transformed this place. It hasn't looked like this for twenty-something years." She looked back at me. "Did you find your father?"

"Yes."

"How did that go?"

"It went well. It was like you said it would be."

"I'm glad for that too." She looked at me. "But you look sad."

"Not everything worked out."

"The girl?"

I raked my hand back through my hair. "Yes."

She nodded. "It's always the girl, isn't it? But then, that's what you write about."

"I would never write this story. But it doesn't matter. That's not why I came back."

She looked at me thoughtfully, then asked, "Why did you come back, Jacob?"

I took a deep breath. "I still don't know. I was looking for answers."

"Answers to what?"

I couldn't answer her. She looked at me for a moment, then said, "You'll never find the answer to what you're really looking for."

"You know what I'm *really* looking for?"

"I'm pretty sure that I do. It's the same thing your friend

Rachel came here looking for. You want to know why you weren't worthy of your mother's love."

I just looked at her. Deep in my heart I knew she was right.

"But more important, it's not *what* you're looking for, Jacob. It's *why* you're looking. You're looking because, deep inside of you, that little boy is still afraid that he's not lovable. So sometimes he pushes love away. And sometimes he tries to earn that love. But then he resents everyone he tried so hard to get to love him. He has to. Because even that little boy knows that love can't be earned. The only true love is grace. All else is a counterfeit.

"So let me answer your question, Jacob. Why weren't you lovable? The answer is something you know but haven't had the courage to believe. You see, it's possible to know things and not believe them. The true answer is this: you *were* lovable. You were a darling, bright-eyed little boy who brightened everyone's lives. Even your mother's. You were immensely lovable. You always were and you always will be. And it was that very love you had that made you so vulnerable."

She looked at me with piercing eyes. "You're still him, Jacob. You're still that sweet, bright-eyed little boy. He's still in you. And he is still loving and vulnerable. Every time I read one of your books, I can feel his sweetness rising up from the pages like groundwater. And it's not just me. So do millions of others. That's why they love you. They feel it too. And so they come to you and you fill their cups. But honey, it's time you forgot about the rest of us and filled yours."

Suddenly I began to tremble. Then tears began to well up in my eyes. Elyse slid over next to me. She put her arms around me and she too began to cry. "You darling, sweet man. I'm so sorry for your pain. I wish I could have taken it from you. But you've carried it long enough. You need to let it go."

I looked up at her. "Rachel left me. She said she loved me. Then she left me."

Elyse nodded slowly. "Of course she did. It doesn't mean she doesn't love you. It just means she fears love as much as you do. She fears abandonment as much as you do. Why else would she have come back after all these years? She's trying to answer the same question you are."

I wiped my eyes. "What do I do now?"

"Love yourself. Respect yourself. And have faith. The older I get, the more I see that things tend to work out. Not always, but usually. Just not in our time."

I looked at her gratefully and she smiled. "I brought you something." She reached into her bag and brought out a cellophane package. Brach's star-shaped chocolates. In spite of my tears, I smiled. "Oh, yes."

"And I have something else." She reached back into the bag and brought out a small polished black box. I lifted its lid. On a bed of cotton there was a glossy pin, a ceramic figurine of Batman. It flooded me with emotion. "I remember that."

"Yes. It was very special to you. I kept it at my house. You'd come over and look at it almost every day."

"The Batman pin was Nick's."

"Yes. He left it for you."

"There was a Robin pin too."

"He kept that one so you could always be the Dynamic Duo. Even when he was in Germany."

I rubbed my finger along the pin. "Such little things could bring such joy."

She looked at me. "They still do." She sighed. "So many memories."

I took her hand. "Thank you."

She slowly stood, holding on to my arm for balance. "Well, I better let you get on with your life. You've got better things to do than listen to the ramblings of an old woman."

"I don't think so," I said.

She looked into my eyes. "May I give you some advice?"

"Of course."

"When Rachel figures things out, don't punish her. She needs grace. Just like you do."

I walked her to the door. She looked out. "Oh. It's snowing again. It's always good to have snow for Christmas." She turned back and smiled. "Have a Merry Christmas, Jacob. I'm so glad you finally came home."

C H A P T E R

Thirty-One

December 30, 1986

Dear Diary,

My sweet baby was born the day after Christmas. She was small, six pounds and three ounces. She's just seventeen inches long. She is so, so beautiful. Her birthday is two days after mine. Christmas will never be the same for me. They took her away from me the same day. Even my breasts are weeping for her. I can't stop crying. I don't think I'll ever see my baby again. How could I? I don't know where they took my baby. My life is shame. Why don't I fight for her? Why don't we fight for what we want?

I wonder if my baby's new parents will ever tell her about me. I wonder if this pain in my heart will ever go away.

Noel

I took a shower, shaved, and dressed, then took one last walk through the old house. One last lap. There were so many memories. Every room had memories. Far too many to take them all back with me to Coeur d'Alene. It was just as well. Many of them needed to be left here, to die with the house. But not all. There were happy memories too, times of laughter and caring. Times of love and tenderness. I just had to uncover them and give them permission to be. To coexist among the pain. Just as I had to uncover the house from my mother's hoarding.

I stood at the door of my mother's room and looked at her bed. I thought of the times I rubbed her feet or scratched her arms and face with the pencil with the toothpicks. She needed grace too. She needed to be left here too.

I took the posters down from the walls of my bedroom and was rolling them up when there was another knock. I walked out and opened the door. Standing on my porch was Rachel.

For a moment I just looked at her. Her eyes were puffy and her cheeks streaked with tears. In spite of her pain, my heart wanted to fire back at her with all the hurt she had filled it with. I remembered Elyse's words. *Grace.*

I took a deep breath. "Do you want to come in?"

Without speaking, she nodded and stepped inside. I gestured to the couch, and she sat down. I sat down across from her. She looked at me anxiously.

"Why are you here?" I asked.

"I wanted to see you."

"You rejected me. Twice."

She looked down, and I could see tears falling from her eyes. "I'm so sorry."

"You said you wanted him."

She wiped her face, then looked up. "You knew the truth."

"I'm not sure I do."

She looked at me, new pain evident on her face. Then she said, "She came."

"Who came?"

"My mother."

I let the words settle. "Is that why you're here? Because Noel told you to come see me?"

"No. I'm here because of something she said to me."

"And what was that?"

"She said, 'Don't make the same mistake I made all those years ago. I let other people write my life story.'" She looked at me vulnerably. "I wanted to see if you could love me again. Like you did. And we could change our story."

I looked at her cautiously. "Change it to what?"

She swallowed. "A romance."

"A romance?"

"Yes, like what you said. Boy meets girl, boy loses girl . . ." She hesitated. "Boy gets girl back."

I looked at her for a moment, then said, "It's a bit formulaic."

"I don't care."

"And the happily ever after?"

"There has to be a happily ever after," she said. "There's always a happily ever after when the girl finds her true love."

I looked at her for a moment, then a broad smile crossed my face. "I can write that. But only if you'll help me."

A smile crossed her face as tears fell down her cheeks. Then she jumped into my arms. "Yes. For the rest of my life, yes."

EPILOGUE

January 11, 1987

Dear Diary,

I'm preparing to go home. My parents have come to see me. They're cold. They did not see my baby. They wouldn't even speak of her. I'm afraid. I'm afraid for my little one. I'm afraid for little Jacob. I wish I could take him with me. It wouldn't be possible. I can't even bring this diary with me. It's "evidence" of a past that everyone has troubled themselves to hide. I can't bring myself to throw this diary away, so I'll just leave it in my bedroom. Maybe it will serve some purpose someday. To my little baby girl: Somehow, if you ever read this, know that I'm sorry for letting you down. To my little Jacob: Know that I will never forget you. And I will never stop loving you. I'll visit you in your dreams.

Noel

I would have liked a redux on that *USA Today* Holiday Roundup interview I did in Chicago. This time I would have much different answers. I'd tell the reporter that Christmas wasn't spent alone drinking eggnog and watching recorded games of college football.

At the last minute I flew everyone up to celebrate Christmas at my home in Coeur d'Alene. By "everyone" I mean the nine of us: Noel and Kevin; my father (yes, he got on a plane) and Gretchen; Tyson, Candace, and their son, Teonae; and Rachel and me. I had invited Elyse as well, but she had obligations with her own family.

There were a lot of stories, a lot of laughter, and a lot of tears. It was a grand celebration of *auld lang syne*.

There was also a lot of caroling as I played my piano for them. I'd had the piano tuned. It was perfect but I wasn't. It had been a while since I'd played the old songs. No one cared. Even out of tune, Christmas carols have a way of sounding sweet. One song I got right was "Greensleeves." Or the Christmas version of it, "What Child Is This?" Noel and Rachel held each other and cried.

Noel was genuinely happy. You could see it in her eyes. You could feel it in her embraces. I was glad. She deserved happiness. After I'd left her home that day, she had told her husband everything. But she did it right. It wasn't a confessional and she wasn't seeking amnesty. It was a reclamation of her authentic self. She was finally claiming her life as her own and standing in the light and power of that truth. No wonder she was filled with such joy.

✦

The next June, Rachel and I had everyone back up to Coeur d'Alene for our wedding at a beautiful resort on the lake. This time Elyse came. And Laurie, of course. All my favorite people in one place. Two months after our honeymoon in Bali, I sent Noel and Rachel off to Paris while I started on my next book. I called it *The Noel Diary*.

I sent my ladies to Paris because I thought it might be a good place for them to get to know each other better. Hemingway went there for inspiration; I figured what better place for them to start writing their own story?

That next year I even found peace with my mother. I realized that, in a twisted way, I had held on to my pain as a way to punish my mother—a woman I hadn't seen in decades. It's like they say, holding on to anger is like swallowing poison and hoping someone else will die. I was ready to let go of my pain and live. The next Mother's Day I took flowers to her grave. I knelt down and kissed her stone and thanked her for life. We chain ourselves to those we don't forgive. For the first time in my life I was truly free. I also poured a bottle of root beer on Charles's grave. He loved the stuff.

I ended up going back to Utah twice that year. Both times to cemeteries. First to see my mother's grave, then for Elyse's funeral. She suffered a stroke in October and passed away. Her family invited me to speak at her funeral. I was grateful for the honor. Nick, her nephew, was there. It was amazing to see him again. Somehow still felt like we were friends. As sad as I was at her passing, I am filled with unspeakable gratitude that she was still there when I came back home. Maybe God is in the details.

I don't have the dreams anymore. I miss them sometimes, but it seems more for nostalgia's sake than anything else. I don't need them. I have Rachel to hold me at night. She's all the love I need. And when I wake up in the morning, she's still there.

Other than in my continued production of books, my life has changed in quantum leaps. *Quantum leaps.* It's funny how often in my writing I use metaphors from physics to describe people or situations: gravity, black holes, magnetism. Perhaps, in the end, life is just a matter of physics. Life is, after all, Newton's first law of motion—the law of inertia. The law states that an object in motion stays in motion in the same direction unless acted upon by an unbalanced force.

That's the way we live our lives. We speed on, happily or not, in the same direction until we collide into something that alters our destination. Sometimes that collision hurts, sometimes it doesn't, but if we're lucky, love is that unbalanced force. Love. There is no greater force in the universe. Now if we'll only learn to stop getting out of its way.

ACKNOWLEDGMENTS

I would like to thank and acknowledge those who have journeyed alongside me with this book: Jonathan Karp, Carolyn Reidy, and the entire Simon & Schuster family. Thank you to my editor, Christine Pride, for great insight as well as remarkable patience and continual forbearance. Also, thank you to my agent, Laurie Liss, who was and is always there for me and my family. Thank you to my bestselling author daughter, Jenna Evans Welch (*Love & Gelato*) for her counsel and help with this book. It's every parent's dream to see their children rise higher than themselves, and Jenna is well on her way. I'd like to acknowledge my staff and friends, Diane Glad, Heather McVey, Barry Evans, Fran Platt, Camille Shosted, and Karen Christoffersen, for their help in sharing my books with the world.

The Noel Diary draws more from my own life than perhaps anything I've ever written. I have my own Noel. I am grateful to her and for all those who have helped to heal my emotional cuts and bruises, especially my courageous wife and friend, Keri.

Again, thank you to my readers. Without you, it's just paper and ink.

ABOUT THE AUTHOR

Richard Paul Evans is the #1 bestselling author of *The Christmas Box*. Each of his more than thirty-five novels has been a *New York Times* bestseller. There are more than thirty-five million copies of his books in print worldwide, translated into more than twenty-four languages. He is the recipient of numerous awards, including the American Mothers Book Award, the Romantic Times Best Women's Novel of the Year Award, the German Audience Gold Award for Romance, five Religion Communicators Council Wilbur Awards, the Washington Times Humanitarian of the Century Award, and the Volunteers of America National Empathy Award. He lives in Salt Lake City, Utah, with his wife, Keri, not far from their five children and two grandchildren. You can learn more about Richard on Facebook at Facebook.com/RPEFans or visit his website at RichardPaulEvans.com.

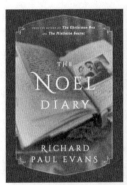
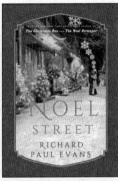
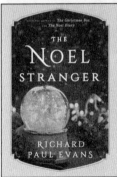
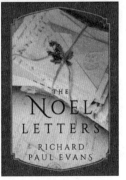

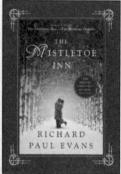
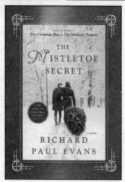

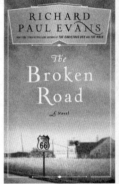
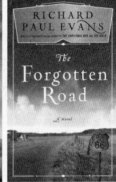
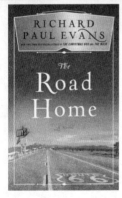